THE SPY WHO Would not speak

THE SPY WHO Would Not Speak

A Morgan Crew Mystery

Arthur A. Lee

Leeward Publishers, LLC
Winter Garden, Florida

THE SPY WHO
Would Not Speak

By

Arthur A. Lee

This is a work of fiction. Names, characters, places and incidents are either the product of the author's imagination or are used fictionally, and resemblance to actual persons living or dead, business establishments, events or locales is entirely coincidental.

Copyright © 2013 by Arthur A. Lee &

LEEWARD PUBLISHERS, LLC.

All rights reserved. This book, in whole and in part, is the property of the author. No part of this book may be reproduced or transmitted in any form or by any means, graphic, electronic, or mechanical, including but not limited to photocopying, recording, taping, or by any information storage retrieval system, without the permission in writing from the author.

ISBN: 978-0615832470

In accordance with the U.S. Copyright Act of 1976, the scanning, uploading, and electronic sharing of any part of the book without the permission of the publisher constitute unlawful piracy and theft of the author's intellectual property. If you would like to use material from the book (other than for review purposes), prior written permission must be obtained by contacting the publisher at

editor@leewardpublishers.com

Silver Cat Press
An Imprint of Leeward Publishers, LLC

**This Book Is Dedicated
To The Memory Of
Tom Davis,
The Spy I Knew.
He Did Very Good Things
In Very Bad Ways**

Other Books by the Author

The Morgan Crew Mystery Series

A Storm In From The Sea
The Las Vegas Murders
A Deadly London Fog
The Four Seasons Murders
The Hawaiian Sunset Murders
The West Texas Murders

The Adventure Series

Three Families

www.leewardpublishers.com

THE SPY WHO WOULD NOT SPEAK
A Morgan Crew Mystery

By

Arthur A. Lee

Contents

ONE - Brown's Farm

The Hudson River Valley of New York State has a history of importance in the formation of the United States during the American Revolution. The British wanted control of the Hudson River in order to divide the New England Colonies from the rest of the rebellious Colonies to the south. The farmers and backwoodsmen of the Hudson Valley fought long and hard to keep the British and their Native American allies at bay. The battles were hard and bloody yet few are noted in the history books, in spite of the importance of these battles to the success of the Revolution.

The Hudson River flows into the Atlantic as it washes against Manhattan Island. Its origins are far to the Northeast in thickly forested mountains as it cuts the majestic valley out of New England granite. The river runs through the Hudson Valley past farms and villages, through mountains covered in trees, past West Point Military Academy.

Seventy-five miles East of Newberg, New York, across the Hudson River, isolated along a thin and winding road that dates back to the days of the Revolution, lies what has been known for 125 years as Brown's Farm. It is a small farm, surrounded by hills and anchored by thick forests that have been untouched and unspoiled for hundreds of years. Brown's Farm has 30 acres plowed and heavy with corn in the season. In the autumn, after the corn is cut and harvested, these acres lie fallow and covered in thick weeds. There are another 9 acres of pasture fenced in tattered and thrown together pieces of used lumber and branches fallen from trees. Eight old milk cows and three aging horses graze peacefully in this pasture. Their days of work being long past, the horses watch as the cows are led to a rickety shed to be milked, if in fact there is milk to be given by the boney and sway back cows.

Barbed wire is entwined through the fence, and at closer inspection one can see old ceramic insulators anchoring the barbed wire to the old fence. The wire is not meant to keep the animals in. The fence carries a voltage charge large enough to disable and throw even the biggest of men into unconsciousness. It would kill the average size person.

A two story house sits near the road. Its dark brown paint is peeling away from the old wood siding. A battered and sagging covered porch runs around three sides of the house. Mismatched asphalt shingles of several different colors on both the roof of the house and the porch cover are bent, thin, and several are missing, waiting to be replaced with yet another assemblage of cheap shingles. Weather beaten Adirondack chairs and broken, rusty metal tables populate the porch, sharing it with cobwebs and dirt on the unswept floor.

Howard and Lucy Redgrave live in the old house and care for the farm. The farm has become too much work for Howard; he is 66 years old now and feeling older than he is after ten years of farming that would barely give the best farmer and his family a living. Every year that goes by now brings more and more undone maintenance. Although 64 year old Lucy tries to help, she has little time after doing what she can to keep the inside of house clean and in order.

Not far from the house is a red barn one would expect to see on any such rural farm. The paint is faded and peeling; a few boards have come loose and hang lazily. A pile of dung four foot tall lay against the western wall of the barn steaming in the afternoon heat. Inside are a twenty year old tractor whose motor starts occasionally when forced to do so, and a few plows and mowers that are aging into more rust than steel. There are nine stalls inside that needed cleaning that day as they have for the past several weeks.

A black Cadillac Escalade, dusty from the long drive into the Hudson Valley and the hills surrounding Brown's Farm, moved slowly along the narrow road. At first it passed the weed filled gravel driveway into the farm. It stopped and backed up slowly, turned and started down the bumpy, rock strewn drive. When the car stopped near the front porch of the house a man, 6' 6" tall, pale hair cut in military fashion, wearing dark glasses, and so muscular his dark suit was ill fitting, jumped from the front passenger's seat and opened the rear door.

From the back seat a woman stepped out into the sunlight and stood on the damp dirt of the driveway, looking down to see if her very expensive custom made Italian hi-heeled shoes were going to be ruined. As her heels sunk into the mud, it became apparent they were going to be ruined if she walked to the house, which she had to do.

She was perhaps 45 years old and too many years of 18 hour work days and seven day work weeks had left little time for her to keep her body in shape She wore an expensive grey suit and simple gold jewelry at her earlobes and around her neck. Her long, thin fingers were bare of rings, including a wedding ring, much to the disappointment of her parents.

She walked around behind the car and started to the front porch. Lucy Redgrave stepped out onto the porch. She was drying her hands on an old kitchen towel, not more than a rag now. Lucy was wearing a washed-out cotton dress that she had worn almost every day for the past year as she tried to keep up on the housework and cooking. Her graying hair was a jumbled mess which she tried to push back out of her eyes so she could be sure who was walking towards her.

Her eyes weren't as good as they were a few years

ago. Age had begun to insert a fog in front of the woman, but she began to recognize her daughter.

"Theresa!" she asked. "Is that you Theresa?"

"Yes, Momma," The woman said.

The woman, known as T. J. to everyone except her mother and father, took the three wooden steps onto the porch quickly and ran to her mother's waiting arms. They held each other lovingly. T. J. was taller than her mother. She bent down to hold the woman to her. Lucy was crying and T. J. fought back a few tears herself. It had been more than three years since they had seen each other.

The two women walked hand in hand through the living room and into the kitchen. Outside, the driver and the two guards who had been in the Escalade with T. J. stood vigilantly near the house, watching everything carefully through dark sunglasses. The driver held an M-16 rifle. Both of the guards were armed with 9 mm pistols at their waists. They were dressed in dark suits and polished shoes that were now covered in mud. Each had an 'earwig' device and each watched their surroundings as if waiting for some jungle monster to spring from out of nowhere.

"Where's Daddy?" T. J. asked her mother.

"Out back," her mother said as they walked into the kitchen, past a sink full of dirty dishes from the day before. "There's always work for him to do. But it's beginning to get to be too much for him. He's not getting any younger. All the work was the right thing at the time. But now . . ."

T. J. thought back to her last visit to the farm, three years before at Christmas. She had stayed for two days. The old house, she remembered, was fresh and neat. The old wooden furniture had been carefully polished, the linoleum floors had been scrubbed spotless. The kitchen, despite the years-old plywood cabinets that had too many coats of paint on them, was sparkling clean. Her mother looked ten years younger three years ago.

"Is it time to leave the farm?" T. J. asked.

"I think so," her mother said as she stepped to the old stove to pull the steaming kettle off the flame. She filled a chipped ceramic tea pot with hot water. "I'm not sure your father would agree."

They sat at the table in the kitchen, the table with one leg slightly shorter than the others. Lucy poured two cups of hot water and added a stringed bag of Lipton tea to each. She slid one across the table to her daughter.

"Do you want milk or sugar?" Lucy asked. "I've got some fresh milk from this morning. Lots of cream in it," she said and smiled wickedly, winking at the secret joke. She knew her daughter wouldn't take anything like heavy cream. She was as near a vegetarian as one could get and anything rich in sugar or fat had been cut from T. J.'s diet many years before. She stood and got a package of hard chocolate chip cookies from the cupboard which she knew her daughter wouldn't eat anyway.

"I hope you like the tea," Lucy said.

"Right now a stiff scotch would be better," T. J. said.

"You know we can't have any liquor around your father."

"Is he still sober?" T. J. asked.

"It's been more than seven years now," Lucy said. "I'm very proud of him. The farm work kept his mind off of the drink. But he's getting too old to do everything all by himself."

T. J. wanted to say that the same might apply to her mother's ability to keep the house clean, but she didn't. T. J. could be cruel, she could be demanding. Many people she worked with would whisper their opinion that she was too often sadistic.

Just then, as T. J. put the hot cup of tea to her lips feigning drinking some of it, the torn screen door at the rear of the kitchen squeaked and her father stepped inside. His boots were muddy and he left a trail as he walked across the cracked linoleum.

"Is that Teresa?" he said smiling his happiness at seeing his daughter again after all those years. "Is that my daughter who hasn't been here for . . . How many years has it been?"

T. J. ran into his arms. "Oh, Daddy," she said. "It's so good to see you again."

She knew this man was her father, but this man was more old and worn than the father she remembered. His hair was thin and white. His skin was red from work outdoors and cracked like old leather. This was not the young and vital man she remembered from just a few years before.

"Come have some tea with us, Daddy," T. J. said, taking his arm and hugging him close to her as they walked to the table. There was a big mug that had seen better days on the table. Lucy pulled it to her and filled it with steaming water and a tea bag for her husband.

"So how are you, Daddy?" T. J. asked. "How are you doing?"

"Just fine, darlin', just fine," he said.

"You look tired, Daddy."

"I guess I am," he said and smiled a little. "I'm not getting any younger, you know."

"You should have never left the CIA, Daddy," T. J. said.

"If I hadn't, I'd be dead right now." He said. "Or maybe just dead drunk." He laughed; Lucy turned her eyes down, sad or maybe embarrassed. "I couldn't handle the life anymore."

****

Michal Kohlski was born into poverty in the Spring heat of early 1944 in an isolated farming town in Western

Nebraska. Karlamiasta is the 150 year old name of the town, settled by Polish immigrants in 1859. In English it is Karla's Town, named for the oldest daughter of the first settler and founder. The young people of the small town often call it 'Karla's Mistake'. The population of Karlamiasta reached a peak of 207 and shrank after December 7th, 1941 when boys and men took the opportunity to leave. Many thought fighting a war would be better than growing old in the middle of nowhere.

Michal's grandfather had seen the family farm go to the bank in 1933 and quickly drank himself to an early death. Michal's father, Gustaw Kohlski, worked the local farms as work was available to support his mother and two younger sisters. School was something the other boys enjoyed while Michal's father plowed behind someone else's horses, milked someone else's cows, repaired someone else's barn, shoveled someone else's dung pile.

Gustaw saw a young girl, the daughter of a farmer who hired him to work the farm, when he was hoeing weeds through acre upon acre of furrowed land. The heat was stifling that mid-summer day and Gustaw was drenched with sweat. He was barefoot because he saved his only pair of boots for church on Sunday. One day, he promised himself, when he had a spare dollar he would by a big straw hat to keep the sun off his head.

The girl, Anna, just sixteen, walked across the dry, rutted field carrying a bucket of water. She smiled at the young, shirtless man. She knew his name was Gustaw but she knew nothing more of him than that her father felt sorry for him and that she found him very physically attractive. He was lean, skinny really. Sinewy muscles formed his arms and ribs overtly laddered his chest. His hair was long for the 30's and hung in wet tangles to his neck. He was a hard worker and always wanted more work. That was a good thing to a young farm girl who needed a good man to provide for her and the children she would raise. And the young girl felt a strange but very pleasant warmth inside her when she looked at his bare chest.

Gustaw turned seventeen in 1943 and had a choice to make. Join the Army or marry Anna. He married Anna because when he did he had a farm of his own to work and would inherit that farm from Anna's father. Anna was pregnant a month after the wedding and Gustaw was drafted into the Army. Gustaw died as he left the landing craft on Omaha Beach in Normandy. Anna gave birth to a son whom she named after her father, Michal. Anna's father passed away six months later, collapsing of a massive heart attack at the plow pulled by his two mules. Anna tried to maintain the farm by hiring labor but she was not a farmer nor did she know much of business. Poverty fell on her for the first time in her life. She married a man quickly, one of the men she had hired, without knowing him, and soon found that he preferred whiskey to work and beating his wife and Michal to everything else. Anna gave birth to two daughters, not as a result of love with their father but after the beatings and rapes their father seemed to enjoy so much.

Michal's early years were filled with hunger and hand me down charity clothes that the other boys made fun of as the farm deteriorated. Violence became the norm, but it taught Michal how to be violent without regrets or conscience. There was one thing Michal had that few of the local boys enjoyed. It was 1957 in the little town school Michal attended, in the eighth grade, when he and his classmates took the State mandated IQ test. When the results of the test were returned to the school, a woman, Mrs. Norma Wozniak, from the Governor's office, delivered them herself. Michal Kohlski, it seemed, had an IQ of 159.

Mrs. Wozniak stayed in Karlamiasta the next three days. At the little three room house the five members of the Kohlski family had made into a home. Michal's mother and stepfather surrendered their bed to her and slept on an old quilt on the floor in the kitchen. Anna said prayers of thanks for the brief relief from her husband's drunkenness and beatings.

But in those three days Mrs. Wozniak convinced Michal's parents to let her take him to a private school in Lincoln, paid for by the State of Nebraska, where his gift could be molded and formed and Michal could be readied for the world outside of the little, isolated town of Karlamiasta.

Michal's mother couldn't bear to see him go so far away; his stepfather knew that this was his only chance to acquire more money than he had ever had had. He demanded money, not a great sum to anyone but the man himself. Mrs. Wozniak smiled and immediately agreed. She knew that if she said 'no' the boy would wind up working in someone else's fields.

At the Lombardi Academy Michal completed four years of High School in eighteen months. Mrs. Wozniak then took Michal out of Nebraska and into the world for the first time. Michael Kohl, as he would call himself, never returned to the place where memories were so difficult to shed from his mind. They visited Harvard University, Yale, Princeton, Amherst, and Stanford. But when Michael and Mrs. Wozniak entered the main gates of the United States Military Academy at West Point, Michael knew immediately where he belonged. There was only one problem, young Michael Kohl was only fifteen years old.

Mrs. Wozniak could easily see the boy's disappointment but she assured him that if he wanted to attend West Point, they would wait for him if he would wait for them. Three years, after all is not a long time, she would tell him.

They were on a train, returning to Nebraska. Mrs. Wozniak said good night to the boy and saw him to his berth in the sleeping car. The next morning she gently pulled the curtain at his berth aside to wake him. But the berth was empty. Michael Kohl had disappeared.

The military life was still attractive to him, and he

couldn't get the idea of guns and uniforms out of his mind. He had searched around for a nice little war that he could enjoy while waiting to turn 18. The only thing he could find was the new revolutionary society in Cuba, so he headed south. 1962 found Michael in Miami.

But once there he couldn't figure out how to get to Cuba. He was broke, hungry and homeless when he set foot on Miami Beach for the first time. He looked for a job, but a runaway skinny kid in dirty clothes wasn't going to be hired by anyone. There were people with money everywhere. There were ladies older than him who approached him for nights of sex, but he couldn't do what they wanted him to do. There were criminals roaming the streets seemingly freely.

Michael thought he could do a good deed for Miami and for America by stealing from these street people and killing them in order to both supply the money he needed to live and to rid the world of criminals. And he became good at it. The first was a drug dealer, a black Cuban almost twice Michael's weight and a foot taller. He wondered if he could actually kill anyone. Fighting was not a problem, hurting someone was not a problem, but he had never killed anyone.

Michael had found a piece of steel at a construction site and sharpened it on a concrete sidewalk. He followed the drug dealer one dark night, in the rain, until they were alone. He found the man's heart. The second, third and on and on, were easy for Michal. No witnesses, lots of cash, and no one left alive to come after him. And to his amazement, there were no nightmares or pangs of a guilty conscience.

He was at a beach-side bar on his seventeenth birthday, drinking a cold beer when a man he did not know sat on the stool next to him. The man ordered a beer for himself and another for Michael. He said his name was Bob Smith, one name of many he used when recruiting agents.

He said he wanted to hire Michael. He offered the young man a steady income and what he described as "adventure." A week later, young Michael Kohl, formerly Michal Kohlski, was in Camp Peary, Virginia, known as The Farm, where he became fluent in Spanish, German, French and Russian, and he learned ways of killing people that were new to him. He became part of Operation Mongoose meant to bring down the Castro Government. Michael learned how to organize levels of espionage, infiltration, and assassination as well as sabotage and the operation of radios and weapons. Before the year was out he was smuggled into Cuba where he killed people that the CIA said needed killing.

He lived in Cuba for three years, never being caught or arrested. He set up three very successful espionage organizations among the Cuban populace who disliked the new Communist regime. He assassinated twenty-three people in those three years, not knowing who they were or why he killed them, only that he received orders to kill them.

The Cold War demanded greater things of Michael Kohl, and he was withdrawn from Cuba and sent to Europe where he met his wife who had been assigned to work with him.

****

"Is it time to retire, Daddy?" T. J. asked.

Lucy spoke up and said, "I've been telling him that for a long time. Theresa, we're not able to handle this farm anymore."

"OK," T. J. said. "Where do you want to retire to?"

"You can do that?" Lucy asked.

"Yes, I can."

T. J.'s father looked questioningly at his daughter.

"What kind of job do they have you doing now?"

"You lost your CIA Top Secret Clearance when they put you on this farm, Daddy. I can't tell you what I do."

Lucy spoke up again and said, "Would we have to keep the name Redgrave? Could we go back to Kohl? I miss my real name."

Lucy reached across the table and put her weather beaten hand on her daughter's. She loved her daughter so much. She had always tried to be a good mother, to take care of her daughter as a mother should. Now she knew the tables had turned and it was time for her daughter to take care of her.

"Once I get you relocated you can use whatever name you want, but you can't use Kohl, I'm afraid. For your own protection. Daddy, you know there are people out there who will never forget what you've done. You can't make it easier for them to find you."

"I know, darlin'. It's just that your mother is tired of the life. She wants out," T. J.'s father said. He looked lovingly at his wife and put his hand softly on top of hers and his daughter's.

Where do you want to go?" T. J. asked.

Her mother said excitedly, "New Mexico . . . Santa Fe."

Howard said, "Your mother has taken up her painting again. She's pretty good at it, too. She wants to open a studio and gallery."

"That's all possible," T. J. said. "It'll take a week or two, but start packing your bags. Someone will be here in a few days to take over the farm. Show them around. And since Santa Fe is more expensive then here, I'll have your retirement pay increased, too."

"Jesus Christ," Howard said. "You must have really made it, honey. Are you happy?"

"Yes, Daddy," T. J. said and smiled proudly. "I'm very happy."

Her mother asked, “Are you seeing anyone? Is there a wedding in the future?”

T. J. grinned mischievously and said, “I date now and then. I even sleep with men now and then.”

“Theresa!” Lucy said and pulled her hand away from her daughter’s.

“Lucy!” Howard said. “Leave her alone. She’s not a child and she has important work to do.”

“I want grandchildren, Howard,” she said firmly.

“You have three grandchildren, dear.”

T. J. asked, “Billy has three kids already?” T. J. had not seen or talked to her brother for nearly twenty years. He berated her for following their father into the CIA and the split seemed like it would last forever.

“William and that wife of his live in Georgia,” Lucy said to her daughter. “He owns three used car lots now. He’s doing very well. His wife is a bitch.”

There was no way T. J. was going to get into that discussion. She changed the subject quickly.

“I need to go down there,” she said pointing downward.

Howard said, “I figured that’s why you came. There’s been a lot of people coming and going. The elevator out in the barn is clean and working fine. It’s back in the work shop. Do you remember how to find it?”

“It’s really muddy out there, Daddy,” she said. “Can I use the tunnel?”

“Of course,” he said. He stood up from the table, and with his daughter following they walked out of the kitchen, through the living room and into a back bedroom.

“It hasn’t been cleaned in awhile,” he said as he pulled a tall dresser away from the wall. “I figured since it’s only an emergency tunnel it wouldn’t be used much and I have too many other things to do.”

T. J. pushed a piece of molding and the dusty wooden wall slid aside revealing a heavy steel door. Michael Kohl touched his thumb to a piece of red glowing glass and the steel door opened an inch or two. T.J. pushed it open. She put her arms around her father, kissed him on his unshaven cheek, and said, “Tell Momma I’ll stay for dinner, OK?”

TWO - I am T. J. Kohl

T. J. Kohl walked as quickly as she could down the three levels of steps and through the dirty and musty grey concrete tunnel. Her footsteps kicked up the layer of dust that covered the grey concrete floor, making little clouds that camouflaged her expensive shoes in the dimly lit hallway. The tunnel was long enough to have eighteen ceiling lights overhead, all protected by thick wire mesh, but they threw off just enough light to keep the tunnel from total darkness.

The tunnel ended at a steel door very similar to the doors that protected bank vaults. There was an electronic keypad lock to the right. She keyed in six digits – six digits that proclaimed her access to every secret facility the United States had. The eight inch thick door swung easily open without a sound. T. J. found herself on the third level of a nine level complex that lay beneath Brown's Farm.

She had a staff of Special Agents from various intelligence and law enforcement agencies waiting for her on Level 8. 'Let them wait', she thought. She would not hurry. It had been important to her to spend a little time with her parents rather than rush to her meeting. She had gotten to the top by being both respected and very feared. The people waiting in the conference room on Level 8 would wait because they feared her anger if they didn't wait.

The elevator was in front of her, across the twelve foot wide hall. She typed in her six digit code and bent to allow the retina scanner to peer into her dark brown eye. The elevator door slid open and she stepped in.

She stepped out on Level 8. Two Marine guards in camo-combat fatigues, each heavily armed, stood at attention, turned and led T. J. to a conference room. Inside, eight people sat around a long, highly polished teak wood table. These were professionals. They had all been at their various jobs for many years. They wouldn't be at one of the most secret intelligence facilities in the United States if they weren't the best.

T. J. walked confidently into the room and stood there waiting for the door to be closed behind her by the guards. She slowly circled the desk, taking a round-about route to reach her chair at the head of the table that was only four or five steps to her left. No one looked at her as she walked slowly; her heals clicked loudly in the closed room.

She sat finally and opened the file folder that had been placed on the table where she would sit. She flipped through the 21 pages inside the folder but she read none of them. She already knew everything that was in the file.

She closed the file slowly, and for the first time she looked at the people gathered around the table. She looked from person to person, her expression telling them she wasn't happy at all.

She began, "I am T. J. Kohl. I am Special Assistant for Intelligence to the President of the United States. The President has put me in charge of overseeing all intelligence matters in the United States that pertain to or come close to terrorist activities. That means I am the God damn fucking boss of the CIA, the FBI, the NSA, Homeland Security, Military Intelligence and any other fucking intelligence agency we have floating around. It also means three other things. Number one, I am *your* fucking boss, too. Number two, I am not happy. Number three, I am not happy with you."

There was silence in the room. Oh, they knew they couldn't be fired. Who would replace them? And although T. J. had ordered people killed before and had killed many people herself, certainly she couldn't order all eight of them killed? So they sat in silence, waiting for the Sword of Damocles to drop on their heads.

T. J. spoke again, "Introduce yourselves, please." She knew everyone, of course. But she wanted them to feel subservient, nervous, and uncomfortable.

A woman began to stand then thought better of it. She remained seated and said, "I'm Elizabeth Blackburn. I'm in charge here, and I'm responsible for everything that happens here."

Elizabeth Blackburn was a very Senior FBI Agent. She rose up from the ranks of the FBI without any special political influence. She had finished a two year Associates Degree in Police Science at a Community College in Kansas at the age of 19 and joined the LAPD as a patrol officer where she was decorated twice for bravery in six years. She received a Bachelor's Degree at night school and a Law Degree also studying at night, part-time. She passed the California State Bar and applied to the FBI at the age of 27. She was 52 as she sat at the table in the conference room, and she was in charge of a Federal Special Taskforce comprised of FBI Agents, Homeland Security Agents, and NYPD Detectives investigating suspected terrorist activity in the North Eastern U.S.

T. J. smiled and said, "Very good, Liz. I'll keep your responsibility in mind."

Sitting next to Liz Blackburn was Theodore Molinari. He introduced himself as, "NYPD Captain Teddy Molinari." Teddy was 58 years old and assigned to Liz Blackburn's Special Taskforce. He was twice divorced and had a 35 year old son who was a drug addicted burglar serving a life sentence in Ossining State Prison for the death of a shop keeper during a break-in at a pawn shop. Teddy and Liz had been lovers for the past year. They had kept their affair very secret. They were sure they had done a good job keeping it a secret. No one knew, they were sure.

"I must apologize to you, Teddy, and to you, Liz," T. J. said. "This whole matter has kept the two of you from sharing a bed for a long time. We'll see if we can correct that. And how is that son of yours? Is he still up in Ossining Prison?" She wanted to be cruel, tough, and unflinching letting everyone know she knew the most intimate details of their lives. The fact that she knew all this shouldn't have surprised anyone, but it did.

Next in line at the table was Ricardo DeMateo. Ricky, as everyone called him, was the ICE Director of Boarder Security for the Federal District of Arizona and New Mexico. He was recruited to join Homeland Security and jumped at the chance. His fluent expertise in Spanish, German, French, as well as Arabic and Farsi placed him on Liz's Special Taskforce.

He used his feigned Latino accent to introduce himself. "Si, leetal senorita. I am Reecky, no? You maybe bring some tacos? I very hungry, si?"

"Thank you, Ricky," T. J. said not taking any pleasure at his put-on accent. "And the next time you want to joke around with me, tell me in advance and I'll fire your ass before you can say anything in that childish phony accent. Don't do it again."

The man sitting next to Ricky stood. He was Paul Hazelton. Paul was an old time cop and NYPD Detective Lieutenant. His idea of investigation and interrogation was to beat the crap out of a suspect until they talked. His massive arrest and conviction record with the NYPD promoted him to Chief of the City's Criminal Intelligence Unit. He volunteered for Homeland Security and now served on the Special Taskforce.

Hazelton glared at T. J. at the far end of the table. For twenty-five years he hadn't taken shit from anyone, and he wasn't about to start now. He said in his usual growl, spitting out the words, "You know who I am, Miss Kohl. You know my reputation. I'll walk away from here before I allow you to push me around."

"Thank you, Paul," T. J. said. "I'll consider that and get back to you on it later." Paul sat.

At the other end of the table, directly across from T. J., sat Dr. Cynthia Erickson. She was a 58 year old, Criminal Psychologist. She held two Doctorial degrees in psychology and a Medical Doctor's degree from Harvard Medical School. She had been teaching at Harvard Medical School when she was recruited by Homeland Security. She served on the Task Force but was looking for a reason to quit and a way to get out safely. She longed for the quiet and peace of a college campus.

After she had introduced herself T. J. said, "I'll want a one on one with you later on, Dr. Erickson. To be honest, I don't understand what's been happening here and I hope you'll be able to enlighten me . . . Psychologically I mean."

Next to Dr. Erickson was Sean Murphy. He leaned back in his chair and smiled at T. J., locking his eyes on hers without flinching. Sean was a Detective Lieutenant with the New York State Police Criminal Investigation Division. He was a ruggedly good looking Irishman, with red-brown hair and emerald eyes with a lightly freckled face.

He was used to women 'making themselves available' to him as he liked to say. Boredom with the routine of the State Police and various location assignments very far from cities of any size caused him to sign up with Homeland Security. He had been assigned to the Task Force because of his investigation skills and because he had a certain instinct when it came to solving crimes. He was very unhappy with his present assignment which he considered out in the sticks, away from available women.

Sean just smiled leeringly at T. J. He said nothing. Finally she said, "OK, Sean. Why don't you try seducing me when all this is over? I like steaks cooked rare and Champaign, but if you're not hung like a horse all we'll do is eat dinner."

The last person at the table was Noah Goldberg. Noah was an Israeli MOSSAD Agent temporarily assigned to the Task Force during the current investigation. Israel had a big interest in the investigation, but the reason wasn't perfectly clear to the rest of the Task Force. T. J. had agreed quickly to his joining the taskforce when the request from MOSSAD came in. She assigned him to the Task Force and Israel expressed profound thanks.

"Noah," T.J. said and smiled honestly. "I'm glad to see you again. Thank you for accepting my offer to be here. I hope you've settled in well?"

No one on the task force had known T. J. had placed Noah with them. They all immediately assumed he was a mole and hoped they hadn't confided in him too much.

"OK," T. J. said. "Now we all know each other. That's a good thing, don't you all think? Anyway, I want the whole story, from the beginning, and don't leave out details you thought were unimportant when you wrote your reports."

****

The Whole Story as Told by Liz Blackburn

Sgt. Joe Fisher of the Montana Highway Patrol was on duty that day. He was driving south on Interstate 15. He had stopped for lunch at Millie's Café just three miles south of the Canadian border. It was his opinion that Millie's bacon cheeseburger was the best in the State. He wished he could enjoy a couple of cold Coors with the burger and fries, but he was a good cop and would not drink on duty.

He was twenty miles north of Great Falls enjoying the sunny, warm afternoon in that late summer. He knew that any day, perhaps even the next day, cold Canadian air would race down into Montana, bringing winter snow with it. But he would enjoy that summer day while it lasted. He kept the windows of his cruiser rolled down.

He passed a car, a blue Chrysler 300. The right rear fender was damaged and the tail light glass was broken. No big thing, he thought, but he ran the Canadian plate anyway. It was a rental, owned by Diamond Auto Rentals which Sgt. Fisher knew was a Canadian company.

No big thing, he thought once again. But he had to stop the car, tell the driver of the damaged rear light and write up a warning that it needed to be repaired. So he pulled behind the car and turned on the overhead lights. There was no response at first. Then the Chrysler suddenly took off.

Sgt. Fisher flipped on the siren and tried to catch up. They reached speeds of over 100 MPH, cutting between and passing other cars on the highway. He radioed in and asked for assistance and soon there were three Highway Patrol and two County Sheriff's cars in pursuit.

The driver of the Chrysler knew what he was doing. He was outdriving and out maneuvering the police. He took an exit ramp and increased speed up the ramp and across the street, through a stop sign, and down the entrance ramp back onto I-15, leaving the police to be more cautious doing the same. He was easily pulling away from the five cars in pursuit until a long-haul truck driver in a cowboy hat who had been listening to the chase on his police band radio decided to help out. As the Chrysler began to pass the truck it swerved and forced the Chrysler off the road.

The car hit the drainage ditch along the side of the road, rose up on the two right side wheels, skidded along for twenty feet and then flipped over on its back. When Sgt. Fisher arrived he pulled a fire extinguisher from his car's trunk and ran to the overturned Chrysler. The engine was still running and he could smell gasoline. There were no flames yet, but he knew there would be at any moment.

Using the fire extinguisher, he broke the driver's side window, reached in and grabbed the key in the ignition, turning the engine off. The driver was slumped down, held up by his seat belt. He was bleeding from his nose and from a gash on his forehead.

Sgt. Fisher tried to open the driver's door but it was jammed shut. He cut the seat belt with his pocket knife and pulled the driver out and away from the car. The two other Highway Patrolmen started assisting with first aid as the two Sheriff's Deputies were using fire extinguishers on the underside of the flipped car to try to cool it and forestall explosions and fires.

As they waited for the ambulance to arrive, Sgt. Fisher looked through the unconscious man's pockets for a wallet with ID. He found nothing except a roll of one hundred dollar bills wrapped in a heavy rubber band. He counted out fifty-one of the bills.

He looked into the wrecked car to see if there was anything there that would identify the man, but all he found was a packet of car rental papers. They listed the driver's name as John Wayne. 'That's gotta be a phony name,' he said to himself.

The ambulance took the unconscious driver to a hospital in Great Falls where he was admitted under a 'John Doe'. He remained unconscious for two days.

The Highway Patrol contacted the car rental agency and learned that the car had been rented by John Wayne who had shown a valid Canadian Driver's License with a home address in Montreal. With the help of the Montreal Police they learned that John Wayne did in fact exist and that he had reported his wallet and all its contents missing three days before.

The Montana State Forensics Lab examined the driver's license and found it had been very expertly altered, changing the photo and the physical description of John

Wayne to match the driver of the Chrysler.

A Highway Patrol Investigator went to the hospital and took finger prints from the still unconscious man. They were run through every record data base in the U. S. and Canada, Mexico, and all South American Countries. As a last resort they requested the prints be run by Interpol which responded they could not match them in their international data base.

At that point the FBI office in Helena, Montana was contacted and an agent arrived at the hospital an hour and a half before the driver regained consciousness. The Agent stood at the man's bedside talking to a doctor when the driver opened his eyes.

The Agent stepped to the side of the bed and asked the driver what his name was. The man stared blankly up at the Agent. He asked again and still received no answer. The doctors said they could find nothing wrong with the man's hearing or speech ability. Other police and Federal Agents tried but the man would not speak to anyone. Eventually, he would not even look up at anyone.

He lay silently for three days and nights. He ate the food brought to him, he drank the water and juice brought to him. He did not fight against what the doctors and nurses did by way of examinations and monitoring; in fact he helped with a small smile on his face. But he would not speak.

The FBI and Canadian authorities tried to find out where he had come from, if he had entered Canada from somewhere. They could trace the man back only to the rental car counter at the international airport at Vancouver, British Columbia. Before that it appeared the man didn't exist at all.

On the third day, a young, low ranking Traffic Investigator with the Canadian Mounted Police linked the Chrysler 300 with a minor two vehicle accident that occurred the day before the wordless man was chased in Montana. The accident happened on Canadian Highway 1 a few miles east of Calgary. It was a minor fender bender that should not have caused a lot of interest on the part of anyone except perhaps the Insurance Company that would have to pay a claim. But when the Canadian Police arrived they found the driver of one of the cars, his wife and his two young children all lying at the side of the road with their necks broken.

The conclusion was that the silent man had flown into Vancouver, B.C., rented the car and tried to enter the US undetected and quietly. Only the minor accident resulting in the smashed rear tail light interfered.

Because of the international aspect, Homeland Security in Washington, D.C. was notified and the man was arrested under a FISA warrant, taken to Washington and eventually to the top secret facility beneath Brown's Farm.

****

At that point in the story, T. J. interrupted Liz Blackburn and asked, "OK. You've had this man here for three weeks and two days. I understand he hasn't uttered a word. Is that correct, Liz?"

"Yes, Miss Kohl. That's correct," Liz answered. Her team's specialty was supposed to be interrogations with a backup of investigations. They had, in the four years since they had been recruited and assigned to Brown's Farm, a 100% success record. They had been directly responsible for stopping six different major attacks on the United States by Al Qaeda. They had sent Special Forces Teams and CIA assassination teams to kill eight people in eight different Countries. But they had been unable to make this man say one single word.

T. J. turned to Ricky DeMateo and asked, "How about foreign Languages? Is it possible he doesn't understand English?"

"I've tried everything I know," Ricky answered. "I even Googled a bunch of languages that only people in remote areas of the world speak. My opinion is that he understands English and he can talk . . . But he won't talk."

She asked Sean Murphy, "Sean, you've run his finger prints through everything there is?"

Sean answered, "Yes, Miss Kohl. I ran his prints all over the world. Even the Chinese and Russians cooperated. I ran them twice through Interpol and asked them to do a manual search. You know how their budget is being cut lately. I figured maybe their computers weren't up to date. Still nothing. I took a DNA sample and ran it through everything we have, military and civilian. This guy doesn't seem to exist."

T. J. next turned to Paul Hazelton. She smiled when she asked him, "And Paul, I assume you've . . . Shall we say questioned the man? . . . In your own special way?"

"Hey lady," Paul said. "I've done everything to that son of a bitch except cut off his nuts. He even seemed to enjoy the god damn water boarding. He ain't gonna talk. That's one tough bastard. I've never run across anybody like him before."

T. J. sat quietly for a moment or two in the quiet room. Then she turned to Noah Goldberg.

"Noah," she asked in a subdued voice. "This is no time to be keeping secrets. Have your operatives in Iran, Syria, Egypt or anyplace else in the Middle East heard anything about this man?"

"Nothing," Noah said. "We've taken chances we shouldn't take to try to find out something. We've done break-ins to get files. We've kidnapped and interrogated people we should have left alone. We've risked all we can risk. There's nothing more we can do and we haven't learned anything about him."

THREE - Off To See The Wizard

T. J. sat staring up at the ceiling, drumming her finger nails on the table top. She had to do something. People were depending on her, as usual. This was important, perhaps the most important job she ever had. The entire Nation depended on how she handled this. It could be, she was sure, that the future direction of the entire civilized world depended on what she would do. T. J. knew this, she was positive about this.

"OK," she said finally. "Everybody please leave . . . Dr. Erickson, please remain."

The people at the table pushed their chairs back and stood, some faster than others. But they all left the conference room and closed the door behind them, leaving T. J. and Dr. Erickson alone.

"Please come sit next to me," T. J. said. The Doctor, who was at the farthest end of the table, rose slowly, uncomfortably, and walked to the chair next to her boss.

"Dr. Erickson," T. J. said. "Tell me what you think about this man."

The Doctor took a moment to think about that. If she said the wrong thing, if she said something T. J. didn't want to hear, then T. J. would be angry and she might fire the Doctor. That, of course, is just what Cindy Erickson wanted, to get out of an environment she hated. She would run as fast as she could back to the peace of a college campus, any college campus.

But having a job termination on her record wasn't a good thing, she thought. Then again, what could they do to her? They couldn't even admit she had been working on Brown's Farm because the facility at Brown's Farm didn't exist outside of a very small Intelligence circle.

So what the hell, she thought and said, "What I think, Miss Kohl, is that we are holding a man here incognito. We have denied him every legal and Constitutional right even the most heinous criminal is assured. And we don't even know who he is. What I think is we have grossly overstepped the bounds of civilized society. We assume this man is dangerous. We have absolutely no evidence to assume that. What I think is that this man may well have committed a civil crime in Canada . . . We don't know that he did, and we don't know that he didn't. That is and should be a civilian police matter, not ours.

"What I think, Miss Kohl, is that we have tortured a man . . . For what? You're asking me my opinion so I will tell you my opinion. We should turn this man over to the civilian authorities immediately and pay the price for having kept him here and tortured him."

"And what about your Nation, Dr. Erickson? What about your Country?" T. J. asked.

"I believe my Country is better than what we are doing here."

T. J. filed all that away in her memory. She would take care of the Dr. Erickson problem later.

"Tell me about him . . . Physically and mentally," T. J. said.

"Without extensive testing . . . Which would take weeks in a hospital environment . . . My best guess is he suffers from total Idiopathic Neuropathy."

T. J. smiled but it really wasn't a smile; there was more of an impatient threat to her upturned lips. "And just what is that, Doctor?"

"It's a condition in which the patient cannot feel pain.

It is thought to be an inability of the nervous system to transmit signals indicating pain to the brain. Most people have limited areas of the Neuropathy; say in their feet or fingers or such. This man, I believe may have the condition throughout his entire body. He simply cannot feel the pain your people have inflicted on him."

"How does one get like that?" T. J. asked.

"Some are born with it; some acquire the disease later in life. Extensive research is being done, but no one knows the absolute truth. There is some speculation that with treatment a patient can have the condition induced, but what I've read on the subject tells me that it can be induced for only very limited periods of time. I don't believe in most things I read on the internet, but there is some pseudo-scientific talk of the Russians having developed a way to permanently induce the condition."

T.J. thought about this for a moment. None of this had been in any of the reports she had read over that past two days. Why? Why wasn't this in the reports and who was responsible for not including it? That was a question she would seek an answer to shortly, but not right then. She needed more answers to other questions first.

"You've given him drugs, truth serums as they're called?" T. J. asked.

"Yes," Dr. Erickson answered. "I've administered several treatments of Sodium Thiopental and Sodium Amytal. Each treatment was in larger doses than the previous. The final dose of each was enough to affect a horse, but they seemed to have no affect on the man. He just smiled when they asked him questions after each treatment."

"How about the new drug the Army has developed? Sodium Banecatin. Have you tried that?" T. J. asked.

"I have refused to administer that drug," the Doctor answered.

"Why?"

"It is untested and unsafe," Dr. Erickson answered. "I've read the reports on Sodium Banecatin. Two of the twelve people it has been used on suffered fatal cardiac arrest and one suffered a massive stroke which brought on death within two days."

"So that means you would refuse to use the drug even if I ordered you to?" T. J. asked.

"Yes," the Doctor said simply and quickly.

T. J. smiled and reached out her hand to Cindy Erickson, but the Doctor refused the offer.

"It's OK," T. J. said. "You have a conscience. I understand that. I wish I had a conscience."

She changed the subject and asked, "Have you examined the man physically and medically?"

"Yes," she answered. "He's the most perfect specimen of a human being I've ever seen. His muscle mass is perfect, and there's not an ounce of un-needed fat on him. His blood tests tell me he's not had any medication or drug or even an over the counter medication inside him for a long, long time. He has no scars. X-rays say he's never had a broken bone. Hell, he doesn't even have a cavity or a filling in his mouth.

"I hooked him up to a polygraph, and all he did was smile when I asked questions. He does smile a lot, by the way. He didn't answer any questions, of course, and the polygraph didn't register the slightest change in breathing, blood pressure or anything when they asked him even the most pointed questions. He had no reaction to anything asked or suggested.

"Physically, he was in better shape when he first arrived here then he is today but he is still a remarkable specimen. Today he shows the results of torture. He's cut and bruised. He has burn marks all over from the electric shock and cigarettes that have been used on him. It's disgusting. But all he does is smile. He won't say a word. He eats everything he is given but has never indicated he was hungry. He drinks water when given water but there's never been a sign that he was thirsty. He's never tried to fight off anything they do to him although by the look of him he could defend himself very well. If he wanted to I'm sure he could hurt anyone here. He even appears to be cooperative no matter what they do to him. But he won't talk."

T. J. stood, made a mental note to get rid of Dr. Cynthia Erickson. She was too soft, too caring, too moral for the work that needed to be done at Brown's Farm. She said, "Alright. Let's go see the man."

The two women stepped out into the pale blue hallway. Waiting there were Liz Blackburn, Teddy Molinari, Ricky DeMateo, Paul Hazelton and Sean Murphy. Only Noah Goldberg was absent.

"Alright everybody," T. J. said brightly. "Why don't you all join us? We're off to see the wizard."

They walked to the elevator following T. J. and the Doctor, no one saying anything. Teddy stepped forward at the elevator and held his eye close to the retina scanner. The door slid open and all managed to squeeze into the car. Teddy touched his index finger to the finger print scanner and the level buttons lit up. The man who would not speak was being held on Level 9 in the Interrogation Section, one level below.

They stepped off on Level Nine, Teddy Molinari in the lead. He turned left and they walked twenty-five yards down the pale green hallway to a room with a heavy steel door, inside of which was a cage ten foot wide, ten foot deep and ten foot tall. Inside the cage, sitting cross-legged on the bare concrete floor was the man. He was naked; his body showed the clear signs of the torture he had endured.

His eyes were closed; his breathing appeared to be regular and soft. He seemed to be meditating. He seemed to be at peace. His eyes opened and he looked up at the group walking into the room. He smiled. T. J. saw the clear, bright blue eyes of the man. He didn't stand, he barely moved.

"Take him to Interrogation Section," T. J. said as she walked out of the room. The man stood without being told to and stepped to the cell door, waiting for it to be opened. He did not seem to be bothered about his nudity. He seemed as if it were normal, as if he was supposed to be naked at the time.

The Interrogation Section was a large room, a nightmare from the Spanish Inquisition. Torture devices both from ages past and the latest thing in hi-tech were everywhere. In one corner was a cold steel chair with heavy leather straps on the arms and on the front legs. Attached to the back was a rod that held a leather cap that would be fastened down on the man's head. The chair was stained in many places with blood that had dried brown.

"Strap him in the chair," T. J. said. She was sitting on a tall wooden stool in the opposite corner.

The man did not struggle; in fact he did what he could to help Teddy and Paul strap him down.

"Before I have them wire you up," T. J. said to the man. "Before I have them turn up the juice so much that it may fry your brain . . . Is there anything you want to say?"

The man smiled at T. J. and tilted his head slightly to the right. There was no fear in his eyes, there was no anger. He seemed to be absolutely without emotion, absolutely at peace.

Suddenly he sat up so straight so quickly that everyone except T. J. jumped a little. The man ran his tongue across his parched lips. He spoke for the first time. In a deep and soft voice, tinged with a very slight accent of some sort, he said, "Morgan Crew."

FOUR - Caroline And Betsy

In the year since I had been in Hawaii I have done a lot of thinking about what happened there. In all that time, with all the thought I've given it, I still don't know if what happened back there was real or a figment of imagination or a nightmare, or maybe just too many years of hiding inside too many tall glasses of Wild Turkey with just a splash of club soda. A year later and I'm not even sure if I was in Hawaii at all. Could all those Hawaiian legends and gods and devils be real? I honestly don't know. The only thing I am certain about is what happened to a good man and father – Hound – is because of me.

When Sandy and Bob Sommers came to Hawaii I tried to put all the bad things behind me. I tried as best I could to tell my wife and my friend what had happened, but it was difficult because any sane person would think I was making it all up. Who would believe that that damn alter and prayer place just disappeared? And although Sandy wanted to believe me, she could not admit that she did not believe me.

We spent two wonderful weeks there, playing in the sun, eating the best fish in the world, sampling strange but terrific rum drinks, and shopping of course. We drove all day to reach the Mauna Kea volcano. And of course the three of us tried to do a hula, after too many Mai Tai's at a couple of hotel sponsored luaus. All we accomplished was making fools of ourselves in front of the others there. But it was all good fun. I could not bring myself to visit Nancy Wong and her children. Inside me, I wanted Sandy to meet Nancy Wong but guilt is a terrible weight to carry.

A lot of other things have happened in my life since coming home to San Marcos. People who know little of my life and nothing about the few days I spent in Hawaii tell me, 'Morgan Crew, you are one lucky son of a bitch.' And in fact I am. I have everything I always wanted in life, and I don't mean all the damn money, either. Most other people would envy me being so rich, but I was thankful for having found Sandy, for having a small circle of good friends, for being able to live in such a beautiful place as San Marcos, and for having the time to go fishing and play golf.

My broken right arm, smashed in an auto accident that saved me from being murdered by Robert Hana, did not heal properly. I had to have it operated on and I spent ten days in a hospital bed. The arm is working well enough but on the golf course I find it impossible to make a full back swing and I have lost twenty-five to thirty yards off my drives. But I still play golf, just with a slightly higher handicap.

A heart attack that caused the sudden and unexpected death of San Marcos City Councilman Howard Mackey also caused me to be appointed to fill his seat for the final ten weeks of his term. And then I lost the election to a two year term on the Council, after my very lackluster campaign which included telling everyone I could that I really didn't want the job.

But the best thing to happen to me was to become a father to the most beautiful little baby girl in the world. Of course I have to give some credit to Sandy for that blessing. She enjoyed every minute of her pregnancy. Although I must admit she wasn't too disappointed when the morning sickness ended. She had a really good time watching me fall all over myself to do everything for her. I cooked, I made sure the house was spotless, and when she wanted a glass of water, I ran to get it for her. I bought her so many maternity clothes that I had to clean all my clothes out of our closet and store them in a guest bedroom. But it was fun for her and it was fun for me.

Old Doc Everett told Sandy she had to exercise every day right up to just a few days before delivery. I objected when I thought he meant she should be going to the gym and working out with heavy weights. Sandy and he laughed at me and he explained that a daily walk and some pre-natal stretching exercises would suffice.

And then there came the night when Sandy woke me at half past one in the morning to tell me it was time. It was shear panic on my part. Oh, I was able to get her to the hospital without crashing the car into a tree or anything like that, but Sandy used her laughter to great effect in order to mask the contractions.

Old Doc Everett had Sandy brought into the delivery room after three very long hours of waiting. I followed but the Doctor was afraid I might pass out and insisted I sit in a corner or leave the room.

I remember saying, “But Doctor! I've got to be near Sandy.”

“Morgan,” he said and patted me on my shaking shoulder. “Sandy is much stronger than you are. If you faint and fall on the floor you'll just be in everyone's way. Everyone will be stepping over you and if somebody trips over you . . . Well, you can just imagine. And Sandy would insist on me taking care of you and I can't have that,” he joked. Everyone in the room laughed except me.

But in short order I was able to stand and hold Sandy's hand. It didn't bother me that she almost broke a couple of my fingers while she gave birth. And I watched as our beautiful daughter came into the world.

****

We were at home that evening, enjoying a drink or two with our good friends Andy and Kay O'Malley. We were headed out to the Country Club for a charity dinner, dance and silent auction for the Northern California Animal Rescue Society. I have let the family accountants work with my old Aunt Viv in deciding which charities get what from the Crew family fortune, but N.C.A.R.S. is something special to Sandy, and she arranges an annual thing at the Club to drain some money from the wallets of the San Marcos rich folks to benefit N.C.A.R.S.

It was the first time Sandy and I had gone out for an evening since our daughter Caroline was born. At first I didn't think it was a very good idea to leave the baby with a sitter. My idea was to keep a close eye on her until her 35th birthday, when I would allow her to start dating boys whom I would select for her after a very careful and very in-depth background check. But Sandy had other ideas, of course.

So giving in as usual, I suggested we start interviewing baby sitters until we found a real life Fräulein Maria from the Sound of Music. But once again Sandy had other ideas. She invited a young lady to our house one afternoon.

I had met the young lady once before. Bob Sommers had asked me some months ago to do some checking on her. It was his subtle way of getting me involved. Bob admitted later that he saw something in the girl. He described it as a spark of something good fighting to get beyond the cloud of the life she was living.

It seems Betsy Concanon had been arrested down in San Francisco with three wallets in her big, tattered, hand-woven bag. None of the wallets belonged to her. Betsy Concanon, you see, is a pick pocket and a very good one at that. Three years ago, when Bob approached me, she was sixteen. She was a run-away from her mother and father who live in San Marcos. She was living with some bikers out near the airport. When she was arrested she was dirty, hungry, and angry. The police returned her to San Marcos after she had entered a guilty plea in juvenile court. She was placed on probation until she turned 18. Bob wanted to know more about Betsy's family before returning her to her parents, and he knew I was the person best able to do that.

So Bob advised the Youth Authorities in San Fran to do some case work and get her a good foster home down there rather than send her home. But the courts decided otherwise and issued an order to return her to the 'loving care' of her parents. Her parents said they didn't want her. They felt some time in "jail" would do her some good.

Her father is a banker who drinks a lot and her mother is a Country Club whore. Both parents had ignored the girl except to chastise her for everything she did. Forget about family dinners and PTA meetings, she was left alone day after day. In Betsy's sophomore year of High School she made it onto the girls' basketball team. Her parents weren't listening when she told them. Betsy was proud at her accomplishment and wanted them to be proud, too. She played one game for the school and then quit the team. She had hoped that her parents would somehow magically appear in the stands to cheer her on. They didn't.

She continually got in trouble, at school, with the neighbors, and with the police; I was sure, as a way to get some attention from her parents.

The first time I saw Betsy she was sitting, arms crossed tightly in front of her, in a corner of a small, grey room at St. Mary's School which is a school for orphans funded by my family. There was no other place Bob could think of to house her in San Marcos until he decided what to do with her. Her parents made no effort to bring her home. They seemed content to leave her at the school. They had told Bob she was too much trouble and they had given up on her.

Sister Coretta phoned me to say there might be some hope for the girl if she could stay at the school. I got Bob to agree to leave her in the care of the Sisters. In fact Betsy did very well at the school once she settled in. She finished High School with good if not excellent grades and she was showing some signs of change.

She was dressed in black that day I went to see her. Her hair was a bright and very unnatural fire engine red. Her face was twisted into as angry a forced stare as she could manage. Sister Coretta walked next to me as she showed me to Betsy's room. I asked the girl a couple of simple questions while trying to smile and sound kind. That's an approach I had learned from Sandy. Betsy would not say anything. She would not look at me. She didn't move.

Betsy, then and still today, dresses in black. She recently has changed her hair color from fire engine red to lime green. She has a gold ring pierced through her right eyebrow and a tattoo of a skull and cross bones on her left shoulder. And she has an attitude towards everyone except the Nuns at St. Mary's School, whom she loves and who show her the only real love she has ever known. She mocks everything she sees as adult and contemporary outside of the borders of the school.

And when Sandy said she wanted to hire Betsy as a babysitter, I said, "Why in God's name would you want to hire a biker chick to take care of our baby?"

"She is *not* a biker chick, Morgan," she said. "She is a bright, intelligent young lady from a really terrible home. She's been working in the kitchen at St. Mary's and taking night classes in business at the City College. I've spoken with her and I trust her. She's been here twice and I've seen her with Caroline. She's really good with the baby. And she deserves a chance."

And so I lost another argument. As it turned out, Betsy proved to be an excellent sitter. I restrained myself from admitting that for a long time. Caroline took to Betsy immediately, and Betsy tried her best to spoil the baby. In fact, she is better than I am at comforting Caroline when she cries. She seems to have an instinct for caring for Caroline.

So the night of the charity dinner we were at home and on our second martini with our friends Andy and Kay while we waited for Betsy. The doorbell rang and I went to answer it.

When I opened the door Betsy said, "BOO!" and laughed.

"Oh yes," I said as I stepped aside to let her in. "Very funny. You're dressed for Halloween again, I see."

Betsy was in her usual black, from neck to feet, which was kind of an artistic statement against her lime green hair. There was a chrome plated chain draped from her thick black leather belt. She was wearing studded black leather gloves that had the fingers cut off exposing her black painted finger nails. She had been wearing less makeup in the last month, setting aside the black lipstick for a pale pink shade and not framing her eyes with black on her brows and lashes. And her black T-shirt was new; at least I hadn't seen it before. It had a large drugged out rendition of some long haired rock star across the front. But the gold ring on her eyebrow was gone!

"Yeah. I do it just to piss you off, man," she laughed.

She was carrying a teddy bear almost as big as she was. "I got this for C," she said.

"Her name is Caroline," I said.

"Yeah, Morgan, I know. But it's a really old fashioned like name . . . And she smiles every time I call her C."

As we walked to the living room I reminded her, "People who work for me address me as Mr. Crew, especially when they are very young people who work for me."

"Yeah, Morgan," she said. "I'll try to remember that."

In the living room Sandy hugged Betsy and introduced her to Kay and Andy who looked suspiciously at the black clad young girl. Sandy took the big teddy bear and told Betsy that Caroline would love it.

"That's a very expensive gift," I said. "Where did you get the money for it?"

"Gosh!" Betsy said. She smiled and winked conspiratorially at Sandy. "My lawyer told me not to say anything. You know. Fifth Amendment and all that stuff."

Sandy and she had a good laugh at that. Sandy hugged Betsy and said, "We're probably going to be late getting home tonight. You better stay the night here, OK?"

"Sure," Betsy said. "I kind of figured that so I've got a bag out in the car."

"Car?" I questioned. "Where'd you get a car from?"

"Don't worry Morgan," Betsy said. "I only hotwired it and I'm gonna' return it when I'm done."

Sandy laughed and hugged Betsy again. "The car belongs to the Sisters at the school," she said.

Sandy and I waited with our friends, finishing our drinks, while Betsy went to Caroline's room.

Andy whispered, "Are you guys sure about her?"

His wife, Kay, said, "Andy, shut up, will you? It's not your business. I've seen Betsy with the baby and she's really good. Don't judge people by how they dress."

Sandy, sensing an argument that would carry into the evening at the Club, said, "Hey! Drink up everyone. We're going to be late."

So we left, and we left our daughter in the hands of Betsy Concanon. At the club I did manage to sneak off and phone several times . . . Just to check to make sure Betsy and Caroline were still OK. On the third call Betsy laughed and said, "Help Morgan! How do I put out the fire?"

FIVE - The Attack

T. J. Kohl waited in the small kitchen of the VIP suite on Level 7. Level 7 was comprised of small living apartments for administrative staff. Levels 5 and 6 were comprised of barracks rooms and a Mess Hall for the fifty-two Marine guards.

Tea sounded good but the Lipton tea her mother had served wasn't what she wanted. She kept a hard to find and expensive Oolong at her home in Washington, DC. But all that was in the kitchen on Level 7 was coffee and only a very common grocery store pre-ground coffee at that. But she needed something while she waited for Noah Goldberg. It had been a long day, and caffeine was the only drug she would allow herself.

She searched through the cabinets for something to eat while the Mr. Coffee did its job. There were two boxes of Saltine crackers, some canned Norwegian sardines, one package of Oreos and three dozen black plastic wrapped MREs. T. J. laughed out loud – something she never did when others were nearby – and said, "Some friggin' VIP quarters."

The coffee was done and she filled a mug and grabbed the Oreos. She was biting into her third when the heavy steel door of the VIP suite opened and Noah Goldberg walked in.

"Close the door, Noah," T. J. said. "Lock it, please. I don't want to be interrupted."

He turned and closed the steel door. There was a small glass window at eye level on the door that was used to see into the hallway. It had a steel shutter over the window that Noah closed and latched. On the wall next to the door was a key pad lock. Noah punched in his own six digit code, and both he and T. J. could hear the four dead bolts slide into place.

He walked to the table where T. J. sat, pulled a chair out and sat.

"Would you like coffee?" T. J. asked.

"No, thank you," he answered. "What are we going to do now?"

"Where is he?" she asked.

"They moved him to a room with a bed and sink. They gave him some clothes and he's eating right now. They locked him in the room. What are your plans for him?"

"How is he physically?" she asked.

"Remarkably good," Noah said. He took a cookie and bit into it, and then said, "I've never seen anything like it. We've questioned the worst of Hamas . . . Never to the extent this man has been tortured . . . And a few of them have died. This man acts like nothing has happened to him despite the scars, burns, cuts, and bruising. I think this man doesn't feel pain."

"How do we find out who the hell he is?" T. J. asked as she pushed the package of Oreos toward her friend. He dropped the cookie he had bitten into on the table and ignored the package.

"I don't know," he said and took a cookie from the package. He looked at it and twirled it around in his fingers, but he didn't eat it. "If I didn't know better, I'd say that son of a bitch doesn't exist. He's like a hallucination . . . A dream . . . A nightmare."

"What about this Morgan Crew?" she asked. "What does that mean?"

"I made a phone call back home," Noah said.

"Mossad tells me he's some super rich bastard. Lives in California somewhere."

"OK. I'll make arrangements to have him picked up," T. J. said. "In the meantime, what do you suggest we do with the man?"

A sudden blaring and ear splitting alarm screeching in the hallway made both of them jump. T. J. ran to a red phone hanging on the wall near the kitchen area.

"What's going on!" she shouted into the phone over the deafening siren. She listened and then said, "Jesus Christ! It can't be! It can't be!"

She stood frozen with the phone at her ear. When the lights in the room went out, the phone went dead at the same time. She let the phone drop from her hand and hang by its cord. The windowless room was pitch-black inside. She fumbled on the wall next to the phone for a flashlight that was hanging there. Flipping it on, she turned to where Noah had been – she could not see him at first but found him standing at the table – and she said, "My God! Brown's Farm is being attacked!"

Noah flipped on a small flashlight he carried and found T. J.'s face. She was frozen with fear, something Noah had never seen in her before. He had worked with T. J. Kohl a dozen times, a few easy and pleasant in sun drenched locals, most in dark and dangerous places where their lives hung by thin threads. Noah had never seen her scared before.

"What do you mean 'attacked'?" he said trying to sound calm. He had been in many, many dangerous situations and had learned to push what could erupt as panic to the rear.

"Attacked!" she repeated. "There's an armed force. They've gotten inside the Levels somehow. Security said they were killing everyone. My God! How?"

Noah walked to her. She was taller then he, and she was shaking visibly. He reached out to touch her shoulder and said, "You have to calm down, T. J.. Look, there's a heavy steel door at this room and no other way in. Is there any place here we can hold up . . . A closet or anything."

"Hide!" T.J. said. "You want to hide? We need to get out there and do something!"

"Do what, T. J.?" he said. "Are you armed? I'm not. There are fifty-two Marines out there and they know what they're doing. We need to protect ourselves now. Tell me. Where can we be safe in here?"

T. J. thought for a moment and then said, "In the bedroom I suppose. Back there." She pointed behind Noah and as she did heavy pounding started on the room's door from the hallway outside. They ran to the bedroom and Noah pushed T. J. under the bed. He quickly slid under and lay next to her hoping that she could remain quiet and not scream like a silly girl. He knew she was more than that, but he had never seen her frightened as she was as they lay hidden under the bed.

She had been with him when they were part of midnight raids on sites in Iraq and Afghanistan on moonless, dark nights. She had done her share of the cold killing and was as good, and sometimes better, than the men they were with. Now, suddenly and without explanation, she was scared.

There was an explosion and the steel door into the VIP suite crashed open. Automatic gun fire exploded and filled the concrete walled room. Then a stun grenade detonated. They felt the repercussion fill the suite.

From under the bed Noah and T. J. saw three men that were mere shadows in the dark room. They were dressed in black from the hoods on their heads to the heavy boots on their feet. They moved quickly and professionally into the VIP suite, firing automatic weapons randomly, spraying bullets everywhere they looked. One of them stepped into the open doorway of the bedroom and fired bullets across the room, over the bed. Noah saw a pale green light coming from the man's head. They were wearing night vision goggles that would reveal his position under the bed if the man were to look down.

The man turned quickly and followed his two companions out of the suite. Noah started to pull himself out from under the bed. T. J. stopped him and put her finger to her lips to tell him to remain silent. She could not see Noah's face because of the absolute dark. If she had she would have seen his forehead wrinkled in wonder at why this woman was so frightened. The woman he knew from years past would have rushed out and tackled the armed men all by herself. Now she lay on the floor under the bed, shaking.

They stayed there for forty-five minutes, until the gunshots and explosions ended. The lights in the hallway flashed on suddenly and absolute silence surrounded them for another fifteen minutes. T. J. slid out from under the bed and Noah followed. Slowly and carefully they peered out into the suite's main room. It was still dark inside but light from the hallway threw enough illumination into the room to reveal the damage done so quickly by the invaders. So many bullets had been fired that nearly everything in the room had been destroyed. Cabinet doors either hung limply on a single hinge or were splintered and lay on the floor. The Mr. Coffee machine was a pile of unrecognizable plastic. The table and four chairs were shattered. Shards of broken dishes were everywhere. Even the bags of MREs were destroyed. Nothing remained undamaged.

Noah stepped quietly to the hallway door and pressed his back against the wall. He carefully and quickly looked to the right and left. He found the hallway empty except for the bullet ridden bodies of two Marine guards. He bent and removed the Beretta pistols from the holsters of the two guards. Their Heckler & Koch automatic rifles lay on the concrete floor next to them. Noah tossed one of the pistols and one of the rifles to T. J. He waved for T. J. to follow him.

There was absolute quiet on Level 7. They went from

room to room and found only destruction and dead bodies. Among the dead were the bullet riddled bodies of Liz Blackburn and Teddy Molinari, who were killed as they lay in bed holding each other. Ricky DeMateo lay in the hallway, his head blown open, along with the bodies of five Marine guards. None of the dead were black clad attackers, however.

"We need to go to Level 9," T. J. said. "I need to know if he's still alive."

They walked to the elevator at the far end of the hallway, carefully avoiding the bodies and the blood. At the elevator T. J. punched in her six digit code and then re-entered it. Nothing happened; the elevator doors would not open.

"We'll take the stairs," she said. The door at the stairs hung open and mangled on its hinges. Together T. J. and Noah started down. There were bodies of Marines littering the stairs, and the walls were riddled with the aftermath of the assault. At the bottom of the staircase the door at Level 9 had been blown open by a heavy explosive and lay in a mangled mass on the floor.

The door to the room where the man had been placed had also been blown open. Inside, the room was empty. The tray of food the man had been given lay on the neatly made bed, the plate and bowl and cup empty. No bullet holes or destruction of any kind had fouled the room. The man was gone.

"This was a rescue," Noah said.

"Yes," T. J. agreed. "But by who?"

They walked to the elevator and found Paul Hazelton's bullet riddled body lying in the doorway of the elevator, the doors sliding back and forth against his lifeless body. That answered the question of why T. J.'s code at the elevator didn't work. Inside the elevator, Dr. Cindy Erickson sat on the floor, her back against the wall, her body riddled with bullet holes from which blood still flowed. Her eyes were wide in the fear of what she had known was about to happen and her mouth hung open in a silent death scream.

Noah and T. J. pulled the bodies out of the elevator and despite the thick pool of blood inside they used it to go to Level 1, which was the small workshop in the barn. The doors slid open and Noah opened the tattered wooden door in the workshop. They walked into the old barn and found Sean Murphy lying on the dirt floor surrounded by his own blood.

"My God," T. J. said. "The whole damn executive staff is dead! Everybody!"

And then T. J. turned suddenly and ran for the open barn door. It was raining lightly outside; the sky was covered with steel grey clouds. She stumbled through the mud, ripping off her hi-heeled shoes and tossing them aside. She ran up the stairs leading up to the old farm house, across the porch, and through the front door. There, inside, she found her parents dead, her mother on the kitchen floor wrapped in her blood stained apron and her father caught in the screened doorway in the back of the kitchen.

Noah walked quietly to her and touched her shoulder gently. She turned and fell into his arms. She was crying uncontrollably and pounding her fists onto Noah's shoulders and chest. He just held her and let her work out her few minutes of heated anger until she collapsed into sobbing and would have fallen to the floor had not Noah held onto her. He hugged her tightly and let her cry.

When her tears began to subside, Noah led her out of the kitchen to the covered front porch. He sat her in one of the weather beaten old rocking chairs. He knelt in front of her.

"T. J.," he said softly. "I'm so sorry. This whole thing is crazy. Your folks had nothing to do with The Levels, for God's sake."

"I was going to get them out of here," she said. "They wanted to retire. They were so good, Noah. They didn't deserve this."

Noah knew T. J.'s parents. He knew their lives before Brown's Farm. He knew her father had once been a CIA sanctioned assassin and her mother, as a young CIA Agent stationed in various embassies in Eastern Europe, used sex and poison to get what she needed. T.J.'s vision of her parents was hers alone. He didn't tell T. J. that he knew who they really were. In fact, he didn't know if she knew her parent's backgrounds. 'Let her memories remain unblemished,' he thought to himself.

"T. J.," Noah said. "Look, we need to do a search of The Levels. And we need to notify Washington."

She nodded as she wiped tears from her eyes. "You go," she said. "I want to cover my folks. I'll phone D. C. You go and meet me back here."

Noah left T. J. sitting on the porch of the old farmhouse. He returned to the barn, to the workshop, and the hidden elevator inside. Level 2, 3, and 4, of The Levels were the Administration offices. As Noah went from office to office and Level to Level he found no one alive. Bodies lay on top of bodies in pools of blood.

Evidence of explosions and bullet riddled copy machines, desks, and shattered glass was everywhere. The rows of file cabinets that held paper information of The Levels lay on their sides, the files emptied from them and piled in the middle of the floor where they had been burned. Noah looked at the pile of smoky ash realizing that every bit of evidence of everything The Levels had been a part of had been destroyed.

Level 5 was the computer section. Again, everyone who worked on Level 5 had been killed. And each of the super-computer mainframes and servers and each of the laptop computers in the room, of which there were dozens, had been destroyed. It was patently apparent that care had been taken to destroy each as totally as possible. Noah wondered if any of the information stored in the mass of twisted metal and plastic could be retrieved.

He spent an hour and a half searching each of The Levels and each of the rooms. He found devastation everywhere. Even the kitchen facilities and dining rooms had been 'blown to hell', as Noah described it in his report to Mossad. If the mission had been to rescue the man, it was also meant to end the usefulness of The Levels. Brown's Farm was done. The billions of dollars it took to build it would never be spent again to rebuild it if it could be attacked and destroyed so easily.

Noah took one last look down the hallway of Level 9 before getting on the elevator to go up to the surface. He wondered if the man, when he had been captured, had been sent to one of Israel's secret facilities, would have eventually talked. What he had seen on Level 9 was little more than brutality. Yes they had tried chemicals and isolation and cold and heat. But if he had been in charge they would have at least tried the psychological means Mossad had become expert at. They would have used Mossad Interrogation techniques that had worked so well for so many years.

Outside, walking through the light rain in the wet soil between the barn and house, he realized how dark it was. He looked at his watch and found it was close to eleven PM. He tried to stamp whatever mud he could from his shoes before walking into the old house. Inside he called out for T. J. In the kitchen her parents lay where they had been killed but T. J. had covered them with old blankets. He walked through the house, into each room both upstairs and down, but T. J. was not there.

Outside he stood on the front porch and called as loud as he could. He walked around the house and barn. He searched everywhere he could. T. J. was nowhere to be found. In the mud at the bottom of the porch were her driver and guards, all dead. But her car was gone. Noah took the satellite phone from his coat pocket and punched in the numbers that would connect him with Tel Aviv.

Noah sat on the porch steps smoking cigarette after cigarette, ignoring the rain that had started to come down heavily. Fifty-five minutes later a car pulled into the unpaved drive to Brown's Farm. Noah's ride back to New York had arrived.

SIX - My Name Is Noah Goldberg

Sandy and I were as late getting back from the Club as we thought we would be. It was almost two in the morning when we finally arrived home. We found Betsy Concanon in our family room, watching a re-run of some PBS Masterpiece Theater show. She was stretched out on my brand new custom made Italian leather sofa, her metal-stud covered motorcycle boots propped up on the soft leather.

"Oh, hi!" she said as we walked into the room. She didn't get up but she did hit the mute button on the remote. She smiled up at Sandy and said, "C was very good tonight. We watched wrestling for about thirty minutes while she finished a whole bottle. Then she fell asleep. She really likes to watch wrestling by the way. You should try it when she's cranky."

"Betsy," I said. "Caroline is a baby. Wrestling is inappropriate for a baby."

"Oh, Morgan," Sandy said and hugged me tightly. "She can hardly focus her eyes yet."

I just couldn't let that slow pitch go by. "Hey. If Betsy can't focus yet she must be doing drugs or something. And if she can't focus should she be trusted with Caroline?"

I thought I was really funny, but Sandy and Betsy didn't laugh. Anyway, Sandy went to the couch and sat where Betsy's feet were, causing Betsy to sit up and put her boots on the floor. Sandy and she talked about the evening at the club. Betsy actually seemed interested.

"You've never been to the club, have you, Betsy?" Sandy asked. She had started to look upon Betsy Concanon as a younger sister. That was easy to hear every time Sandy spoke to her.

"Oh, Morgan," Sandy said, excited like a little girl. "We've just got to take Betsy to the club for dinner some time. I think she'd love it there."

"Sandy my dear," I said. "How many times have you told me how much you hate the San Marcos Country Club and all the terribly snobbish people who hang out there? I have to drag you there for dinner yet you think Betsy is going to like it there?"

"Oh, Morgan! I love you when you're dumb. We'll take Betsy to lunch tomorrow. OK, Betsy? And Caroline can come too."

All I could do was to sigh deeply, shrug my shoulders at the mystery, and leave the room. I went to my daughter's room and carefully opened the door enough to look in. There was a small lamp, a dim night light near her crib. Caroline was asleep, one arm outside her pink blanket. I stepped lightly to her and carefully pulled the blanket up to cover her little arm.

I looked around her room, filled with toys and stuffed animals. Betsy had straightened up the room, putting everything away. There were clean baby clothes piled neatly on top of the small dresser. Betsy had done Caroline's laundry.

As I looked around the room and at my beautiful daughter, I began to think that maybe Betsy wasn't all that bad after all. Caroline started to stir and made some little mewing sounds. I recognized that as her beginning to awaken. I started to her when the door opened and Sandy and Betsy walked in.

"Oh, hi Morgan," Betsy said. She was carrying a

bottle. She went straight to Caroline. "C's like clockwork," she said as she picked up the baby. "She's gonna be a big eater, wait and see."

"I thought you wanted to breast feed her?" I said to Sandy who was standing next to me, smiling.

"Too much champagne," she said. "You don't want a drunk baby running around the house, do you?"

We left Betsy holding Caroline gently and lovingly cradling her in her arms. She rocked back and forth in an antique white rocker Sandy had found on a shopping trip to San Francisco. She was humming softly. Caroline relaxed in her arms and enjoyed her 2 AM feeding.

"Come on, Morgan," Sandy said. "Let's go to bed. They're fine."

****

We awoke at 9 AM to the smell of coffee permeating throughout the house. Sandy poked me. "I think it's time to get up," she said.

We threw on bathrobes and old slippers and raced toward the coffee. In the kitchen Betsy was sitting at the table, Caroline held in one arm and a large mug filled with the coffee she had brewed in her free hand.

"Good morning," she said brightly and smiled at us. "C was very good last night. She finished her whole bottle, had a little fun while I changed her clothes, and then she went right back to sleep."

I poured coffee into a couple of mugs for Sandy and me. "You couldn't have gotten much sleep yourself," I said.

"Enough," Betsy said. "I just love being with C. Look, I made up some pancake batter and I was going to toss in some fresh blueberries. Want some? I got some fat sausage to go with it . . . If you guys want some disgusting meat that is."

Sandy asked, "Where did the blueberries and sausage come from? I don't remember having that stuff here."

"Oh, I had some things delivered last night," Betsy said. "You know, milk and stuff you guys were short on. I'm gonna start on the pancakes," she said and handed Caroline to Sandy.

Betsy was starting the sausage when the doorbell rang. It rang twice more before I could get to the door. I opened it and found a man standing there. He was a foot shorter than me, maybe more pudgy around the middle than I am, and not very imposing. But there was something about the man, something I could sense, that told me he was dangerous.

"Mr. Morgan Crew?" he asked.

"That depends on who you are," I said. I couldn't let this little man know I was worried about who the hell he was. I have this little voice in the back of my head. Whenever danger is near the little voice starts screaming, "RUN AWAY! RUN AWAY!" It started screaming as I stood in the doorway.

"My name is Noah Goldberg," he said and held his hand out. I didn't take it. I put the mug of coffee to my lips and pretended to drink instead.

"Nice to meet you," I said. "What do you want?"

"I need to talk to you," he said. "May I come in?"

"Once again," I said. "That depends on who you are and what you want. If you're selling something, I'm not interested."

"I'm not selling anything," Noah said. "Has the FBI been here? Homeland Security? Anybody?"

"The FBI . . . What the hell!" I said.

"Look," Noah said. "Let me come inside. This is important. I really need to talk to you."

He was looking over his shoulder, looking up and

down the street as if he were expecting someone. I kept my hand on the door and stood in the open doorway hoping to look intimidating in spite of the way I might have looked in a tattered bathrobe and old slippers.

"Hey," I said. "Whoever the hell you are . . . Until I know you're not some drugged out maniac, you're not getting inside my house. Now I'm going to give you one more chance. Who are you and what do you want? Make it quick because I'm going to phone some friends of mine on the City Police in just about 30 seconds."

"Who is it Morgan?" Sandy asked from behind me.

"Go back in the kitchen."

"Go back in the kitchen?" Sandy said incredulously. "Did I hear you order me back into the kitchen? Am I all of a sudden your good little obedient wife?"

"Sandy," I said. "I don't know who this guy is or what he wants. Now please . . ."

Rather than leave the room . . . Which I should have known she wouldn't do . . . Sandy pushed her way in front of me and stood in the doorway, her arms folded in front of her and a mean scowl on her face.

"OK," she said. "Who are you?"

"I'm Noah Goldberg," he answered.

"That's your god damn name, not who you are. Now tell me who you are and what you want here," she demanded.

"Let me in, please," the man said. "I need to talk to Morgan."

Sandy smiled that wicked little smile of hers that I'd seen so many times, right before she gets violent.

"My husband," she began, "would slam the door in your face. Me? I'm gonna' punch you in your god damn balls if you don't tell me who the hell you are and what you want."

I started to pull Sandy back, away from this little man who I felt was dangerous. I knew Sandy wasn't lying when she threatened to punch this guy, and I couldn't let her get hurt.

But before I could he said, "I'm an Israeli Government official . . . That's as far as I can go right now. Mr. Crew's name has come up in a very sensitive investigation . . . Regarding national security."

"Israel's national security?" Sandy asked.

"No." he said. "Your Country's national security."

It was time for me to step in. Once again, Sandy had accomplished what I could not. But this was getting serious, and we needed to start working together. Sandy and I always learn more when we work together.

"OK," I said. "You can come inside. But I warn you that if this is some kind of scam . . . If you try anything . . . I'll see you either in jail or dead. Understand?"

We stepped aside and let this little man into our home. I waved him into the family room and to a chair in a corner near the fireplace. I wanted to keep him in a corner, and I wanted me to be between him and my family. Sandy and I sat next to each other on the couch Betsy had been using the night before.

Noah leaned back in the chair and looked from Sandy to me and back to Sandy. It took a moment but finally he asked, "Has a woman been here? Has a woman contacted you?"

"A woman?" I asked trying to sound as sarcastic as possible. "There must be hundreds of millions of women in the world. Which one are you talking about?"

He ignored my sarcasm and asked, "Has anyone contacted you in any way about a security issue?"

Sandy and I looked at each other. We were thinking the same thing. This guy was either insane or once again we were in trouble. That little voice in the back of my head was screaming again, "GET OUT! RUN AWAY!" That little voice had been 100% right every time I was close to danger. But once again I chose to ignore it . . . Unwisely it would turn out.

Sandy spoke up, "You've told us your name and you said you're with the Israeli Government. So back up and start at the beginning. What agency are you with, and we need to see some ID."

Noah hesitated and then said, "I can't tell you what agency I'm with. I don't carry an ID."

I stood and said, "OK . . . Whoever the hell you are. Get out before I call the cops. Maybe they can find out what asylum you escaped from."

"Wait," he said. "Sit down . . . Please. I'm going to tell you some things you probably shouldn't know. But I have to get your cooperation before anyone else approaches you."

He paused once again, looked down at the floor and twisted his hands together nervously.

"Pick up your phone. Dial information. Get the number for the Israeli Embassy in Washington, DC. Dial that number and when the operator answers say 'Operation Ruhiger Mann'."

I looked questioningly at Sandy. She shrugged and I picked up the phone. I got the number and punched it into the phone. A woman answered and I said simply, "Operation Ruhiger Mann". I was put on hold and within seconds a man with a heavily accented and very deep voice came on the line.

"Who is this?" he asked.

"I'm Morgan Crew," I said.

"How did you get the name Ruhiger Mann?"

"There's a man in my house. Says he's Noah Goldberg," I answered.

"Describe the man," the voice said.

"He's about 5 foot six or so. Maybe 180 pounds. Dark, thick hair . . ."

"Let me speak to him," the man said.

I tossed the phone at Noah and he listened to the

deep voice on the other end. After half a minute Noah pushed the end button on the phone, placed it carefully on the side table next to his chair, and then said, "About a month ago a man was picked up by your Homeland Security people. He had crossed into the States from Canada. He was . . . He was questioned for some time but said nothing. He could not be identified by anyone anywhere. After heavy interrogation this man said only two words. He spoke your name Mr. Crew. Nothing else."

"So what?" I said. "Are you asking if I know who this guy is?"

"Do you?" Noah asked.

"How the hell am I supposed to know? I know lots of people. If you want me to look at this guy, I guess I can do that."

"Wait a minute," Sandy interrupted. "We're getting ahead of ourselves here. Let's get back to who the hell you are, Mr. Goldberg."

"I told you," he said. "I'm an Israeli Government official. The Embassy verified that."

"Not good enough," she said. "What government agency are you with?"

He hesitated once again but finally admitted, "I'm with Mossad."

"Oh! Right!" I said. "And you flew into town on some top secret space ship from the planet X. Right?"

"Mr. Crew," Noah said. "You phoned my embassy. I'm here to help you if I can. You may be in great danger . . ."

"Please," Sandy said interrupting him. "Let's skip all the back and forth crap and get down to why you're here. So, some un-named guy mentioned my husband's name. So what?"

"You must trust me," Noah said.

"Trust you? Trust you?" I said. "Right now the only thing I trust is that you probably escaped from some loony bin."

Sandy put her hand on my knee which I had come to understand was her way of telling me, very gently, to shut up. So I sat back and let her take over. But I was going to let this go only so far.

Sandy said, "Get back to your story. You said some man was being questioned and he mentioned Morgan's name."

"Questioned, yes. But he was tortured terribly. The people who had him knew all the techniques but those techniques were out of date. The man suffered every pain they inflicted but would not talk. A woman . . . She was in charge at the time . . . Arrived where this man was being held. When he saw this woman he spoke his first words in a couple of weeks. He said your name, Mr. Crew."

"Alright," Sandy said. "Now just how does that put us in danger?"

"Not you, Mrs. Crew. Only your husband," he said.

"Now it's you who doesn't understand," she said. "We are together and when one of us is in trouble the other is, too."

Noah chose to ignore that for the time being. He went on with his story.

"I was there at the end," he said. "The place where the man was being held was attacked by a very professional group. Everyone was killed . . . Except for myself and the woman. And of course the spy who would not speak. He apparently was the subject of the attack. He was rescued by the attackers."

"How did you escape?" Sandy asked.

"We hid and they didn't find us."

"Now wait a damn minute." I said. "A professional group of killers attacked this . . . Place or whatever. They kill everybody but you . . . You *hide*? Sandy, this guy is either wacko or he's been playing too many games with the other children."

"You're probably right, Morgan," Sandy said. "But we're never going to find out if you lose your temper. Calm down now, OK?"

I sat back on the couch and took a deep breath. As usual, Sandy was right. Little could be accomplished via temper. But I felt I had to be ready to defend Sandy and Caroline, just in case we had let a maniac into the house. The big question was . . . How the hell do I defend them?

Sandy spoke to Noah again. "This woman. Who is she?"

"First, let me ask you once again," Noah said. "Has anybody spoken to you about any of this before me?"

Sandy and I looked at each other and then she said to Noah, "No one has told us anything about this. Why?"

"I was afraid of that," he said. A worried and concerned shadow crossed his face as he looked from Sandy to me and back to Sandy. "Her name is Teresa Jean Kohl. She is known as T. J. She is a very high ranking Intelligence Agent for your Government. She was in charge of the facility where the man who would not speak was being held. Her parents were sort of care takers at this facility. They were among the scores of people killed. That is the part that has me worried."

"Why should that worry you?" Sandy asked. "If she's a Government official there shouldn't be a problem."

"I'll try to be clearer," he said and sat forward in his chair. "She and I were the only survivors . . . Except for the man who would not speak, of course. T. J.'s parents were killed in the attack. She and I are the only people now alive who know the man spoke your name, Mr. Crew. The FBI . . . Nobody . . . Has come to question you about this, which tells me T. J. has not reported the fact to anyone. She is withholding that critical information. The question is why? And knowing T. J. she may well be thinking about vengeance on whoever was responsible for the attack. If I'm correct, it's only a matter of time before you meet T. J. and you really don't want to do that if she thinks you had anything to do with the murders of her parents."

"OK," Sandy said. "Suppose we believe you. Why haven't you reported all this to the FBI . . . Or somebody?"

"I told you, Mrs. Crew. I am an Israeli Agent. It would cause an international incident if it became public that I was at the facility. In fact, the existence of the facility itself would cause an uproar in your Country. Your own Government would be torn apart."

"And just where is this facility?" Sandy asked.

Noah didn't answer right away. He was thinking again, he was weighing whether or not to tell us where this top secret facility was. Finally he said, "I guess I can tell you that. Brown's Farm will not be used again. By the end of the month it won't even exist."

"Your top secret whatever is a farm?" I asked incredulous at the man's story.

"From the outside, it is . . . Or was . . . A farm. Underground there were nine levels. It was used as an intelligence filtering station. There were super computers and receivers for satellite reception. There was electronic monitoring of everything, everywhere. Much of what was done there was illegal but sanctioned by the highest level of U.S. intelligence. It was also a holding and interrogation facility for the most dangerous suspects."

"Again," Sandy said. "Where is this place?"

"In New York," Noah answered. "In a very rural area of the Hudson River Valley."

SEVEN - You Need Me

The three of us sat in complete silence for a minute or two looking at the floor and then at each other, not knowing what to say or do next. Those couple of minutes seemed like an hour. I broke the uncomfortable silence by saying, "Sandy, we need to talk. You," I said to Noah, ". . . Whoever you are . . . Stay here."

We walked into the kitchen where we found Betsy holding little Caroline while the sausage burned in the skillet. She was standing at the door with a worried look on her face.

"Hey," she said. "You guys are in trouble, right?"

Sandy went to the stove and pulled the pan off the flame. I watched as she tossed the charcoaled sausages into the sink and ran water on them.

"This doesn't concern you, Betsy," I said. "Take the baby to her room, ok?"

"I don't think so," she said. "What are you guys gonna' do with C while you get yourselves outta' trouble? You need me."

"What are you talking about?" I asked. I think I had an idea of what she was getting at but I needed to hear it from Betsy. I wasn't going to admit that I had slowly been changing my mind about the girl. At first glance, the first time I had met her, I saw an anti-social, out-of-control child who would benefit from extensive professional psychological care. But I had gained some experience seeing her with Caroline and how she and Sandy interacted. I had begun to see them acting like sisters. Maybe she would make a good . . . What? . . . Babysitter? . . . Something else?

"I'm saying I need a place to live," Betsy began. "I need a chance. You need someone you can trust to look after C. I want a job. I know all about you two. I've heard all the stories. I know all about the trouble you get yourselves into. You can't take C with you."

"Are you asking for a full time job?" I asked her.

"Yeah," she said and smiled anxiously. "I don't want to go home. There ain't no . . . I mean there isn't any future there for me. I like it here. I like Sandy and you. I really like C. I just need a chance. I want to make something outta' life, you know?"

I looked at Sandy and she looked at me. She nodded and grinned knowingly. I turned to Betsy and said, "OK. You are now a live-in Nanny. Room and board and say five hundred a month? How does that sound?"

"I want to continue with school," she said. "But we can work out a schedule. And a thousand a month would be good."

"A thousand a month!" I said. "You're going to live here rent free and eat our food. Why the hell do you need a thousand a month?"

"Morgan!" Sandy shot back. "Watch your language! The baby!"

"Caroline can hear all the four letter words I know and she wouldn't know what any of them are," I said. "She's not even a year old yet, dear."

"I don't care," she argued. "Watch your language."

"Look," Betsy said. "I'm probably going to spend most of that on C . . . What I don't use for school, that is. And I need some clothes and stuff."

Sandy put her arm around Betsy's shoulder and said, "A thousand a month is fine. Now why not take Caroline to her room while we go back and talk with that man again."

Betsy was smiling as she started for Caroline's room,

stopped at the door, turned and said, "There's pancake batter ready . . . Over there by the stove . . . After you guys are done, I'll do up some breakfast for us."

Sandy and I waited until Betsy and Caroline were out of sight and then we returned to the living room. But Noah Goldberg wasn't there. I went to the front window and looked out. There were no cars on the street.

"He's gone," I said. "Did you hear anything?" I asked Sandy.

"No," she said. "What do you think? Was he serious or was this some kind of scam?"

"I don't know," I said as I went to the phone. "I'm going to talk to the Embassy again."

I dialed the number and the same woman whom I had spoken with before answered.

"Operation Ruhiger Mann," I said.

I waited but heard nothing but a very low and faint buzzing on the line. I waited and then said, "Hello? Did you hear me? Are you there?"

"I'm sorry sir," the woman said. "What did you say?"

"Operation Ruhiger Mann," I repeated.

"I'm sorry, sir," she said. "Is there someone you want to speak with?"

"I phoned a short time ago," I said. "Operation Ruhiger Mann."

"I'm sorry, sir. But I don't know what you're talking about. Is there someone you wish to speak with?"

"Yeah," I demanded. "I spoke with some guy about Noah Goldberg. This concerns Operation Ruhiger Mann."

"Look, sir. I can't tie up the line all day. There is no one at the Embassy named Noah Goldberg and I have no idea what Operation Ruhiger Mann is. If you don't have someone you wish to speak with . . ."

"OK," I said. "Is there anybody there with Mossad? Israeli intelligence? Anybody like that?"

"OK, sir. I have to hang up now. This is an Embassy,

not some James Bond movie." And the phone line went dead.

I held the phone in my hand, turned to Sandy and said, "I don't get it. Didn't I phone the Israeli Embassy just a few minutes ago and talk to someone there? Wasn't there some guy called Noah Goldberg here? Am I having a mental throwback to that nightmare in Hawaii?"

"No," Sandy said. "You ain't crazy, babe. But what's happening may be crazy. They never heard of Operation Ruhiger Mann?"

"And it was the same lady's voice," I said. "Last time she transferred me instantly. This time she never heard of Ruhiger Mann. What the hell does Ruhiger Mann mean, anyway?"

Sandy shrugged her shoulders. From the doorway Betsy said, "Ruhiger Mann is German for quiet man."

We turned to her and I said, "You speak German?"

"Yeah, a little," she said. "School, you know? Look, C has had her morning bath and she's got a nice warm bottle. She's gonna' sleep for awhile. I'm hungry and I'm gonna' do up some of them blueberry pancakes. You guys want some?"

The three of us sat at the kitchen table. I watched as Sandy wolfed down six blueberry cakes and then reach for two more. She is amazingly slim, trim and fit . . . And don't forget sexy . . . But I've never seen anyone eat the volume of food she can put away. I missed the sausage that had been put down the disposer and asked if there were any more. Betsy said there weren't and Sandy mumbled between bites that they were too greasy anyway.

When we were done and enjoying cup after cup of really good coffee, I asked, "So what do we do now?"

"There's not much sense in trying the Embassy again," Sandy said. "Do we know anybody in the spy business?"

"No, of course not," I said. I really wanted a cigarette,

and even though it was still morning I really would have liked a strong bourbon. But I knew what would happen if I reached for the bottle. Sandy had relented enough to allow me the occasional expensive illegal Cuban cigar at the Club with our friends, but cigarettes would always be out of the question.

"How about political connections?" Sandy asked. "There must be somebody high up in D.C. that owes us a favor."

"I can try," I said reluctantly. "But what if that Noah guy was just running a scam? And what if he wasn't and I start some international incident? No, I think we need to get more facts, first."

"OK," Sandy said. "Like what?"

"We know the name of that woman . . . Teresa Jean Kohl I think he said, right? He called her T. J. He said she's with some Intelligence Agency. U. S. Intelligence. And we know that place . . . Brown's Farm. We know there was a prisoner there who was being tortured and gave them my name. We don't know who runs Brown's Farm. Noah Goldberg may not be that guy's real name, but somebody at the Israeli Embassy knew him, described him, and spoke with him. Somebody knew what Ruhiger Mann was. I think that's all we have to go on."

"And what does all that mean to you, my love?" Sandy said with a sly grin on her beautiful face.

"It means I'm headed off to New York, to Brown's Farm in the Hudson River Valley," I said.

"You're not going alone," Sandy said. "Not after what happened to you in Hawaii. I'm going with you."

Now, I could have argued that we had Caroline, a baby less than a year old. I could have argued that there might be risk and some danger and I didn't want her involved. I suppose I could have argued a hundred different things but none of it would have made a difference. Sandy was going to come with me . . . Like it or not. So I didn't waste my time. I resigned myself to the fact that I would have company in New York.

"The only problem we have is," Sandy said, "where the hell is Brown's Farm? The Hudson Valley must be a really big place. Do we just drive around until we stumble on it?"

Betsy got up from the table, left the kitchen and came back with a laptop computer. She turned it on, waited a few seconds and then said, "Let's start simple. I'll Google Brown's Farm and see what we get."

"You know about that computer stuff?" I asked her.

"Yeah. Remember? School?" she said sarcastically. "OK, there's a ski place in Washington State and a lot about John Brown's farm but that's up in Lake Placid. There's something about Brown's Berry Patch . . . But nothing specifically on a Brown's Farm. Let me try some other things."

She worked the keyboard and said, "There's no New York State business or corporate records . . . The State Agriculture Department has nothing on it . . . The Post Office has nothing on it. My guess is," she said, "if that place really is some Government facility it's pretty well hidden and off the record."

"So I guess we just drive around until we stumble onto it, like you said," I said, resigned to the fact that we might be on a wild goose chase.

"Wait a minute, Morgan," Betsy said. "I've got it, I think. There's something called the Hudson River Valley Revolutionary War Historical Society. Looks like a pretty obscure group . . . The website hasn't been updated for almost two years. There's a member's list and there are only nine members. But there is a reference to Brown's Farm. Seems there was some shooting there when the British tried to take the valley. Here, I'll write down where the farm is located."

I was still uncomfortable with being called by my first

name by my employee but I didn't have a problem with Betsy giving us a head start.

We sat in silence for a minute or two; both Sandy and I were thinking and Betsy was waiting to hear what we were going to do. I broke the silence by asking, "Are you absolutely sure you want to take care of Caroline while we're gone?"

"Hey, Morgan," Betsy said. "That's what I've been saying here. Listen up, OK?"

I looked at Sandy and she nodded slightly. She turned to Betsy and said, "We'll only be gone for a day or two."

"Just in case," Betsy said. "Get me a cell phone. That way you can have 24/7 access to me and you can be sure I'm not taking C up to North Harbor and making a crack ho' out of her."

EIGHT - We May Really Be In Trouble

We had been driving for a couple of hours. We had the street address of Brown's Farm that Betsy had found for us, but few of the farms and houses in the area were marked with a street address. We had a GPS that was working fine. The problem was that we were in some really, really backwoods, rural country. As we drove deeper into the boondocks we kept loosing the satellite signal. We stopped twice and asked directions, first an old man leaning against a rail fence smoking a pipe and then a teenager fishing off of a beat-up old concrete bridge over a still pond. Neither said they knew of Brown's Farm and neither was very helpful in suggestions, either.

The area was pretty enough; thick forests of tall trees that often blocked out the sun and sky; a few green pastures here and there; a picture perfect little stream idling over and around big rocks; and hills everywhere. We were about forty miles west of Newberg where we had spent the night. The thin road we were on twisted and turned so we drove slowly. After more than two hours Sandy suddenly shouted, "STOP!"

I slammed on the brakes and she told me to back up. She rolled down her window and pointed. "Look there," she said. "Look at that mailbox."

There was a rusted and dented mailbox hanging by one nail from a rotted wooden post near what appeared to be a gravel driveway that was filled with weeds. The painted numbers and letters on the mailbox were hard to make out, but after we got out of the car and looked closely at it, we both were certain it was the street address Betsy had found. And under the numbers the faded letters read 'Brown's Farm.'

"We found it!" Sandy said proudly.

Looking down the gravel drive, we saw a two story house sitting near the driveway amongst tall weeds. Its dark brown paint was peeling away from the old wood siding. A battered and sagging covered porch ran around three sides of the house. Dark and molding asphalt shingles on both the roof of the house and the porch cover were bent and thin, and several were missing. As we walked closer to the house we saw two weather beaten Adirondack chairs and three broken metal tables on the porch. They were dirt and dust covered and occupied by cob webs and dead bugs. But we didn't see any people. In fact, Brown's Farm looked deserted.

"Do you think we should go inside?" Sandy asked.

"If this is really the place that Noah guy was talking about, we need to go inside. We need to find somebody or something to let us know he wasn't lying or crazy. If he was telling the truth, we might be in some trouble. If this place is just some deserted farm, we can go home."

And so we made our way through the ankle deep weeds towards the front porch. I stepped on something hard and looked down. It was a brass shell casing hidden under some broad leaf weed-thing. Looking around, there were hundreds of shell casings lying all over the place. I pointed down and when Sandy saw them she said, "Oh damn! We may really be in trouble."

We stepped cautiously onto the covered porch. The front door was open a few inches. I pushed on it and it squeaked open on rusted hinges. Inside was dark and musty, and it smelled of mold and age. Shades had been drawn over windows to hold out the light of day.

I was kind of waiting for Sandy to go inside first since she's really the brave one in the family, but I could wait only so long before my manhood started to slip away. So inside I went and Sandy followed. The front room was small and had three doors leading from it, one on the right and two on the left.

For no particular reason I turned to the right and found myself in the kitchen. The kitchen was a throwback to the 1950s. The cabinets were cheap plywood and one of the doors was missing. The counter tops were green vinyl, cracked and dirty. The floor was avocado green and gold linoleum and was sporting a tear down the middle of it. And on the linoleum were two unmistakable dark brown stains of dried blood. One was near a small wooden table and one near a torn screened door that led to the back of the house.

"We've seen stuff like that before," Sandy said looking at the brown stains.

"Yeah," I answered. "I'm getting pretty close to believing Noah."

"We should look through the rest of the house," Sandy said as she turned and led the way. As we walked we opened shades and curtains. Daylight did little to improve the small farmhouse. It needed a good cleaning. Every room, upstairs and downstairs, was the same. It was hard to believe that maybe people actually lived there . . . Before the attack Noah described that is.

In a back bedroom I noticed that a tall dresser had been pulled away from the wall and then slid back. Scuff marks in the dust on the floor revealed the fact. So I pulled the dresser away just to see what was behind it. And we found a small steel door that the dresser had been hiding.

There wasn't a handle or knob on the door and I couldn't see any kind of lock. The door seemed not to be closed, so I just gave it a push and it opened. Behind it was dark but we could see the first of concrete steps that went down . . . But to where?

"Is there a light switch?" Sandy asked. I found one on the wall to my left. Switching it several times did nothing.

"The power's been switched off," I said.

"Let's go see if we can find a flashlight or something," she said.

"You don't mean you want to go down there, do you?" I asked.

"Of course. You're the one who said we need some kind of evidence. We need something to take to whatever authorities we can go to."

We searched through the ground floor of the house and the best we could come up with was an old Coleman lantern. Rooting around in kitchen drawers, I found some matches and I was able, after fiddling with it, to light the lantern. So down the stairs we went.

We walked down the steps, finding three landings to the bottom. I figured we had to be three floors underground. At the bottom of the stairs a cold, grey tunnel began. It was absolutely dark in the tunnel and there was no way for us to know how long the tunnel was. "Let's walk," I said.

The lantern lit the tunnel enough for me to see and count eighteen lights running along the ceiling's length. None of course were on. The tunnel ended at a vault-like steel door. There was a keypad lock at the side of the door.

"I guess that's as far as we go," Sandy said.

I pushed on the door and it swung, slowly, open. "Just a guess," I said. "I figured since there wasn't any electricity it might just be unlocked."

Sandy pointed to the edge of the door, at three heavy, bank-like dead bolts. "If the power were off," she said, "the dead bolts wouldn't have opened all on their own. Somebody unlocked the door and left it unlocked."

On the other side of the door was a hallway and directly across the hall was an elevator with a key pad lock, the same kind of lock as on the door. "Even if those doors open," Sandy said, "I'm not getting on an elevator down here. Where the hell do you think we are?"

"Noah said this was some sort of top secret installation. This place sure fits the bill. What I don't like is it being open and easy to get into," I said.

The hallway ran left and right. I held the lantern high over head and asked, "Which way dear? Left or right?"

"How about up?" Sandy said.

"We're here," I said. "Might as well go on." So we turned right and started slowly down the hall, walking into the pitch black.

Then ahead of us we saw a faint glow of light floating across the floor. We stopped and I whispered, "There's someone there."

Sandy pointed at the lantern and I turned it off, taking her meaning. We walked slowly toward the light and stopped at a door under which the light escaped. I put my hand on the door knob and looked at Sandy, silently asking if I should open the door. She nodded and took a step back, away from the door.

I gently turned the knob and eased the door open quietly. Light from inside flooded into the dark hallway. As it opened I carefully stepped into the doorway and jumped back as seven men in combat camo fatigues stood and pointed M-16 rifles at me.

****

Sandy and I were ordered to sit in what turned out to be a break room where the soldiers were. Our hands had been secured with plastic zip-cuffs behind our backs. All seven of the soldiers stood in a circle around us, pointing their guns at us. I was amused, almost at the point of laughter, at the thought of what they would do to each other if they started shooting. What's it called? A circular firing squad?

We sat, side by side on uncomfortable metal chairs, quietly and peacefully for over an hour. There was a table at one side of the room that had paper plates of half eaten food and open cans of soda on it. This, I thought, had to be a lunch room for the soldiers. But I wondered why they were there.

Then an eighth soldier in camo fatigues walked into the room. This man wore silver eagles on his collar and an aura of meanness all over the rest of him. He wore a green beret at a proud angle which told me he was in The Special Forces and a full Colonel at that. He stood in the doorway, filling the room with his presence, and looked at the guards surrounding us.

"What the hell are you misfits doing?" he growled. "Put the god damn guns down and go park your asses in those chairs! Finish your damn baby food lunch, you friggin' idiots!"

The seven soldiers meekly but quickly did as the Colonel had told them. He shook his head and walked to us. He circled us twice; I imagine trying to make us nervous which he was doing very, very well.

He stopped in front of us and said, "I am Colonel Mark Huntsinger. Who the hell are you?"

I spoke up before Sandy could start yelling because I could sense she was getting angry. Her gorgeous face was flaming red; her big blue eyes were clinched tightly. "I think we need to speak with our lawyers first," I said and smiled hopefully.

"Lawyers!" Huntsinger yelled. "You want friggin' lawyers! You just broke into a Federal Facility! Do you know what happens to suspected terrorists?"

Sandy and I looked at each other and then I replied as meekly as I could, "Guantanamo?"

Huntsinger laughed too loudly and robustly to even

suggest it was a real laugh. He said, "Gitmo, hell! I've got this little place in Asia . . . Where all those funny little Countries that end in 'istan' are . . . You know! Little out of the way place that nobody ever heard of. I like to call my little resort Hurts-like-hell-istan! I'm gonna' put black bags over your friggin' heads and sit your tight little asses on a jet and fly you out there, and nobody will ever know what the hell happened to you! You'll just disappear!"

Sandy and I looked at each other again and then Sandy said in a little, meek voice, trying to imitate me, "Can I ask a question, please?"

"Sure, lady," he said. "Go ahead."

"I gotta pee. Is there a ladies room nearby?"

I closed my eyes and said out loud, "Oh no."

"OK," Huntsinger said. "I'm gonna' get that friggin' jet ready. You two will be gone in a couple of hours."

"Wait a minute," I pleaded. "We want to cooperate with you but we don't know what's going on around here. Tell me what you want."

"Who are you?" Huntsinger demanded.

"I'm Morgan Crew," I said. "This is my wife."

Huntsinger looked like he had been hit in the chest with a baseball bat. I would bet my last million he had never been lost for words or a quick and insulting comeback before. He finally said, "You're who?"

"I told you," I said. "I'm Morgan Crew. Why?"

"Oh shit!" he said. "Why . . . How . . . You're here? How the hell did you get in here?"

Sandy smiled and said as snidely as she could manage, "You left the door open, Colonel honey."

"OK," he said. He was rubbing his temples, and beads of sweat started to appear on his forehead. "I gotta' report this. Shit!" He turned to the seven men sitting around the table. "Watch them," he said. "And for God's sake don't point your friggin' guns at each other! Didn't you guys get any basic training?"

And so we sat, our hands tied, in the chairs until Huntsinger returned twenty minutes later. He stood in front of us, looking down at us and looking mean and angry. From his boot he pulled a big and nasty looking knife.

"Wait a minute!" I said, thinking he was going to decapitate us or maybe something even worse. "You can't do that!"

Huntsinger walked behind us and cut the plastic cords that had been stopping the blood flow to our hands.

"You can get up," he said. "Stretch your legs. Do you want something to eat? Water?"

NINE - I'm Afraid That's Not Possible, Mrs. Crew

We stood slowly, thinking maybe this was all just a trick. Maybe they had a rule that they didn't shoot people who were sitting down with tied hands? I said, "What I really want is to know what the hell's going on."

"They'll be some people here soon . . . To talk to you," Huntsinger said. "You got me in big trouble, you know."

"How?" Sandy asked. Knowing her, she wasn't really concerned; she was probably hoping to do over and over again whatever got him in trouble.

"These idiots here," he said pointing at the seven young soldiers sitting at the table, "These friggin' idiots left the damn doors unlocked. I'm in charge here. Everything that happens here is my friggin' responsibility. They give me some God damn part-time friggin' reserves and they expect great friggin' stuff from me."

"Hey, look," I said. "I think we're the ones in trouble around here. What's going to happen to us?"

"Hell, I don't know," Huntsinger said. He strode across the room not unlike John Wayne in his prime. With his back turned to us he pulled a dark leather cigar case from his fatigue pocket, took a long, thin cigar from it, lit it and blew a cloud of smoke toward the ceiling. He turned and walked slowly back to us. He pulled a chair away from the table and sat. The seven soldiers at the table got up immediately and stepped away, leaving their rifles on the table and a few lying against the wall nearby.

Huntsinger laid the cigar on the table's edge and sighed deeply. He put his head in his hands and shook his head. "What the hell is wrong with you children?" he said to his soldiers. "Didn't anybody ever tell you not to leave your friggin' piece laying around where a prisoner can get to it? PICK'EM UP!" he screamed and they did.

To tell the truth I was beginning to feel a little bit sorry for Huntsinger. He was, I was sure, a very professional soldier stuck in a very unprofessional situation. I walked to him and pulled a chair away from the table. "Can I sit down?" I asked.

"Yeah, sure," he said.

I sat and asked, "What are you guys doing here?"

He looked up at me for a moment and then said, "You wanna' know what I'm doing here? What the hell are you doing here?"

"You reacted like you know me when I told you my name."

"I know who you are," he said. "You're the friggin' reason I'm here doing janitor work."

"I'm the reason?" I asked. I really didn't understand, and if Sandy and I were ever to get out of there, we had to understand what was happening. Working in the dark wouldn't get us anywhere. Chances are we could trick the seven part-time soldiers we had stumbled onto. But I felt sure we couldn't fool Huntsinger, and there were probably more like Huntsinger outside this room.

"Hell," Huntsinger said. "I guess it won't hurt. It don't mean nothin' anyway. Them putting me in charge here tells me my career is just about over. So, I'm supposed to tear this place apart. Make sure there's nothing left. I just got here yesterday with this superlative group of friggin' latrine commandos. They give me twelve reserve idiots. Can you believe that?"

"But you said I'm the reason," I said. "Why? I don't understand."

"You're one hot item, Mr. Crew," he said. "The people who will be here soon will either explain it all to you or shoot you in your friggin' head. If it were up to me . . . I'd shoot the both of you right now. That would put an end to it all. For right now, I'd have some water and some food, if I were you. It might be a long time before you see any."

There was a small refrigerator next to a cabinet and sink near the table we were at. Sandy went to the fridge, opened it and looked inside. There was bottled water; she took two and tossed one to me. There were some bananas and apples; she took one of each and I took an apple.

Colonel Huntsinger stood up, growled at his team to follow him, leaving two of them to guard us. He left the room, closing the door behind him. I don't know what happened to the Colonel. I've not seen him again since he walked out of the room.

****

And we waited once again. We ate what was there; fruit and potato chips and what was left of a jar of sour pickles. We drank water and paced around the concrete room. The two guards stood nervously in a corner watching us. They didn't speak to us or to each other. They held on tightly to their M-16 rifles. There were big banana clips in each rifle; I wondered if they had bullets in them.

An hour crept by and then another. We were getting really bored and a little angry. So finally I took Sandy's arm and walked to the door. I turned to the two guards and said, "If this door isn't locked, we're going to go home now. Say goodbye to Huntsinger for us."

Neither of them moved and neither said anything. I

think they were a little confused and a little scared. I tried the door knob and it turned. I looked behind me and the guards hadn't moved yet. So I pulled the door open and they still did nothing. But before we could step into the hall a man walked to the open door and stood smiling broadly at us.

"Why, thank you," he said. "Not many people would open a door for me. Don't you agree that simple courtesy is becoming a thing of the past? How many times do you see a man open a door for a lady? I do wish we could go back to the days of ladies and gentleman, don't you?"

Sandy said, "You ain't no lady."

"Ah, yes," he said. "Well . . . That can't be helped."

I can recognize expensive, custom made European suites and shoes. This man was wearing some of the best I have ever seen. The suit was a navy blue pin stripe. The shoes were Italian. His shirt was a creamy colored silk. His tie was also silk, an 'Old School' stripe, and tied in a perfect Windsor. And he wore an impressively large diamond ring on the little finger of his right hand.

He was as tall as I am but he didn't carry all the extra weight I do. There was an elegance about the man, right down to his manicured fingernails and the white rose he wore on his lapel. His hair was thick and grey and expertly coiffured. There was the slightest suggestion of jowls below his cheeks. All this told me he was older than he appeared at first sight.

Plus he was wearing a slightly sweet aftershave, perhaps it was more than that. Perhaps it was cologne. Perhaps he was sporting something more feminine. Maybe he was more than just older than me?

The three of us stood facing each other, the man smiling and looking from one of us to the other. We just stood there.

"May I come in? Let's not talk in the doorway, shall we?" he asked. His voice had an accent to it that I recognized. Too many people in my family had attended Ivy League schools and left with post graduate degrees and an Ivy League accent. But I had a strong hunch this man's accent wasn't feigned. Plus there was a touch of sophisticated upper-class Boston somewhere in the background.

We stepped aside and he walked past us slowly, very assuredly. He said to the guards, "Would you gentlemen mind terribly? I'd like to speak with Mr. and Mrs. Crew alone." And they left, very quickly, closing the door behind them. They even remembered to take their guns.

"Shall we sit?" he suggested and we followed him to the table and chairs on the other side of the small room.

"It's such a great pleasure to meet both of you," He said, smiling graciously.

Sandy, in her usual 'get-to-the-point' manner asked, "Who the hell are you?"

"Oh, I am sorry," he said. "I haven't introduced myself. My name is Mathew Collins. I'm an agent with the Central Intelligence Agency."

"Oh! Ain't that just great!" I said. "First we get Mossad, then some hypertensive Special Forces Green Beret, and now the CIA! Hey Sandy, we're working our way up the ladder!"

"I gather you're slightly skeptical, Mr. Crew?" Collins asked.

"Skeptical isn't the word. But let's cut to the chase. Are we under arrest? We want to leave here and go home," I demanded.

"At the present time I'm afraid you can't go home . . . Initially for your own safety. But also because there is a matter of national security we must clear up. You said Mossad. Has someone from Mossad contacted you?" he asked.

Sandy could sense I was losing my temper. She knew that when the situation called for it, she would get obnoxious and sarcastic. In those same situations I would often let my temper get me in serious trouble. So she started to take over. She put her hand gently on my knee to tell me to keep quiet. She said, "Yes. Noah Goldberg came to our home."

Collins sat in silence for a moment or two, smiled his ever present smile, and then said, "I'm afraid that's not possible, Mrs. Crew. You must be mistaken."

"No," she said. "I'm certain that was his name . . . And the Israeli Embassy confirmed it was him."

"I see," he said reflectively. "Well, I think we should go now," he said and stood.

"Go where?" Sandy asked. "Are you taking us to some secret prison somewhere?"

"Oh my! No! Of course not! I suggest we go to my home. I have a little place down in Virginia. I think you'll be more comfortable there than here."

I decided I needed to ask some questions, and I tried to be as nice and calm as possible while I did.

"Do you have some ID Mr. Collins?" I asked first.

"No," he answered. "The CIA doesn't issue credentials to Field Agents. I'm sure you can understand the secrecy that is needed."

"And are you to be our interrogator?" I asked.

"Interrogator? Why no, of course not!" He laughed. "How do I say this without sounding braggadocios? Oh well," he said and paused. "I guess you might say I am much too high on the totem pole to be doing that." He laughed at his little joke.

"OK," I said. "And what if we don't want to go to your home in Virginia? What then?"

"Well, I suppose you might stay here," he said. "However, it will take two days for this facility to be emptied of everything. There isn't much food here and the sleeping accommodations are very basic. After emptying everything from this place the house and barn will be burned to the ground. This entire facility will be wired with very large explosive charges and blown into oblivion. If you decide to stay . . . Well, need I explain further?"

"And if we decide to go home?" Sandy asked.

"As I already explained, at the present time, that won't be possible. Perhaps in a few days, but not right now. I'm certain you will be quite comfortable at my home. And I assure you, you will be quite safe there."

We asked Collins if we could speak in private and he immediately stood and walked to the other side of the room, standing with his back to us.

I whispered, "As quietly as you can . . . This place might be bugged . . . What are your thoughts?"

"I think we're in a trap," Sandy spoke softly. "I don't think we have a choice. I think they'll kill us before they let us escape. Let's just go along with it all until we know the truth."

So we reluctantly turned and told Collins we were ready to go with him.

"Oh, that's fine. There's a helicopter waiting. Shall we go? We'll be home in time for a light dinner." he said and led us out, into the hallway. What had been an absolutely dark tunnel was now lit and bright. The power had been turned back on. It was the same grey concrete in the hallway as was the room we were in. As we walked, following Collins, he said without turning to us, "Do you ride?"

"Ride what?" I asked.

"I raise Arabians at home," he said. "I don't spend much time in the States but when I do I truly enjoy a ride before breakfast. Stirs the appetite. Perhaps you'll join me tomorrow?"

TEN - What Shall I Call You Today, My Dear?

The helicopter set down on a green and white landing pad behind Mathew Collins' home. We looked around as the helicopter settled slowly. The property was beautiful. The house was not grand, but it fit the landscape perfectly. It was a sprawling Ranch-Type, white with a red tile roof and some red brick out front. To our left was a stable that was a twin to the house.

There were white fenced pastures, not overly large, but big enough. And there was a pond, actually larger than a pond but smaller than a lake, surrounded by rocks and water loving plants. And there was a wooden walk out over the pond with a covered and screened gazebo at the end.

Collins saw me looking at the pond and said, "I keep it stocked with trout. When I'm here I enjoy a few hours of fly fishing. I'm not very good at it, but I enjoy it. Perhaps you'd like to try your luck?"

I didn't answer, mainly because I didn't intend to be there all that long. Instead I said, "Suppose we just took off running right now? I mean, are you going to stop us all by yourself?"

"Of course not," he said, smiling his sophisticated little smile that was starting to get really old. "You wouldn't get very far on foot. You don't know where you are or how far it is to the nearest town. And I can have people here in minutes. But most importantly, I'm looking forward to visiting with you, and I would miss not having you here."

We walked behind Mathew Collins toward his house as the helicopter took off and flew away. I silently pointed to the left and with a questioning look asked Sandy if we should just run. She shook her head, put her finger to her lips to tell me to keep quiet, and we continued into the house.

Inside we found an expensively decorated house without it being overdone. It was simple, tasteful, and elegant all at the same time. Only the best had been infused in Collins' home. As we stood in what must have been the living room, Collins walked to a small bar and said, "It must be five o'clock somewhere in the world. Will you join me?"

Before we could answer, a tall, statuesque woman walked into the room. At one time she could have been a highly paid fashion model. Today she retained her beauty and grace at perhaps forty years of age. She was dressed in riding jodhpurs and a tan shirt, sleeves rolled up to her elbows. The outfit accentuated her slim body. She walked across the polished wood floor in white athletic socks, no boots or shoes. Her hair was blond and long, but that day she wore it tied back in a pony tail that hung to her shoulders.

Collins saw her and said, "Oh, wonderful, my dear. I didn't know you were here already. Mr. and Mrs. Crew, this is my assistant . . ." he paused for a moment and asked her, "And what shall we call you today, my dear?"

"I was thinking of Henrietta," she answered.

"Henrietta!" Collins said laughing and clapped his hands. "That's wonderful! Haven't used that one before, have you?"

"No, sweetums," she said as she strode in royal fashion to the bar. "And what shall I call you today, my dear?"

"I was using Mathew Collins," he answered and then kissed her lightly on her cheek.

"Oh, dear," she said sounding rather disappointed.

"You've used that one before. Tsk-Tsk."

"Wait a minute," I said. "You mean your name isn't Mathew Collins?"

"Of course not," he said. "Security, you know. It's a strange life but it's the life we've chosen."

"So if you lied about your name, how do we know you're telling the truth about being with the CIA?"

"I suppose because I told you," he answered.

Sandy said, "At least Noah Goldberg confirmed who he was. We spoke to the Israeli Embassy."

"My dear Mrs. Crew," Collins or whatever his name was said. "Noah Goldberg is . . . Or should I say was . . . A top Mossad Agent. One night five years ago he went into Gaza on a mission. He never came out. His body, what was left of it, was found draped over a fence on the border three months later. Noah Goldberg is dead. Whoever you spoke with was not Noah Goldberg."

"Then why did the Embassy confirm who he was? They even spoke to him," I questioned.

"The Israelis do unusual things, Mr. Crew. And although they are and should be our friends, they often work alone, without letting us in on their actions. I assume there was some kind of code word? A phrase or something to break the ice as it were?"

I looked at Sandy and again she shrugged her shoulders. She said, "What have we got to lose at this point."

I said to the man, "Operation Ruhiger Mann."

"Ahh! Silent Man . . . How appropriate but not very imaginative," he said. He turned to his assistant who was being called Henrietta that day, and said, "Let's inform Langley on that."

'Henrietta' nodded and left the room.

When we were alone, Collins-whoever-he-was said, "Now, won't you join me?"

Sandy said, "I think we'll pass. I have a feeling we're

here so you can learn stuff from us and it's probably better if we keep a clear head."

"You are as perceptive as you are beautiful, my dear," he said. "Shall we sit then? Let's be comfortable anyway."

Sandy and I sat next to each other on an upholstered couch and what's-his-name sat on a beige leather armchair next to the couch. He hadn't stopped that incessantly sophisticated smiling yet. From his pinstriped suit jacket he retrieved a gold cigarette case and offered us one. I really could have used a smoke or a drink or something, but Sandy is my conscience and she stopped me. But he lit one with a small gold lighter that had small diamonds running up both sides, and delicately blew a cloud of smoke towards the ceiling.

"Alright," he said. "Let's start at the beginning. I'm sure you know that a man was being questioned back there at The Levels."

"We were told he was being tortured," Sandy said.

"Terrible," he said. "All these years and I'm still not used to that. But it is done, my dear. Unfortunate, but not the point here. The man being questioned mentioned your name, Mr. Crew. Why?"

"Now that's a good question," I said. "If you ever find out why, I'd really like to know, too."

"Not good enough, I'm afraid," he said. "He must have gotten your name from somewhere."

"So who is this guy?" I asked.

"That, Mr. Crew, is the ultimate question. We don't know and that is precisely what we need to find out."

"We were told that what you call The Levels was attacked and this man was rescued, or at least taken. Who did that?" I asked.

"Oh, Mr. Crew," he said. "None of that now. I'll ask the questions, if you don't mind. You almost got me there. You are good, aren't you?"

"All I'm trying to find out is what the hell is going on," I said. "It seems we're somebody's prisoners and we don't know what we did."

"What you did was to have your name mentioned in a National Security matter. I need to find out why. I suggest you simply cooperate and you and your wife will come out of this in fine shape."

"Mr. whatever your name is," Sandy said. "It seems useless for us to keep telling you we don't know anything and we don't have the answers you need. You want us to prove a negative and you must know that's not possible."

We sat silently for a couple of minutes that dragged on and on. I decided to break the tension. I said, "Maybe if we cooperate? You tell us a few things and with that maybe we'll come up with something that will help you? Let's start with something Noah Goldberg told us. Who is T. J. Kohl?"

"Alright," he leaned forward a little. "T. J. is very intelligent, very politically minded, and a very dangerous person. She is both a cold blooded killer and a respected leader in the Intelligence Community. Her position today is classified as Top Secret so I'm afraid I can't tell you that, but rest assured she has a position about as high up in Washington as one can get."

"This man, Noah, seemed concerned that she might be coming after us, to do us some harm," I said.

"If she is, Mr. Crew, you are in very deep trouble," he answered. "Now let me ask you. Have you ever heard of her before?"

"No, absolutely not," I said. "And I kind of think I don't want to meet her either."

"So then," he asked. "Why would she wish to harm you?"

"That's a really good question," I said. "My family is quite wealthy and influential in politics. We support a lot of politicians. But as far as I know, we've never been involved in anything like what we're apparently involved in now."

"Well," he said. "I think I have an answer for you.

See if this helps. T. J.'s parents were killed in the rescue at The Levels. If she believes you had anything to do with that . . . Well, I hope you understand."

"Revenge then," Sandy said. "But if she's as smart as you say, why would she just run off to kill people without thinking it through? And if she's as highly placed as you claim, she must have huge resources available to her. Why act alone?"

"Did I ever say she was acting alone?" he said. "There must be hundreds of people in the world who owe her favors."

"And why aren't you doing something to stop her?" I asked. "If you're high up the totem pole, as you say, you must have some influence. Do something."

"Things are being put into play that cannot be discussed with you," he said. "But I need to get back to this man. How does he know you?"

I looked at Sandy. She turned to the man who wanted to be called Collins and said, "Tell us about the man. Maybe something will click."

He told us about the man who would not speak; how he had come to the U. S. from Canada and how he had been captured. He told us there was no record of the man and how interrogations, torture, and drugs could not make him talk. He described the man physically in great detail. But nothing told us who the man was or how he came to know my name.

"I am very disappointed," he said and I believed he was telling the truth. His face reflected sadness, concern, worry.

'Henrietta' returned to the room. "All has been arranged, darling," she said. "Shall I have some dinner prepared?"

"Yes, my sweet," the man said. "Something light, please. I don't think any of us are ready for a big meal."

He was slouched in his chair now, his shoulders were

slumped. He said to us, "I suppose we must make the best of a delicate situation. May I show you around the property? The stable is quite interesting."

"Mr. Collins or whatever your name is," Sandy said. "I have a child at home. I'm not staying for dinner. If you're done with us, we should be going. We'll need a ride to the nearest airport."

"Mrs. Crew," he said and pushed himself upright. "I think you know that's not going to happen. Tomorrow you and your husband will be taken from here and placed in the custody of people not as nice as I am. For now, you should, as I said, make the best of a delicate situation."

I figured I might be able to take Collins if I didn't fight fair. I was sure Sandy could beat the crap out of the middle-aged model. That is if they weren't some kind of James Bond super karate experts. But after that, what? They would be sure to notify someone and we'd be lucky to put a mile between us and Collins. Sandy has taught me patience and I decided that biding our time was the better part of valor.

Sandy pulled her cell phone from her purse and said, "I'm going to phone to check in and see how the baby is doing." It was not a request; she was telling Collins. He nodded.

"Hello, Betsy. This is Sandy," she said after dialing Betsy's new cell phone number.

""Hi Sandy," she said. "You OK?"

"Yes . . . Sort of. How's Caroline?"

"She's fine," Betsy said. "She misses you but she's doing fine."

"Look, there's a chance we won't be home tonight. We'll let you know what's happening in the morning."

"Hey Sandy," Betsy said. "Me and C had to leave the house. There was this really strange woman come to the house. I told her you were out shopping and for her to come back tonight. Meantime I packed up some stuff and we're gone."

"Oh my God! Where are you?"

"Hey, it might be smart not to say over the phone, ya'know? I've seen enough spy movies and stuff. They listen in on phone calls. Don't worry. I'm with good friends and nobody will find me. I'll check-in with you every day." And the line went dead.

I asked her what that was all about. She said, "Betsy had a caller earlier today. I think it may have been this T. J. woman. Anyway, Betsy has taken Caroline and is staying with friends. Morgan, we need to get out of here."

Collins spoke up. "Mrs. Crew, there is no one who wants to see you go home more than I. But we must know your connection. It is a National Security issue."

"Screw National Security," I said. "Our child may be in danger. If we have to fight our way out if here, we will."

"Then tell me the truth," he answered simply and calmly.

"God Damn it!" I yelled. "I'm telling you the truth! Hook me up to a damn polygraph if you have to!"

'Henrietta', or whatever her name was, came back into the room, this time holding a very large pistol. She had it pointed at Sandy and me. She said, "Shall we lock them up until the morning, darling?"

"I think you're right, my love. The back room, would you agree?"

"Absolutely," she said and waived the gun menacingly, telling us to get up and go to a room where we would be locked in for the night. The room turned out to be small, no larger than about ten by ten. There were no windows and the door was thick, solid wood with a quarter inch thick steel plate riveted to the inside of the door, covering most of it. There was a single chair, on wheels, like you would find in an office, and a bare mattress on the floor. It was old and stained. Sandy and I had the same thought at the same time. Blood? A single light bulb hung from the ceiling. Other than that, the room was bare.

When the door was locked, and we were alone Sandy asked, “OK, what do we do now?”

“We get out of here,” I said.

ELEVEN - Report To Langley

Henrietta carried a silver tray down the narrow hallway to the backroom. On the tray were a silver coffee service, two glasses of freshly squeezed orange juice, and a glass decanter of ice water. It was a few minutes past seven AM and she needed to get Sandy and me ready to be transported.

She stopped at the door and balanced the tray on one hand as she took the key that was on a cord hung about her neck and unlocked the door. She took two steps into the room, stopped and dropped the tray on the bare wooden floor. Sandy and I had left during the night.

She ran from the room screaming, "Patrick! Patrick!"

Patrick, whom we had known as Mathew Collins, came from his bedroom, tying a maroon and gold tasseled cord around his Chinese patterned silk bathrobe.

"What is it, Susan?" he asked, calling her by her real name, as he held onto her by her shoulders.

"They're gone!" she screamed. "They're gone!"

"What!" Patrick said, bewildered and wondering if she were dreaming. He pushed Susan aside and ran to the back room where we had been locked-up. The door was open and we were not there.

****

The 'Tech Team' arrived at Patrick's house in exactly twenty-seven minutes. It had taken Patrick and Susan a half an hour to work up the courage to phone Langley and report the loss of Morgan and Sandy Crew. But twenty-seven minutes later the 'Tech Team' arrived and started working to determine just how we had escaped.

Patrick Chesterson and Susan Kipman had been flown in from London a day before we had been caught in The Levels. Patrick had been on the 'Consult Team' at CIA headquarters in Langley that would decide the fate of The Levels. It didn't take much discussion for the seven-member 'Consult Team' to come to the conclusion that no evidence of The Levels could remain. Nightmare visions of the world learning of an ultra-secret intelligence gathering and torture facility, outside the realm of law yet inside the United States, filled the thoughts of all seven.

Patrick knew The Levels were in the process of being destroyed that day we had escaped. All paper and computer records would be stored securely in vaults deep below CIA headquarters in Langley. But how was he to explain the loss of us, Mr. and Mrs. Crew? He tried to think of a way that would place the entirety of it on Susan's shoulders, but he realized that was futile dreaming. He was in charge. He would accept the blame and retire. He had enough money tucked away in various banks throughout Europe. He would be fine, he knew.

Patrick and Susan sat on the back patio, drinking coffee and smoking the Turkish cigarettes Susan preferred. They didn't speak; there was nothing worth talking about. Their silence was broken by John Malcolm, in charge of the 'Tech Team' that examined the scene and collected forensic evidence. Their goal was to find out just how the hell we got out of there.

Malcolm walked out onto the flagstone patio and strode back and forth, his hands behind his back. He said, "We took the door lock apart. There are scratches on the tumbler pins. They picked the damn lock."

He waited for Patrick and Susan to say something but neither did.

"You did search them before locking them up I suppose?" he asked.

Again, neither answered.

"That's what I thought," Malcolm said. "It appears they used wire from the ceiling light to bypass a window's alarm contacts in the living room. That's how they got out. They completely destroyed each surveillance camera in the front and back, as well on each side of the house. We have no way of knowing which direction they went in. Mrs. Crew did leave a message for us using the last camera before they smashed it. She has an attractive middle finger."

Susan lit yet another cigarette. Patrick looked towards his stables remembering that someone needed to tend to the horses there. He would call old Manny Gonzales who took care of the horses when Patrick was away.

"Alright," Malcolm said. "Both of you pack up and report to Langley first thing in the morning."

Patrick and Susan smiled at each other. That was a big relief for both of them. They were being given time; time to run if they thought that was their best tactic. It would also seal their guilt. No, later that day, when they were alone, they agreed they would report to Langley and surprise everyone.

Patrick struggled to push himself up from the chair. Age had never been a problem before. But this whole affair – a strange man who would not speak, two people whom he was sure had nothing to do with the strange man, ugly torture, and now his downfall from a career filled with success after success. But his prized Arabians needed to be cared for and that was most important to Patrick.

Five Days Later

Patrick Chesterton and Susan Kipman had been called to meet with Ian McCauley who had been named Agent-in-charge of the file named Silent Man. The Company, as the insiders like to call the CIA, had borrowed from the Israelis and named the file Silent Man. Everyone agreed it was as good a name as any.

They had reported to Langley and were told to meet with McCauley in Los Angeles at the office building of Kirkwood Industrial Manufacturing. K.I.M., as it was known, was a CIA front and their basement offices were commonly used as a meeting place.

Patrick and Susan waited outside the basement meeting room, in the hallway where there were no chairs. Patrick paced back and forth in front of the steel door to the room. Susan leaned against a wall and watched him. All the possible moves of the game of chess she was playing ran through her mind. She had several options rolling around in her head that might clear her and hang Patrick. And Patrick had his own plans on what to do to clear himself and hang Susan.

They had successfully come through three days of questioning in Langley and now they were about to find out what plans had been devised for them. Thoughts ran through Patrick's head. Weeks before he had been a respected and very independent Field Agent who never failed an assignment. Now he had become a pawn. Susan, on the other hand, was tired of being a pawn, of being Patrick's 'assistant' as he often referred to her. She wanted more, and when the opportunity presented itself, she would grab for more.

The door opened and Ian called their names. They walked into the room and the door was closed behind them by Thomas Christopher. Tom was a former Navy Seal who worked as a contract agent for the Agency. Tom was big, he was intimidating, he was a killer, and he worked with Ian for those reasons.

The room was big, bright, nicely furnished; it had an aura of comfort about it. There were old master paintings – prints really, but nicely framed – on the walls. There were bookcases full of the books Ian loved. There was a big bar with several crystal decanters filled with expensive liquors. At the far end of the room a big, flat screen TV hung on the wall; a CNN reporter was speaking, but the sound had been turned off. This was where Ian did all his important work.

Ian sat behind a polished teak wood desk. In the room with Ian were Donald Stevens and Edward Burns, both Agents with the Company as Ian preferred to refer to the CIA. He waived Patrick and Susan to chairs and said, "I hope you know Donald and Edward? They will be working with you."

"Working on what?" Patrick asked anxiously. "We have a new assignment? Susan and I will be working together?"

"You have a new assignment," Ian said. "Actually, you have two assignments. You'll be reporting to Donald and Edward. Tom there will be available for dirty work."

"OK," Patrick said. He sat forward in the chair, leaning his elbows on his knees. He would live another day, and maybe if he could do what Ian wanted, he would live long enough to really retire with a Company pension. "So what and where?"

"First, T. J. Kohl has gone rogue," Ian said. "She needs to be stopped. Find her."

Susan asked, "What do we do if . . . I mean when we find her?"

"Tom will take over," Ian said without emotion. Susan knew that meant T. J. Kohl would be killed.

"And second," Ian said. "Find Morgan and Sandy

Crew. Don't hurt them . . . Bring them here for questioning."

"Are they in the States?" Susan asked.

"The States is where you will start," Ian said. "Follow wherever they take you but find them."

Susan fidgeted uncomfortably in the deep cushioned chair and said, "I'm on record as not liking assignments in the States. You know that we cannot operate in the States. It's the law. If we get caught . . . Well, you know what will happen."

"Don't get caught," was all Ian said. He tossed a manila folder on the desk toward Patrick and Susan. Susan retrieved it, tucked it under her arm, and she and Patrick stood.

"Donald and Edward will contact you," Ian said. "Review the file . . . If you need anything, contact them, not me. Good Luck."

Both Patrick and Susan knew that meant they would be breaking the law by working inside the United States, and Ian McCauley was insulating himself from that Federal crime. They stood in the hallway after the door was closed. In a whisper, Patrick asked, "What do you think, my dear?"

"I think we're pretty close to being useless enough to be eliminated. I think we'd better find T. J. and find her fast."

"Go home, Susan," Patrick said. "I need to make arraignments for the horses. Come to my house in three days. I'll make up a list of people who are close to T. J.. We'll start there."

TWELVE - I Don't Want To Hurt Any Of You

Susan kept an apartment in the Georgetown district of D. C.. Susan Kipman came from a wealthy family who had provided her with the very best Ivy League education. Her father and his father had been influential high level employees of the State Department. Susan joined their ranks, found intelligence gathering working for the State Department to be fun. She was good at it, and soon she was recruited by the CIA. The fun was gone after she had joined the Company.

She had never met T. J. Kohl, but T. J.'s reputation was well known and talked about within the intelligence community. She was a dangerous woman but also a woman of great power and influence. It was rumored that she was acting as a Special Assistant to the President when The Levels was attacked. It was all just a rumor, not unlike so many rumors floating around about T. J.. But if only a few of the rumors she had heard were true, why would T. J. go rogue? Would she so willingly give up so much so quickly?

Susan had one day left of the three days before she was to meet Patrick at his home in Virginia. Three days to relax and think about her future. Resignation was always a possibility, and in fact she had typed up several versions on her laptop computer. All she had to do was submit one, a non-offensive version, and she could be gone.

Dinner at her favorite Georgetown restaurant, l'ami de

Michael, was what she needed. She showed up without a reservation, but they knew her and sat her at a small table, in spite of the line of people waiting. She enjoyed a salad, a plate of garlicky mussels, some of their delicious French bread, and at least two glasses of very cold champagne. She felt good enough to walk home that night.

As she turned the corner to her street, a van pulled to the curb; three men jumped from it and grabbed her. She felt a sharp pain at the side of her neck where the hypodermic needle was stabbed. They pulled her into the van as black unconsciousness overtook her.

Susan awoke in a cold, dank, stone cell. There was no window in the cell, no light save for cold grey light filtering in under the rusty metal door. She was lying on a solid metal bunk that had no mattress or padding and was hung from the wall by thick, rusty chains. Her hands were cuffed behind her back. Her head was throbbing; her throat was as dry as a desert. She had no idea how long she had been unconscious or where she was. But she knew all about the many secret prisons where people disappeared.

She pushed herself up to a sitting position. As she stood, she found her feet were bare as they touched the icy-wet stone floor. She was dressed in a grey jump suit that although it was new to her, must have been worn by several other people before her, based on the acrid, unwashed smell of it.

She walked to the door and yelled, "Hello! Is anybody there?"

From the ceiling an angry and very frightening voice growled, "Shut up, bitch!"

Susan slunk back to the bunk and sat. There was nothing to do but wait. Her CIA training at The Farm taught her survival techniques and how to manage confinement. Quiet and calm, that was best. Eat and drink anything given to you. Don't cooperate. Endure torture only as long as you can. Only a fool would die a painful death rather than live to escape. Tell them partial truths and only lies that could be true and would be hard to verify. Find a friend amongst the captors. Become one of them until escape was possible.

And so she waited. It was impossible to determine the passage of time, but eventually a trap door opened at the bottom of the cell's door and a tin plate with food was slid in. The trap door slammed shut immediately. But how to eat it?

She tried to slide her hand cuffed arms under her legs, but her model's legs were too long. Giving up, she knelt on the floor and ate the food dog style. The food, some kind of stew or soup, was half liquid and half solid and all indeterminate in taste. After licking the plate clean she pushed herself to her feet and went back to the metal bunk. Rest, she thought. Quiet and calm. Wait.

She slept, but she couldn't tell for how long. When she woke she needed a bathroom. "Oh Christ," she thought. "Now what?" She wondered if she could stand to be in constantly urine-wet clothes. So she tried once again to bring her cuffed hands from behind her back. They had showed her how to do it back on The Farm. She lay on her side and pulled her knees up to her chin. She pulled her arms around . . . First as far as her bare feet . . . And then she dragged the metal handcuffs across her heals scraping them raw, finally by twisting her feet up, she managed to bring her hands to the front.

Her eyes had become acclimated to the dark. As she unbuttoned the jump suit she looked around and saw in a corner away from the door, a hole in the floor. It was difficult but she managed to pull the suit down far enough to urinate, hoping that there was not a camera with people at the other end watching her.

Time became a fantasy that didn't exist. She tried counting seconds into minutes into hours but the task, she was afraid, would drive her crazy. Quiet, calm, wait, was all she could hope for.

Tin plates of food were slid under the door, one after

another. With her hands in front of her she was able to eat sitting up rather than on her knees. She counted the plates – there were five and then six – but it was impossible to determine how regularly they appeared. Day and night were just a distant memory.

She was sleeping when the screaming woke her suddenly. It was an anguished scream, a tortured scream from someone hoping to die soon. She sat up and the icy cold stone floor sent a shiver up her spine. Then the screaming stopped and quiet fell like a cold sheet folded all around her. More sleep was fleeting and whatever reality time might have been was dragging by. Six more times she was awakened by the screaming. It seemed like every time she would fall into sleep the screaming would start again. So she fought off sleep.

She paced in a tight square around the cell. The icy-wet cold was stingingly painful. Soon she could no longer feel her feet beneath her. But she kept it up – for how long she did not know – until she was ready to collapse. She fell onto the metal bunk and sleep came quickly despite her shivering from the cold.

She jumped from a nightmare when the steel door to her cell slammed open. Two big men, dressed entirely in black and grey camouflage fatigues with black ski masks covering their heads, ran into the room and dragged her from it. They held her tightly by her upper arms and pulled her backwards roughly. She struggled to get her bleeding feet under her to no avail.

In the hallway a third man, also hidden in black and grey camo and ski mask, pulled a heavy black bag over Susan's head and roughly drew a draw string too tightly around her neck.

She was dragged, still backwards, on her bare heals, down the hallway. She counted one right turn and one left turn, and then she was pushed down onto a hard chair. She felt heavy leather belts being tied around her waist and her left arm, still handcuffed to her right, was strapped down to an arm of the chair.

Waiting there she began to hear other people. At first there was just breathing and then faint moaning. Without warning the hood was ripped from her head. She quickly looked to her left and right. Hand cuffed and secured to chairs as she was, dressed in dirty grey jump suits as she was, were Patrick Chesterton, Ian McCauley, Donald Stevens, Edward Burns, and Thomas Christopher.

Four men in black and grey camo, wearing ski masks, left the room, closing the door after them, leaving the six people alone. They looked at each other, back and forth, and finally Ian spoke. "What the fuck is going on?"

No one had an answer so no one said anything. They each tested the leather straps holding them to the chairs. And they each found the chairs were bolted to the floor. Each looked like they had seen better days.

Before they could speak to one another, the door opened again and I walked in with another man who was dressed in black and grey camo but without the ski mask. He wore a pistol at his side.

I said, "For those of you who don't know me, I am Morgan Crew."

A six foot long table and two chairs were brought into the room. My companion and I sat with the table between us and our captives. I felt good. I felt really good, as I always do when a plan of mine comes together.

Ian McCauley spoke first. He said, looking at my companion, "That's Colonel Masterson. He's a filthy, throat cutting mercenary."

I turned to the Colonel and asked, "Are you really a filthy, throat cutting mercenary?"

He smiled and said, "Yep. 'Fraid so."

I looked from captive to captive and said, "So let's get one thing straight right from the start. I get what I pay for and if I pay to have you shot in the head, you will be shot in the head."

Ian asked, "What do you want? Do you know what you've done?"

"Mr. McCauley," I said. "I want the truth. Now, you've been honest enough to admit knowing my friend the Colonel. Can I trust you'll be honest enough to tell me what I want to know?"

"Screw you," he said and spit on the floor.

I called for two of the masked guards who were standing in the hallway at the open door. They stepped into the room.

"Take Mr. McCauley back to his cell," I instructed. They pulled a hood over his head, undid his leather straps and pulled him to his feet. One of them punched him hard in the stomach. Ian buckled over as his breath was forced from him. The two men dragged Ian from the room. The five remaining watched as he was punched again in the stomach and at the back of his head. They turned into the hallway, and the five listened to the sound of Ian being beaten again and again. Finally, quiet filled the room.

I waited until it had all sunken in, and then I leaned forward, elbows on the table, and I said, "Look, I have a family to protect. I was dragged into this because of something I know nothing about. All I want is out. All I want is for my family to be safe and left alone by you bunch of idiots. I don't want to hurt any of you . . . But I will if I have to. Now, who is going to help me get what I want?"

No one answered. I stood and the Colonel stood. We left the room, closing and locking the door behind us, leaving the five alone. In the hallway we were met by Ian McCauley and the two guards. He was standing, unshackled, waiting for us.

"I'm sorry we got so rough with you, Ian," I said and shook his hand.

Colonel Masterson said, "I told my people to make it look real, but not to hurt you. I'm sorry if they went overboard."

"That's OK," he said and grinned like a kid. "I've had worse."

We walked down the hall to a room that I had converted to a comfortable office. Sandy was waiting for us there, relaxing on a comfortable couch.

"Mrs. Crew," Ian said. "I'm very happy to see you again. How are you? And how about little Caroline?"

"She's fine," Sandy said. "Betsy took her down to San Francisco. She has some friends there. Not the best people in the world, but her friends were there and they hid and protected Betsy and Caroline. She and the baby are here with us now, out in the main house."

Colonel Masterson sat with Ian, Sandy and me at a round table in the middle of the room where good, strong coffee was waiting along with sandwiches and even a plate of warm chocolate chip cookies. Next to the food was a small speaker. The Colonel switched it on and we ate as we listened to the five people we had left secured in the other room.

Patrick Chesterton was speaking, ". . . Anybody know how long we've been here?"

Edward Burns said, "It's SOP in these situations to institute time deprivation. Breaks down normal rationalization."

Susan asked, "Did anyone hear that man screaming? Sounded like he was being tortured."

No one had heard what Susan had heard. Burns again had an explanation. "Fear," he said. "Get a trapped rat scared and he'll do just about anything to get away."

Donald Stevens asked, "Can anyone slip out of these restraints?"

No one answered but I assumed they were all twisting their wrists around, trying to see how secure the straps were. There was silence coming over the speaker. Then Ian said in between mouthfuls of a cookie, "One of those bastards is a traitor. I hope they slip up soon."

"And if they don't," I asked. "What do we do then?"

"T. J. is one of the best," Ian said. "She can hide out in the open, in broad daylight, and no one will find her. She can kill in a dozen different ways. We don't know why she went rogue, but the best we can do is assume she believes you and Sandy had something to do with the death of her parents. This place is secure; she won't get in here. I just hope that we don't have to wait too long for the traitor to slip up. One of those people knows where she is and what she's doing."

Colonel Masterson said, "I think you may be forgetting something. This T. J. woman may be a threat but what about that guy you had at The Levels? He's still missing. The people who rescued him are still out there. Who are they and who sent them? And why did that guy come to the U.S.? What was his mission?"

Ian said, "Whoever the traitor is in that room may know that also. There were only a handful of people who knew what was happening at The Levels or that the levels even existed. Everyone who knew, except the five people in that room, is dead. Someone had to at least reveal secrets, if not actually plan and run the attack. Someone in that room knows who the team was and where they came from. Someone knows who financed it. Someone knows who the man is and what his assignment was . . . Or maybe still is."

"And suppose that person doesn't give it up?" I asked. "How long can we keep them here?"

"Technically," Ian said. "They'll never leave if that becomes necessary."

"That's sanctioned?" Masterson asked.

"From the top," Ian answered.

We listened in to what the five said for three hours and learned nothing. The coffee pot was dry, the sandwiches and cookies had been eaten. Ian finally stood and while pacing around the room he ordered that the five be returned to their cells. They were hooded once again and forcefully dragged back to their cold, wet cells. Each cell had a hidden microphone and speaker, and each was monitored 24/7.

Time once again became meaningless. Each of the five prisoners was fed questionable food at irregular intervals. Blazingly loud acid rock music was piped into each cell at irregular intervals followed by total silence for long periods. Extreme heat and extreme cold alternately filled the cells, again irregularly. The pitch black of the cells were suddenly lit with extremely bright lights, then back to black after hours that could have been days as far as the five could tell.

No human contact was given to them and when any one of them yelled or tried to attract attention, the same barely human, growling voice filled the dark room telling them to 'shut up'. All this was meant to confuse and twist thought process, to instill fear and to make each lose hope.

On the evening of the eleventh day I was enjoying a pleasant dinner with Sandy and Betsy. Caroline was making happy noises as she lay in a colorful crib. We were listening to some good jazz from a collection of CDs provided by The Company and had opened a second bottle of almost good wine. We were laughing and making believe we could sing. We were happy and we felt safe there.

The prison was in a South American Country but the Company would not tell us which Country it was in. It was one of many around the world, in "friendly" Countries or in places so isolated they could go undiscovered. We had flown in on a Company jet in the dead of night. The shades had been locked down so we could not see outside, even if there had been something to see. When we climbed off the jet I saw that there were mountains all around, and it was raining hard as we were driven to the prison. It was easy enough to figure out that the prison was isolated; there was nothing anywhere but jungle and mountains, and a muddy dirt road.

At the prison we saw armed Marine guards everywhere. Combine the guards with the isolation and the contracted mercenary force that Colonel Masterson had brought with him to secure the site, and I felt sure T. J. Kohl could not get to us. My only question was – how long could we stay there.

Ian McCauley broke the spell of good fun and good food when he walked into the room. "I think we have to accept the fact that it's not working," he said. "We're not getting anywhere."

"Alright," Sandy asked. "Since this was all your idea, you came to us, we didn't come to you, what do you suggest we do next?"

"I frankly don't want to think about what we do next," Ian said. "We've done in-depth financial investigations. If the traitor received money it's hidden under a mattress somewhere. We exhausted all other means and still nothing."

"So what?" I asked. "Sandy asked a really good question. What do you want to do?"

"There's only one course left to us," he said. "We need to bring in interrogation specialists."

"You mean torture?" Sandy asked.

"It may be necessary."

"Not while I'm involved in this, Ian," she said. "I'm gone if you start that."

"I have to do something," he said. "In the last three days two people way up The Company chain have died . . . By accident, the reports say. One man, Upper Level Operational Planning Section, fell down a flight of stairs and broke his neck. The other, Logistical Management Section, was killed by a hit and run driver. Both had incidental and minor connection with The Levels. Neither one knew details of any kind. T. J. is hunting and killing."

THIRTEEN - Bait

Sandy was right of course, as she usually . . . Or should I say as she always is. There are limits to what either of us will do. I needed to protect my family but could I, in good conscience, stand by and watch people suffering extreme inflicted pain? I didn't think so. But I had an idea that I had been thinking about, keeping it to myself, for two days.

I asked Ian to sit with us and offered him a cup of coffee, which he declined. I looked at Sandy and Betsy sitting next to her. My little daughter was mewing happily after Sandy had given her breakfast. I thought about San Marcos and all my friends there. I thought about my life and the future and all I wanted for everyone. There was no way I could justify risking all that. So I knew I had to put myself at risk once again, for other people's safety this time.

I leaned forward and said, "Look, I've got an idea."

Sandy shot back, interrupting me, "No! Whatever you're thinking, NO!"

"You don't know what I'm thinking," I said.

"I know you, Morgan Crew. You've got some harebrained scheme that will get you hurt or killed. I say, no way!"

"Hear me out, anyway," I said. "This place is very, very secure. It would take a miracle for T. J. to get in here. I feel that Sandy and Caroline are safe here. I feel safe here. But being safe can't last forever. I don't intend to live my life out here, nor do I want to have Caroline grow into adulthood sheltered here. I want to bring this to an end."

I paused for a moment. Sandy said, "Oh shit! Here it comes!"

Ian said, "So what? What do you suggest?"

"I want to go home," I said. "I want to go back to San Marcos. I want to go back to my territory. I want to be somewhere that I'm familiar with. If someone is hunting me, I want them to hunt me on my territory. I want T. J. to find me there."

Sandy jumped to her feet and shouted, "And you want her to kill you!"

"No," I said, trying to stay calm and hoping calm would rub off on Sandy. "I want her to find me and I want her caught when she does. And I want Colonel Masterson and a couple of his people there to keep me alive and catch her when she shows up."

"So you want to be bait," Ian said. "Are you crazy?"

"We're here," I began, "because you approached us. You suggested this means of protecting us while stopping T. J. Kohl. Your plan isn't working. Do you have a better suggestion . . . And don't start with the torture thing because that won't happen as long as Sandy and I are here and part of this."

Ian said nothing. He sat at the table with his hands folded together, his knuckles turning white from the grasp. For the first time in his life he didn't know what to do. Somehow he had to be successful. It wouldn't be the first time he had used bait but never civilian bait. Oh, others in The Company had perhaps less scruples than he had. But he had to be successful.

Sandy said, "I'm afraid there's no changing his mind. He does this stuff all the time. We'll leave first thing in the morning."

"You're not coming with me," I said.

"Yes, I am," she said firmly. "I'm going to leave

Caroline with Betsy . . . I'm going to leave them here. And I expect them to be safe," Sandy said looking directly at Ian. "You don't want me after your ass, Ian. Keep them safe."

****

The next morning there was a car waiting for us at the entrance to the prison owned by The Company. Two very large and very well armed Latino men loaded our luggage into the car and drove us to the little airfield a half hour away. A Gulfstream jet was waiting there for us. Before boarding I asked the two Latino men who had taken us there what Country we were in.

They laughed together and one of them said, "No speakee' Americano, dude".

The jet was equipped with a large thermos of coffee, some donuts and pastries, several bottles of booze but no Wild Turkey, and window shades that would not open. So we ate and drank but we had no idea what direction we were flying in or any idea of where we might be. The flight took a little over five hours, and we landed at a small private airfield outside of Sacramento. A car was waiting for us with two men, equally as large and equally as tough looking as the two who drove us from the prison. They wore blue jeans and black t-shirts. They openly had large, semi-auto pistols at their sides. I glanced inside the open front door of the car and saw two really nasty looking automatic assault rifles.

"The Colonel sent us," the driver said. "He'll join you at your home tomorrow. We're to stay with you."

The drive to San Marcos was long and hot in spite of the A/C being turned up to maximum. We sat in the back seat, Sandy on my right. She stared out the right side window; I stared out the left side. The only words spoken by either of us were from Sandy when she whispered, "I miss

Caroline."

****

Masterson showed up at our house the next day as promised. He brought two large duffle bags with him. Inside the first was an assortment of really dangerous and scary looking fully automatic H&K MP5Ks and MP5Ns. There were pistols, night vision headgear, knives, and a dozen different kinds of explosives from hand grenades to shape charges and even small "toe cutter" land mines.

"You're not planning on planting those things in our yard, are you?" Sandy asked.

"That's the idea," Masterson said as he spread his toys out on the living room floor. "These we plant under your windows. They won't kill but we'll hear a lot of screaming."

I gave him a guided tour of the house, the terraced decks running down the hillside behind our house and overlooking the harbor, the sparsely built neighborhood in the hills, and the two roads that lead up to the house. Masterson confided that he didn't like the neighborhood.

"Don't get me wrong," he said. "It's a beautiful place to live but a hell'uva place to defend. It's too isolated. There's too many trees and too many ways to get here without being seen. I know Kohl and she's one of the best. If she wants you she's gonna love the terrain."

The second duffle bag Masterson brought held wireless CCTV cameras and a half dozen small monitors. There were heat sensitive sensors and alarms, and spools of hair-thin trip wire. His two men took that bag and started placing the cameras, sensors and alarms around the exterior perimeter of our house. They hid a wireless camera in a tree fifty yards down the south road to our house and another one fifty yards down the west road.

In spite of Sandy's protestations, Masterson prepared for a battle. The two men who met us at the airport stayed with him, and a few hours after he arrived two more men joined them. Sandy and I sat on the couch and watched as they field stripped and cleaned and loaded each of the weapons. They placed hand grenades at strategic places inside around the house and buried the toe cutters outside under each window.

Then Colonel Masterson sat on the couch with us and gave us basic instruction on the use of the guns. "Leave the grenades alone," he said. "I don't want you tossing one in my direction. And remember to point the guns away from you *and* me."

Sandy asked Masterson a question that had been rolling around in my mind also. "Why is all this stuff necessary? It's like you're expecting a war."

"Mrs. Crew," he began. "T. J. Kohl is almost an army all on her own. When she comes you'll be very happy we are here with all this . . . Stuff. Plus, The Levels was attacked by a very professional group of very professional soldiers. I don't know who they were, although there are rumors out there. I have to protect you against the worst and hope for the best. If we never use any of the equipment here, I'll be very happy."

"You said rumors," I asked. "What rumors?"

"OK. Understand that these are just rumors. There is no evidence to back them up. But what I've heard is that the attack group was actually a super-secret CIA Delta Force."

"Wait a minute," I said. "You mean the CIA attacked itself?"

"The Levels wasn't a pure CIA operation. It was multi-divisional. NSA ran electronic eavesdropping. Air Force OSI Intel ran a system of surveillance satellites. The FBI provided ground surveillance and phone taps. There were others, but Homeland Security was in a position of overall management. All of this was sanctioned but outside current law. The rumor is that someone inside the CIA is a mole left over from the old Soviet Union. And that there is an intelligence unit and Delta Force group inside the CIA that even the CIA doesn't know about. And that this mole organized this super-secret force."

"And Ian McCauley is trying to find that mole . . . Back wherever we were?" I asked.

"That he is," the Colonel said as he started to field strip a Sig Sauer 9 MM semi-auto pistol for the second time.

"By the way," Sandy said. "Where is that place? Where were we?"

"I'm sorry, Mrs. Crew. That's classified."

"But you're not in the CIA," Sandy said.

"I'm on contract. A very lucrative contract. I don't want to lose it," he said as he took the pistol apart without looking at it and without much thought.

Sandy and I searched through the refrigerator and cupboard and found enough food in stock for a late lunch – a wedge of good cheddar cheese, what was left of a beef roast, and some deli sliced turkey to make sandwiches for the seven of us. As an afterthought, Sandy suggested we make enough for more than seven as Colonel Masterson's men looked like they could eat enough for two or three each, which in fact they did. A large pot of coffee was refilled twice and everybody had their fill.

Hours later, as we started wondering if we had enough food to feed Masterson's men dinner, the phone rang. Sandy picked it up and then handed it to me.

The man on the phone asked me to wait a moment and then T. J. Kohl came on the line.

"Mr. Crew, this is T. J.," she said. I had heard a lot about the woman. And most of it scared the hell out of me. Maybe it was just my imagination, but just hearing her voice started me sweating. "I've been hoping to speak with you."

"Well," I said. "You know where I live. Come around and we can talk."

"Did Colonel Masterson suggest you say that? Mr. Crew, please. I didn't make it to where I am . . . Or should I say to where I was . . . Because I'm stupid. We can meet and talk or . . . Well, you probably don't want to know the alternative."

"Actually," I said. "I feel pretty safe where I am."

"Ask Masterson about Bosnia. Ask him about Kuwait. Ask him about Somalia, Peru, Indonesia, or a dozen other places. Ask him how safe you really are. His little toys and hired guns aren't going to stop me if I come to see you. The best thing you can do for yourself is cooperate with me."

"What do you want from me, Ms. Kohl?" I asked her. Masterson was rushing to hook up a recording device to the phone. One of his men was on a cell phone ordering a trace on the line.

"I have to go now," she said. "Tell Masterson that I'm using a one-time throw away cell phone. Tracing is a waste of time and effort. When I call back I'll be using a new phone and I'll be in a different location."

The phone line went dead. I told the Colonel what she had said.

"That makes sense," he said. "I didn't think she'd be stupid enough to allow a trace. But it's worth a try. Nobody's perfect."

An hour later, Sandy picked up the phone and dialed in Betsy's new cell phone number. It rang five times but the voice mail didn't pick up. She let it ring another five times and still no answer.

"She's probably changing diapers or something," I said.

"Yeah, probably. I'll try again later."

The day dragged on . . . Slowly. One of Masterson's men tried to light a cigar but stopped the lighter short when Sandy yelled at him. He stepped out onto the deck. It was approaching evening, the air was cool, the sun was crashing into the Pacific, and there was a hint of approaching rain. I decided to sneak outside and see if the guard could spare a cigar for me to enjoy while hiding from Sandy.

She was rooting around in the kitchen trying to find something for dinner while I played secret commando slipping outside. The guard's cigar was burning a scar on the wooden deck. The guard lay on his back, blood pouring from the bullet hole in his forehead, above his left eye.

I yelled into the house, "Get out here! Masterson! Get out here!"

The Colonel ran out onto the deck, looked down at his dead soldier and grabbed me by my shoulders. He shoved me back into the house as a bullet tore into the side of the house. Had it not been for Masterson, the bullet would have opened my head.

The phone was ringing as I was pushed back into the house. Masterson stopped Sandy from answering it. He rushed to turn on the recorder and start the trace. He nodded and I picked up the phone.

"Mr. Crew," T. J. said. "I hope this will convince you to cooperate with me."

"You almost killed me," I said.

"If I wanted you dead . . . You'd be dead. That was just a message. I can get you anytime I want."

"OK," I said. "So tell me what you want."

"I want to know your connection. I want to know why that son of a bitch spoke your name. I want to know who killed my parents."

"I'm not connected," I said. "I don't know why my name was tossed around. I don't know who killed your parents. Is that an end to it?"

"Bullshit!" she said without trying to hide the menace in her voice. "You're lying, and that's going to get more people killed."

The line went dead once again.

Masterson had left the living room as soon as T. J. had disconnected. Sandy reached for the phone and tried

Betsy's cell again. She let it ring even longer than the last time and still there was no answer.

"You did set up voice mail on her phone, didn't you?" she asked me.

"Yes, I did. But remember where they are. Mountains all around, jungle and all that kind of stuff. Maybe there's really bad cell reception there. Let's not worry yet."

Masterson came back into the room with one of his men who had changed clothes. He was dressed in black from head to toe and had covered his face and hands with black camo paint. "This is Master Chief Dick Simmons, U.S. Navy SEALs retired. It's getting dark out there. He's going out there and get T. J.."

Masterson handed Simmons a short, automatic H&K MP5 assault rifle with a silencer attached. In the kitchen Masterson turned off all the lights and shut all the doors. Simmons quickly and quietly moved outside like a snake on the hunt.

An hour crept by and then another hour. Masterson was pacing around the living room and the kitchen. His two men were equally nervous. A third hour passed in silence and then we heard a muffled BOOM from the front of the house. Masterson turned off all the lights in the house and quickly opened the front door. Sandy and I followed him and his two soldiers. To the right, lying on his stomach on top of the softly exploded toe cutter mine was Master Chief Simmons. Masterson carefully turned the body over and we saw that the man's throat had been cleanly and deeply cut. His body had been tossed on the toe cutter but he was dead before that.

Masterson said, "Back inside. Everybody."

Sandy asked, "Are you just going to leave him there?"

"Bringing him inside isn't going to help him, Mrs. Crew. We'll wait until it's light outside."

FOURTEEN - I'm Beginning To Believe You

The phone rang again. Colonel Masterson told us to wait until the recorder was turned on and he could start a phone trace. He nodded to us and I picked up the phone on the fourth ring.

"Mr. Crew," T. J. said. "I hope I gave the Colonel enough time to start the trace. You might mention to him that I'm using yet another one time use cell phone."

"Why are you phoning this time, Ms. Kohl?" I asked.

"To be honest, I was pretty lucky killing that man. It's been a number of years since I've slit a throat. Now, if my count is right there are just three left to protect you. But I hope you see that they really can't protect you."

"Protect me from you?" I asked. I wanted to keep her talking this time so that Masterson could complete the trace.

"I really don't want to hurt you or Mrs. Crew . . . Or that beautiful little baby of yours."

"How do you know about our child?" I asked. Sandy grabbed my arm in fear.

"Oh please," T. J. said. "I've read the file on you. And by the way, you have an impressive background."

"So what do you want?"

"I told you," she said. "I want you to tell me your connection. How did that very strange man know you? Who killed my parents?"

"Ms. Kohl," I said. "How many times do I have to tell

you? I don't have a connection and I don't have answers to your questions. Now why not just go away and kill people in some other town?"

"Alright, Mr. Crew," she said. "I have to go now. Tell Masterson when I call back it's just a waste of time to try to locate me using these throw away cell phones."

Masterson and I paced back and forth around the house. He checked that all the windows and doors were locked, and that all the windows were covered. We talked about what to do next.

"I think we have to face the facts," I said. "That one woman has us trapped like rats. I mean, how long are we just going to wait locked up in here?"

"The point is, how long will she wait?" Masterson said. "Sooner or later she will try to get in here. I'll kill her when she does."

"Now wait," I said. "The plan was to capture her."

"She's killed two of my men, Mr. Crew. If I get close enough to her . . . She's dead."

Sandy interrupted us. "I just tried Betsy's cell again and again there was no answer. I'm worried."

Masterson walked to the phone in the living room. I watched the buttons he pushed and realized the area code he used was not one I was familiar with. He didn't use an international call number. It was a standard 10 digit number and without a '1' in front. While he was waiting on the line I went to the kitchen and looked in the phone book. The area code didn't exist, at least not for the general public.

Masterson was talking in a whisper on the phone; Sandy was nearby trying to listen and looking scared. He hung up the phone and said, "There might be a problem. No one has been able to get through to the prison by phone or radio."

"Oh my God!" she gasped. "Caroline!"

The Colonel tried to ease her fear by saying, "A group has been sent there. A Delta Force detachment. They'll be there within two hours. I'm going to get an immediate report. Look, that place is isolated and old. Anything could have happened to eliminate communications. A storm could have knocked out power temporarily. I'm sure there's no real problem. And besides, there are fifty-five Marines there as well as eighteen of my own men. It's a safe and secure place."

Sandy's eyes were filling with tears. She said in a fear filled, shaking voice, "If anybody hurts my baby I'll . . ."

She started crying; I took her into my arms and tried to comfort her as best I could, but I was scared myself.

She looked up into my eyes and said, "Morgan, I've never felt so afraid and helpless in my life." I shared her feelings but I couldn't tell her that. I felt that she needed someone to be strong. I wished it could have been me. It wasn't me; I was as scared as she was, but I had to at least make her believe I was strong.

The phone rang again, and I didn't wait for Masterson to tell me to answer it. I wanted to hear the report coming to him myself, and I was beginning to feel that it was about time to start taking control. But it was the Kohl woman again.

"Damn it!" I said. "I really don't have time for you right now."

"What? What happened?" she asked.

"None of your friggin' business lady."

"Morgan," she said, using my first name for the first time. "Listen to me. I'm beginning to believe you're being used here. I'm beginning to believe you're a red herring that's meant to distract me and a lot of other people. Tell me what happened."

I'm still not sure why but my gut was telling me to confide in Kohl, at least a little. I told her that our daughter may be in jeopardy and of our inability to contact anyone at the prison.

"OK, Morgan," she said. "That answers a lot of questions. I'm going to take a chance here. Tell Colonel

Masterson I'm leaving now. I won't bother you anymore. And tell Masterson I'm sorry for killing his people. He and I have worked together several times in the past. I respect him and I'm sorry."

The phone line went quiet. I told Masterson that Kohl said she was leaving. I decided not to tell him anything else, even though he had recorded the conversation. He quickly told his two remaining men to search the area around the house. He went out the back door and eased his way down the three levels of the deck, jumping over the lower rail and moving down the hillside.

While he was out, I told Sandy what Kohl had said. She agreed that it was time for us to start taking some control over the situation. We have learned over the years that when we are in trouble we never trust anyone, except ourselves, with everything. Sandy took the tape from the recorder that was attached to the phone. It had T. J. Kohl's words on it, and I agreed with Sandy that Masterson didn't need to know what she had said. She slid it under the couch cushion she was sitting on, and put a blank tape in the recorder.

Masterson and his two men were gone nearly an hour. They returned to our house one at a time, Masterson being the last. They conferred quietly for a few minutes and then Masterson said, "She's gone."

"No disrespect," I said. "But I think we knew that. Look, I want to thank you for all you've done, but I think you need to leave, too."

"She might come back," Masterson said. "She might be lying."

Sandy stood and said, "We'll take our chances. And please remove those explosives from under the windows."

The Colonel shrugged his broad shoulders and began packing up all his guns and grenades and bullets and electronics. His men carefully dug up the toe cutters and retrieved the two cameras that had been placed down the road. He put everything in the back of his van next to the bodies of the two men murdered by T. J. Kohl. He asked one more time before he walked outside, "Are you sure? This might be a foolish move."

"Before you go, Colonel," Sandy asked. "Our daughter may be in trouble. Where is that prison we were at?"

He thought for a moment, weighing whether or not to reveal a state secret to us. He said finally, "I can't tell you that. But maybe someone will. If someone does, it'll be by phone." He winked conspiratorially and he left our house.

****

It was ten past three in the morning when the phone rang. We had tried to sleep but found sleep impossible. I was pacing around from room to room, looking at each phone as I walked passed it, hoping it would ring. Sandy made a pot of really strong coffee which helped, but didn't make us feel any better.

"Morgan?" T. J. Kohl said.

"Oh for God's sake, lady. Leave us alone, will you?"

"I was speaking with Colonel Masterson," she said. "The prison is in Colombia."

"Where is our daughter?" I asked. "Is she still there? Is she OK?"

"I don't know where she is, but I'm told she's not in danger nor has she been harmed. I want to speak with you," she said. "When will that be possible?"

"I'm not sure that is possible," I said. "To be frank, I don't trust you."

"Morgan," she said. "If I wanted to, I could be in your house right now and both of you would be dead already. I've moved beyond that. When and where can we meet?"

I cupped my hand over the phone and told Sandy what Kohl said.

"Tell her to come here and come here now," Sandy said.

"Do you think that's a good idea?" I asked. "I mean, she's killed two people already."

"Morgan, it's Caroline. We have to find out where she is. My God! I'm going crazy here!"

"Where do you want to meet?" I asked T. J. "Make it someplace very public."

"Come down to the harbor," she said.

"Alright," I agreed. "But not until the sun is up. Do you know where Cap'n Nick's Tavern is?"

"I can find it," she said.

"At the head of the pier. There are a couple of restaurants there and there'll be a lot of people around. There's a popular place called Monahan's that does breakfast. It's crowded most of the time. Be there at half past eight. Get a table. Wait inside. If when we get there you're not alone, we won't stay."

"Agreed," she said.

And so we waited. The hours dragged by and we started on the second pot of coffee.

FIFTEEN - Hello, Ms. Kohl

It seemed like an eternity before the sun came over the eastern hills and started lighting up San Marcos and the harbor below us. Sandy tried Betsy's cell phone a dozen times and heard nothing but the unanswered ringing. No voice mail, nothing. When we were tired of sitting, we walked around the house until we were tired of walking, and we sat again. I needed a really big bourbon but Sandy, right as usual, said I needed to keep a clear head, and booze on an empty stomach would do neither of us any good.

Seven AM finally arrived. Neither of us gave any thought to changing clothes or cleaning up. We agreed to wait another hour and then leave.

"Morgan," Sandy said. "I think you need to get that gun you've been hiding. The one I didn't want in the house."

"You're right," I said. "We might need it. But you knew I didn't get rid of it?"

"Of course," she said. "And right now I'm glad you didn't."

"I've been thinking," I said. "Maybe we should have Bob Sommers with us?"

Bob is my best friend. We go back to our college days when we chased girls together. We are as close as brothers. He is the only detective the San Marcos Police Department has. I have trusted him with my life more than once.

Sandy thought about that one and then said, "Not this time. Our daughter is too important. We have to do this ourselves and not have anyone who might do something that will get her hurt."

So I went to our bedroom and pulled boxes of stuff we'd never use but couldn't throw out – old sweaters and other out of date stuff – from the shelf in the closet. Inside a small box on the bottom of the pile was the Colt .38 Police Special revolver I had hidden there. There was a box of Winchester ammunition next to it.

We sat at the kitchen table, the loaded pistol lying there between us. We finished the last dregs of what had once been good coffee. My stomach was rebelling at all the coffee and lack of food. The clock on the wall seemed not to be moving, but eventually it was eight in the morning.

We took Sandy's new Corvette because it was fast and maneuverable, and it could get us out of trouble if needed. My old MGB looks better and faster than it really is. I had the gun tucked in the waistband of my pants, and as I slid behind the wheel I took it out and handed it to Sandy. In spite of her general dislike of firearms, she held it as if it were a close friend, something she was prepared to use to its best effect.

I drove slowly down the hills, through Downtown, and into Harborside. There was a parking space only a block away from Monahan's. Pulling to the curb on the opposite side of the street from the restaurant, we sat and waited and watched. It was exactly half past eight.

Sitting in a booth at the back of the restaurant, next to the restaurant's windows and with her back to the wall, was a woman. She looked neither young nor old and she looked tired. She was drinking coffee and rubbing her temples. Her hair needed the assistance of a comb. She seemed to be keeping watch on the street outside the window and inside the restaurant. We agreed that the woman had to be T. J. Kohl.

We waited fifteen minutes before getting out of the Corvette. If she weren't alone, they would have assumed we weren't going to show up. The people with her would approach her, or she would contact them, and they would start to leave thinking that we had changed our minds. But she remained alone, looking at her wrist watch every ten or fifteen seconds.

I saw her reach under the dark denim jacket she was wearing and adjust something. Sandy saw it, too. "She ain't adjusting her bra strap," she said. "She's got a gun."

We got out of the car and closed the doors without locking them, knowing that we might have to get back inside quickly. I was wearing a light wind-breaker jacket that comfortably covered the pistol that I had tucked back under my belt. Sandy went to the sidewalk on the right, and I crossed the street to the sidewalk on the left. As I reached the restaurant door Sandy stood across the street and watched. If anything unusual happened she would go for help. What help she would go for we weren't exactly sure of, but she would go anyway, and it was important to me that she not be hurt. One of us had to stay safe . . . For the baby.

I opened the door and stepped inside. T. J. looked up and saw me, but she didn't smile or make any recognition of me. I had seen her adjust her shoulder holster with her right hand. When I saw her lift her coffee cup to her lips with her right hand, I walked to her booth and slid in while she held the cup. Holding the cup intentionally with her right hand was a signal to me that she wasn't going to kill me then and there. Maybe later, I thought, but not then and there.

"Hello, Ms. Kohl," I said. I made it very obvious that my hand was on the pistol under my jacket.

"Morgan, I'm glad to finally meet you." She slowly put the cup of coffee on the table and extended her right hand. I ignored it and kept my hand on the .38 at my waist.

"Let's make this short," I said. "I told you I know nothing about any of this shit. Why are you making my life difficult?"

She lifted the cup once again, with her right hand, took another sip of coffee and said, "I recommend something besides the coffee, Morgan. It's not very good. And please, let's have your wife join us. The morning air must still be cool outside."

I turned slightly and waived for Sandy to come inside. She walked slowly, glancing left and right as she crossed the street. I stood, letting her slide into the booth. I stepped to the side of the booth where Kohl was seated and said, "Slide over". When she did, I sat next to her and carefully pulled the revolver out, holding it below the table top and pushed it against her ribs.

"Slowly," I said softly, trying not to sound too nervous and scared. "And very carefully. Take your gun out with your left hand and hand it to my wife under the table."

"Why?" she asked.

"Because I have enough influence in this town to put a bullet in you and walk away a free man," I said forcing a smile. "Now do it."

She smiled, put the cup down and with her left hand, as I had told her, she pulled her Glock .40 semi-auto from its holster and held it under the table. Sandy took it and held it in her lap.

"That's fine," I said. "Now, you wanted to talk. So talk."

"There was a man who we suspected of being in the Country to complete some terrorist act . . . Possibly an assassination . . . Maybe worse. He was questioned . . ."

"You mean tortured," Sandy said interrupting her. "We were told."

"Who told you?"

I spoke quickly, "You said you wanted to talk to us. No questions until you talk to us."

"Alright." She said as I nudged my gun into her ribs. "This man . . . And we have no idea who he is . . . said nothing except your name, Morgan. Then there was a raid on the facility where he was being held. My mother and father were there. They were killed by whoever the raiders where. My only connection to whoever did this was you. But I'm beginning to believe you really had no connection."

"The man was taken away by whoever attacked your place?" I asked.

"Yes," T. J. answered. "He wasn't there when we searched the entire facility. Dozens of bodies were lying about, but not this man."

"Were you there during this attack?" I asked.

"Yes," T. J. answered. "We managed to hide, and we weren't killed."

"And who was with you?" I asked.

"A man I sometimes work with."

"Who? What is his name?"

She was silent for a moment, until I again nudged her with my gun. "Noah Goldberg," she said.

"I doubt that," I said.

"Why?"

"Because Noah Goldberg died five years ago . . . In Gaza," I said, feeling really pleased with myself and what I knew.

"And who told you that?" she asked.

I looked at Sandy wondering if T. J. should know who we had been with. Sandy nodded and said, "Two very strange people. Mathew Collins and a woman called Henrietta. But those aren't their real names. They're Agents with the CIA." It was a test. I wanted to see just how much T. J. knew. If she knew their real names I would know she might be for real.

"Never heard of them," T. J. said. "Where did you meet them?"

"We had gone to what you folks call The Levels," Sandy said.

"Wait a minute," T.J. said. "You mean the two of you found The Levels? You got inside? That's ridiculous!

You're lying!"

"We're not lying," I said. "Some soldiers caught us, and those two agents took us for a helicopter ride to Virginia."

"Virginia?" T. J. said. "Was it a horse ranch? Was the man about fifty or so, gray hair very well groomed? He was well dressed? Very European looking? And the woman was tall, a model type, maybe forty or so?"

"That's them," I said. "Do you know them?"

"That's Patrick Chesterson and Susan Kipman. I thought they'd retired that flaming fag Chesterson. And Kipman, she's a very strange dyke. She likes leather and whips and that sort of thing. They team them up because they know there won't be any sexual attraction to screw things up."

She looked at both of us and then said, "I've got a cell phone in my left pocket. I'm going to reach for it very slowly."

Without waiting for either of us to say yes or no, T. J. retrieved the cell phone and punched in a number. "Yes," she said into it. "Come on over, it's O.K."

A man who had been sitting in a far corner of the restaurant with his back to us stood and turned, and we watched as Noah Goldberg walked to our booth. He wanted Sandy to slide over and let him sit next to her, but she is too smart to be backed into a corner. She stood, let Noah see the pistol she held, and motioned for him to sit and move to the window.

A waitress came to the booth and smiled down at us. I didn't take my eyes off of Noah and I didn't take the pistol away from T.J.'s ribs. Sandy stared at T. J. and kept the Glock pointed at Noah. No one said anything to the waitress. Sensing she wasn't wanted, she walked away.

"T. J.," Noah said. "Would you like me to take the gun away from Mrs. Crew?"

"No, thank you," T. J. said. "Morgan here has a gun

jammed very uncomfortably in my side. Let's talk, and maybe later we'll take both the weapons and kill them."

"Keep your hopes up, Ms. Kohl," I said. "For now, Mr. Goldberg, quietly hand your gun to my wife."

Noah didn't move. He looked from me to T. J. and then to Sandy and back to me. I knew what he was thinking. I knew he was weighing the chances of killing both Sandy and me. I said, "I am now cocking the hammer on my little gun. I have it pointed up slightly so that when I pull the trigger the hollow point Winchester Silver Tip bullets this gun is loaded with will tear upwards, into Ms. Kohl's chest and most surely kill her instantly. I can pull this trigger faster than you can do anything. Now give your gun to my wife."

Sandy added, "I have Ms. Kohl's gun. I have it pointed at you, Mr. Goldberg. Please don't underestimate what a mother will do for her child. I will fire every bullet this gun holds and there won't be enough of you left to scrape off the floor."

T. J. said, "Go ahead Noah. Not here. I need time."

Noah reached into his brown tweed jacket, on the left side of his waist, and took out a Sig Sauer semi-auto and handed it to Sandy under the table.

"Would you like the Beretta from my ankle holster?" he asked. "And how about the knife strapped to my left wrist? Oh, and let's not forget the pen in my shirt pocket that has an explosive and detonator inside?"

"Gosh, I'm impressed," I said. "Just remember that your girlfriend here will be dead if you try anything. Now reach down and get the Beretta. Hand it to my wife."

After Sandy had the third gun lying in her lap I said, "OK, Noah. Now pull up your left sleeve so I can see the knife."

When he pulled up his sleeve, I reached across the table and took the knife.

"Now the pen," I said.

"I was just kidding," he said and laughed. "I saw that

in a James Bond movie once. I'm not stupid enough to carry explosives over my heart." He pulled his jacket aside to show me that his shirt pocket was in fact empty.

"OK," I said. "Now tell me what you think you're going to do?"

"I'm not going to do anything," Noah said smiling very casually. "Not now, anyway."

"That's good . . . Whoever you are," I said. "We were told you were killed five years ago. So who are you?"

Noah looked questioningly at T. J. who said to him, "Go ahead, Noah. You're out now. Too many people know."

He turned to me and said, "My death was part of a plan to eliminate a couple of mid-level Hamas killers. All that's over with now. Hamas knows I'm still alive and now you know, too."

"How do I know you're telling me the truth?" I asked.

Noah smiled, but I saw a frightening hint of viciousness hidden behind the smile. "You phoned my Embassy and they verified that I am who I am."

"And we phoned a second time," Sandy said. "They never heard of you and they never heard of Operation Ruhiger Mann."

"That makes sense," he said. "Denial is normal in my business. But the first time, they knew me and Ruhiger Mann, and I spoke to . . . To who I was speaking to."

"All that's true," I said. "Assuming you are who you say you are, what are you going to do to solve our problems?"

"Me?" Noah said. "I'm not going to do anything for you. If I can, I'm going to help T. J. find out who the traitor is. If doing that solves your problems . . . Then alright. If not . . . I'll kill you if you get in my way."

"Alright," I said. "I guess I can accept that. Now that we're all here and we have an understanding, I want to know how to get you two out of our life."

Sandy said, "Not so fast, Morgan." She looked T. J.

square in her eyes and said, "I want my daughter back. Nothing is going to stop me from getting her back. You help me get her back or I will kill you before you have a chance to kill me. Agree or you're dead."

"I think," T. J. said, "that getting your daughter back and me finding out who is responsible for my parents is the same thing. I have a suspicion. But I need a free hand to find out if I'm right."

I said, "Yes, well, we're not exactly going to go home and drink tea. You tried to kill us. You killed two people at my house already. Do you really think I'm going to let you walk away as easily as that? For us, what we need to know is why no one can contact anyone at that cute little prison you people have down in Colombia."

Noah said, "That, Mr. Crew, is the same thing we need to find out."

"The best thing you can do," T. J. said, "is to let us take care of this. There's a traitor inside The Company. Only someone on the inside would know about The Levels."

"Colonel Masterson told us that," Sandy said. "And you plan on finding the traitor and doing what?'

"Whatever is necessary," Kohl answered.

"That's not good enough," Sandy said. "If there is such a traitor there's a very good chance he has my daughter somewhere. I won't let anything happen to that person until I get my daughter back safely."

"I understand . . ." T. J. began.

"Do you have children, Ms. Kohl?" Sandy asked.

"No, I don't. It's the job . . ."

Sandy stopped her again. "Then you can't understand. Don't try to bullshit me. I will not let you kill whoever this man is . . . At least until Caroline is back with me."

T. J. thought for a moment and then said, "OK, alright. I'll take you to Colombia and we'll see what's going on at the prison."

"Nothing personal," I said. "But I've got an IQ of 137. I've taken the test several times. You and your friend here can always try to kill us when we're 30,000 feet up. You might try to have us take that first long step off the plane. I imagine you've got a fifty-fifty chance of success. So now we're going to get up . . . Very slowly and easily and then we're going to go back to my house."

Noah asked, "Why? What are you going to do?"

"We're going to talk and think this thing out," I said. "I guess my wife and I have to decide what to do with you."

"*You* have to decide?" Noah said. "What makes you think you have any decision in all this?"

"The fact that my wife and I have all the guns," I said.

"Do you really think that's going to stop me?" Noah asked threateningly.

T. J. said, "Noah, not here. Let's just go to their house."

SIXTEEN - The Missing

When we arrived at our house in the hills overlooking the harbor, you would have never guessed a small war had taken place the night before. It was as peaceful as usual, and the trees cast enough shade to cool the growing heat of the day.

T. J. and Noah drove the rental car they had arrived in. Sandy and I . . . And all the guns . . . Followed in Sandy's Corvette. When we pulled into the driveway next to their car, I got out quickly and held Noah's Sig Sauer so they could see it as they stood near the closed garage.

"Sandy," I said. "Go unlock and open the front door. You two follow her inside. I'll be at your backs."

Inside I told T. J. and Noah to sit on the far side of the living room, in a corner, on a couple of chairs on either side of our stone fireplace, away from any doors and windows. Sandy and I were about to pull a couple of chairs together as far from them as possible when we heard Betsy's voice from behind us.

"Hey!" she said. "You're home finally."

"What the hell!" was all I could think of saying.

Sandy ran to her and took her in her arms. "Oh my God!" she said. "What happened? Where's Caroline?"

"She's fine," Betsy said. "She's in her room, asleep. Everything's alright."

From the kitchen a man stepped into the living room. I didn't know whether I should call him Mathew Collins or Patrick Chesterton. He looked the same as when I had seen him last. He was dressed in an expensive, custom made suit of European design. His longish salt and pepper hair was perfectly combed. He held a sandwich in his left hand, so delicately, his pinkish pinky finger held up, that he could have been in the best London Tea Room.

"Well," he said jovially. "So good to see the two of you again. And I see you've brought guests."

T. J. said, "Patrick you old fag. How'd you get here? You're supposed to be in the prison in Colombia."

"Watch your language, T. J." he said. "There are children present."

Behind him, from the kitchen, Patrick's partner – Susan Kipman or Henrietta as I first knew her – stepped into the room. She held a pistol in her hand and said, "Patty, darling. Shall I kill her?"

"Not yet, my dear," Patrick said. "Maybe later we can shoot her in her head together. Wouldn't that be fun, Suzy darling? Remember that time in Chechnya when we had target practice on those five Russians?"

"I do remember, Pat my love," she said and pouted like a little child. "I also seem to remember that you never paid the twenty dollars you owe me for that little contest."

"Oh, cut it out," Betsy said. "You two are going to scare somebody pretty soon. They might think you're serious."

"How did you get here?" I asked her. "You're with these two . . . People?"

"I'll let Patrick explain," Betsy said. "I need to put a load of wash in. They didn't have any washing machines down there at that place in Colombia. Can you imagine that?"

Patrick and Susan sat next to each other, too close to each other, on the couch. She wrapped one arm around his shoulder and with her other hand, she massaged his thigh . . . Too far up his thigh as a matter of fact. If they were actually gay as T. J. had said, they were a very weird couple of gay people.

Patrick said, “Susan my lovely, shall I begin?”

“Oh, please do, Patrick,” she said happily. “You tell a story so much better than I.”

“Thank you, dearest. Anyway,” he began, “we were in these horrible little cells, as you know. Mr. Crew, you are a bad little boy for kidnapping us. But my darling little Suzy and I are not the kind to hold grudges. So anyway, there we were, and for the longest time we heard nothing and no one gave us food or water. No one came to get us although we were expecting torture of some kind.”

“I was so hoping for something nasty,” Susan said interrupting him as she licked her lips hungrily.

“And then this lovely young lady . . . Betsy . . . You know . . . She opened my cell door. Just a crack; just enough to ask if I was willing to help. Naturally, I said yes although I had no idea what she wanted help with. And she let me out of the cell. She pointed to the other cells along the hallway. All were open and empty except for one, in which my beautiful and sweet Susan was secured. Betsy had keys which unlocked the door, and Susan and I followed her to a kitchen some distance away. Your beautiful little child was there, gurgling away happily. But the thing is, there weren’t any guards anywhere.

“Inside, little Betsy told us that in the big room where we were secured and you spoke to us . . . Do you remember? . . . Good. In that room she said there were three bodies. All had been shot. I went there and found Donald Stevens, Edward Burns, and Thomas Christopher lying on the floor, all having been shot many times. All were dead, of course.

“I started from the room to return to Susan and Betsy, and wouldn’t you know, Ian McCauley turned a corner and found me. Ian had a gun! Would you believe that? He was surprised to see me and asked how I got out of my cell. Before I could answer my darling Susan hit him on his head with a thermos bottle from the kitchen.

"As he lay there, she and I made a quick search of the facility. We were alone as it turns out. So, we retrieved Betsy and the darling little baby and skedaddled out of there just as fast as we could."

Susan interrupted again. "I wanted to cut Ian's throat but of course Patrick wouldn't hear of it. He never lets me have any fun," she pouted.

"Susan love," Patrick said and patted her on her knee. "We don't know what was going on there. Ian may be a good guy."

"Maybe not," she said. "Besides, I really wanted to kill someone . . . For being kept in that cell for so long."

Not that I really wanted to involve myself in their conversation but I had to ask, "How the hell did you get back to the States? To my house?"

Susan said, "That was easy. There was an old pick-up truck outside. I hotwired it and we all crowded in. It was several hours to Medellin where my wonderful Patrick has a sometimes lover who is associated with the cartel there. Patrick's wonderful and beautiful lover, Tomas . . . What's his last name, darling? . . . Oh well, no matter. Tomas flew an airplane up to the Mexican border where some friends of Tomas drove us to Phoenix along with a few pounds of cocaine. From there we flew commercial . . . First Class of course as Patrick simply refuses to fly coach. And here we are."

Betsy came back into the living room and said, "Look, you're going to have to keep it down if you don't want to wake C. She's had a hard couple of days and needs her sleep."

Sandy asked, "Did you hear anything of what they said? About how you got here?"

"Oh sure," she said. "Everybody's being too loud . . . Like I said."

"Is all that true?" I asked.

"Yeah, of course," she said as if I asked her the time of day. She turned around and left the room.

Sandy and I looked at each other in unbelieving astonishment. Sandy whispered, "Are we dreaming?"

At the time I wasn't sure, but I asked Patrick and Susan, "What would you suggest we do now?"

Susan answered quickly, "I think we should take T. J. out and beat the truth out of her. I know some fun stuff that she won't like."

Noah spoke up and said, "That's not a good idea."

"And who the hell are you?" Patrick asked.

Since Noah would only smile and not say anything, I spoke up. "He's Noah Goldberg."

"Oh Suzy darling dearest! We're seeing ghosts now!" he said. As he spoke, he pulled a small pistol, brightly chrome plated and with an ivory handle, from under his jacket and held it casually, pointed at Noah.

T. J. spoke up for the first time saying, "He *is* Noah Goldberg. You aren't high enough on The Company's food chain to know operations he's involved in."

"Damn!" Susan said. "I was hoping I could kill him. I suppose now I won't be able to. Damn!"

It occurred to me that Sandy and I were standing in the middle of the room with what seemed like completely mad killers on both our left and right. But we also had guns from T. J. and Noah. I wondered if that would be enough to stop these four *very* strange people from going at each other's throats . . . And more importantly, at our throats.

"Hey folks," I said, hoping my voice didn't give away the fact that I was really scared. "Let's get down to business. Now, my wife and I have our child back. That's the most important thing to us. All we need to know is that you and all your little friends are going to get out of our lives. Can we agree on that?"

T. J. said, "Patrick told me what I think I'm after. Ian McCauley . . . And I'm about ninety percent certain of this . .

. Ian is the traitor I've been looking for. For the time being I'm going to leave you and your family alone. I'm going to go to Colombia and from there I'm going to find Ian."

"Oh, T. J." Patrick said. "I'm so very, very sorry. But you've gone rogue my dear. And I'm not exactly on good standing with The Company. I'm afraid I'm going to have to take you back to Langley. I hope you appreciate the fact that when I walk you in, I'll be back and good as gold once again. I think I will even request an assignment in Paris. Suzy, darling, wouldn't you just love to go to Paris with me?"

Noah leaned forward. Even I could sense the electric current of menace being emitted from him. I came to the conclusion after being around these people for as long as I had that Noah Goldberg was the person to be really feared among the four of them. Patrick and Susan were crazy, but knowing that, I could be ready for them. T. J. was an experienced killer but she was a cool, careful, planning assassin; not a person to act rashly. Noah was the one who, I felt certain, was capable of attacking and killing all of us right then and there, without warning. I felt he was not insane; he was not a long distance assassin; I felt he was a trained and dangerous killing machine.

Noah said, sounding threatening like a rattle snake about to strike, "I'm afraid I can't let that happen, Patrick. T. J. is a friend of mine. I'm here to help her. I will stop you."

Suzy asked, "Are you sanctioned or rogue?"

"I am sanctioned without limits," he said as he sat back and relaxed in his chair.

Suzy answered, "Oh that's too bad. 'No limits' is a rare thing. Maybe I will have to shoot you in your head just to protect my lovely Patrick and myself."

"Suzy, sweetums," Patrick said. "Killing him would cause an international uproar."

"Who would know?" she asked in a little child's pouting voice.

"Witnesses," Patrick said simply, looking at Sandy

and me.

"Not if I kill them, too."

"Well," Patrick said, choosing to change the very dangerous subject. "If you really are Noah Goldberg . . . That will present a problem. How would you suggest we work that problem out?"

Noah turned and looked at T. J. He was waiting for her to say what she wanted everyone to do. I guessed that to Noah, T. J.'s loss of her parents by an Agent gone bad was what everyone should be concentrating on. That rogue agent was at the center of the destruction of The Levels. Mossad was a part of The Levels, although Noah knew that Mossad was often pushed aside when it recommended more modern interrogation techniques. In any case, the ultra-secret of The Levels was no longer limited to a few people. The web of secrecy had been broken and the incident had to be closed before Israel's enemies learned of The Levels.

T. J. said, "You need to let me go. I need to find Ian and find out if he instigated the attack. If he is responsible . . . I will kill him."

Patrick thought about this; he quickly weighed all his options and which of those options would be of best benefit to him. To Patrick the best part of working for The Company was playing the different jobs like a game of chess, knowing all the possible moves on the board many moves ahead, and making the right moves to benefit Patrick only, even if that meant making others suffer.

And so he said, "If you find him and he is the traitor . . . Bring him in and reinstall yourself with The Company. Vengeance is mine sayeth The Lord. You've heard that one, I suppose?"

"Since when have you gotten religion?" T. J. laughed.

"Then find him and let me bring him in," Patrick said hopefully.

"He killed my parents," she argued.

"And what do you think will happen to him after we

bring him to Langley?" Patrick said. "Do you think he'll be given an attorney and brought to trial? Do you really think Gitmo is in his future? The Company can't let knowledge of The Levels reach the media. He'll be disappeared . . . You know that. If you're nice to them, they might even let you kill him and erase all record of him. And you and I will be reinstated with honors."

T. J. seemed to be absorbing what Patrick said. She, too, was considering all the moves on the chess board. Like Patrick, like Susan, and probably like Noah, they all wanted success for themselves regardless of what their success did to the others.

She asked, "And suppose I find out that Ian isn't the traitor?"

Patrick smiled and looked up at me. When he did a shiver crept up my spine. He said, "Well, my dear. If Ian is not the traitor you're looking for . . . Then you have only one clue left. Mr. Morgan Crew."

"You're right, of course, Patrick," T. J. said. "I haven't forgotten about Mr. Crew."

"Look lady," I said, maybe a little too loudly. "I told you I don't know anything about anything you people are involved in. I don't know anything about that guy you folks were torturing."

"Look, Morgan," she said. "You've got the money to finance the operation that killed my parents. It wasn't a cheap, buy-'em-off-the-streets operation."

"And your employer also can fund such a thing," I argued.

"I doubt you can come up with a reason why The Company or any other Federal Agency would want to destroy its own very top secret operation. No, it was planned and somehow financed by an inside traitor or by you, Mr. Crew."

"Why me?"

"That's what I intend to find out," T. J. said resolutely.

Betsy walked into the living room carrying Caroline. That simple occurrence, seeing my child, struck a chord inside me. I had to protect her. I had to protect Sandy. It was like an explosion inside my brain when I realized I had to kill these four people if that's what it took to protect my family. I felt my arm, holding Noah's big gun, moving upwards involuntarily. I had to stop myself before I killed all four of them in front of my family.

"Ahhh, the beautiful little child," Patrick said.

Susan, looking covetously at Betsy, said, "Yes, and the baby is beautiful, too."

I had to take a chance. I had to come up with something short of trying to shoot dead the four of them without getting Sandy and Caroline and Betsy hurt. And as usual, it all came down to money.

I spoke up, "I have an idea."

Sandy took Caroline into her arms from Betsy and said softly, "Oh my God! Here we go again!"

"Patrick, Susan," I began. "You're on your employer's shit list, correct?"

They both nodded but neither said anything.

"T. J. You're outside, gone rogue as everybody says. Noah, if you screw up here there will be an enormous international incident that won't do Israel any good. Sandy and I just want out of all this. It seems to me that we will all benefit if we work together."

Everybody was silent. Everybody stared at me. T. J. finally said, "OK, what's your plan?"

"Patrick and Susan," I said. "You'll look good if you bring T. J. in to Langley dead or alive. Correct?"

"Correct," Patrick said.

Susan, not surprisingly, said, "I'd rather bring her in dead."

"T. J.," I said. "If you expose what you believe to be a traitor inside the CIA and find out why The Levels was attacked . . . You'll be back and resume your life as a spy.

Correct?"

She said simply, "Yes. Maybe. I've been thinking I might need a friend really, really high up . . . Maybe."

"Noah," I continued. "The only way for you and Israel to come out of all this without having the world even angrier with you folks is to very quietly expose the traitor along with T. J. Correct?"

"Of course," he answered.

"Alright then," I said. "Patrick and Susan, I will pay you $100,000 in cash to stay here and protect Sandy, Caroline and Betsy. I will hire you to kill T. J. if she comes back here without me and tries to hurt my family."

Patrick and Susan looked at each other and then Patrick said, "A hundred thousand won't last us very long if we're forced into retirement. Make it a quarter million and you've got a deal."

"Ok," I agreed. "A quarter million."

"In advance," Susan said.

"Not a chance," I said. "You folks live on lies and cheating. I don't trust any of you. You succeed by causing confusion. You get paid when I get back."

"Get back from where?" Sandy asked rather snidely, knowing that I was going to suggest something that would drag me to the edge of the cliff once again.

"I'm going with T. J. and Noah to find Ian. And if Ian isn't who they're looking for, I'm going to stay with them until they find who they're looking for. I'm going to finance the search. I imagine T. J.'s money won't last forever."

Sandy handed Caroline to me. She was wrapped in a soft pink and white blanket, her delicate arms and hands fidgeting about as she made happy little noises. Every time I held my daughter, I couldn't believe how happy I was, and I thanked God for where my life had come to.

Sandy let the baby hold her finger as she adjusted the blanket. She said, "There's only one thing wrong with your plan, Morgan."

I waited for her to say what I knew she was going to say and what I knew would be useless to argue about. After a moment or two I said, “OK. Go ahead. Tell me.”

“I’m going with you,” Sandy said.

SEVENTEEN - Here We Go Again

"Sandy," I said. "Things have changed. We have a baby to think of. You can't go."

She smiled up at me and said, "I suppose you're gonna' bet your last million on that? Look, we're going to be gone maybe a week and we've hired Betsy for just this sort of thing. Patrick and Susan brought her home when they could have left her and the baby to rot in that prison. I think we can trust Betsy and them to take care of Caroline for a few days. Besides, do you remember what happened to you in Hawaii? You need me to take care of you. Caroline needs a father, and if you get killed what will she do?"

Oh, I suppose I could have stood there in front of those four killer-spies and argued my head off. I would have embarrassed myself and wound up looking like a fool. The four of them would have laughed at me and I would have lost a lot of male prestige and ego. So I decided to take the easy way out, once again, and just give in to Sandy.

"OK," I said without trying to throw my chest out too much in a manly fashion. "I guess I can let you come along. But I'm in charge, understand? I hold the guns and we do it my way. OK?"

"Oh sure, dear," Sandy said smiling as she took Caroline from my arms and turned and walked away. "Anything you say. I think the baby needs a feeding, so excuse me, please."

Betsy stood next to me, grinning excitedly, and looking around at the four very strange people in my living room.

I asked her, "Betsy, are you OK staying here with Caroline and Patrick and Susan?"

"Oh sure," she said happily. "I like them. I've got this thing for unusual people, you know? They're fun to be with. They got me home and I love a little adventure now and then. I'll take care of C. Ain't nothing gonna happen to her."

****

I leased a Gulfstream jet with more than enough fuel range to get us to Colombia. Getting back might be a problem, so I told the pilot to go on to Bogotá to refuel. T. J. and Noah knew where the prison was. The pilot dropped us at a small runway near a village a few miles from the abandoned prison in a remote valley of the Andes mountain range. The runway, cut out of the jungle, was used primarily by drug smugglers to quickly move their product out of the thatch-roofed group of huts where processing the cocaine was the only industry.

It wasn't a long runway; it took a lot of brakes to stop the jet from running off the runway at landing, and the pilot revved the engines up high before releasing the brakes at takeoff. But he was good, and we watched as he banked the jet and lifted the nose sharply to get over the mountains.

The CIA owned and used the old stone prison. The Company ignored the smuggling operation in order to not have trouble with the local cartels. The Company paid to have several vehicles and supplies stored out of the weather in the little village. We managed to talk a few of the dirty and vicious looking cartel guards into letting us take one of the bigger Humvees. Of course, the two one-hundred dollar bills I gave them didn't hurt the negotiations.

Noah drove; T. J. sat in the front passenger seat.

Sandy and I sat in the rear with the guns. The road was mostly rutted mud. The rain coming from the fast moving black clouds that darkened sky didn't improve our ride. We drove through thick jungle, up hills that would have been impassable without the four wheel drive of the Humvee. And then we would slide almost sideways down the other side of the slick hill.

As we bounced and slid along about as slowly as the big Humvee could move, Noah looked in the rear-view mirror at us and said, "I've been meaning to tell you. Sooner or later I'm going to take those two guns away from you."

"That's nice," Sandy said. "Be sure to let me know when because if Morgan doesn't kill you, I will."

Noah laughed but said nothing. In good weather the drive would have taken less than forty-five minutes. In the really bad weather we were enjoying, it took an hour and a half to reach the prison. As Noah drove with his foot on the break, he and T. J. were looking carefully all around them. They knew ahead of time, and I learned from their reaction, that there could be a trap waiting for them. Neither T. J. nor Noah had any contacts at the time in the CIA. Both were listed with The Company as having gone rogue. Neither knew if The Company had anticipated their return. I realized that it could be a death trap not just for them but for Sandy and me, too.

Noah stopped the Humvee a hundred yards from the front gate of the red stone prison. The big, rusted, iron gate was hanging open. Mold and jungle ferns had found homes on the stone, but it didn't appear that any other living things were there.

T. J. opened her door and turned to speak to Sandy and me. "I'm going to take a look around. Noah's going to stay here with you. It would really help if I could have my gun back."

"Oh sure!" I said as sarcastically as I could manage, considering I had no idea what was going to happen to us.

"I'm supposed to fully trust you to not take your gun and kill us. I think not, lady. Sandy will stay here with Noah. She will sit behind him. He will keep his seat belt fastened. She will have Noah's gun . . . Cocked and pointed at the back of his head. If he makes any move that she doesn't like, she will shoot his head off. You and I will go exploring."

The rain had slowed to a fine mist, but the air was cold and wet. I had on a light tan Izod windbreaker jacket that had seen a lot of time on the golf course. T. J. had on the same jeans, grey sweatshirt and denim jacket she had been wearing for the past two days. The hundred yards from the Humvee to the prison gate was all red clay turned to sticky mud. I almost lost one of my loafers to it.

I let T. J. walk ahead of me. I held her gun cocked and ready to fire quickly. But in my mind I had some doubts that I was ready to do what needed to be done. I didn't have the training or experience T. J. had. I hoped I could react as quickly as she could. I tried to guess what would be a safe enough distance between us, enough that she would not be able to spin around and kick the gun out of my hand like I've seen done in spy movies.

We sloshed our way slowly toward the gate and stopped as we reached it. Inside was a small courtyard that was overrun with weeds and blown down leaves and branches. A big lizard was munching on some greenery. He or maybe she looked up, saw us and ran away towards some trees near the left hand wall. At each corner of the wall was a guard tower rising above us. I couldn't see anybody inside, but that didn't mean there wasn't anyone there.

T. J. turned to me and said, "Look, if there's anybody in here . . . Are you going to be ready to kill? Maybe you should give me the gun?"

I didn't answer; I motioned with the gun that she should walk into the courtyard. I followed her, staying six feet behind her, which I hoped was far enough to keep her from turning and grabbing the gun out of my hand. I figured if there was anybody waiting for us, she, being known to whoever might be there, would be shot at first, giving me time to protect myself.

There was a second rusting iron gate on the other side of the courtyard, at the entrance to the building. It was closed, but when T. J. pushed on it, it opened noisily but freely. It squeaked, and she pushed until we were able to walk inside. It was dark, dank and dirty inside, as I remembered it from the last time I was there. T. J. went straight to a series of light switches on the wall to her right and threw all of them on, lighting up the inside of the entire building.

She turned to me and said, "That's good. If anybody was here, they would have been in the dark. But don't count on certain people not liking the light. Some assassins prefer working in broad daylight."

I thought she was saying that just to scare me . . . Or maybe not. Either way, she scared me. We walked inside very slowly, both of us looking and listening.

Having been there before, I knew my way around pretty well. There were five hallways off the entrance. I was surprised, even though I shouldn't have been, when T. J. walked directly to the hallway where the kitchen was and around the corner where the cells were. That told me she had been there before, probably for a similar reason for me having been there – to lock someone in a dank cell where they could rot away with no one knowing they were there.

T. J. found the door to the kitchen, opened it and switched on the light. It was empty, neat and clean. Next she went to the big room where I had spoken to the people who Ian McCauley had kidnapped and brought to Colombia. That was the room where Betsy had found the three bodies. It was empty and clean, without blood stains, and it showed no sign of death. Each of the cells was open and empty.

I followed T. J. as she walked each hallway, looked in

every room, and searched every broom closet so to speak. There was nothing, and there was no sign that anyone had been there recently, except for the fact that the hundred year old prison was as clean as a hospital.

We ended our search at the main entrance. T. J. turned to me and said, "I don't get it. This place is used all the time. Every Intelligence Service has access to this place. I expected to find *someone* here."

"So what is this place commonly used for?" I asked her.

"Extraordinary rendition," she said nonchalantly.

"You mean it's a place where people are brought to secretly? For questioning?" I asked but I knew the answer of course.

"For torture," she said casually. "Most often by Colombian Secret Police. But we have our own experts, too. Executions when necessary, also. All in extreme secrecy. It's one of many such places."

"You talk about this kind of thing like it's supposed to be normal," I said. "Doesn't it mean the same thing to you that it means to me?"

"Morgan," she began. "If you knew what I know . . . If you've had the experience I've had . . ."

I interrupted her and said, "Is there no limit? Do we do anything in this war?"

"You think this war is against a few hundred radical extremist Muslims . . . Al Qaeda? You think a handful of backward miscreants with rusty AK-47s who learn to crash an airplane into a building is the only enemy we have? Morgan, the United States doesn't have many friends around the world. We are a wealthy nation and our freedoms are unusual. What we have and what other people don't have causes jealousy and envy. That jealously and envy in turn causes hatred. In Europe . . . In South America . . . In Africa and certainly in Asia, too many people and governments want what we have and they intend to get it by taking it away from us by force. And they aren't all Muslims. They are Catholics, Protestants, Buddhists, atheists, anything. They all have their own causes. But in common, they all want to redistribute our wealth around the world. They want to end our religious and political freedoms. If you want your daughter to inherit the Nation you've enjoyed, then understand that we have to fight with the same weapons our enemies fight with. They use terror openly. We can't be overt so we must use terror covertly. It's as simple as that."

"In some ways, I agree with you," I said. "But it's not that simple. Would it change any minds if we built schools, hospitals, that sort of thing?"

"If you think you can buy friends," she said. "Then you're as naïve as I think you are. The only thing these people respect is strength. If they fear us enough, they'll leave us alone. They're like animals. They can smell fear, and when they do, they attack. You can throw as much money as you want at them. Hell, you can give them every red penny the U. S. has, and it wouldn't make them like us. They want us destroyed. They don't want the U. S. to exist anymore."

"And is that the attitude of the Government? Washington?"

"You've got to be kidding," she said and laughed. "In D.C. they all think they can talk our enemies into being our friends. They haven't grown out of their hippie beliefs that all you need to do is make love, not war. It's up to people like me . . . Like Noah out there . . . And hundreds of others like us, to keep our Nation and families free and safe. I'm thinking that maybe you might be the type to join our little group once you know more details and secrets."

"Don't count on it," I said. "I'm here to protect my family, nothing more."

"And I'm here to protect your family, too," she answered. "What do you think will happen to your daughter if the United States surrenders to Sharia Law? Do you know there are people in Washington . . . High up in government . . . People who think it would be a good idea to give Sharia Law an equal standing with our Constitution? They actually think that if we do, the Muslims we're fighting will love us."

"And this is why you want to kill whoever killed your parents?"

"Whoever organized the raid on The Levels is a traitor to our Country and responsible for the deaths of my mother and father. The people who are in charge at The Company have named the file on that guy at The Levels 'Silent Man'. The considered analysis at The Company is that he's an assassin. Someone sent to murder someone very high up. Maybe even the President himself. I have an idea that once the truth is discovered, they'll change the name to 'The Spy Who Would Not Speak'."

I asked, "So you think this guy is an agent of some Government?"

"Maybe a Government . . . Maybe a quasi Government. Someone sent him here to do harm. When I find him, I'll know who the traitor is and I'll know who sent him. I talked to the people at The Levels, a very knowledgeable Doctor. She's dead now, but she thought there may be a connection with the Russians, the former KGB, maybe the remnants of the KGB that is now called the Russian Mafia. She believed these people had been experimenting with drugs that affect the human body that would make an ordinary man into something like a . . . Hell, like a superman if she's to be believed. It's all just speculation now since all the records at The Levels have been destroyed."

"Superman," I said, trying not to laugh. "You've got to be kidding."

"I'm not kidding," T. J. said looking up, straight into my eyes. "There are things out there that you would not believe even if you saw them. If people knew what was really happening, there would be riots all over the world.

Governments would fall. Fear would take over."

There wasn't much sense in wasting time talking about secrets that may or may not be true. And maybe it would be better, I thought, to not know. Sometimes ignorance really is bliss.

"So all this has worldwide implications?" I said. "You think maybe this guy was sent by the Russians to kill somebody here? And this guy was saved by a CIA traitor? So that leads you to believe that killing the traitor will solve the problem and avenge your parents as well as make the world a better place? I asked.

T. J. answered, "Exactly," like it should have been a foregone conclusion.

"That guy . . . Who wouldn't talk . . . He's still out there. Don't you want to find him and stop him? Not just kill him. Arrest him or whatever you folks do. Since you're such a patriot, I mean," I said.

"I know that," she said a little sadly and looked down at the floor. "But my folks! They're dead!"

"And what's the best vengeance?" I said. "Killing Ian if he's the traitor or stopping the assassin and helping your Country?"

She stared at me and I hoped she was thinking about what I said. She moved quickly and made me jump as she started for the door and said, "Let's go back. I need to talk to Noah."

At the Humvee we found Noah still strapped into his seat belt and Sandy still holding the cocked pistol, pointed at the back of his head. Noah said, "Will you tell her to take her finger off of the damn trigger. That thing has a light trigger pull. She'll blow my brains out if she sneezes."

Back inside the car T. J. told Noah, "The place is completely empty. There's no one there and no sign anyone has been there."

"So what do we do now?" he asked.

"I don't know," she said. "I was hoping you had an

idea."

"The only thing we can do is go back to Langley," Noah told her. "They have to have been in on this. They will know what we don't know."

"Wait a minute," I said. "Look, you guys are more into this spy stuff than I am, but isn't it reasonable to think that if there's one traitor inside the CIA, there might be others? If you go there now, you might not come out."

"And what do you suggest, Mr. Morgan Crew?" Noah asked.

"Colonel Masterson had some of his men here, didn't he?" I asked. "Where are they? Who told them to leave? Are they still alive? I get the impression Masterson cares about his people even though he expects them to take risks. At the least, he likes to be in charge. I think you need to find him and talk to him. He must know why his men aren't here anymore."

Noah and T.J. looked at each other. As Noah said, "What have we got to lose?" a shot rang out, and without bullet-resistant glass on the front window someone would be dead right now. We stared at the spider web of cracked glass in front of us and then Sandy yelled, "Get us the hell outta here!"

Noah started the engine and floored the gas pedal. He ignored the mud slick dirt road and sped all the way back to the airfield. It would be at least an hour before the Gulfstream returned from its refueling mission. We had no choice but to wait in the little village of drug runners and killers.

"So who was that?" I asked.

"Could be Ian," T. J. said. "Could have been just some cartel thug. Could have been some kid taking target practice. Who knows?"

"And what do we do now?" Sandy asked.

"We wait," was all Noah said.

EIGHTEEN - Mi Jefe Quiere El Dinero

It was late afternoon; the sky was showing the first signs of dusk coming on. Clouds began to race in from the western Andes, and before the Gulfstream returned, rain started again. The jet was late; each of us in turn checked our watches and then checked them again. Four men, ugly, dark, and dangerous looking men with AK-47s, were standing together under a thatch roofed porch. They were looking our way, talking quietly, smoking whatever they had to smoke, and double checking that their rifles' magazines were fully loaded.

A fifth man, shorter and older, fatter and meaner looking, with salt and pepper hair down to his shoulders and a graying beard, carrying a long machete, walked through the rain to the four. They gathered in a circle under the thatched porch roof and seemed to be arguing. The older man seemed to be winning and after a few minutes one of the four walked from under the protection of the roof towards us.

Noah watched the man walk slowly in the rain. He said quietly, "You'd better let me have my gun."

"I still don't trust you, Noah," I said. "Could be these guys know you. I think I'll keep the gun and see what they want."

The man reached the side of the Humvee, and I rolled

down my side window halfway. "What do you want?" I asked.

"Señor," he started and spoke in broken and halting English. "My boss . . . He say go."

"Go where?" I asked. "We're waiting for our plane."

He stood there with a blank look on his weather beaten face. It was obvious he didn't understand what I was saying. Sandy leaned towards the window and said, "Estamos esperando nuestro avión."

The man smiled showing off a couple of rows of broken yellow and brown teeth. He turned and walked back to his fellows under the thatch roof. There was more talk, and then the same man walked back to us. He said, "Mi jefe quiere el dinero."

Sandy said, "He wants money. Morgan, give him a couple of hundred and they might leave us alone."

I handed the man two one hundred dollar bills from my money clip. He smiled broadly, waved the bills over his head in the rain and ran back to his friends. The older man snatched the bills from him and walked slowly back to where he had come from. The other four ducked low through the small door into the hut, and we didn't see them again.

****

We heard the sound of the jet engines before we saw the jet emerge from the clouds, nose down over the mountain, and glide into the valley. There were no lights on the landing strip but the pilot managed to bring the Gulfstream down safely and to a stop before it ran off the rutted and wet tarmac.

The rain was slowing as we jumped from the Humvee. I told Noah to leave the keys with the car for the cartel's people to use. I figured it might be payment enough to keep them from shooting at us as we took off. We ran to the jet, slipping and sliding on the mud. The door swung open and stairs were lowered down for us. I waived my gun to T. J. to board, then Noah. I boarded, and Sandy followed closely behind me. As we had on the flight down, T. J. and Noah sat at the front of the plane, and Sandy and I sat behind them.

The co-pilot closed the cabin's door and asked us, "Where to?"

I leaned forward and asked Noah and T. J., "How do we get in touch with Colonel Masterson?"

"There's a phone number," T. J. said. "Sort of a business agent. Handles Masterson's business."

"Where's this guy at?" Sandy asked.

"It's a computer generated phone number. I've tried having it traced but it goes through so many servers all over the world, it takes hours to trace, and then we find it's being call forwarded to a cell phone. A different cell phone every time, and a different cell tower somewhere in the world every time. Some day we might get lucky but no one really wants to. Masterson does good work for us."

I looked up at the co-pilot and said, "Let's go home."

****

We landed at San Fran International before sunup and drove up to San Marcos. T.J. had been told to drive, and Noah sat in the front passenger seat so we could keep an eye on them. We rode in silence most of the way, but I could see that Sandy was thinking about something. Her forehead was furrowed and she was staring out the side window without looking at anything passing by. Twenty minutes into the drive she said, "Whoever shot at us back there . . . At the prison . . . I don't think it was a drug runner or some kid taking target practice. I think it was a message to us. I think someone was telling us to stay out of whatever is happening."

Noah and T. J. looked at each other in the front seat; they shared a look of acknowledgement. Noah said, "I think you're right. And who do you think sent the message?"

Sandy turned and looked out the window again. Her brow furrowed again, and then she said, "Could be Ian . . . Maybe somebody else. I just can't help thinking that Ian is too obvious a choice. You people don't live in the obvious. Your lives are like an English garden maze, full of twists and turns that can get somebody lost. Look, Patrick said he turned a corner back there when Betsy opened his cell door. He said Ian was there, holding a pistol. Susan hit him from behind apparently before he could say anything. Stevens, Burns, and Christopher were all dead, and we're assuming Ian did it. But what about Betsy and Caroline? Why did Ian leave them as witnesses? It would seem they would be the easiest targets. But they were left alone."

She paused for a moment or two and then went on. "And what happened to the Marine guards and Masterson's mercenaries? Somebody had to call them off. Could Ian have done that? Maybe, but maybe there's somebody out there with more authority."

"So what does all that mean?" T. J. asked.

"If you find and kill Ian without knowing he's the person who is responsible for all this, you'd be making a big mistake. If he wasn't responsible for your parents' death than you've killed an innocent man and accomplished nothing."

"And . . . What do you suggest?" she asked Sandy.

"First we need to contact Colonel Masterson and then we need to go speak with people at . . . What do you people call it? . . . The Company? Noah's right about that. It's where we will find answers."

"And what if I'm right," I argued. "What if there's more

than one traitor and we walk into that traitor's office?"

"Morgan," she said. "We know nothing right now. All we know is if T. J. doesn't find what she's looking for, she's going to come after us. Am I right, T. J.?"

"You're right," T. J. said. "But to be honest, it wouldn't be fun. I've actually come to like you."

We drove five more miles in complete silence, all of us thinking and considering and wondering just what the hell we should do. We each had our own goals, and none of those goals were shared. Sandy took my hand in hers, and she smiled that wonderful smile of hers. We were together on this, with one goal of our own, and whatever it took, we would do.

I broke the silence by saying, "When we get to San Marcos, phone Colonel Masterson. If he wants to be paid, I will pay him. Get him to our house so we can talk to him face to face. I don't want to talk to him by phone. If nothing comes of that, then we're going to go to Langley. I'll go with you if that will make any difference."

NINETEEN - Terry Two

It was nearly three in the morning when we pulled into the driveway of our house in the hills. I hadn't come to trust Noah and T. J. yet. I knew both were capable of taking the guns from us if we gave them the chance. So I was careful, more so considering we were in the dark of the night, and there were no witnesses nearby.

From the back seat of the car I said, "Stay in the car. Sandy and I will get out first. Sandy will go to the house and open the front door and turn on some lights. Then you two get out and walk slowly into the house. We've come this far. Don't make me kill you now."

They did as I told them, and I followed them to the house at a safe distance. Betsy came from her bedroom, dressed in flannel PJs with pink and yellow ducks all over them. She was rubbing her eyes, and when she could focus on us she said, "Oh, hi! I wasn't expecting you guys back so soon. Everything OK?"

Sandy said, "Yes. How's the baby?"

"Oh, she's just great as usual. That's the nicest little kid I've ever seen. She only cries when she's hungry and when she's crapped in her pants. So I keep her fed and her pants clean."

"Where's Patrick and Susan?" I asked. "Did they take one of the guest rooms?" It wouldn't really have surprised me if the two gay spies were sleeping together.

"No," Betsy said. "They got a phone call last night and left."

"Left! Where did they go?" T. J. asked. "Who was the phone call from?"

"Hell, I don't know," Betsy said. "They got a call. They left. I'm OK here alone, ya' know. I ain't no helpless little kid. I'm going back to bed," she said and went back to her room.

"OK," I said to anyone who would listen. "What's that all about? Who phoned and where did they go?"

"Knowing them," T. J. said. "It could have been anybody. Maybe some fag orgy down in San Francisco."

"They gave up a quarter million dollars to go to a sex party?" Sandy said. "I don't think so. I think I might even trust them more than I trust you. I mean, they brought Betsy and Caroline back from Colombia safe and sound. What have you done for me except make me worry that you're going to find a way to kill Morgan?"

The four of us went to the kitchen where Sandy started a pot of coffee. I told the two to sit at the table and keep their hands on top of the table.

"Suppose I gave you my word we wouldn't do anything?" Noah asked.

"To be frank, Noah," I said. "I haven't gotten any closer to trusting you since we left the restaurant. Just stay where you are."

Sandy filled four mugs with extra strong coffee. We had been awake for going on two days and it was beginning to be hard to keep thoughts straight in my head. The coffee was good but sleep would be better.

I tossed my cell phone toward T. J. and she caught it with one hand. She was quick even after two days without sleep.

"Phone Masterson's number," I told her.

She did and waited a few seconds for someone to answer. Then she spoke her name and a phone number which she told us was her cell phone. When she disconnected she said, "He'll call back."

We drank coffee, and then Sandy made a second pot, and we drank that down, too. My eyes were burning, and I was pacing around the kitchen trying to stay awake. Sandy had fallen asleep in a chair; her head lying on the table. T. J. and Noah were awake, and I was sure watching for their chance to jump me. I figured, and I guessed they figured also, that as tired and sleepy as I was, I could still kill one of them before the other could kill me.

I woke Sandy and said, "I've got to get some sleep. Go to the garage and get that roll of duct tape."

"Duct tape!" Noah said. "You're going to tape us up? You've got to be kidding!"

"I'm perfectly serious," I said. "Do you really believe I'd go to sleep and let you two just sit here? I'd bet my last million you'd slit our throats before I could start snoring."

And so we used almost an entire roll of duct tape on T. J. and Noah. We walked them to beds in a guest bedroom. We taped their ankles, their wrists, their knees and elbows. And we put a couple of layers of tape over their mouths. I locked the bedroom door as we left and we headed for our bedroom. I fell onto the bed and I was asleep immediately, without bothering to take my clothes off.

****

I forced my eyes open and tried to focus on the red numbers of the clock on the bedside table. The room was lit in bright sunlight so I assumed the 2:00 on the clock meant 2 PM. I nudged Sandy who had managed to pull herself under the covers while I slept on top of them. She grunted and rolled over. I mumbled, "Time to get up."

"You get up," She grumbled. "I'm gonna' sleep."

I got up and stumbled into the bathroom. Splashing a lot of cold water on my face helped, but coffee would be better. In the kitchen I found Betsy holding Caroline on her lap and shaking a rattle for her. She was enjoying it and laughing happily. Sitting next to them was Colonel Masterson, this time in civilian clothes - tan slacks, a pale blue golf shirt, and brown loafers.

"Well, good afternoon, Morgan," he said. "I've been waiting for you to wake up."

"What the hell are you doing here?" was all I could think of saying.

Betsy stood and said, "I'll make some coffee." She put Caroline in my arms and handed the rattle to me. "You entertain C," she said. "She's had lunch, and she's gonna' get her afternoon bath soon."

Masterson pushed a chair out for me and I sat. I buckled Caroline into a small rocker that was set atop the table. She was gurgling and making happy baby sounds. I said to Masterson as I shook the rattle for Caroline, "I don't get it. What's happening?"

"I'm here," he said. "You want to know what's going on, don't you? So I'm here."

Before I could say anything, Sandy walked into the room, her beautiful eyes full of sleep as she wrapped a soft and fluffy white robe around her. She picked up Caroline and made some silly baby talk that made Caroline smile.

"I heard the two of you talking," Sandy said. "Nice to see you, Colonel. By the way . . . Now don't be too surprised . . . But I stopped by the back bedroom where we left T. J. and Noah. They're gone. Lots of duct tape lying around, but they're gone."

Masterson laughed loudly and said, "You duct taped them! And you thought you were going to keep them here by duct taping them! Those two have escaped from really deadly situations all over the world, and you thought duct tape would keep them!"

"Hey," I said. "We're not spies and black ops people. Besides, we were up for two days running."

"Morgan, let's understand," he said. "Black ops Company people and the men who work for me can stay awake for days, not eat anything except maybe a lizard and a few worms, and live on a mouthful of muddy swamp water. They stay sharp and dangerous. I heard about your little trip to Colombia, and thank God luck was with you. Those two could have . . . And probably should have . . . Taken their guns back and killed you. I have no idea why they didn't."

What he said stirred a thought in my mind and I went to our bedroom. I had put the guns we had taken from T. J. and Noah in the drawer of a night stand. The guns were gone. Back in the kitchen I decided not to mention that fact in front of the Colonel. I didn't need to make myself feel any more foolish than I already did. Instead, I got right to the point.

"How did you know we went to Colombia? And how the hell did you know we had their guns?"

"It's a small society in the unadvertised war community," he said. "Remember those nasty looking guys at the landing strip down there? The old guy . . . The guy you gave the money to . . . He's on the Federal Payroll. Those guys you saw there work for him. You were being watched by them, and they reported by satellite radio to Langley. I heard from my people there."

"And they took a shot at us?" Sandy asked.

"No," he said. "That was a local from the drug cartel. The old man had him caught and questioned. He unfortunately died before saying who ordered the shot."

"Was it a warning shot, or was someone trying to kill us?" Sandy asked.

"I'm told the best guess is a kill," the Colonel said. "You were lucky the Humvee had bullet resistant glass."

"And who do you think ordered us to be killed down there?" I asked.

"Hard to say," Masterson said. "I'd put my money on whoever T. J. Kohl is hunting."

"When we went to that prison in Colombia, we found it empty," I said. "No one was there. But you had some of your mercenaries there. Where did they go?"

"I received a message from Langley," he said. "I was instructed to pull my men out. And by the way, mercenary is sort of a bad word in my business. We prefer professional soldiers."

"Soldiers for hire," Betsy said as she filled four large mugs with coffee.

"Young lady, I get paid a lot of money for doing very tough jobs that very young, under paid and inexperienced soldiers might be called upon to do. I spent my career in the military, and I saw too many young men get killed in the prime of their lives for something they didn't understand, for something that did nothing to change the world for the better, and for a paycheck that was a disgrace. My people are the best trained special ops people in the world. They are highly paid, and they know what they're doing and why they're doing it. We have a one hundred percent success rate at everything we do. And we have a much lower kill rate than any uniformed military unit in the world, mainly because we're good at what we do. So we are soldiers for hire, but we are the best soldiers in the world for hire. OK?"

"Whatever," Betsy said. "I'm just the nanny here, you know? But I'm not dumb enough to like war and killing."

"And that's great," the Colonel said. "If enough young people thought like that, the world might actually change. But there have to be young people all over the world who know that the world will never change and will put their lives on the line for people who feel like you do. Because whether you like it or not, there are other young people out there who want war and want to kill you."

"Hey, let's get back on the subject," I said. "Who at Langley told you to leave?"

"They assign people to contractors like me. They call them 'Handlers'. My handler is a woman I know as Terry

Two. They all use phony names. She phoned, and I contacted my people down there. I had one of my helicopters that was nearby pick them up that day and take them out."

"*One* of your helicopters?" I asked. "You have more than one of your own helicopters?"

"Actually, my company owns five in operation and two in the shop for maintenance."

"How do I buy stock in your company?" I asked trying to make a joke cover my amazement.

"You can't," Masterson said. "I don't plan on going public."

"OK. Anyway, this Terry Two, did she say why you were being pulled out?" I asked.

"No and I don't ask. If the assignment makes sense, and the details are left to me, I just do what they want," he said.

"What about the Marine guards?" Sandy asked. "They were pulled out, too."

"I don't know who told them to leave, but they were packing up when my people were packing. They were offered one of my helicopters but refused. I don't know how they left."

Betsy had been leaning against the counter near the sink, listening and drinking a glass of water. She took a step forward and said, "Can I ask something?"

Sandy smiled and said, "Sure, what do you want to know?"

"I'm confused," she said. "The last time you were here, Colonel, you said you couldn't tell Morgan and Sandy anything because you didn't want to lose your contract. Now you're telling them everything they want to know. What's changed?"

"Now that's a really good question," I said and smiled at our young nanny.

"I was told to coöperate with you," Masterson said.

"Whatever you want to know, I'm supposed to tell you."

"Who told you that?" Sandy asked.

"Ian McCauley."

TWENTY - Nom De Guerre

"Ian McCauley!" I said, astonished. "Ian McCauley? The Ian McCauley I know? He told you to cooperate with us?"

"Yes," Masterson said. "After my men were pulled out I spoke with him. He said I was to go to you and tell you whatever you wanted to know."

"Before or after T. J. phoned your agent?" Sandy asked, and I immediately saw where she was going.

"Agent?" Masterson asked. "What agent? I'm not some Hollywood type. I don't have an agent."

I grabbed my cell phone - the phone T. J. had used to make her call to what she said was Masterson's agent. I pulled up the last number dialed and pushed the 'call' button. A woman answered. "Monica's" she said.

"I'm sorry," I said. "I must have the wrong number. Is this an agent's phone?"

"Agent? Sweetie, this is my hair salon. Do you need an appointment?"

I hung up and told everyone who T. J. had phoned. Betsy laughed, and Sandy swore. Masterson didn't seem surprised at all.

"My God!" I said. "How do you people stay sane living in lies and deception like this? My head is swimming trying to keep it all straight."

Colonel Masterson, still with a very serious look on his face and not finding any humor in all this, said, "Some don't stay sane."

Sandy was pacing around the kitchen, holding Caroline who was the good little angel she always is. She stopped and looked out the kitchen window. She said without turning around, "Correct me when I'm wrong, please Colonel. This man they had at The Levels was rescued by a very professional group of what were probably soldiers of one kind or another. Were they yours, Colonel?"

"No, they weren't mine," he said.

"And you're telling the truth?"

"I'm being paid to tell the truth, Mrs. Crew. I always do what the money buys."

"And how do we know you're not lying when you say you're not?" Betsy asked.

"I guess you don't," Masterson said without emotion.

"OK. Assuming you're telling the truth, we were told only a few people . . . Outside those at The Levels . . . Knew about this man. Everyone at The Levels except T. J. and Noah were murdered. Did you know about The Levels and that man?"

"I knew about The Levels," Masterson said. "I didn't know about that guy they had there."

"Mr. McCauley told us that the five people you kidnapped for us and brought to Colombia were the only people who knew about that man," Sandy said, still staring out the window. "Ian also knew, so there were six people altogether. Assuming you aren't lying."

"That's about right," Masterson said and added with a grin, "Assuming I'm not lying."

"About right?" I asked. "What does that mean?"

"Nothing that ever happened at The Levels had a paper trail. Everything was highly encrypted and stored on servers completely separate from anything else The Company has. If someone had a Top Secret clearance, their clearance wouldn't be high enough to know anything about The Levels. However, the CIA and several other Federal Intel Agencies hire the best computer geeks and encryption people in the world. If someone wanted to get into those files, they probably could without leaving a trail."

Sandy said, without turning around, "So Ian lied to us."

The Colonel, surprised, said, "How did he lie?"

Sandy turned finally and said, to everyone, "He told us only those five people you kidnapped . . . And he, of course . . . Knew about that man who they couldn't get to speak. But T. J. and Noah knew. They were there, for God's sake, when the place was attacked."

Masterson thought about that for a moment and then said, "Maybe he wasn't lying. Maybe he knew it would be nearly impossible to find a rogue agent and a Mossad buddy for kidnapping? Maybe since T. J. is hunting the traitor, he assumed she wouldn't be the traitor?"

"And that's another point," Sandy said. "If three of the five are dead and T. J. is still out there . . . Hunting as you say . . . That leaves only four obvious possibilities. One, you Colonel, because you have the capability to arrange that very professional raid on The Levels. Two and three, Patrick and Susan. Four, Ian himself. Of course if someone out there was able to hack into those super-secret computers, then anybody in the world could have done it, and I don't think T. J. or anybody else will ever find out whom."

"And in the meantime," I said, "T. J. could be around any corner waiting to kill me."

Betsy spoke up, speaking softly, in a hesitating voice, and maybe a little bit unsure of whether or not she should say anything at all. "You're forgetting one person, Sandy. How about that Noah guy? Could he be the traitor?"

Sandy and I exchanged a look, without speaking words, but knowing that from the very beginning we had not believed or trusted Noah. Betsy realized what should have been obvious to us but wasn't. There was too much misdirection, too many lies, too many confusing mazes to get lost in.

Sandy smiled and said to our ever so young nanny, "That's good Betsy. Keep it up."

I asked Masterson, "What about that? What do you know about Noah? What do the people in the CIA think about him?"

Masterson said, "I've worked with Noah Goldberg twice before. He's one helluva' fella'. He's been a liaison between Mossad and the CIA for years. He's worked with CIA agents many, many times."

Sandy asked, "Just out of curiosity, is Noah Goldberg his real name?"

"I doubt it," Masterson said. "Everybody in this business uses a nom de guerre. Backgrounds on everyone are fictitious. Security and protection override everything, even personal lives."

Betsy grinned as if she already knew the answer to her question, "Is Colonel Masterson really your name?"

"Of course not," he answered. "I have a private life, too. I have a family that I need to protect and keep out of all this. When I was a kid, I used to love reading books on Bat Masterson . . . You know . . . the Old West gunfighter? So I took his name."

"Are you a real Colonel?" Betsy asked.

"I was," he said. "Marine SOC. My men use the title now out of respect."

I poured another cup of coffee and tried to think through all the fog surrounding us. That little voice in the back of my head was screaming once again, '*Run away! Run away!*' But there had to be a way of cutting through all the crap and obfuscation. My first thought was to pack up my family and head to some little corner of the world where the sun was bright and the beaches were lined with tall palms. But I also realized that these people had no worldly limits. They recognized no boarders. They would go anywhere; they would do anything to kill whomever they thought needed killing. Running would do no good. I had to take control and end this in order to protect my wife and child.

"I want to talk to Ian," I said to Masterson. "Can you arrange that?"

"He specifically said he wanted to speak with you. He wants to arrange that ASAP."

"You know," I said, grinning like a fox who suddenly realized there might be a reason for it being too easy to get into the chicken coop. "I'm starting to think like you folks. I know why I want to see Ian. But the big question is why does he want to see me? He wouldn't want to get me alone in some lonely, dark place with no witnesses around, would he?"

"I'm being paid to tell you what you want to know," Masterson said. "To tell you the truth . . . I don't know. I suggest you name the place and time. Someplace where you feel safe."

I was born in San Marcos, California . . . Too many years ago to admit to readily. My family, going back a couple of generations, have had summer homes here. My Grandfather built a mansion in San Marcos where he and his third and forth wives respectively lived. My father and mother inherited the twelve bedroom drafty old place, and I called it home as I grew up.

San Marcos used to be a quiet little town, a place where once my childhood friends and I could play outside after dark in complete safety. But wealth came to San Marcos and things changed. The quiet little Downtown of small shops and Mom and Pop groceries became a city with tall buildings. Children now have to be watched and protected both day and night. North Harbor, once the place where the middle class built small summer homes, is now the home to drug dealers and addicts, prostitutes and grimy bars. The Harbor, still the home to a few remaining commercial fishing boats, needs repair and maintenance. The newest addition to San Marcos is one of those God-awful mega-shopping malls.

I imagine a tremendous amount of time, effort and corporate cost, by probably a large executive sub-committee of very highly educated people, went into coming up with a name for the mega-mall. After maybe months of meetings and discussions they decided to call it 'The San Marcos Mall'. Brilliant! But for my immediate purpose there was one very good element to the brand new mall. There is a big and very popular food court right in the middle of the damn thing. On any day of the week, from 11 AM to 7 PM, the food court is filled shoulder to shoulder with people wolfing down hamburgers and imitation Asian food.

I told Colonel Masterson, "Tell Ian I'll meet him tomorrow in the food court of the San Marcos Mall at precisely fifteen minutes past noon. Tell him to come alone."

TWENTY-ONE - Something Of Great Interest

Patrick Chesterson and Susan Kipman stepped off the small plane at the landing strip that passed for an airport just a few miles outside the town of Salmon River Bend, Idaho. During the salmon season prop planes and small jets brought fishermen, and during the hunting season they brought hunters. When Patrick and Susan arrived it was between those seasons, and they were alone.

Susan, being an experienced pilot – she had flown everything from a single engine piper to F-15 fighter jets, to C-17 Globemasters, to Apache Gunships and nearly everything in between – had flown the rented Cessna 340 from San Francisco to Salmon River Bend. They stood on the barren concrete runway amongst the weeds that were sprouting everywhere through the hundreds of cracks. They were looking for someone, for anyone. The wind was blowing wildly and was pushing dark clouds toward them from the mountains to the west.

"Are you sure?" Susan asked.

"He said Salmon River Bend, Idaho," Patrick said. "He said he has a hunting lodge somewhere around here. There can't be more than one place with a silly name like Salmon River Bend in such a silly place as Idaho."

There were five Quonset huts along one side of the runway. Four were locked with rusting padlocks. The door on the fifth was open slightly. As the cold rain started, Patrick and Susan ran for the open door. Lightning struck nearby; Susan ignored it, Patrick jumped.

Inside the hut it was dark and musty smelling. They left the door open behind them to let remnants of light in. Patrick reached out and touched the wall next to the door, searching for a light switch. Before he could find one a deep voice, metallic and almost disembodied, spoke softly.

"Please do not turn light on," the voice said. "Leave door open and no talk, please." There was an accent to the voice; Eastern European, perhaps southwest Russian, Patrick thought.

Four extremely bright flood lights flashed on from the far side of the hut, pointed at Patrick and Susan, blinding them.

"It is I who want you here. I must talk to you. There is car behind building with map on front seat. Drive car and follow map. Is one hour to lodge. If you are not there in one hour, I leave."

The lights went dark. Both of the agents were momentarily unable to see anything, but sight returned quickly. They left the Quonset hut; Susan ran through the rain to lock the Cessna while Patrick ran as quickly as his old, chubby legs would carry him, breathing hard after only a few steps, to get to the car behind the hut. The car was painted black, a new Jeep 4 X 4. Keys were on the driver's side seat, and a map was folded neatly and lying on the passenger's side seat. Patrick got in and drove around the building, stopping to pick up Susan.

"Do you want me to drive?" she asked, standing in the rain at the driver's window.

"Oh, yes dear," Patrick said. "You drive so much better than I do."

As Patrick slid to the side, Susan got in, and they drove off. Patrick opened the map and gave her directions. Their route took them toward the mountain range to the west. The paved road turned into a muddy mess as Susan switched on the 4 wheel drive and slowed the Jeep. Patrick kept track of the time and realized they were going to be late. He didn't voice what he thought, but he wondered if this trip would be a waste of time. Would the man be there when they finally arrived?

It was twelve minutes past the given travel time when they pulled to a stop at the grand, log-built hunting lodge. It was big to say the least. There was a green stained wood shingle roof over the two story building. A covered porch ran the front length of the lodge. A man, dressed in an ankle length black fur coat that he was pulling tightly around him, stood on the porch. He was smoking a cigarette that was held in a four inch long silver holder. He wore thick glasses and his hair was as white as snow, although his thick black mustache was only peppered with grey.

"Hello Patrick and Susan," he called out brightly and waived to them. He was smiling broadly but that meant nothing. Patrick had been a spy – he preferred 'agent' to the James Bondish title – since graduating from Columbia University first in his class thirty-two years ago. He well knew that nothing was real in his world. Nothing could be taken on face value. Fabrication and mendacity were the norm, and therefore the man's seemingly friendly and welcoming smile meant nothing. He adjusted his Smith and Wesson semi-auto pistol that was tucked under his belt at his waist before getting out of the Jeep.

"I'm sorry we're late," Patrick said. "The weather . . . And these roads were terrible."

"Not to worry, Patrick," the man said. He stood on the porch at the top of the five wooden steps, holding his hand out in welcome. "And you should never say apology, it is sign of weakness." He laughed loudly at that and said, "I do love your John Wayne. He says that in great cowboy movies that I love. Come . . . Come inside out of rain."

Inside was grand in a carnivorous hunter fashion.

The furniture was twisted wood with deep cushions of bright colors. The floors were highly polished with rustic carpets tossed randomly. And hanging on the walls were the trophy heads of animals.

"Come in," the man said. "Come in. I have tea. You want tea?"

Susan stayed a step or two behind Patrick. She was more unsure of all this than Patrick was. When they had received the phone call at my house Susan wanted to ignore it. Whoever had phoned them said a friend wanted to speak with them and told them to go to Salmon River Bend, Idaho. Susan argued that it was a trap; that meeting a stranger without any reason for the meeting in such a remote place was too obvious. But as usual she deferred to Patrick, and off they went. And so she stayed a pace or two behind Patrick and was ready to pull her 9mm semi-auto from under her jacket if needed.

Patrick said, "I think I'll pass on the tea, thank you. Why are we here?"

"Come, sit down," the man said. He pulled his heavy fur coat off and tossed it across a chair. He was dressed casually but Patrick quickly recognized the silk shirt and wool pants as European and expensive. "Sit by fire. It will warm you."

There was a stone fireplace against one wall. A log fire cast a welcoming heat into the room. Patrick took one chair on one side of the fire; Susan took one opposite. Splitting a target might assure one of them would not be killed.

The man took a seat on a couch facing the fire. He leaned back and smiled again. "It is good to meet you at last," he said. "I have heard so much of both of you."

Susan and Patrick looked at each other, both sharing a similar thought. Susan voiced that thought, "Who the hell are you?"

"I am Anton Evgeny Fedoseev," he said.

The three sat in silence for a few moments and then Patrick asked, “Why are we here? What did you want to talk with us about?”

“I sent a man to your beautiful Country. He is now missing. I want him back. Do you wish something to drink? I have good vodka” – he pronounced the V as a W – “and some whiskey.”

“Nothing for us,” Patrick said. “Too early in the day. But what makes you think we can give you this man? Do you think we have him hidden somewhere?”

“Ahh,” Anton Evgeny Fedoseev said in a sad sigh. “In my Country vodka is a curse. But Patrick and Susan, of course you know where my man is. You will tell me, yes?”

“I’m afraid you’ve made a mistake, Anton,” Patrick said. “My Suzy and I don’t have your man, and we have no idea where he is.”

“So, I hear you say you know of my man, Patrick. You know my man he was at this place you call The Levels,” Anton said.

“You know about The Levels?” Susan asked, surprised because The Levels was supposed to be one of the utmost secrets in the U. S. This man was obviously Russian or perhaps from one of the old Soviet satellite nations. That meant The Levels wasn’t as secret as it should have been. That meant that the traitor inside the CIA was working for Russia.

“Oh my dear Susan,” Anton said. “Secrets they are so very difficult to keep secret!” He laughed at his little joke.

Patrick asked, naming the Russian Intelligence Agencies, “Are you SVR? FSB? Maybe GRU?”

“Patrick my friend,” Anton said. “I was once KGB . . . But that was long time ago. My English is poor, but I think you say . . . Is independent the word?”

Anton Evgeny Fedoseev had studied these two people in depth before having them come to him. He knew their sexual proclivities, their strengths and most importantly their weaknesses. He knew their working history with the CIA; the files they had worked, the people they had murdered, many of them people he knew. He knew how well they worked together. Patrick was the brains and Susan was the muscle. Susan was strong, and Patrick was starting to get old and concerned about the future. He knew that when they received the phone call any other agent would have never run to him as they did. That was because, Anton knew, their brains were warped from their sexual lives of so many years. Their thirst for ever more strange and exotic sex was never quenched. Clear and reasoned thought that they used to enjoy was becoming clouded as if drugs were common to them. Patrick alone could be used. Susan could not.

He stood and said, "I have something of great interest. You will learn facts of great importance."

He walked around behind the couch to a writing table near a window. He pulled open a drawer and reached inside. Quickly, he turned and shot Susan; one bullet squarely in the center of her forehead. She fell over backwards and lay on the carpet, her blood and brains staining the fabric forever.

Patrick stared down at his friend, unbelieving what had happened. "Why?" he said weakly. "Why?"

"Quite simple," Anton said. "You, Patrick, I can deal with. Susan I could not. I think it is time to get down to the business as you wonderful Americans say. Now give me gun you have at belt."

TWENTY-TWO - To Prove A Negative

At twenty past eleven I walked into the San Marcos Mall where I was to meet Ian McCauley at fifteen minutes past twelve. I found a dark corner to stand in inside the lobby of the ten screen movie theater that was the meeting place of teenagers on Saturday nights. From there I had a view of the entire food court. A young man, I'd bet fresh out of High School, who worked at the theater asked me three times if I wanted to see a movie and if not what I was doing. I shooed him away and watched as three men and one woman took up positions around the court.

One man pretended to be a janitor type whose job it was to clean and wipe tables. But this man concentrated on five tables in one corner of the court, wiping each over and over, going from table to table even though each was clean and unused. The second man bought a cup of coffee and sat in yet another corner and opened a newspaper. He flipped through the pages but rather than read the paper and drink the coffee, he continually scanned the food court. The third man stood at the parking lot entrance to the food court. He held an iPhone and pretended to text someone without looking at the iPhone, as his eyes were fixed on the food court. The woman walked in from the mall. She carried two large shopping bags, one from Nordstrom's and one from Wilson's. Having been dragged through the mall by Sandy several times, I knew there was a Nordstrom's but there wasn't a store named Wilson's. She sat at the first table she came to and started to look through her two shopping bags as she, too, scanned the food court.

At fifteen minutes past twelve, the food court was filling up with moms and children and retired folks with no place else to go. Ian walked in from the parking lot. He passed the texting man without looking at him. As he walked past, the texting man spoke into his shirt sleeve. The three others all responded, speaking into their own shirt sleeves.

Ian sat at a table in the center of the court. He waited and watched and waited some more. At half past twelve he stood and spoke into his sleeve getting a spoken into-the-sleeve response from his four people. The four left the court by separate routes not acknowledging each other or Ian. Ian walked back to the parking lot entrance, and I followed him. Outside, Colonel Masterson's Mercedes SUV, driven by Sandy, pulled quickly to the curb in front of Ian. Masterson jumped out and pulled Ian inside. I ran and jumped in behind him. Sandy floored it and we took off like a bat out of hell.

****

Betsy had readied Caroline for her afternoon nap, put her in her crib, and was now making sandwiches for everyone. Ian, Colonel Masterson, Sandy and I sat around the kitchen table.

"I still don't think it was necessary for you to kidnap me," Ian McCauley said. He was enjoying the bottle of cold beer I had given him.

"And I thought you were going to meet me at the mall all alone," I said. "Your people were too obvious."

"Morgan," Ian said. "T. J. is still out there. I had to

protect myself."

"Alright Ian," I said. "You told Colonel Masterson to tell me anything I wanted to know. Can I assume you will be as forthcoming with me?"

Ian hesitated for a few seconds and then said, "To some extent. There are things I can't tell you . . . But if it concerns you and T. J. and this whole damn mess . . . Yes, I can tell you almost everything of what you want to know."

"Let's start with that guy you had at The Levels," I said. "He seems to be at the center of all this. Tell us what you know about him."

"We think he's an assassin," Ian said. "We think he came to the States to kill someone very important but we don't know who."

"That's it!" Sandy said. "You're supposed to be the best spies around and that's all you know about that guy?"

"Ian," I said. "We're not dumb. You've been calling in favors all over the world. You've got more on him than that. You know it, and we know it. Now tell us."

Ian looked at Masterson, and the Colonel said, "You might as well tell them. I figure they're going to find out sooner or later. Maybe they can be of some help. And I get the impression they're not the type to give up and walk away."

And so Ian shrugged his shoulders and said, "Back in the days of the Soviet Union, the KGB was experimenting with biological warfare."

"As was the United States," Betsy injected.

"That's true," Ian said without apologies. "Anyway, rumors have been flying for decades that their bio-warfare labs came up with a series of drugs that could be used intravenously and would alter DNA at the most basic level. They supposedly were close to making supermen, so to speak. Strength, memory, mental abilities, even altered moral beliefs.

"The Levels was, as you know, ultra-secret. Nothing

was supposed to leave The Levels. All records were supposed to be kept on site to limit access. But Dr. Cynthia Erickson, a medical doctor assigned to The Levels' staff, sent me a report independently. She was in complete objection mode to the torture, which I didn't care about. Once on staff, she knew there was no such thing as a resignation. But as part of the report she mentioned that she thought the man being tortured might have an extremely rare disease she named Total Idiopathic Neuropathy."

"What's that?" I asked.

Betsy spoke up and said, "A condition where the person cannot feel pain. Has to do with nerve sensors and transmissions to the brain."

"How the hell did you know that?" I asked her.

"Hey Morgan. College, remember? I'm thinking of pre-med maybe. I read a lot, too."

"She's right," Ian said. "We have files full of rumors collected over three decades concerning these Soviet projects. We were never able to confirm any of the rumors. The projects were so secret that we lost a dozen top agents trying to get inside the research facilities. Anyway, when Dr. Erickson mentioned her suspicion it struck a chord in my memory. I pulled up some of the old files. She may have been right."

"So you think this guy is some kind of genetically altered superman? From the old Soviet Union?" I asked.

"Could be," Ian said. His bottle of beer was empty. He held it up, silently asking for another which Betsy retrieved, opened and handed to him.

"And how did he know Morgan's name?" Sandy asked.

"That's a really good question," Ian said. "A bunch of our analysts have been arguing over that. We simply have no other reason than that you were involved in this somehow. Maybe not knowingly. Maybe one of your companies is involved. Maybe you made an investment in something related to it. We just don't know."

Masterson spoke up, "And maybe he just read about Morgan in some newspaper. Hell, I've done that. He seems to be a magnet for trouble."

"That could be," Ian said. "But if all he did was read about Morgan Crew, why say his name?"

"It might be a military maneuver," the Colonel said. "Cause a distraction there so you can attack over here. Very standard stuff."

"One more question, Ian," I said. "Did you order the attack on The Levels?"

"Me? You think I did that? Why would I?"

"You would if you were the traitor inside." Sandy said bluntly. "And because you're high up inside the CIA, you probably have the means to order some secret military group inside the CIA to make the raid."

"Without admitting that we have Special Operations people inside, how could I order that raid using them without a hundred other people inside knowing about it? The Company may be a secret intelligence organization, but that doesn't mean we don't have accountants and budget people and payroll and a whole lot of management above me that need to put their stamp of approval on everything that happens out in the field."

"How about private soldiers?" I asked. "Colonel, you must have competition out there? Other professional groups?"

"There are a lot of businesses like mine . . . I like to think I don't have any competition. But most do security work . . . Executive protection, things like that. There are a couple of small groups who make a living doing wet work. But there aren't enough of them to put together a raid as was done. The Mexican and South American drug cartels have their own special ops people. They have guys who enlist in their Government's military. Many are trained in special operations right here in the U. S. by our own military. They go back home, desert, and join the cartels that can pay them four and five times more than their military can. Which only goes to prove what I say, you can't buy friends. It wouldn't be hard to buy their services."

"So Ian," I said. "Is that what you did?"

Ian sat in silence, a very serious look on his face. After a few moments he said, "How do I prove a negative? I'm telling you I had nothing to do with that raid."

"So who did?" Sandy asked.

"I have no idea. And I'm not revealing any big secret by saying that no one inside The Company knows, either."

TWENTY-THREE - The Killing

FBI Special Agent Michelle Grassley woke at 3 AM and rolled over to check the time on the alarm clock at her bedside. She rolled back onto her left side and carefully let her hand move across the sheets to be sure that Anthony was still there. More than once he had slipped out of her bed without waking her and was gone when her alarm clock woke her. She hated that.

They had been sharing a bed once or twice a week ever since Anthony and his wife separated. It was nice when they shared breakfast. It really pissed her off when he was gone in the morning. And he would never tell her where he went. Michelle felt sure he was going back to his wife and kids.

But that morning he was still there, breathing deeply and slowly as he did when soundly asleep. She smiled and closed her eyes, but sleep evaded her. Three AM turned into half past three, then a quarter past four, and then five AM. Michelle turned onto her right side, and then to her left again, doing it as softly as she could so as not to wake Anthony.

In truth, she felt sorry for Anthony. He was a commercial financial analyst for a Private Bank in Beverley Hills. His boss, a 56 year old woman, hated him according to Anthony. His wife was draining away everything from him he ever had. Life, he complained, was hard. Michelle tried to sympathize and make him feel good about himself, but nothing seemed to be enough. Thoughts were running through her head that maybe it was time to send Anthony on his way.

At six AM the clock buzzed. She let it buzz for a long time, until Anthony woke and grumbled about the buzzing.

"It's time to get up," Michelle said. She reached out for him and tried to pull him close to her. But he pulled away roughly.

"I don't need to get up this early," he growled. "Wake me when you leave."

Michelle tossed the blanket aside and got out of bed, bouncing and shaking the bed as much as she could. 'To hell with him,' she thought. She left the bathroom door open so the noise of the shower and the bright lights over the double sinks filtered into the bedroom.

She stood under the water, turning the faucet so the water was very hot. Her temper was rising and she began to think up the words to tell Anthony not to come back. 'Just tell him the truth,' she thought. 'Hell, you're great in bed but a lot of men are great in bed,' she would tell him. 'But you've got too much baggage you're dragging around.'

Maybe that was too hard, she thought. Maybe she should be easier on him and just tell him they had to move on? Maybe suggest that they see each other for dinner once a week and nothing more? Maybe tell him that they could maybe get back together after he finally really divorced his wife? Whatever, Michelle was sure that they were done.

She stepped out of the shower, wrapped a big towel around her, and walked determinedly back to the bedroom. Now is the time, the right time. Tell him to leave and not come back.

The bedroom was still dark. She pulled open the drapes and the early morning sun flooded in. There was enough light for Michelle to see the blood stained blanket covering Anthony. She pulled it away and looked down at him. His throat had been cut and blood gushed from his carotid artery. She turned quickly and started for the bedside table where she had put her gun the night before. But she was stopped by someone grabbing her from behind. The man's strength was unusual. He was able to hold her with one arm so tightly he cracked two of her ribs. In spite of all the self-defense training she had, she could not get away from the man's grip. He laughed when she elbowed him in the ribs. He laughed more when she reached down and grabbed his penis and balls. She saw his right arm move slowly in front of her face. She could see the knife he held. She screamed but her breadth was stopped suddenly as the knife cut deeply across her throat.

The man tossed her aside like a leaf in the wind, onto the bed where she lay, life draining from her, next to Anthony.

****

The National Security Agency has the task of protecting the U.S. National Security Systems and to produce foreign signals intelligence information. What that means is that the brightest and best from the computer science, computer engineering, and electronic engineering fields are recruited to spend a lifetime working in this most secret organization.

Cryptography and computer/electronic monitoring are specialties of the NSA. Agents monitor worldwide computer traffic. They monitor satellite signals and the cell phone calls of known and suspected terrorists and foreign agents. And they break the most sophisticated cryptographic codes while designing cryptography of our own they hope our enemies cannot break.

Timothy Newark had spent the last twenty-one years of his life working for the NSA. He hated the name Timmy but that's what almost everyone called him. Not because anyone who called him Timmy liked the name, but because they knew Timmy hated the name. He was a nerd. And he was a coward, afraid of almost everything. In fact he was afraid of absolutely everything.

His school years had been hell for him. He was classified as a daydreamer. Paying attention was impossible. And when his teachers sent notes home about him, his father would beat him after drinking himself into a mood mean enough to hurt the boy. Children would pick on him and make fun of him. He had no friends. But when it came to mathematics and sciences, he didn't need to study. It all came naturally to him.

After near perfect SAT scores he was recruited by MIT under the unspoken auspices of the NSA. He thrived in the community of geniuses who lived in their own little world of computers and mathematics. Required text books were, to Timothy, a waste of time, money and paper. He knew it all already.

After graduation with a PHD and Summa Cum Laude Honors, he was put on the payroll of the NSA. He never cared about the reasons for what he did at NSA. All that mattered was that he was doing something so very easy and something he loved doing.

Cryptography was fun, like playing games. As he broke codes and designed new codes, he would laugh loudly and clap his hands, oblivious of the fact that others in the office were laughing at him.

He had a little glassed in cubicle in a NSA office in Arlington Heights, Illinois. The locale wasn't important. He had no social life and his days were taken up working on his computers, breaking codes, designing systems, doing what he was told to do. He had a small apartment four blocks from his office. The NSA arraigned to pay his rent directly to his landlord because Timothy could never remember to pay it. The first of the month was just another day with no special meaning to him. Weekends were meaningless to

Timothy; if asked what day of the week it was, he would not know. His time was divided between the apartment and the office. He hated the out-of-doors because it reminded him of his childhood.

All too often Timothy was at his desk well into the night seven days a week; he had trouble keeping track of time. When that happened, old Nestor the janitor would touch Timothy's shoulder and say, "Hey, boy. Time to go home."

Timothy would look up and smile at Nestor and say, "Oh sure. Time to go home."

That night the air was warm, but Timothy didn't notice as he walked the four blocks to his apartment. His mind was filled with computers and mathematics. Up the five flights of stairs and unlock the door was his unnoticed routine. Inside he would switch on the lights, but the lights didn't come on that night. He worked the switch over and over but still nothing. The reason eluded him.

The man inside Timothy's apartment grabbed him and pulled him inside the dark little room. He slammed the door shut while holding Timothy's arm in a one-handed, vice-like grip. When Timothy was a child and the boys ganged up on him, he fell to the ground and rolled himself into a protective fetal position. He tried to do that but the strength of the man was extraordinary. The man was able to pull Timothy up, his feet off the ground, with one hand. And when he pulled Timothy up, he dislocated Timothy's shoulder and nearly tore Timothy's arm off. The bone under his shoulder broke and ripped through muscle and skin.

A diet of takeout hamburgers and junk food and cakes and candy had put 295 pounds of fat on Timothy, yet the man was able to hold him with one hand, pick him up, and toss him around like he weighed nothing. He took hold of Timothy's belt at his back and picked him up. He took three steps and threw Timothy through the closed window. He looked out and watched Timmy fall the five stories and land hard on the concrete below. His body was twisted unnaturally. Blood spewed from his head. His dead eyes stared at nothing.

****

Martha Stigler was a newly retired clerk who had spent thirty years typing and filing at CIA headquarters. Martha had signed the standard secrecy agreement as all personnel did, so she couldn't tell people where she worked or what she did. She did tell people she was a Government employee, and because she hated to tell lies, she told people she worked in McLean, Virginia, which is where CIA Headquarters is actually located. It is commonly believed that CIA Headquarters is in Langley, Virginia but the building is actually next door in McLean. So she wasn't telling lies when she told a part of the truth.

Martha had married young when she said yes to her Traverse City, Michigan High School sweetheart. Six weeks after they married he was driving home from work at the old gas station where he worked as a mechanic when a drunk driver T-boned his six year old Chevy and killed the boy. Martha never re-married. She left Traverse City and took a Greyhound bus east. After eight months of looking she finally landed a Government job at something called The Central Intelligence Agency. She had no idea what that was on her first day of work.

At work she was steady and reliable, and her work was always accurate and neat. Thirteen years of occupying the same desk, typing and filing, brought her a promotion to supervisor of a staff of twenty-three clerk-typists. Computers were not her friend. And when the CIA started putting more emphasis on computer record keeping, she was thankful for the promotion. As a supervisor all she needed to do was learn how to fill out computer forms. Others would do the actual work on the machines that baffled here.

She was known as Aunty Martha among the staff, but never to her face. She didn't want to be mean or overbearing to the young women who worked for her. But she wanted good, error free work. She had three friends in The Company, three ladies her own age who were also on the administrative side of the business. They ate lunch together, and once each year they took a two week vacation together. Martha liked the three ladies; they were fun and smart, and they made no demands on her.

After twenty-one years of working for The Company, she decided to retire. She gave up her apartment, the one she had lived in for the last twelve years, and returned to Michigan. Her parents had left her their vacation home, and she decided to live out her retirement years there, in peace, quiet and solitude.

Since her retirement she had kept a close contact with her three friends from the office. Each was now retired and the four ladies had agreed to share their retirement lives travelling. Martha was sitting in a rocker on the porch of her home facing Turtle Lake outside of Traverse City. She was writing a note inside a birthday card to one of her lady friends when the man walked around the corner of the house.

Martha jumped when she saw him from the corner of her eye. "Oh my God!" she said. "You scared me. What do you want?"

"I come for you lady," the man said.

Martha jumped up from the rocker and ran into the house. She bolted the door and ran for the phone but there wasn't a dial tone. She threw the phone down and ran to her bedroom where she kept her Benelli 20 gauge shotgun leaning on the wall next to her bed. She pumped a round into the chamber and turned towards the sound of the front door crashing to the floor.

The man walked slowly to the bedroom door and easily kicked it open. He was smiling cruelly. Martha felt the tears filling her eyes. Her hands were shaking and she had a hard time holding the long barreled shotgun upright.

"What do you want?" she stammered. "Don't rape me! Please, don't rape me! Take whatever you want! I have some money and jewelry . . . You can have it all . . . But don't rape me!"

"Put gun down, lady," the man said in a deep growl. His voice was heavily accented and strange.

With a trembling finger Martha pulled the trigger but the man moved so fast she could see only a blur as he bounded from the line of fire. Her frightened eyes could not keep up with his too quick movements as he jumped across her bed and then bounded onto Martha, pushing her under his weight to the floor. He pressed the barrel of Martha's shotgun down on her neck stifling her screams. He put all his weight and extraordinary strength on the shotgun. He heard bones crack, her wind pipe break, and the woman went silent.

****

There is a hospital east of Seattle, Washington. It is named The Hospital of St. Thomas of Verona. To date, no one has bothered to research just who St. Thomas of Verona was. Were someone to look him up on a list of Saints, they would find there is no Saint by that name. But no one has ever bothered to do that.

From the outside it appears to be like every other hospital, perhaps a little nicer because it is a private facility. The landscaping is pretty but not extravagant, and very well maintained. There is a large grassy area in front under tall vine maple and red alder trees. Patients who are ambulatory are brought outside on those rare sunny and warm days untypical to Washington State.

The one unusual thing about The Hospital of St. Thomas of Verona is the high wall surrounding it. It is a thick wall, seven feet tall, of grey stone topped with broken glass embedded along the top. There is a big, very thick and heavy, black-painted, steel gate at the hospital's only entrance. It is closed and locked 24/7. A guard in the uniform of a private security firm that does not exist opens the gate for only selected people.

The hospital is privately owned and totally funded by the Federal Government via the top secret and unpublished budget of the Central Intelligence Agency. Most patients, Intelligence Agents of one kind or another, are there for long term recovery – from severe injuries or gunshot wounds. There is a wing to the hospital, at the rear, away from general sight, where psychiatric patients are cared for. The wing has eighteen rooms, all light, airy, and nicely decorated. The staff of orderlies at the psychiatric wing are chosen firstly for their size. All are big, well muscled, and confident of their strength. Secondly, they are chosen from the ranks of the various Special Forces Units; all were medics in their SOC Groups. Their jobs were threefold: 1. To care for the patients; 2. To keep the patients from escaping; 3. To keep the outside world out.

The patients in the psychiatric wing – there were only four that day – were all from U. S. Intel Agencies. Nervous breakdowns, brains warped by drugs, or psychotic episodes of both short and long term duration, were what brought patients to the wing.

One of the four patients that day was Henry Willis. That, of course, was his 'Company Name'. His real name did not appear on hospital records. His reason for confinement at St. Thomas of Verona Hospital was officially classified as paranoid schizophrenia and extreme long term depression. Henry was treated well, but he was watched constantly. CCTV cameras in his room were monitored 24/7. An orderly checked on Henry every fifteen minutes, whether he was in his room or in one of the 'social rooms'. His file was noted as 'Suicide Risk Very High.'

Three times a week, on Mondays, Wednesdays and Fridays, Doctor Spenser Williams spent an hour or two with Henry. They spoke of whatever Henry felt like talking about, which was baseball most of the time. Doctor Williams tried, gently, to move Henry into talking about his years as a CIA Field Operations Manager. Henry argued that he wasn't crazy and he wasn't suicidal. All he wanted was for people to listen to him, to believe what he believed.

Not too long ago Henry had started writing reports about a traitor inside the CIA. They were rambling diatribes most of the time. He had no real evidence, just what was seen by others as more and more the incoherent writing of a man who was succumbing to the pressures of years submerged in the whirlpool of secrecy at The Company. The decision was made to relieve him and send him to one of the agency's hospitals.

Henry was watching Boston play the Yankees on the TV in his room that day. He was sitting in his brown leather recliner, his blue bathrobe tied over his grey hospital pajamas. They wouldn't allow him to have beer, but he had a small fridge filled with decaffeinated and sugar free sodas. Anything with stimulants was forbidden.

The door opened and a man walked in. He was well dressed, very European, and he smiled like an old friend who hadn't seen Henry in years. He carried a box of Belgium chocolates, Henry's favorite thing and something else he was not allowed to enjoy at the hospital.

"Hello Henry, my friend," the man said. "I have gift for you. The good candy you like so."

Henry looked up at the man. He was big, muscular, and handsome, but Henry couldn't remember who he was.

"I'm sorry," Henry said. "Do I know you?"

"I am Johann," he said and handed the box of chocolates to Henry. "You remember me, yes?"

"I'm really sorry," Henry said. "I should remember you . . . But my memory . . . I think it's the drugs they give me here."

"I am Johann . . . from the Bundesnachrichtendienst. We work together many times. You remember, yes?"

He spoke with a deep and heavily accented voice. Henry tried to recognize the accent. He thought it might be Eastern European or Russian. It could be German, but more likely not.

"You're with the BND?" Henry asked. "German Intelligence?"

"Of course," the man said. He pulled a pale green painted wooden chair close to Henry and sat. He patted Henry on the knee and said, "Is good to see you again, my good friend."

"You and I . . ." Henry started. "We worked together? On what?"

"Henry my good friend," the man said. "We cannot speak of those things. People might hear. You have forgotten, yes?"

Henry opened the box of chocolates and ate one, then another. They were good, better in fact then he remembered, but it had been a long time since he tasted the rich luxury. He offered a piece to the man, but he declined.

"Why are you here?" Henry asked. Dr. Williams had told him he needed to start trusting people, but Henry couldn't bring himself to trust anyone. He had tried to trust people within the CIA when he had discovered some indications of a traitor. But they laughed at him. 'Yuri' they said was a myth. The stories of a Russian born American who had infiltrated inside the CIA were years old. They had become urban legends of a sort, the stuff Company people laughed at over lunch.

But Henry had compiled enough evidence to convince

himself and he thought any reasonable person, that there was an American traitor. Not a Russian mole, but someone who had sold out to the Russians. He had so convinced himself that he saw this traitor in every shadow, in every person who laughed and denied that such a traitor existed. He reached that point where he didn't trust anyone anymore. Anyone could be the traitor and would try to kill him to keep the secret. He didn't trust this man.

"We have been on the work of . . . How you say? . . . The spy? . . . Is that word I need?"

Henry took another chocolate while he was thinking. Finally, they might start to believe him. Finally his suspicions might bear fruit. The chocolates were delicious and he had missed the years without them. One more and he asked, "The mole? The traitor?"

"Yes," the man said and slapped Henry's knee jovially. "That is word I wanted."

"You have a lead?" Henry asked.

"Yes, lead," the man said. "We have lead and we have need for file."

"File? You mean my file? How do you know I have a file?"

The man laughed and leaned back in his chair. He said as Henry ate two more chocolates, "Everyone knows, Henry my good friend. We need file to work on lead for traitor mole."

Henry's head began to hurt. Drums started beating at his temples and his eyes were losing focus.

"Did you poison me?" he asked. His voice was difficult, his throat was dry and becoming tight, his words were becoming slurred.

"Poison!" the man said. "No my good friend! Is simple drug to help you remember and speak of where file is."

Henry's head was spinning and he was having a hard time focusing his eyes and thoughts. But he was certain he should not talk to this stranger. The problem was controlling his mouth that seemed to want to say everything.

"I can't," Henry muttered. "Can't . . . Won't . . . No."

"Henry old friend," the man said as he grasped Henry's knee and squeezed hard. The man's strength was profound, and Henry tried to scream under the pain as his knee cap cracked and broke under the vice. "You tell me where file is."

Henry tried as hard as he could to scream for help. The orderlies would help him. His weak voice did little however. And it wouldn't have mattered anyway. The three orderlies on duty as well as Dr. Williams and the nurse at the front desk were all dead.

Henry kicked and struggled to little affect. The man stood and took Henry's shoulders in his hands. He lifted Henry out of the chair and threw him onto the bed. Henry landed hard and hit his head on the metal headboard. Blood streamed from the stinging cut. The room was spinning and Henry could no longer see the man.

The man lifted Henry again by his arms, squeezing his elbows so hard his left elbow was dislocated and the bones splintered. He shook Henry hard, holding him up off the floor. Blind anger overtook the man. His mental acuity was twice what it had been; his strength tripled since he had been given the treatments. But there were ever increasing periods when uncontrollable violence overtook him. There was no stopping it. He didn't even try anymore. He just let the black fury take over.

He threw Henry, like a soft pillow, across the room and against the far wall. Henry cracked the wall as his head crashed against it, splitting his skull open. He slid to the floor. His lifeless eyes stared into nothingness.

TWENTY-FOUR – It's A Dangerous Dark World

A month had passed by quietly and peacefully since I kidnapped Ian McCauley from the San Marcos Mall. I had wanted to talk to Ian and he was willing to talk with me, but he had nothing to tell me. At least, he said, there was nothing he *could* tell me. Too many secrets.

I wanted to know what they were doing to catch and stop T. J. Kohl . . . But Ian said he couldn't tell me that. I wanted to know what they were doing to dig out the traitor T. J. was hunting . . . But Ian said he couldn't tell me that. I wanted to know if anyone had a suspect or list of suspects . . . But Ian said he couldn't tell me that. In fact, there was nothing he could tell me.

It didn't take long for a bunch of Ian's people to show up at my door, guns in hand. Ian did manage to calm them. Sandy, Betsy and I breathed a sigh of relief that we wouldn't be dragged off to Gitmo or some such place like that prison in Colombia.

Colonel Masterson, Ian, and Ian's four people stayed until midnight. There wasn't much sense in spending the night arguing and fighting, so I put some chicken and hamburgers on the bar-b-que while Sandy and Betsy drove down to the store to replenish our stock of beer.

The month since they left saw us spend a lot of time playing with Caroline. Betsy and Sandy went shopping a couple of times, and Caroline and I had a ball watching whatever ESPN had on TV.

Sandy and I were on the floor playing with Caroline while Betsy sat nearby trying to read one of her school text books. Caroline had been crawling around and pushing herself up to sit without help. She could take a few steps if she could hold onto someone's fingers for support.

Caroline is a happy child; she finds reason to giggle and laugh at almost everything. But when the doorbell rang that evening, she seemed to sense that something that would not be fun was about to happen. The grin disappeared, and the giggling stopped. Betsy tossed her book aside and took Caroline in her arms.

I told Sandy and Betsy to stay in the living room while I went to the door.

Sensing that I should be careful, I took a quick look out a window before going to the door. T. J. Kohl was standing there, looking around nervously. She rang the doorbell again and knocked on the door. I ran to my bedroom and got the little .38 revolver from the bedside table drawer.

She rang the doorbell twice more before I could get to the door and open it. When I did she pushed me aside and stepped into the house.

"I was hoping you'd think no one was home and go away," I said as I closed the door.

"I saw the lights and heard sounds. I knew you were home," she said and looked down at the pistol in my hand. She laughed derisively and walked ahead of me into the living room. Betsy was holding Caroline tightly, and Sandy was standing in front of them defiantly.

"What the hell do you want?" Sandy demanded.

"I'm not here to hurt any of you," T. J. said. She was wearing a not cheap grey jacket with a gold circular pin, studded with small diamonds, on the lapel. Her black slacks and short heeled shoes looked equally expensive. I guess I assumed that someone on the run from all kinds of spies and Government Black Op killers would have been dressed a little less well - maybe in wrinkled and dirty clothes from sleeping in back alleys. But I wasn't a spy, and I had no idea how these people lived and thrived.

"Why are you here, then?" I asked.

"Can I sit?" she asked. "I'm a little tired. I've been awake for thirty hours now."

I told her to sit in a chair as far from my family as possible.

"Where's Noah?" Betsy asked. It has become normal for Betsy to ask questions that are so obvious I should have asked them first.

"He was recalled to Israel," T. J. said. "I think he may be in trouble for helping me. I hope not, but he's a valuable asset to the Israelis, and they won't punish him too much."

Betsy asked if she should make coffee, which I thought was a good idea since it would take her and Caroline out of the living room.

Sandy and I sat next to each other on the couch on the other side of the room. I kept my revolver in plain sight, and we waited for T. J. to say something.

She closed her eyes for a second to two, opened them, yawned, and said, "There have been four murders in the last few weeks. All of them, I believe, have been linked to the traitor who killed my parents."

"So what does that have to do with us?" Sandy asked.

"Let me explain," T. J. said. She sat up straight and leaned forward. "A little over three years ago a Field Operations Manager, his Company name was Henry Willis, collected some disjointed evidence of a traitor inside the CIA. It was all very cursory stuff, a lot of assumptions derived from a few facts and the like. He tried to get his superiors to take interest but what he presented seemed . . . Unlikely to say the least . . . Crazy and laughable stuff maybe. But Henry persisted and wrote more and more memos to more and more people until the joke got tiresome.

He wound up in a mental hospital.

"Before Henry was hospitalized, he found what he thought was a piece of code in a waste basket. It apparently was just a scrap with some numbers and symbols on it, but Henry was sure it was code. No one would help him with it; no one would believe that a spy within The Company would be stupid enough to toss a piece of code in a waste basket. So he went to a NSA Cryptanalyst. One of the best. A savant sort of guy named Timothy Newark. Newark was able to decode what little was there. I don't know what it said, but Henry added it to a file he was keeping.

"Many of the memos he wrote and the contents of a file he kept were dictated to and typed by a clerk, Martha Stiggler. She's retired from The Company now. I can't be sure if she fully understood what she was typing and what the file she was putting together meant. Many of the clerks just do their work blindly and forget what they've seen.

"The FBI and the CIA aren't exactly friends. They are constantly in competition for funding and headlines. After 9-11 Congress tried to get them to work together and outwardly they often do. But if one can screw the other, they will. The FBI got wind of Henry's suspicions. They sent an agent, Michelle Grassley, to make contact with him away from Langley. She spent a couple of weeks following him, looking for routine. But Field Agents are trained not to have routines. Covert contact was necessary so that Company managers wouldn't find out that the FBI was interested.

"Henry was good; I knew him well, and I know that he never took the same route home or to work. He never even used the same dry cleaner twice in a row. He would switch cleaners every time he dropped his suits off. He never bought groceries at the same store twice in a row. But he had one obsession . . . Fine and expensive Belgium chocolates. He ordered them online most of the time, but when he was completely out and couldn't wait for a delivery, he would go to a small candy shop somewhere in the D.C.

area. Michelle made contact there, and within days he was confiding in her . . . Without letting his Company bosses know."

She ended her story and sat back, I imagined waiting for us to say something. So I asked, "And what does all that mean? Why are you telling us this?"

She said, "In the last few weeks all four of these people have been murdered. There are no suspects, but the murders were all so violent, and the four of them all had unusual injuries . . . Crushed bones. Not just broken but actually crushed. I think the killer was the man we had at The Levels."

Sandy said, "What does all that have to do with us?"

"I believe that the file Henry Willis compiled exists. I don't know who has it or where it is. There is one more person who Henry contacted and knows something about his file. Henry approached an Intel Analyst. A young man with a remarkable brain named Ryan Russell, his real name, not a Company name. After reading Henry's file, Ryan added up the numbers and made some connections with reality. He wrote a report and got himself in trouble for taking on the file without his boss' OK. I'm told that Ryan is now being protected," she said. "He's in a safe house somewhere, but none of my contacts know where."

"Again," Sandy said. "What does this have to do with us?"

"I need your help," T. J. said. "I need you to go to Langley and find out where Ryan Russell is, arrange for me to speak with him and get a look at Henry Willis's file."

"You've got to be kidding!" I said. I was astonished and almost choked on my words. "You want me to walk into CIA Headquarters, and someone is going to just tell me some top secret stuff, just like that? Are you crazy, lady?"

"I can't go there," she said. "If I walk in right now I'll never walk out. I believe the man we had at The Levels is now out and doing what he was brought into this Country for.

He is killing everyone who had anything to do with Henry's file and he wants to, I believe, find and destroy that file. The reason he's doing that? Obviously because Henry Willis was right, and if The Company picks up where Henry left off, the traitor will be found. Whoever sent this man into the States wants the traitor protected. Whoever this traitor is, he or she is sending good stuff . . . Important intelligence . . . to somebody."

"OK," I said. "I think I agree with you on the facts. You may be right. That being said, you're still expecting me to walk into CIA Headquarters and get what you want. Once again lady, are you crazy?"

"Mr. Crew," T. J. said and sat forward once again. "You have contacts in Congress. Use those contacts. Make demands through those contacts. Call in some favors. You've done that before."

"If I do then you realize this whole thing will be made public," I said.

"If it goes public, then so be it. What matters to me is exposing and killing the person who killed my parents. Nothing else matters," she said. "But The Company has ways to keep things out of public sight. No matter what you do, I don't think anything will go public."

She sat in silence and looked back and forth between Sandy and me. Then she said words that sent an icy chill of fear up my spine.

"If you won't help me . . . Then I have to assume that when the man said your name it was more than just pulling a name out of the phone book. I have to assume you are involved in this somehow and you should assume that I *will* make you talk."

"Don't forget, T. J.," I said. "I have a gun."

She laughed.

****

T. J. drank a cup of Betsy's very strong coffee, tried rubbing the sleep from her eyes, got up without another word, and walked out of the house, ignoring my gun.

Sandy turned to me and said, "I don't know Morgan. I still think this whole thing is a dream of some kind. These people can't be real can they?"

"Unfortunately my dear," I said. "These people are all too real . . . And all too dangerous. I need to figure out a way to do what T. J. wants. If I don't . . . Well, let's not talk about that now."

Sandy held her arms out and took Caroline from Betsy. Our young nanny sat in the chair T. J. had occupied. She looked concerned if not really frightened.

I saw this, and I wanted to give her an open door to get away, if she wanted to. I said, "Betsy, you've been a blessing to us. I don't know what we would have done without you. But there's no need for you to be a part of this. Why don't you sort of take a vacation, and when all this is over, you can come back to us?"

"Are you kidding, Morgan?" she said. "The only way I'd leave you guys and C now is for you to throw me out physically . . . And I think I might just be able to kick the crap outta' you, old man."

I looked at Sandy, and she smiled and shrugged her shoulders. Once again I was forced to do what the ladies told me to do. But I had a responsibility, too. I had to protect my family.

"OK," I relented. "You and Sandy stay here while I go to see the spies."

****

Senator Kelly Hubbard was a college friend of my mother. They shared a dorm room at Wellesley College for two years and, so the story goes, Kelly bailed my mother out of jail one night when she had too much to drink and tried to drive back to the campus at three in the morning from a Harvard fraternity party. She was my mother's Maid of Honor when my mother and father married.

After years as a Representative in the House, Kelly was elected to the U. S. Senate, and after a couple of re-elections, she had worked her way up to be a prominent member of the Senate Select Committee on Intelligence.

I made arrangements to meet Sen. Hubbard in Washington on the Friday following our visit with T. J.. She explained that Fridays were typically days off for Senators. I knew that Mondays were also days off most of the time for them, and the three days in between did not leave a lot of time for any real work, but I wasn't going to share that opinion with Sen. Hubbard.

I booked the Presidential Suite at The Willard which is very near the White House. I found myself trying to think like a spy. My thought process was becoming twisted and disjointed. I figured a spy, trying to look inconspicuous, would book some back alley five dollar a night flop house. A spy-catcher would be watching all the flop houses, if there were any in D. C.. And if I booked a standard room at a hotel away from any Government office, that too might be watched. So I booked the most expensive place I could find in the most overly-conspicuous place I could find. Not that I figured I could blend in with a bunch of diplomats and over-paid Government officials. I just figured no one would look for me there. Hide in plain sight seemed illogically logical. The craziness was rubbing off on me.

I had a silver coffee service and pastries waiting when Sen. Hubbard arrived at half past ten in the morning. She hugged me like an Aunt would and told me I was looking good except that I should lose some pounds, something I get tired of hearing from everyone. We talked about Sandy and Caroline, and she promised to visit soon as she had not seen Caroline yet.

After a delicate china cup of coffee and a bite or two from a pastry, she asked, “So what did you want to see me about?”

“I need your help, Senator,” I said.

“Well, your family has always been a big help to me,” she said. “You know, when your mother passed away, she asked that I keep an eye on you. She predicted that you would always be in some kind of trouble. And Morgan, dear, she was right. I’ve read the news stories about you and your . . . Shall we say adventures. What can I do for you?”

“I’m glad you’re sitting down, Senator,” I said and swallowed hard. “I hope you’re ready for this. I need to speak with a CIA analyst, Ryan Russell, who is currently being protected in a safe house. I don’t know where that safe house is.”

“Why?” she asked simply and directly, apparently not surprised at what I was asking. I guess she really had been following my “adventures” as she put it. If so, she must have known I was never far from trouble.

“There’s a file that may be classified as top secret. I’m going to need to see that file. I believe this Ryan Russell can lead me to that file.”

The Senator poured another cup of coffee from the silver pot but didn’t drink it. She took a small bite of the pastry and laid the crusty remains on a thin, gold rimmed china plate. She was looking out the big window, through the fine shears covering it and filtering the bright sunlight. I let her think about what I had asked. There wasn’t much sense pushing.

Finally she said, “I know about Silent Man. I’ve read the file, and we’ve had closed door hearings on the subject. The Levels was something that was put together without Congressional oversight. Heads are beginning to roll. The media will have all that in a matter of months. I know your name was brought up."

I tried not to show the surprise I felt. That this whole mess was beginning to blow up wasn't a surprise, but the fuse was burning faster than I thought it would. I figured, naively I guess, that the Feds would be able to keep this whole thing quiet for a longer time. But secrets and conspiracies are hard to keep secret. I remember someone telling me of an old Sicilian Mafia saying, 'Three people can keep a secret if two of them are dead.'

"This has to do with your file Silent Man," I said. "Can you help me?"

"That's quite impossible," she said. "The file is definitely classified at the highest level."

"It's not the Silent Man file I need to see," I said. Withholding the truth would do no good. She would know the truth or would eventually know that truth. So I said, "There's another file. A file put together by someone with a Company name of Henry Willis."

"I don't understand," the Senator said. "What kind of file? I don't know what you're talking about."

"It all started with what you know as Silent Man . . ."

I told the Senator everything that had happened since that day when Noah Goldberg first appeared at our house in San Marcos. As I heard myself relate the story, I began to realize how crazy it must all sound to anyone who wasn't involved in it. The whole thing sounded like a not too well done Hollywood movie. But it was all real to me. It was all too real.

When I had told her everything, she said, "My God! What the hell is going on here? There's a couple hundred people out looking for T. J. Kohl, and she comes and goes from your house freely? That damn mercenary Masterson is out there killing and kidnapping when anybody tells him too? I've not taken the side of those who want a top to bottom revamp of Intelligence. I'm beginning to change my mind on that."

"So," I asked. "Will you help me?"

"I need to use the phone," she said. "Would you excuse me for a few minutes?"

I took a fresh cup of coffee with me, and as a secret rebellion against Sandy's dietary restrictions, I took two of the pastries also. I waited in the bedroom, leaving the door open a crack, but still I was unable to hear anything Sen. Hubbard was whispering on the phone. There was an extension on the bedside table, and I was very tempted to pick it up and listen. But I couldn't risk screwing this up. Kelly Hubbard was the only chance I had to get anywhere. And I had to be successful or figure out a way to kill T. J. Kohl.

I had eaten both pastries and wished I could get a refill on the coffee when the Senator called my name. I carried the delicate gold rimmed china cup with little pink roses on it with me as I walked back to the sitting room. I took the seat I had left and waited for Sen. Hubbard to say something.

She gently laid her cup on the table and said, "A man will be coming here to speak with you. He works for my Committee. He is a former CIA Field Agent. His name is Nathan Strasburg. He's very good, in fact he's the best there is."

"Is that his real name or Company name?" I asked. I was actually trying to sound smart, like I was some kind of insider knowing that Agents always used phony names.

But Senator Hubbard didn't catch the joke, or she decided to ignore it because she said simply, "It's his real name. He'll be here in about an hour."

She stood, and the look on her face told me she was very worried. It was clear that she and her Committee, which was supposed to be the oversight of all U. S. Intelligence operations, had no idea that The Levels existed until the attack and the murders. They had no idea of Henry

Willis' file or his suspicions, and may never have learned of it without me telling the Senator. I wanted to ask her what she was going to do, but I knew she wouldn't tell me anyway.

"Morgan," she said. "It was good seeing you again. Please be careful. I know I can't stop you, but please be careful. It's a dangerous dark world out there."

TWENTY-FIVE - Maybe I Should Have Waited

The sun was bright, but there was a coolness to the air at Anton Evgeny Fedoseev's hunting lodge in the foothills of Salmon River Bend, Idaho. Patrick had not yet gotten over the death of his Suzy, his good friend and partner. He had buried Susan behind the lodge. Anton Evgeny did not help, even to carry the body outside, but he did stand by and watch Patrick dig the grave.

As Patrick dug, Anton Evgeny smoked a long Cuban cigar, one of that Country's prime cigars; the same as Fidel used to smoke. In one hand he caressed the cigar; in the other he held his pistol.

A month had passed and Patrick, little by little, became content with his position. Anton Evgeny had deposited five hundred thousand dollars into Patrick's bank account in Luxemburg. For this Patrick became a source of insider information. At first it was about old cases, from years before. Meaningless things, Patrick thought. But he knew the routine. Start by getting small, old things, and slowly work up to the important things.

He passed the first days reading and walking outside, but not too far from the lodge, and always with Anton Evgeny not too far behind. He walked ahead of Anton Evgeny downstairs to the basement at night where Patrick was locked in a tool room, where he slept on a rickety old cot that had seen better days.

But Patrick ate well; Anton Evgeny was a very good cook. The lodge was well stocked with excellent wines, scotch and the best Russian vodka. Patrick was eventually allowed to walk outside when he wanted to, after being reminded that the lodge was more than twenty miles from its nearest neighbor and Anton Evgeny had the keys to the cars.

On this day Anton Evgeny called to Patrick to return to the house. Patrick had been sitting under a tall tree. He was reading something, he really didn't know what. The words all ran together and meant nothing to him. Thoughts filled his head. Thoughts of how he might kill Anton Evgeny.

Patrick put the book down and pushed himself out of the very uncomfortable wooden Adirondack chair.

"What do you want?" he called back loudly.

"There is man here. You should meet. Please, come to house, my friend Patrick."

Patrick's steps were slow and heavy. He resented having to reveal secrets that had been part of his life for so many years. But he knew his days with the CIA were over. He would never be allowed back in, and he would be lucky if they let him retire. A bullet behind his ear was the most likely retirement he would face. The money Anton Evgeny gave him would see him through. That, added to the 1.75 million he had squirreled away over the years, would keep him comfortable and secure someplace warm and quiet. But he had decided to demand more from his captor. Maybe this new person would be the opening to more money?

Anton Evgeny was waiting on the porch at the rear door. He stepped aside to let Patrick in. Inside a man was waiting. He was big, muscular and his eyes seemed very strange. Patrick thought upon first seeing the man, 'Death walking'.

Anton Evgeny told Patrick to sit in an overstuffed chair in a corner. He and the man stood in the center of the room, facing him.

"Patrick my good friend," Anton Evgeny said and smiled broadly as he always did when demanding information from Patrick. "I have need to know of man named Henry Willis."

"But . . . I've already told you about Henry," Patrick stammered. "You know. The Belgium chocolates . . . The hospital."

"Yes, my good friend Patrick," Anton Evgeny said and smiled again. "You did good. Now I have need to know of this Henry's file."

Patrick paused before answering. He knew where this was going and he had to be very, very careful. There was a line separating selling information and being an unredeemable traitor who would be hunted throughout the entire world. There would be no place to hide.

"File?" he started. "What file? My God, there must be millions of them."

"Oh now, my good friend Patrick," Anton Evgeny said. He smiled viciously and took two steps closer to Patrick. Those two easy steps were threatening. Patrick had to speak carefully.

"I assume you mean Henry's stupid file on the traitor inside The Company?" he asked.

"Stupid?" Anton Evgeny laughed. "Is file stupid to you my good friend Patrick?"

"It is . . . Unless you believe there actually is a traitor inside the CIA."

"And do you believe?" Anton Evgeny asked.

"Of course not," Patrick said quickly. He had to be very careful now. Revealing too much would eventually be a certain death penalty. "My God, they put Henry in a mental institution. He's crazy. Do you believe what he was dreaming about in his dementia, Anton?"

"Of course I believe," he answered. "My good friend Patrick. You have been good help to me. I think I tell you some things. This man," he said flicking his thumb over his shoulder at the man. "This man, he has . . . How do you say? . . . Is 'limitade' word?"

Patrick thought for a moment and then said, "You mean eliminate?"

"Yes! Yes, my good friend Patrick. This man has eliminate the four names you have given. Now he must find and destroy file. There must be no record left of traitor."

"So there really is a traitor inside The Company?" Patrick asked. "Who? Who is it?"

"My good friend Patrick," Anton Evgeny said, this time with a serious, almost sad look on his face. "I do not know. Your man has been giving to us . . . To Russia and others for many years. Each we pay and each time money is put in different bank account. Money is transferred so many times and so fast that we cannot trace. Very smart man, that traitor of yours."

Patrick asked, "So you want to find out who he or she is?"

"No! No! I want he . . . Or she as you say . . . to be secret for long, long time. Your CIA must not discover him . . . Or she as you say. So you tell man here where to find file, yes?"

"What makes you think I know where the damn file is?" Patrick said.

"You can give the man here . . . How do they say it on your TV? . . . Lead? Yes?" Anton Evgeny said and smiled again.

"OK," Patrick said. "First understand that I have no idea where the file is or even if there ever was a file. I've never seen it. Right now . . . If it exists . . . And it's not been run up the ladder to upper management . . . I suppose the most likely person to have it . . . Or maybe know where it is . . . Is Ian McCauley."

Anton Evgeny looked at the man standing next to him and nodded. He then asked Patrick, "Why this Ian person?"

"Ian McCauley is the head of all Black Operations for

The Company. If there really is a file, and if they believe what's in it . . . Then a Black Op file will have been opened and the traitor is being hunted."

"How this Ian McCauley be found?"

Patrick said, "He spends most of his life in the office. Twelve . . . Fifteen hour days are his norm. I don't know where he lives. Addresses are highly restricted to everyone. He doesn't have any lusts or routines that I'm aware of. I guess the best chance of getting to him is simply waiting and being patient. Follow him home."

"Is good," Anton Evgeny said. He patted the big man's shoulder. He and Patrick watched the man walk away, out of the lodge.

Patrick sat forward. He was scared, there was no sense denying that. The truth was he had no idea if Ian McCauley had the file . . . If it existed at all. He knew Ian's job was a mid-level Operations Manager, not in charge of all Black Ops. But he had to keep Anton Evgeny pacified. He had to keep feeding him information, truth or lies. He knew that when Anton Evgeny was finished with him, he would kill Patrick unless Patrick could kill him first.

"Look, Anton," he started, hoping to change the subject. "I'm going to need more than half a million if I'm going to hide from The Company. How about you come across with another hundred thousand or so?"

"Is no problem, my good friend Patrick," Anton Evgeny said. He lit another of his big Cuban cigars. "I will have money put in same account, yes?"

****

That day Patrick returned to his chair under the tree in spite of the cold air rushing in from the mountains. He held the book in his lap, his back turned to the lodge where Anton

Evgeny was preparing a lunch of beluga caviar, smoked salmon, and the Goose foie gras that Anton Evgeny loved so much. He uncorked a bottle of 1999 Leflaive Chevalier – Montrachet and put it on ice in a silver bucket.

For two days Patrick had sat in the hard wooden chair under the tree, reading the book that lay in his lap. Patrick needed a weapon. Anton Evgeny was at least ten years younger than Patrick, and Patrick's long life of indulgence had left him overweight and out of shape. He could not hope to kill Anton Evgeny without a weapon, and he had to do it from behind.

Under his book he was using the edge of a coin to slowly, painstakingly, cut a piece of wood from the seat of the chair. After two days of work he finally was able to rip the pointed shaft from the chair. He held it and tested its weight. It was about ten inches long; long enough he thought. He hid it under his shirt, got up and walked back into the lodge.

Patrick had quite a few classes in self-defense and escape and how to kill quickly, although he had always left that sort of thing to Susan, who enjoyed killing more than Patrick ever could. He knew almost anything that could be held in one's hand could be a weapon. A tightly rolled up newspaper, used as a stabbing weapon at an opponent's neck, could break a windpipe. A simple thing like a pencil or ball point pen could be deadly if plunged into a neck at the carotid artery, or via an eye into the brain, or at the temple again into the brain, or under a rib into a heart. A simple key, held between one's index and middle fingers, makes the perfect killing weapon when used at the neck or eye. The shard of wood he had with him was ideal for what he had in mind.

"Is lunch ready?" he asked Anton Evgeny.

"Yes, my good friend Patrick," he said. "You are here in time. Sit. Please sit. We have very good wine today."

Anton Evgeny was just finishing his careful

arrangement of the thinly sliced salmon on the platter. Patrick walked to him and pulled the pointed wood from his shirt. Using his weight he stabbed Anton Evgeny low in his back, hoping for a kidney. He stabbed Anton Evgeny seven more times as Anton Evgeny fell across the food platter. He made no sound, and he didn't fight. Patrick just kept stabbing him, over and over, until his hand, his arm, and his chest, were covered in blood from Anton Evgeny.

When Patrick stopped and stepped back, away from Anton Evgeny, the Russian slid to the floor. Patrick began to pull splinters from his hand as he watched life drain from Anton Evgeny Fedoseev. Patrick thought, "Maybe I should have waited until he transferred that extra hundred thousand."

TWENTY-SIX – Run Away, Run Away!

Nathan Strasburg arrived at my suite at the Willard as promised. Nathan, Senator Hubbard told me, was a retired CIA Field Agent. If a person were to think a spy should look like James Bond, dapper and dangerous, then Nathan would not fit the part. He was grey haired, average height, maybe a little overweight with a paunch, and absolutely nothing distinguishing about him. He wore inexpensive plastic rimmed glasses. His scuffed shoes were from a discount store and needed a coat of polish to knock off some of the dust and dirt. His suit, complete with flecks of dandruff on the collar, was off the rack, not nearly new, and it needed to be introduced to a dry cleaner and an iron.

"Mr. Crew," he said when I opened the door for him. It wasn't a question, rather a statement of fact, maybe just in case I had forgotten who I was. He didn't smile and he didn't offer to shake hands with me. His eyes shifted around everywhere except to meet my eyes. He stepped inside without being asked and without waiting for me to step aside. But he carefully avoided touching me as he walked by.

Inside, he looked around the suite, turning slowly so as to take in the entire room and all its very expensive furnishings. I closed the door and asked, "I assume you're Nathan Strasburg?"

"Of course," he said, finally looking at me. "Were you expecting someone else?"

"No . . . I guess . . . I'm not sure . . ." I stammered.

"You OK?" he asked.

"Yeah," I said. "I guess so. Sit down . . . Anywhere."

He looked from chair to couch to chair and finally settled on a tall backed executive chair at the workstation near a window. He sat, looked out the window and then got up and walked across the room to an upholstered chair and sat again.

"Window," he said softly, almost talking to himself. "Gotta' be careful."

I sat on the couch not too near Nathan. He said nothing; he was watching his feet move in motion to some music maybe only he could hear.

"Mr. Strasburg," I said. He looked up at me. "Senator Hubbard said you work for her Committee. She said you are a retired CIA Agent?"

"Kelly said that?" Nathan asked.

"Kelly? You call her Kelly?" I said.

Nathan chose to ignore what I said and asked, "She said you needed to see a CIA analyst who is stashed away in a safe house somewhere. Who is this guy?"

He was having a hard time sitting still. His feet danced a nervous step and he couldn't seem to keep his eyes on one subject for more than a second or two. He was avoiding eye contact with me, which I attributed to nervousness, but it could have been a sign of a life dwelling in lies.

I was confused. Senator Hubbard said this guy . . . If this guy was in fact Nathan Strasburg . . . Worked for her Committee and was 'the best there is'. But this guy seemed completely out of it. Pictures of all these spies and spooks that had come into my life ran through my mind. There was a lady who was a stone cold killer, two flagrant gays, a short and slightly overweight Mossad Agent, a killer for the highest bidder mercenary and his private army, and now someone who seemed mentally disjointed from almost everything.

The only man who was close to being normal was Ian McCauley. Maybe, I thought, I should just dump this guy and go directly to McCauley?

The phone rang before I could say anything. I picked it up on the first ring. It was Senator Hubbard.

"Did Nathan get there yet?" she asked.

"Yes," I said. "Are you sure about this?"

"You mean he's coming across . . . Unusual shall we say? Don't worry. He's the best, as I said. He knows everybody and he knows where all the bones are buried. He can find Mr. Russell for you. He'll get you what you want. And when you get it, I need it, too. I've decided to join the group that wants to clean house."

I agreed and hung up. So I decided I had to trust Strasburg, regardless of what he appeared to be.

I said to him, "I need to speak with a man named Ryan Russell who is supposedly being protected by the CIA. I don't know where this man is being held . . . A safe house, I'm told. This concerns a file a guy called Henry Willis put together. It has to do with a traitor inside the CIA."

"That file!" he said and came almost close to grinning. It sounded like he thought the file was a joke, something very funny, but his face didn't smile, in fact his blank poker-face expression barely changed. He just kept looking around the room, blankly taking in everything and maybe nothing. "If this guy is in protective services with The Company and not the Marshall's Service, he's gonna' be hard to find. And if that file really does exist it's gonna' be highly protected and almost impossible to get."

"I thought you were the best?" I said. "Senator Hubbard said you could do anything."

"Well, she's right," Nathan said. "I said the guy would be hard to find, not impossible to find. And the file would be *almost* impossible to get. If it exists, I can get it."

"Ok," I said. "Alright . . . I guess I'd like to know how you're going to get it."

He stopped looking around the room and looked at me. "Need to know," he said. "You don't have a need to know."

I guess spies and spooks and killers and mercenaries all have a different way of thinking about things. Maybe if you're normal . . . Whatever that is . . . Like most people I guess . . . Then you couldn't make it in a spy's world.

"What do I do?" I asked him.

He stood slowly, struggling to push himself to his feet like old men do, and said, "Stay here. It'll take a day or two."

****

I woke up early on the morning of the fourth day as I waited to hear from Nathan or anybody for that matter. I was getting bored. I phoned Sandy three times a day just to make sure she and Caroline were alright. I didn't worry her with the truth; I just said I was OK, that I missed them, and I'd be home in a day or two.

I was looking over the room service menu, trying to decide which of the sandwiches or hamburgers to have that day. The doorbell buzzed before I could order anything. When I opened the door, I was greeted by two men, both dressed in dark suits, blue ties and starched white shirts. They could have been twins. I'd seen their kind before.

"Let me guess," I said. "FBI, right?"

The one standing slightly in front of and to the side of the other raised his hand which held his badge case. The small gold badge and ID card confirmed I was right.

"Morgan Crew?" the Agent asked.

"You know I am, my good man. Hey that rhymes!" I said trying to joke but not being very successful. "Come on in."

I walked ahead of them and sat on a cushioned chair

near the work station desk. The two of them stood, not too close and not too far away, just close enough to tackle me if I tried to run.

"I am Agent Morrissey. This is Agent Chandler," Morrissey said. "You asked Nathan Strasburg to find a man. The matter concerning this man has been classified Top Secret."

I said nothing. I just sat and looked from one to the other.

"Did you or didn't you?" Morrissey asked.

"I'm sorry," I said. "Was that a question? It sounded like you were telling me something I already know."

"So you did ask Nathan Strasburg to find a man and arrange for you to speak with him. A man who works for the Central Intelligence Agency." Morrissey asked again.

"You know I did," I said. "Or you wouldn't be here."

"Morgan Crew, I am placing you under arrest for violation of U. S. Code Title 18, illegal communication of classified information. Please stand."

Before I could stand, the phone rang. Morrissey reached for it.

"Yes . . ." he said and listened. "Agent Morrissey . . . Yes, Senator . . . Yes . . . He's here with us . . . Yes . . . Alright, I'll hold." He kept the phone to his ear and stared at me. After a moment or two he said into the phone, "Yes Director . . . Agent Morrissey, sir . . . Yes . . . I understand . . . Yes, sir . . . Thank you, sir."

He put the phone down and said, "Mr. Crew. I'm told to apologize to you. You are not under arrest. I'm told that if there are any questions we can answer for you, we are to answer them truthfully."

"Why?" I asked. "What happened? Why?"

"Senator Kelly Hubbard and FBI Director Stanley Calendar have told me that I must cooperate and assist you. What do you want?"

What do I want? Now that was a good question and

one I had to think about. To give myself some time I said, "I want the two of you to sit down, relax, and let's order some lunch."

Morrissey and Chandler did, in fact, sit and relax. They took off their jackets, revealing big and dangerous looking semi-auto pistols in holsters tucked under their left arms. They were actually thankful for a chance to have some lunch. I asked them what they wanted and phoned the order in. After that I went to the suite's bar. They refused anything alcoholic but took a couple cans of Pepsi. I took a bottle of cold beer and a second one before the lunch arrived.

As we waited for lunch I asked, "So you're going to tell me anything I want to know. How about telling me something I want to know but I don't know to ask?"

Morrissey said, "What does that mean?"

"Tell me some secrets . . . Stuff I don't know about this Ryan Russell guy."

Morrissey asked, "Like what?"

"If I knew, I would ask," I said. "Look, you're here because something has happened. Sure, Nathan Strasburg is supposed to be getting me in to see Ryan. Maybe he got caught, but he works for the Senate Intelligence Oversight Committee. No, something else has happened that I'm not aware of. What?"

"Ian McCauley has been killed," Agent Chandler said. "What do you know about that?"

"Ian? The Ian McCauley I know?" I said, unbelieving what I was hearing. "Why? How?"

"He was driving home the night before last, Morrissey said. His car was hit by a .50 caliber bullet, we believe at long range from a sniper rifle. It exploded and burned completely before help could arrive. Ian was nearly cremated."

"Jesus Christ! I don't believe it. Do you know who?" I asked.

"Not yet," Chandler said. "The police are investigating."

Lunch arrived and the three of us sat around the workstation table eating and drinking. Between mouthfuls I asked, "Are you guys aware of the four people who were killed recently? Grassley, Newark, Stigler and Willis?"

Morrissey said, "Yes, we are aware. Do you see a connection?"

"Do I see a connection? For God's sake . . . Don't you see the connection?"

"Tell me," Chandler said.

I explained, "Henry Willis supposedly put a file together that would lead people to maybe believe there is a traitor inside the CIA. I think you guys know the connection of the other three to Henry Willis. Now Ian McCauley is dead, murdered obviously by some expert. I think that if Willis' file really exists, Ian McCauley might have had it and the traitor inside knew this. Someone is killing everyone who has had access to that file. I think there is a traitor inside the CIA and that traitor is killing people who could expose him or her. I think the traitor might now have the file or at least know where it is. And I think the file might be destroyed or amended to keep this traitor safe."

Both Morrissey and Chandler sat in silence. Neither would say I was right or wrong. But I knew I was at least close to the truth.

I said, "This Ryan Russell is the only other person who had access to Willis' file. The CIA is now protecting him, which tells me they've connected all the dots. I need to speak with Russell so I can connect the dots and get my hands on that file. Nathan Strasburg is trying to find Russell now and get me access to him. What do you know about that?"

Morrissey looked at his partner and nodded. Chandler told me, "Nathan Strasburg is missing. We believe he has been kidnapped. We think that he may have been taken out of the Country. We don't know where he is. Senator Hubbard is demanding his release. So far, CIA Directors are denying knowledge."

Chandler again looked at his senior partner who again nodded. Chandler continued, "The FBI believes Strasburg may have been taken by the same people who raided The Levels."

Once again I felt that I was sinking in a swamp with alligators chomping at my ass. That little voice in the back of my head was screaming as loudly as it ever has, 'RUN AWAY! RUN AWAY!' But as usual, I had good reason not to run. T. J. Kohl was still out there and still a very real danger to Sandy and Caroline. The people I was dealing with were not normal in any sense of the word. Whether it was an acquired abnormality or something they were born with, I could not trust that she would come after *just* me. So I had to stay involved and disregard my fears.

"So what do I do now?" I asked them.

"What do you know about Nathan being kidnapped?" Morrissey asked.

"What do I know?" I said, amazed that they would even ask. "I don't know anything more than what you just told me. I've been sitting here for four days waiting for him to get back to me. Check the hotel's phone logs. Check my cell phone logs. Check the video surveillance records the hotel keeps. And when you do all that then don't imply I kidnapped the man who was going to help me protect my family from T. J. Kohl."

"T. J. Kohl is after you?" Morrissey asked without hiding any surprise in his voice. T.J.'s reputation was widely known. A lot of people respected her and a lot of people feared her.

"You guys didn't know that?"

They didn't answer. But after looking at each other again Morrissey said, "Go home, Mr. Crew. We can send some Marshalls to protect you, or we can relocate you and your family and give you new identities."

"You've got to be kidding!" I said and laughed loudly. I had a hard time stopping my laughter. "I appreciate the offer but you guys would find the job of hiding me absolutely impossible."

"Then at least go home and leave this to us," Chandler said.

They both stood in synch, and without another word, they left the suite. I tried to phone Senator Hubbard at her office but I was told she was out. I asked that she phone me as soon as possible but I knew she wouldn't. The message that the two FBI Agents left was from her; 'Go home.' I was being told that I was now out of this whole mess. Nothing more would be volunteered; nothing more would be opened for me. I would get no more help finding Ryan Russell and no more help in finding Willis' file.

So I packed my two suitcases and checked out. At Reagan National I bought a ticket to San Francisco and waited in the First Class lounge where I enjoyed a couple of good – but not Wild Turkey – bourbons.

I sat in 3A next to a window on the jet that would take me home. The flight attendant brought me a glass of ice and three of those little bottles of Jack Daniels. I sat back, relaxed, and I felt good about going home. But I couldn't shake that little voice that kept shouting, 'RUN AWAY! RUN AWAY!'

I was staring out the window, enjoying the second of the little bottles of Jack, when I felt someone sit in 3B, next to me. Whoever it was wore a strong and overt perfume, maybe cologne. Whatever, I could smell it, and I didn't look forward to smelling it all the way back to California.

I had been hoping I would be alone for the cross Country flight. My seat mate was probably either a pest of an insurance salesman or a little old lady with a hundred pictures of her grandchildren that she knew I wanted to see, I thought.

I turned to see which it was and found Patrick Chesterson sitting there, grinning slyly at me.

TWENTY-SEVEN - The Inside Guy

"What the hell are you doing here?" I didn't know whether to be surprised or angry. "How did you . . ."

"Morgan," he said. "I would really like a drink first. It's been a tough couple of days for me."

Patrick waived to the cabin attendant and asked for a double vodka on the rocks. He drank the whole thing down in one mouthful. He held the empty glass up and another drink was quickly brought to him. He threw that one down as quickly as the first.

The jet started to pull away from the gate. "I hope they have something good for dinner," Patrick said. "I'm starving."

"Forget that!" I said. "Tell me what the hell you're doing here!"

"I'm exhausted, Morgan," Patrick said. He slouched down in the seat and closed his eyes. "Let's talk when we get home, OK?"

"Home? What the hell do you mean 'home'?"

"Well, alright," he started and yawned deeply. "Your home then. Wake me when they serve food."

He was asleep almost instantly, breathing slowly and deeply. All the years of working in the shadow world of stressful and dangerous jobs had taught Patrick to sleep when he could, to eat when he could, to kill when necessary. The jet started to taxi and then turned onto the runway. We rose quickly above the clouds, and Patrick snored softly until the meal service started. I poked him, and he woke quickly.

"Ah, good," he said quickly, as if he hadn't been asleep at all. "I'm famished. Did I mention that?"

"Where's Susan?" I asked. "Did you make her sit in coach?"

Patrick looked serious for a moment and then smiled and said, "Not here. Too many ears around here. Let's talk when we get home . . . I mean to your home, of course."

My dinner was a passable green salad, very average shrimp with sort of a roasted potato seasoned with something I couldn't identify, and some over cooked broccoli. Patrick had a small steak which he said was good and by the look of it, that may have been an overstatement. I can remember the days, not too many years ago, when meals in First Class were really good; something I used to look forward to on long, boring flights. Today, First Class meals are what the people in Coach got back then. Coach passengers now suffer through a bagel and a bag of pretzels.

But the wines were good, and the booze is still complimentary up in the front cabin. So Patrick and I had our fill of a good California Cab for him and an Oregon State Chardonnay for me.

We were a half hour late getting into San Fran International, thanks to a head wind that we couldn't get enough altitude to lose. Ninety minutes before we landed, I phoned ahead and had a driver and limo waiting for us. The drive up to San Marcos was made longer than it actually was by the tension I could feel. Patrick wouldn't talk. He stared out the window, and it wasn't hard to see that he was troubled, perhaps sad, maybe upset about something.

At home I found Sandy and Betsy on the floor of the living room playing with Caroline. The baby was having great fun playing with a half dozen toys that made noise and a little music. Sandy jumped up and ran to me, throwing a great bear hug on me. Before Sandy, coming home was just a way of getting away from the world, of hiding from all the grasping and demanding people. But my world has changed since Sandy and our baby entered it. Coming home is now something I looked forward to. There is happiness there now rather than loneliness.

Patrick stood aside, near the front door, as I picked up Caroline and spun her around to her delight. After a few minutes Sandy recognized that Patrick was standing, waiting patiently.

"I'm sorry, Patrick," she said. "Please come in. Sit down. Would you like anything? Coffee? Maybe something stronger?"

"Vodka would be nice," he said. "Large if you don't mind . . . No ice please."

He walked slowly across the room, his head down and a very sad look on his face. He took the overstuffed chair by the fireplace that is my favorite chair. Oh well. Sandy brought his drink, and she and I sat next to each other on the couch.

"Betsy my dear," Patrick said. "Please take the baby into another room."

Sandy nodded, and Betsy carried little Caroline out of the living room.

When we three were alone Patrick said, "My darling little Suzy is dead."

"What! Susan! How!" Sandy exclaimed. "Oh my God!"

"We received a telephone call from someone who said he could tell us who the traitor is. We went to see him . . . In some remote place somewhere in the mountains. Anyway, he killed Suzy and I killed him. So here I am . . . All alone and wondering what I should do now."

"And you came here hoping that we would tell you what to do?" I said.

Sandy, once again using good sense instead of the

anger that I use too often, asked, "Who killed Susan? Who phoned you?"

"I really don't know," Patrick lied. "He had a Russian accent though."

Patrick felt he had to protect himself. If it was learned that he had cooperated with Anton Evgeny Fedoseev, his life would be over. No one could ever find out. But he also knew that the very strange man who was at the lodge, who was sent out to find and kill Ian McCauley, could expose him.

"Russian?" Sandy said sort of to herself. She was running everything through that wonderful brain of hers, trying to come up with a plan that most importantly would protect our family. "What did this Russian guy want you to do?" she asked Patrick.

"He wanted secrets . . . He wanted names . . . He wanted me to reveal everything."

"Did you?" I asked.

"Morgan," he said. "I've been in the business a long time . . . A very long time. I gave him bits and pieces of truth interspersed with a lot of lies and half truths. I told him nothing that would be useful," he lied.

"Can I refresh your drink?" Sandy asked and got up to refill his glass.

While she was doing this I asked, "Do you know about the murders?"

"What murders," he asked very innocently.

So I told Patrick what had happened over the past few weeks; the murders of Henry Willis and the three people who had come into contact with his file. I told him about Ian McCauley's murder. I told him about Ryan Russell.

Patrick asked, and the question surprised me but at the time it did nothing more than surprise me, "The file . . . Henry's file . . . Who has it now?"

Sandy answered, "We have no way of knowing that."

I said, "Patrick, you need to go to Langley. Tell

everything to your boss. I'm not sure why you're not doing that right now."

"Morgan," he said. "I'm not a young man anymore. I'm 59 years old. I've never been without my darling Suzy. I'm scared."

"Scared of what?" I asked.

"As a Field Agent, when I'm not on some special assignment, I'm supposed to check in with my Operations Manager weekly. On a special assignment, I check in daily. I haven't been doing that while having been kidnapped. Will they believe me? Will they believe I told that damn Russian nothing? Maybe they'll think I'm the traitor? My darling little Suzy has always been there to protect me. Now she's gone, damn it."

"What's your alternative, Patrick?" Sandy asked as she handed him the vodka. "Are you going to run the rest of your life? You can't hide forever."

"You're right of course, Sandy dear," Patrick said as the front doorbell rang twice.

I got up to go to the door and opened it. Two people, a man and a woman, in dark blue windbreakers with yellow letters 'FBI' emblazoned on each and blue baseball type caps also with large yellow FBI on them, stood there.

"Morgan Crew?" the man asked.

"That depends on what you want," I answered. I have spent most of my life challenging authority when authority needed to be challenged. My attorneys at Harper, Harper, Jascro and Nettles, who have been described more than once as a wolf pack, have gotten me out of every scrape I managed to get myself into. I wasn't about to cave in to a couple of Federal Cops who had their sights set on me . . . Not yet anyway.

"Cut the crap, Crew," the woman said. "We're not here for you. We want Patrick Chesterson. He's here. We know it. Now, do you let us in or do we assume you are assisting a man in avoidance of being apprehended? A man wanted for questioning in a very serious National Security matter?"

She pushed me aside and strode into my house. The man she was with just shrugged his shoulders kind of apologetically and followed her inside. I was going to ask to see a warrant before she shoved me out of her way. I figured I would just let well enough alone. There would be a time for me to file a complaint of warrantless entry against them.

They walked directly into the living room and found Patrick slumped in my favorite chair, holding the empty glass Sandy had just filled with vodka.

"Patrick Chesterson," the female agent said. "I am Agent Diane Hartford. This is Agent Edward Jenks. We need you to come with us to answer questions regarding your disappearance and how it relates to a National Security matter."

I spoke up, "Do you want a lawyer, Patrick?"

Agent Hartford said quickly, "Lawyers are not permitted. He's not being arrested nor are charges filed against him . . . Yet. If charges are filed, he will be read his rights at that time, and he will be allowed to confer with an attorney. Now, Mr. Chesterson, will you come peacefully or do we have to handcuff you?"

"What about The Company?" Patrick asked.

"We are working with the CIA on this," she answered.

"One question before he leaves," I said. I turned to Patrick and asked, "Who ordered that prison in Colombia to be evacuated?"

"No questions, please," Agent Hartford said. Patrick smiled and nodded slightly. He was telling me he knew. All I needed to do was find the opportunity for him to tell me.

Sandy stood and said, "You know, I think it would be nice if you could show us some ID. Isn't that what you're supposed to do?"

With that Agent Hartford pulled up the loose fitting

jacket and pulled a mean looking semi-auto pistol from the holster at her waist. The man she was with did the same.

"I don't have time for all this crap," Hartford said. "Get on your feet Chesterson. And the two of you keep out of this, understand?"

Sandy and I have gotten into a lot of messes and dangerous situations over the few years we have been together. One thing we have learned is never say 'no' to a big gun. So we stood aside as Patrick was pulled from his chair by Jenks, handcuffed and led out while Hartford followed, walking backwards to keep her gun in our direction.

The door closed behind them and Sandy asked, "So what do we do now?"

I said, "Sandy, my dear, you've got me. This whole thing has my head swimming. None of these people live in the world you and I know. I can't figure them out. I mean, why even try? I can't think like they do, and I know you can't."

"But we still have T. J. Kohl out there," Sandy said. "And if she doesn't find what she wants . . . Then she's coming after us."

Betsy rounded the corner and walked into the living room, carrying Caroline. Sandy smiled happily and took the baby into her arms. Betsy was a little reluctant to interfere but she did say, "I was listening. I hope you won't get upset if I stick my nose in here, but you guys need to get a look at that file thing. That seems to be the center of all this. I mean everybody's looking for that traitor guy. They aren't going to leave you alone until they find him."

"You're absolutely right," I said. "The problem is getting my hands on the file. It seems everyone who comes close to it winds up dead. Everybody so far except for Ryan Russell. At least we can safely assume he's still alive. And that being the case, whatever high up management there is in the CIA probably has the file right now."

Betsy grinned and said, "I don't think so. Look, if they

have the file, then they already know who the spy-spy guy is. They would have arrested him, or whatever they do, already. This Ryan Russell guy wouldn't be in some safe house, he'd be back at work. They wouldn't still be out there trying to find out who the bad guy is, and that Kohl woman wouldn't still be out to get you. No, I think the file is hidden somewhere and not at spy central."

Sandy and I looked at each other. Our little biker chick - punk rocker - nanny was right.

"OK, Sherlock," I said. "So how do we find it?"

"I guess if it was me, I'd look where this Willis guy would have hidden it," she said. "Find out what he did, who he was, what he liked and disliked. Find out everything you can about him and you might find out where he could have hidden the file."

"And how do we do this?" Sandy asked as she bounced Caroline in her arms around the room.

"You only have one inside guy left who will talk to you. I doubt even that Senator lady will talk to you anymore. Too much . . . I was going to say a four letter word . . . Too much stuff is going on. Go get that Masterson guy and pay him to help you," she said proudly. "And while you do that, I'm going to give C her bath."

TWENTY-EIGHT - The World Isn't Big Enough

Patrick Chesterson sat in the back seat of the pale blue Chevy Tahoe. Agent Jenks sat next to him, looking at the landscape passing by as Agent Hartford drove. Patrick knew something wasn't right. The FBI might actually own a few Chevrolet Tahoes, but none of them were pale blue in color. And he also knew that if The Company wanted to pick him up and bring him in for questioning, they would do it themselves. They have very good people for that sort of thing. They would not have lowered themselves enough to ask the FBI for help. He was being kidnapped . . . Again.

After taking the twisting roads down and up and around the hills from my house, Patrick asked, "So who are you?"

Hartford didn't take her eyes off the road when she said, "Shut up."

Patrick had known something wasn't right when they walked into my house, but he also knew that everyone there – I, Sandy, Betsy and even the baby – could be in jeopardy if he didn't go with the two quietly. So he did. But now he needed a way out. If only Suzy were there, he thought.

He took note of where they were going. Interstate 5 South would take them to the airport in San Francisco. They were headed for the Interstate, and when they reached the junction, they turned to the North.

"So we're not going to catch a plane," Patrick said.

"What is it? Probably not Oregon. Maybe Seattle?"

Hartford said, again without turning or looking in the rear view mirror, "Shut up."

Jenks looked at Patrick, frowned and put his finger to his lips, telling Patrick to be quiet, but saying it in a nicer way than the woman had. He reached behind him, into the storage area of the Tahoe, and pulled a black plastic bag from a box. He stripped off his FBI jacket and took off his FBI hat. He shoved them into the bag. Hartford did the same while trying to keep the Tahoe from running off the road. She tossed them back to Jenks who added them to the bag and threw it back into the storage area.

Patrick smiled although he was scared and said, "I guessed you weren't FBI. You probably fooled Morgan and Sandy . . . But you couldn't fool me."

The woman driving didn't say 'shut up' that time, so Patrick decided to push the envelope. "I guess I'm dead. I mean, I'm too old to take you on so I guess I can't escape from you."

Again neither of them said anything. Patrick took another step. He said, "Do I disappear or will I be found somewhere. Honestly, I'd like a good funeral. So if I can be found, I'd be a lot happier."

Silence.

He said, "I'm old and I'm tired. The love of my life is dead. The Company won't take me back. I don't have enough money to last a good long life. So maybe you're doing me a favor."

Silence from both of them.

"Or maybe I can buy some more years and maybe earn some money at the same time?" Patrick said. He was sweating now and hoping they didn't notice. He was fighting for his life and he was scared. "I know things," he said. "I know secrets. I know things. Your people won't have to hurt me to learn things . . . For my life and a little money I'll tell you what you want to know."

The woman glanced in the rear view mirror and her eyes met Jenks'. Jenks nodded, turned to Patrick and asked, "Why did you kill Anton Evgeny Fedoseev?"

"Why? He killed my darling little Suzy. He was holding me and forcing secrets out of me."

"Forcing?" Jenks asked. "He paid you a lot of money."

"He killed my darling little Suzy," Patrick argued.

"Yet you offer secrets now without payment?" Jenks asked.

"I had to get away from him," Patrick explained. "When he had enough from me he would have killed me."

"And we won't kill you?" Jenks asked.

"In our business, contracts are honored. If we have a contract . . . I believe you'll honor it," Patrick said hopefully.

Jenks and Hartford spoke in Ukrainian. Patrick knew it was Ukrainian but he could only understand a few words. Many Russian dialects he understood; Czech and Slovakian dialects were fairly easy. He could get along in many Eastern European Countries. But Ukrainian he had very little experience with. Suzy on the other hand, he remembered, was fluent in Ukrainian as well as many other languages. He managed to understand a few words, enough to know they were discussing whether or not to kill him then and there.

"Take me to your people," Patrick said. "Contracts aren't hard."

****

Finding a guy who runs a private mercenary army, one would think, might be easy to do. After all, if somebody wants to hire his own army, one would have to have a way of finding Colonel Masterson. He had to advertise somehow. I found it not easy at all.

I had to recruit the services of Harper, Harper, Jascro and Nettles, Attorneys extraordinaire. All my life they have been my backstop, the people who handle the family's invested billions and have gotten me out of trouble. It took some time but they were able to find the Colonel.

Peter Jascro, the Managing Partner of the firm and a childhood friend of my father phoned with the news. He has been like a doting old Uncle and stand-in for my father since my father and my mother passed away years ago.

"What the hell have you gotten yourself into now, Morgan?" Peter demanded. "Mercenaries this time? My God!"

"OK, Peter," I said. "Sandy and I have gotten in a little deep . . . But because of nothing we've done. Did you find Colonel Masterson?"

"Yes, I had some people work on it, and they found him. He's going to phone you at your house today," Peter said. "Please Morgan. Whatever it is you're involved in . . . Get out. Get your family on a plane and fly away."

"As much as I'd like to do that, Peter, I can't. The world isn't big enough this time," I said and hung up. I couldn't explain to Peter, and I knew he would push me to tell him what was happening if we kept talking. It would be hard to say 'no' to him; it would be like saying 'no' to my father.

Sandy and I played with Caroline while we waited. Betsy retired to her room to read and do "some stupid stuff on the computer." Time slipped by slowly. A couple of hours later Betsy took the baby, and she and Sandy gave Caroline a dinner of some really disgusting looking strained carrots out of a jar. They bathed her and put her to bed. When she was asleep, they both joined me in the living room.

I was enjoying my third Wild Turkey bourbon with just a splash of club soda in each. Sandy mixed up a shaker of martinis and sat close to me on the couch. Betsy sat with her legs crossed under her in my favorite chair next to the fireplace. She tried reading a book, but I could see that she had her mind on other things. No one said anything for quite a while.

The doorbell broke the silence and made all of us jump just a little. Betsy made no movement to leave the room to leave us alone with our caller, and neither Sandy nor I told her to. She had been a help, and I guess we both thought she might be more of a help.

I went to the door and opened it. Colonel Masterson stood there in civilian clothes once again. He wore a really nice navy blue blazer with a fancy gold and red patch on the breast pocket and good quality tan slacks. He had a white silk golf shirt on under the jacket, and he had a big cigar clamped in his teeth.

"Sandy isn't going to like the cigar," I said.

Masterson took it in hand and tossed it behind him into the street. "Shit. That was a twenty dollar cigar."

I followed him into the house. Sandy pointed to the chair on the opposite side of the fireplace from Betsy.

"Would you like a drink?" she asked. "I just put a couple of martinis together."

Masterson looked a little sheepishly at the offer. I said, "I've got some good bourbon and scotch, too."

"Bourbon on the rocks," he said. "A little club soda if you've got it."

A man who drinks what I drink can't be all bad, I said to myself.

He drank some of my Wild Turkey and smiled. Then he said, "OK, I'm here. What do you want?"

"How much do you know about what's happened in the past weeks?" I asked.

"Not much," Masterson answered. "I had a little job in Uganda. I've been away for three weeks."

Between Sandy and me, we told him of the murders,

of the file Henry Willis had put together, of Ryan Russell, and of Patrick and Susan.

"And then Ian McCauley was killed," I said. "We think he may have had his hands on Willis' file."

"What! Ian you say!" Masterson said. He was ready to laugh and my first thought was that he and Ian may not have been the best of friends. Maybe he was happy to see the guy dead? "Ian was with me in Uganda," he said. "We flew back together on my jet two days ago. We had a breakfast meeting this morning in D.C.. He isn't dead."

We were speechless. What a world these people lived in. They seemed to be unable to extricate themselves from the web of lies they wove around themselves and everyone who got close to them. Nothing could be counted on to be the truth. Did they even know what the truth was and what the lies were? Or were they all lost in the fog?

"Who told you Ian was dead?" Masterson asked.

"A couple of FBI Agents," I said. "You mean they were lying?"

"Let me make a phone call," he said and pulled a satellite phone from his inside jacket pocket.

We heard him say "Hello, Ian. It's me . . . Yes . . . Look, I'm in California at Morgan's house . . . Yes, they called and I'm here . . . They were told by the FBI that you were killed while we were in Uganda . . . Yeah, killed . . . That's what they said . . . That's what happened? . . . Yeah . . . OK . . . I'll bring Morgan with me . . . Tomorrow . . . I'll call when we get there . . . That Spanish Place? With the tapas bar? . . . Yes, about 7, is that alright? . . . OK, see you then."

"Ok, Morgan," Masterson said, grinning like a kid with a big secret. "You and I are going to Virginia."

****

Patrick tried to stay awake while they drove North on Interstate 5. But it was a long drive, stopping only for gas at the California – Oregon border and again as they passed by Medford, Oregon. Patrick woke each time they stopped. He asked if he could get something to eat or at least some bottled water, but neither Jenks nor Hartford would speak to him. So he slept.

He awoke as the door to the warehouse closed leaving him alone in the back seat of the Chevy Tahoe. Neither the woman nor man who took him there were in the car with him. There were no sounds after the steel door closed. The dark was absolute.

Patrick waited, wishing his Suzy could have been there. She would have rushed out and killed whoever was there. But she wasn't there; she was dead, and never again would she save Patrick's life. He sat and closed his eyes, remembering the first time they had been paired on an assignment.

****

It was 1979, in the Communist sector of Berlin. Susan was just a child, barely twenty years old, but she was a born killer and very smart, with a photographic memory. They were to meet and turn a German Stasi Colonel. Colonel Dieter Muller was, simply stated, a drunk. The East Berlin Sector had a thriving criminal element dealing not only in the black market goods that kept many East Germans from starvation, but also supplying drugs and women to the political elite. Colonel Muller, while drunk, had a taste for young girls, ten to thirteen were the best.

Working with Jurgen Zimmermann, a leader in the East German underworld, the CIA was able to film Colonel Muller with several of the young girls Zimmermann supplied.

Patrick was to meet Muller and blackmail him into working as a double agent for the west. Three years of steady work would be rewarded, Patrick told Muller, with a home in the west wherever Muller desired, as well as a pension and a lead to people who could supply him with young girls.

The problem, unknown to Patrick and the CIA, was that the Stasi and the KGB knew of Colonel Muller's predilections for alcohol and little girls. They accepted it as not being as bad as some of the corruptions of so many others in the Stasi and the KGB lucky enough to be assigned to East Berlin. In those days, East Berlin lived on the black-market, criminal activity, and every kind of sex even the most twisted mind could dream up. Russian elite from the KGB and military paid huge bribes to be reassigned to East Berlin.

Patrick set up a meeting with Muller in a room in a disreputable, flea and rat ridden hotel near The Wall. He had set up a projector and screen and was ready to show Muller the film. But Muller arrived with three burley uniformed Stasi brutes, former Hitler Youth street thugs. Patrick was surprised and although he could not admit it, he was scared.

But before Muller and his people could hurt Patrick, Susan stepped from a closet holding a silenced and very large semi-auto pistol. One of the Stasi guards tried to pull his pistol from its holster but Susan shot him squarely between his eyes and watched as the man slowly slumped to the ground with a bewildered stare from the three eyes on his face.

She quickly shot the other two uniformed men and then stepped hurriedly so that she was between Muller and the door to the hallway. Without a word, Patrick switched on the projector and the three of them watched Muller with two children. Muller laughed and told them his boss would like a copy to take home and watch with the little boys he enjoyed. Patrick shrugged and Susan shot Muller in the back of the head. They had failed but no one in the East would know.

****

He sat in the back seat of the Tahoe in total darkness. Should he get out? Should he call out to someone, anyone? But before he could do anything, a disembodied, metallic voice, speaking in a whisper, filled the dark room.

"Hello," the voice said. It was a male voice, soft as a pillow of clouds, gentle, slow and almost reassuring; but Patrick knew he was not there to meet a new friend over champagne and rare Russian caviar. "Patrick . . . May I call you Patrick? . . . I'm so glad you could come here. I'm not happy that you killed Anton Evgeny, but there is a cost of doing business, and in our business the cost is often the lives of valuable people. But that can't be helped or undone. There is a replacement for Anton Evgeny on his way now."

"He killed my little Suzy," Patrick said.

The voice said calmly, "I'm very sorry about that, Patrick. I know how much you must miss her. Would you mind rolling your window down? I'm having a hard time hearing you." Patrick did as the voice suggested.

"As I said," the voice said with a little sad tinge behind it, "There is a cost of doing our kind of business. But now we must come to some arrangement, Patrick. I must ask you to do a small favor for me."

"And if I refuse?" Patrick asked. His eyes were beginning to become adjusted to the dark. He was able to see a little, and he could smell engine oil. He reasoned correctly that he was in some type of truck warehouse or mechanical repair shop.

"Well," the voice said in almost a very sad whisper, "Then you will become another unfortunate cost of doing business."

"May I get out of this car?" Patrick asked.

"Oh, of course," the voice said. "I'm so sorry. It was a

long drive, wasn't it? You must need to stretch your legs. It's been a terribly upsetting few weeks for you, hasn't it? And if you need to relieve yourself, I'm afraid there isn't a rest room here. Just go anywhere . . . It doesn't make any difference."

Patrick opened the door and stepped carefully onto what he felt must be a concrete floor. It was slippery, but it didn't feel wet. Oil, grease he affirmed. He walked carefully, holding his arms out in front so he wouldn't walk into any walls. He found a couple of cold and slightly slimy steel I-beam columns and little else. Wherever he was, it was a large building, but as much as he walked around, he found nothing but the Chevy he had arrived in.

"Patrick," the soft metallic voice said, "You won't find a light switch. There aren't any. It's unlikely you'll find a door. There's only one door and it only opens from the outside."

"Why am I here?" Patrick asked. "What do you want of me?"

"I have a job for you to do, Patrick. You will be well paid if you accomplish the task. You will disappear if you do not accomplish the task."

"And what is this task?" Patrick asked.

"When you leave here," the voice said, "You will drive the car you arrived in. On the passenger seat you will find an envelope. Inside is a first class ticket from SeaTac to Washington, D.C. You will also find a Glock 9MM pistol in the glove box. Before leaving for the airport you will kill the two people who brought you here. They are just outside. Leave their bodies in the street to be found.

"There is a rental car waiting for you in Washington," the voice continued. "You will turn yourself in to the Senate Intelligence Oversight Committee. You will tell the Committee everything that has happened to you, including our little conversation here. Withhold nothing. You will tell them that you killed Anton Evgeny in Idaho and that you escaped from me, not that I let you go. You will tell them that you killed your kidnappers in order to escape. The local police will verify that, and I've arranged for the Idaho authorities to find Anton Evgeny."

Patrick waited for the voice to say something else. Seconds passed into a minute and beyond. Patrick paced carefully around the pitch blackness. Then he asked, "Why? I don't get it."

The voice answered, "After you've done what I've told you to do, you will be accepted back into the Intelligence Community. Once inside . . . And I fully expect that will take only a day or two, as you will be seen as a hero who escaped capture . . . Then you will find out where Ryan Russell is being hidden for me."

"Why me?" Patrick asked. "You must have other people who can do that."

"I need distance between me and the person doing this task for me," the voice said.

"Then you're the traitor everyone is looking for?" Patrick asked.

The voice said rather jovially, "One man's traitor is another man's Investment Professional putting money aside for the future."

Patrick was careful as he started doing what the voice said to do. He wanted to look closely at the Tahoe before getting in and starting the engine.

"I need some lights," he said into the darkness.

Within seconds the warehouse was flooded with bright lights. Patrick was blinded momentarily. But when he could see, he pulled the hood of the car up and peered inside. It looked normal. He struggled to get his soft, overweight, out-of-shape body onto the dirty floor and pulled himself under the Tahoe. It, too, looked normal. Finding a bomb, he hoped, would be easy. Suzy would have known and done a better job at making sure the Tahoe was safe.

If Patrick's little Suzy had been there, she could have helped him to his feet. But she was dead, and Patrick had to push himself up with great effort. A loud grinding noise accompanied the steel door that rolled up behind the Tahoe. Bright daylight and cool, clean air raced in. Patrick hauled himself up into the driver's seat. He saw the envelope on the passenger seat and reached over to the glove box. From it he took the Glock and pulled the magazine from it. It was full. His hand hovered over the key. He knew that turning it might well set off explosives.

But why, he asked himself. He could have been killed at any time on the drive from California. And if the voice really wanted him to find Ryan Russell then why would he kill Patrick then and there?

He turned the key and heard the engine come to life. He put the gear shift in reverse and slowly backed out of the warehouse. The woman was standing on the sidewalk to his right, the man to his left. Patrick pushed both the buttons to let the passenger and driver's side windows down. He stopped and called to the woman. "Where am I? How do I get to the airport?"

The woman took a single step towards the Tahoe and as her mouth opened to answer, Patrick shot her, a single head shot. He quickly pulled the Glock to his left and shot the man, again a single head shot.

It took some time for Patrick to find out where he was and to find his way to SeaTac Airport. Hours later he stepped off the jet in Washington, D.C. and found the rental car that was waiting for him. He soon was on his way to Capitol Hill.

TWENTY-NINE - Sweep The Spider Webs Away

Colonel Masterson and I stepped off the jet at Richmond International Airport as Patrick was asleep in the back seat of the Chevy Tahoe, about an hour before he entered the dark warehouse. It took us forty-five minutes to get to the Spanish restaurant outside Richmond where Ian McCauley said he would meet us. It was a little past one in the afternoon, and the restaurant was still crowded with business men and women enjoying their extended lunches.

We waited twenty minutes for a table in a back corner of the crowded restaurant, and then we waited for Ian to arrive. He rushed in, fifteen minutes late, breathing hard.

"I'm really sorry," he said. "I was in a meeting that ran long and then this damn traffic." He pulled a chair out and sat, taking in a deep breath after running a block from the cab to the restaurant.

We ordered some sangria, which is not a favorite of mine but which my two companions seemed to enjoy.

"So," Ian said after drinking some of the wine. "Who told you I was dead?"

"FBI Agents. Morrissey and Chandler," I said. "Why would they tell me that?"

"I guess because that's what was supposed to happen. Only a handful of people knew I was going to Uganda. I drive a Company car, as do a couple score of other people. Whoever took the shot thought he was killing me as I was leaving Langley for the day. The car was permanently assigned to me, but because I was out of the Country they had given it to a young guy who didn't have a permanent car. He was killed and burnt to a crisp in the car fire. The company has kept this all very quiet."

"I guess you were very lucky," I said. "But the guy who thought he was killing you is still out there. Aren't you worried?"

"Morgan, I've been doing this for twenty-two years. If I spent a lot of time worrying, I wouldn't accomplish anything. You get used to it."

I guess I had to accept that. These people were unlike any I'd ever met before. I'd been involved with criminals, murderers, drug dealers, maniacs, every kind of warped, twisted mind there is. But I'd never met people like these. They live their life in a miasma of lies in which life itself is cheap. The death of someone means little or nothing to these people. They manipulate everything and everyone who comes in contact with them or who can contribute to the success of their assignment. All in the name of National Security and protecting the people of the United States. And was I being manipulated? I knew I was.

T. J. Kohl had me in her gun sights and was manipulating me for her own ends. I had a feeling everyone I'd come into contact with was manipulating me. In the past I'd found people I could trust. I had people who would help me, who would protect my back, so to speak. I didn't trust anyone in that whirlpool I was trapped in. If for no other reason than to keep my family and me alive for another day, I had to do what T. J. wanted. But while doing that, I assured myself I would also do whatever it took to protect my wife and child. If that meant killing T. J. or anybody else, I would do that.

"Nathan Strasburg is missing," I said. "Ryan Russell is supposedly in a safe house somewhere, but he could be dead for all I know. Henry Willis' file is . . . Somewhere, and everyone associated with it is being killed off. Patrick Chesterson was taken by a couple of very unusual FBI Agents who I don't think were FBI, so he's now missing, too. His partner, Susan Kipman, is dead, killed by a Russian type out in Idaho. T. J. Kohl is out there killing whoever gets in her way, and she's going to kill me if she doesn't get answers. Someone is out there who wants you dead, Ian, yet it seems you couldn't care less. All those people we brought to Colombia are dead. My friggin' head is spinning."

Ian sat silently, sipping at his sangria, staring at me almost blankly with hooded eyes as if he were bored stiff. "So what do you want me to do about it, Morgan?" he asked calmly.

"What do I want you to do?!" I said a little too loudly for the small restaurant. "I want you to clear the fog! I want the spider webs swept away! I want to know everything, damn it!"

"Well," Ian said. "I can't tell you everything. But I can tell you a few things. First, no one knows where Willis' file is . . . Or even if it really exists. We and the FBI have searched everywhere without results. Second, Ryan Russell is at a safe house . . . A very safe house. Even I don't know where he is. But I've had reports on what he's told us. I can't tell you what those reports contain. Lastly, no one knows where Patrick Chesterson is. The consensus is he's either the traitor we all want to catch, and he's left the Country, or he's dead, or he's being tortured for what he knows. Of course, I think he may have gone rogue and independent. The truth is, if the fat fag ever shows his face again . . . He'll disappear, so to speak."

"How about T. J.?" I asked.

"There are a couple of our Delta Force Hunt Teams looking for her," Ian said. "The FBI has a nationwide BOLO out. But the fact is she's the best there is. She spent eight months in Bosnia, and no one could catch her. She spent three months in Iraq, and no one could catch her. She's going to be out there until all this is over. Get used to it."

"What about Senator Hubbard's guy, Nathan Strasburg?" I asked.

"That's why I was late getting here," Ian said. "I was trying to explain to the Senator that we don't know what happened to him."

"He was going to see someone at the CIA . . . I think he was, anyway," I said.

"That's right," Ian said. "He was coming to see me, in fact. Up there in DC."

"So what happened to him?" I asked.

"I told you," Ian said. "I have no idea. I waited and he never showed up."

"Who else knew he was coming to see you?" I asked Ian.

His wrinkled brow told me he was thinking for a moment or two and then said, "I have to keep track of every non-operational meeting I have. Company rules to keep track of work time . . . The bean counters in DC . . . And to make it hard to meet people you shouldn't be meeting with. I phoned my secretary and she entered the meeting into the system. From that point on . . . Christ, anybody could have seen the meeting schedule. There is a separate, classified and restricted system for keeping track of operational matters. There is very limited, need-to-know access to that system. But the normal, unclassified stuff is easy to access."

"So, since everyone now seems convinced there really is a traitor inside your agency," I said. "That traitor could have seen the meeting with Strasburg and got to him first."

"Right," Ian said. "I guess that could happen. Look, meetings outside of operations are considered non-confidential . . . Unless they are associated with something that could be operational, of course."

"And how is that decision made?" I asked.

"Agents have to make that decision themselves," Ian

said. "Agents are supposed to be smart enough and experienced enough to make those decisions without going to management. And if they screw up . . . I think you can guess what happens."

"Why was Strasburg coming to see you, Ian?" I asked.

"I don't know," he answered but I could see a worried cloud cast a shadow across his face. "He works for Senator Hubbard. I don't refuse to see anyone associated with Senate Oversight when they ask to see me."

"Ian," I said. "Nathan wanted to see you at my request. It all has to do with all this stuff that started at The Levels. He wanted to ask questions for me. Operation Silent Man is still operational. Yet you made public a meeting with Strasburg concerning that Operation. Did you screw up without knowing it?"

Ian lowered his head. His forehead became beaded with sweat. The glass of sangria slipped from his fingers and bounced off the table top onto the floor where it crashed loudly, attracting a lot of attention. Ian rose to his feet and said, "Shit!" He walked out of the restaurant, almost running.

Colonel Masterson and I sat and watched Ian run across the traffic filled road. He disappeared from our sight as he rounded a corner.

Masterson drained his glass of the sweet, fruity wine and asked, "OK, what now?"

"I need to see Senator Hubbard," I said. "I appreciate you setting up the meeting with Ian, but I don't think there's anything else you can do right now. Go home. Send me your bill. And please, give me a way of contacting you quickly . . . In case I need your kind of help."

He gave me a cell phone number which I wrote down on a cocktail napkin from the tapas bar. I was hungry, and Sandy was three thousand miles away. So I stayed after Colonel Masterson left. I ordered a bunch of stuff that I'd never heard of before, that Sandy probably would chastise me for even thinking about, and washed it down with three bottles of very good Spanish beer.

The tapas bar was still crowded with people enjoying their two hour and sometimes longer lunch hours. Wine and martinis were flowing freely and the noise level was increasing with every glass refilled. After eating, I used my cell phone to call Senator Hubbard's office. Her receptionist said she had a full afternoon but I was entered onto her calendar for two in the afternoon the next day.

It was a short flight on a small jet from Richmond to Washington. I managed to find a very over-priced suite at the Mandarin Oriental. D.C. was always crowded with people who wanted something from the American taxpayer. Only the most expensive hotels had even one free room at exorbitant prices on short notice. But I had to stay, and I hated small hotel rooms anyway.

I had a few ideas, hunches really, and I needed to find out if I was right. I had an idea where I might find Willis' file, but I needed more details. I had an idea who the CIA traitor was, but I needed more details. I had an idea how the killer . . . Who I was sure was the man who had been held at the levels . . . How he was being controlled, who was doing the controlling, and how he might be captured, or better yet as far as I was concerned . . . Killed . . . but I needed more details. And more important than anything else, I had an idea how best I might protect Sandy and Caroline, but again, I needed more details. Despite all that, I was beginning to feel good knowing that I was getting close.

I checked into the Mandarin Oriental, and before doing anything else, I phoned Sandy.

"Hey babe," I said. It was really good to hear her voice again. A few hours away from Sandy seems like interminably long days. Having her next to me, as we relaxed at home, as we slept, as we travelled, as we tried to extricate ourselves from the trouble that always seemed to follow us, made my life worth something. Before Sandy, I felt I was just wandering, lost in a world I didn't fully understand.

"Morgan!" she said brightly. "Are you on your way home?"

"No," I said. "I'm going to stay here a day or two. I need you here. I think all this may end in a short time."

"I'll leave right away," she said. "I'll take Betsy with me to help with Caroline."

"No," I said. "Tell Betsy to take the baby back to where she had gone before. Don't ask her where she's going. Tell her to keep her cell phone on but not to try to contact us or to phone anyone using it. Cell phones are too easy to trace. If she has to phone anyone, tell her to find a pay phone on the street. Tell her not to leave any trails. Tell her to drive to wherever she's going. Give her five thousand in cash from the safe in the bedroom. Tell her not to use credit cards. Use the company AMEX card from Harper, Harper, Jascro and Nettles to rent a car for her. Nothing flashy . . . Just basic and a dark color. Tell her not to contact anyone, and she should just show up wherever that is. Tell her to stay inside wherever she is. Being seen too often on the streets can be dangerous. Caroline has to be safe."

"I hate to leave the baby," Sandy said. "Would it be better if I took Caroline somewhere safe?"

"Sandy, you can't hide the way Betsy can. Too many people know you. Betsy knows people outside of society. She can go underground . . . You can't. She has friends who live outside the norm. She can disappear; you can't. I miss Caroline, too. But it's more important that she's safe. If one of these people gets their hands on her . . . Well, you can imagine what they can do. We're dealing with some very dangerous people here. Life to these people means nothing. I need to protect you, and I need you to protect me. Most importantly, I need that brain of yours. I need help. Just do as I ask, and come to DC, please. I'm at the Mandarin Oriental. Don't phone me about your flight. Take a cab from the airport and be sure you're not being followed. Switch cabs several times if you have to. Take buses and the subway if you think you're being followed. Just be careful."

I hung up before she could say anything else. I knew she would be with me the next day.

THIRTY - I Need To Run Away

I took the evening to think. The bottle of Wild Turkey 101 I ordered from room service didn't do much to help the thought process, but it did help me to ease my mind . . . Temporarily, anyway. Later in the evening guilt caused me to order a turkey sandwich on whole wheat with coleslaw on the side, thinking I would brag to Sandy what a good, healthy, and light dinner I had. And then an hour later I raided the honor bar and ate several candy bars and some greasy, cheese flavored chips. That I would keep secret.

After at least a half dozen large bourbons – maybe more – I don't remember going to bed that night, but my sleep was rough and filled with dark nightmares. I woke up at ten to seven in the morning, soaked with sweat. My stomach was struggling to hold in an earthquake from the bourbon.

I tossed the sheets aside and threw my feet onto the floor. I knew I left the slippers provided by the hotel somewhere, but without opening my eyes I couldn't find them. I risked opening one eye and the light was like a bolt of lightning splitting my head in two. So I closed my eye and fell back onto the bed.

"Are you OK?" a voice asked.

I shot up and ignored the pain of light filling my eyes. In the fog of my hangover, I saw a man sitting in the armchair in front of a window, his legs crossed and a cup of coffee in his hand.

"You won't pass out, will you?" the voice asked. "I dare say I wouldn't mind giving you mouth to mouth but not if you're going to vomit."

I rubbed my eyes, trying to get them to focus. The mist started to lift, and I saw what I thought might be Patrick Chesterson sitting in my bedroom.

"Patrick?" I asked. "Patrick? Is that you?"

"Of course, Morgan," he said. "Damn, you look bad. Too much to drink, right?"

"How did you get here?" I asked. "Where have you been?"

"I think some coffee and maybe a small bite of food first, Morgan. You need to get a clear head."

If the voice belonging to the hazy figure sitting on the other side of the room was actually Patrick Chesterson, he was right of course. I needed to get some strong coffee inside me and allow it to clear away the cobwebs.

After the third cup, I managed to keep down two slices of wheat toast that Patrick had ordered with the scrambled eggs that he ate when I couldn't. My head was still a little out of tilt but at least I could see.

"OK," I said. "Now tell me what the hell's going on. How'd you get here?"

"It's a long story, Morgan," Patrick said. "I'm not sure I believe it all. But anyway, at your house those two people who pretended to be FBI weren't, of course. They took me on a terribly long and very boring drive. I was very frightened. They had me in the back seat of their car . . . They wouldn't talk to me except to say 'shut up' . . . They wouldn't let me use a bathroom . . . They wouldn't let me eat or drink. I thought I was going to be killed. They took me to a warehouse or something. It was dark and smelled of motor oil. There were no lights at all. The floor was slick, the air was heavy. Then this voice started talking to me."

Patrick stopped speaking and just stared at me. For a moment I thought he was going to cry.

I asked, "What did he tell you?"

"That's what I thought," he said and forced a smile.

"What?" I asked. "What are you getting at?"

"You said 'what did *HE* tell you'."

"So what," I said. "What the hell are you trying to say?"

"You set me up," Patrick said. And as he said it he pulled a small, shiny chrome pistol with pale pink mother of pearl grips from his coat pocket.

"Are you crazy?" I asked. "I set you up? What the hell . . ."

"You had me kidnapped and brought to the prison in Colombia. You had those two people take me from your home, too. You knew it was a man's voice. You could've said, 'What did the voice say'? You could have said anything, but you knew it was a man."

"Do you have any idea what you're saying? That's just the way people talk, Patrick. You must have heard people talk like that before. Now put the gun away and let's talk rationally," I said.

His hand was shaking visibly. His eyes filled with tears that were about to burst free. His hand wiped the sweat from his cheeks and forehead. It wasn't hard to see that he was near his breaking point. Honestly, to this day I don't know how these people maintain any semblance of sanity year after year of working the jobs they do.

"Did you have anything to do with murdering my darling little Suzy?" he asked.

"Of course not," I said. I stood slowly, still in the underwear I had slept in, and stepped slowly to Patrick. I bent down to him and put my hand on his shoulder. I said softly, "Let me help you, Patrick."

I truly felt sorry for the man who was older than his years. He had lost the only friend he thought he had. He had spent his life in the grey world of spies and lies. I imagined he felt lost.

Patrick let me ease the small gun from his hand as he started to cry freely and loudly. He pressed his head against my waist and hugged me to him tightly as I stood in front of him. I let him cry it out, and then I pulled away and poured a cup of coffee for him. I added a strong dose of Wild Turkey to the cup and handed it to him. He smiled and sipped at it approvingly.

"That's nice," he said and tried to smile bravely. "I'm sorry, Morgan. I guess I'm just tired . . . Exhausted really. I know you aren't responsible for any of this. Hell, you're being hunted, too."

I refilled his coffee cup, half with coffee and half with bourbon. He drank it thankfully and smiled again. I sat on the edge of the bed and watched patiently as he drained the cup and put it on a small table next to his chair. I didn't ask if he wanted another because I needed to keep his head somewhat clear. Calm was OK but drunk wouldn't help at all.

"Start at the beginning," I said. "Tell me what happened."

Patrick spoke slowly as if he were trying to be detailed about everything. He told me of the gasoline stops, of each time he spoke and each time he was told to not talk.

"I awoke in the back seat of the auto," he said. I could see clearly that even remembering brought back the fear. "I was in absolute darkness. There was a very faint buzzing sound, sort of electric, you know? I thought for a minute that I might have died and awoken in Hades. After so many years of doing the nasty work that my darling Suzy and I did, I know that the fires of hell are awaiting me.

"Then I heard a voice. It was not a normal, human voice. It was the kind of voice I'd heard many times before. It was masked electronically. I've used such devices before. I know what they sound like. And I think I know who was speaking. I mean, having used the device before, I can hear beyond it, so to speak. Do you know what I'm saying,

Morgan?"

"I guess so," I said. I really didn't know, but I didn't want him wasting time on an explanation.

"By the way," Patrick said and smiled slightly. "I killed the two people who took me from your home. It's OK because they weren't FBI, as I said. I wouldn't worry about them. My darling little Suzy and I used to kill a lot of people. I miss her, did you know that?"

"I'm sorry," I said. "Go on, tell me what else happened."

"Knowing who it was speaking tells me who the traitor is, Morgan. That's why I'm here. I can't go back to Langley . . . I've been around long enough to know that in the last few days my file has been added to. I am now persona non grata so to speak. If I enter that building I will never leave."

"I guess I've heard that," I said.

"I need to run away, so to speak," Patrick said. "I need to hide. I have some money . . . But not enough. I need money, a great deal of money."

"And you want me to give you money?" I asked.

"Of course," he said as if I had asked a really stupid question that I should have known the answer to.

"OK," I said. "I'll make a deal with you. Tell me who the traitor is. If you're right I will give you what you want."

"How much?" Patrick asked. He sat up straighter in the chair and smiled, knowing that he had a chance to live a few more years. The morning sun was pouring into the room through the window behind him. But before I could tell him how much I would pay, the window exploded and the front of his head was blown away. The bullet that tore through his skull smashed into the wall, shattering a framed picture. Patrick fell backwards at first, then he slumped forward and crashed onto the table and tray that had carried the coffee and eggs.

I fell to the floor and found myself laying on broken glass and bits and pieces of Patrick's face. I crawled away as fast as I could to the wall under the broken window as Patrick lay bleeding on the carpet. I hadn't heard the shot, and the noise of the glass breaking wasn't loud enough to attract attention outside the suite. The phone was on the other side of the room, and I had to get to it. But I knew that the sniper who had killed Patrick could still be out there, waiting for a shot at my head.

Remembering a few old war movies I'd seen, I crawled like a soldier through the jungle and pulled the phone off of the bedside table. As I did, another silent bullet shattered the bedside table. I grabbed the phone and pulled it with me as I crawled back against the wall. Whoever was shooting would not be able to get me there . . . I hoped. I dialed 911 and decided it was much safer to stay flat on the floor as I waited for the police.

Patrick was lying on his side. He had no face left. Blood and brains were everywhere. His feet and hands were twitching, but that stopped quickly. I couldn't tear my eyes away from his lifeless body. And I couldn't clear my mind of the life these people lead. Most, I am sure, do their particular kind of work out of love of and dedication to their Country. Some probably just like the life. But to risk life itself day after day, year after year, swimming with sharks in a black ocean of deceit . . . I just didn't get it.

I heard some commotion finally, outside, in the hallway. But there was no way I was going to get up and open the door for whoever was there. I hoped it was the police or at least hotel security. So I yelled as loud as I could, "Kick the damn door in!" and they did just that.

A half dozen uniformed cops and as many hotel security guards rushed into the suite, guns drawn, looking for somebody to shoot, and then through the open door of the bedroom where Patrick and I were on the floor. I pointed at the broken window with the curtains blowing in the breeze. I didn't need to say a word. One of the policemen carefully approached the window, hugging the wall, and pulled the drapes across to block out the sunlight and keep the killer from seeing into the room.

I stood finally and found the nearly empty bottle of bourbon. There was enough for one stiff drink which I downed quickly, not bothering with a glass. I had seen police handle crime scenes before, and I watched as they did what they do. A pair of plain clothes detectives walked into the room, one an older, grey haired man, the other a woman who apparently liked to over indulge in food. They looked down at Patrick's faceless body and walked to me. I was standing, leaning against the suite's bar, still in my underwear, holding the bottle by its neck, finishing what little was left of the bourbon.

They both held gold badges up, and the man said, "I am Detective Lieutenant Ben Herman. This is Detective Sam Waterbury."

"Sam?" I asked.

She said, "Short for Samantha . . . But I prefer Sam. Detective Waterbury to you."

"You're Morgan Crew?" Detective Herman asked.

"Yes," I answered and finished the bourbon in one long swallow, letting the empty bottle slip from my grasp and fall to the floor. "And that's Patrick Chesterson. He is . . . Or should I say *was* . . . with the CIA."

Waterbury turned to his partner and said, "Better call that in. They'll want their own people here. Better notify the FBI, too. They'll want in."

Detective Waterbury nodded and walked to the phone that still lay on the floor. Her partner called out to the uniforms, "It's Federal, guys. Don't bag anything yet. But take lots of photos and make notes of everything. We may be able to keep the body for autopsy."

He pulled a small, wrinkled notepad from his jacket pocket, searched for a pen in several other pockets, and when he found one he asked me, "So what happened?"

I said, "Patrick came to see me . . . "

"Are you with the CIA . . . Or some other Fed thing?" Detective Herman asked.

"No," I said. "Just a passerby."

"Why did he come to see you?" he asked. So far he hadn't written anything down in his little notebook.

"I don't know," I lied. "He was killed before he could tell me. He was sitting in that chair, across the room, with his back to the open window. Someone outside took a shot and blew his head off."

"Why did he come to see you?" the detective asked once again. He was implying that I was lying to him. I, of course, was.

It has been my experience that when I am involved in what could be serious criminal charges filed against me – I had to assume the police were looking at me as at least a suspect if nothing more serious – the best thing I could do is keep my mouth shut. I am not against telling fabrications and half-truths when necessary, so I said, "I don't know. As I said, he was killed before he could tell me."

"Did you kill him?" he asked.

"Oh man!" I said mockingly. "You got me copper. Yeah. I done it! I climbed outside that there window . . . On the ledge . . . Twelve stories up . . . In my underwear. And I asked Patrick to sit very still while I shot him in the head."

Detective Waterbury came back, looked at me and asked, "Why are you in your underwear?"

"Well," I said sarcastically. "I normally sleep in the nude, but I didn't last night. Do you see anything that interests you, Detective?"

THIRTY-ONE - The Cleaners

Before either of the Detectives could smack me up beside the head, as I knew they were tempted to do, two old friends walked into the suite. FBI Agents Morrissey and Chandler smiled knowingly as they stepped between the two Detectives and me. They faced the two cops, and Morrissey said, "Thank you for showing up, but we'll take it from here. Please tell your people . . . And the security guards . . . to pack up their things and not to touch any evidence."

"This is a homicide," Detective Herman said flatly as if he were used to the argument he must have lost a lot in the past. "You're Feds. You don't do homicides."

Agent Morrissey said, "This is a National Security matter. An agent of the Federal Government has been killed. We do handle that."

The two Detectives, Ben and Sam, turned dejectedly, and without another word they waived at all the uniforms in the room and led them out of the suite.

Chandler watched them leave, followed them to the door, closed it, locked it, and walked back to the bedroom. "You wanna' put some clothes on?" he said to me.

I took the hint and grabbed my clothes off the foot of the bed and pulled them on. As I did, I found it difficult to pull my eyes away from poor Patrick, lying on the floor having spilt his brains and blood all over the carpet. I was fully aware of the life's work Patrick had done. I could only imagine the lives he had torn apart using blackmail and extortion in service to his Country. And he and Susan certainly had committed many murders, probably too many to count. What would bring a man like Patrick Chesterson to want to be a field agent?

Morrissey and Chandler stood near the open door of the bedroom, looking into the suite's sitting room, their backs to me, talking too quietly for me to hear. I walked to them, still barefoot but wearing wrinkled slacks and shirt, and I asked them, "When are your forensic people going to get here?"

Morrissey and Chandler exchanged looks. Chandler nodded almost imperceptibly and Morrissey shrugged his shoulders. Chandler said, "There won't be any forensics. There won't be any Crime Scene people. There will be a Cleaner Team here in a few minutes. They will take the body; they will clean or replace the carpet and replace the window and anything else that needs to be replaced. There won't be any record of what happened here."

"But the police?" I asked.

"This is DC, Morgan," Morrissey said. "The DC police are used to this sort of thing. They've already gotten a phone call, and all records of this are being destroyed as we speak."

"Is that the same thing that happened when you guys told me Ian McCauley was murdered?" I asked.

"That was necessary," Chandler said. "You're new to this. Get used to it."

"I've got a very good killer out there threatening my life and the lives of my family," I said. "I'm in this to win this . . . You guys get used to it. You can lie to me, you can threaten me, you can do whatever you're inclined to do, but I'm not going anywhere. If I have, to I'll start buying what I need. I've done it before, and I can do it again. Now, you guys can either start cooperating with me, as your boss and Senator Hubbard told you to do, or get the hell out of my life."

Chandler was having a hard time holding back his

laughter. He went to Patrick's body and pulled the sheet the police had left in a bundle at Patrick's feet over the poor guy's head. He went to the dressing table and sat in the chair, covering his mouth with his hand to keep from laughing.

"OK, Mr. Crew," Morrissey said. He wasn't laughing however. "Have it your way. But remember that the best advice you're likely to get is to go home . . . Go away . . . Leave this to the professionals. What do you want to know?"

"Let's start with the personnel file on Henry Willis. And don't tell me there isn't such a thing. Every Government agency there ever was keeps too much paper."

"Why?" Morrissey asked. He pulled a pack of Marlboros from his jacket pocket and lit one. "My wife would kill me if she knew I was doing this," he said.

I answered, "Has his file on the traitor been found yet?"

"No," Morrissey said.

"I think I know where he hid it," I said. "But I need some personal information about him to be sure."

"Tell me," Morrissey demanded.

"No, I don't think so," I said maybe a little too smugly. "When I get it and read it and I'm done with it, I'll give it to you. Not before."

That set Chandler off. He couldn't hold back the laughter any longer. He burst out laughing and slapped his knee.

"What the hell's wrong with you?" Morrissey asked, obviously not too happy with his partner.

"I've never seen anything like this before," Chandler said. "The biggest National Security threat in years, and this guy is running the show. That's just plain amazing and very, very funny."

"And what would you do about it?" Morrissey asked pointedly.

Chandler stood, his laughter ended, and he walked

towards me. He stopped about two inches in front of me, his eyes locked on mine. He was maybe an inch or two taller than me, maybe ten years younger and a helluva' lot tougher than me. But I stood my ground in spite of that little voice in the back of my head telling me to run away.

He said menacingly, "I'd take this son of a bitch out of the Country, turn him over to the Saudis . . . The Egyptians . . . Maybe the Iraqis, with instructions to find out what he knows and then kill him."

"Yeah," Morrissey said as he took a big, deep drag on his cigarette. "That would be great. I'd do that, too. But we've got specific instructions."

Just then the soft, melodic chime of the suite's doorbell rang. Morrissey went to the hallway door and opened it. Five men, dressed in white coveralls and long, blue rubber gloves, walked in. Each was carrying some kind of tool or cleaning buckets and sponges. They went to work immediately.

A black body bag was pulled from a case, and Patrick was unceremoniously dropped inside. The bag was zipped, and two of the men walked out carrying the bag at the head and foot. They came back a few minutes later and joined the others in cleaning blood and brains, replacing the glass on the window, cutting out a large portion of the thick beige carpet that was stained beyond redemption and replacing it professionally so that no seam could be seen. The smashed picture that had been on the wall was replaced within the gold painted frame that had been undamaged.

Morrissey, Chandler and I stood aside and silently watched as they did their work. We said nothing while they toiled, even though I was bursting with questions that I needed answers to. Morrissey smoked three more Marlboros, and I was very tempted to bum one from him, but I didn't. I went to the suite's bar and found a can of cold Coke in the small refrigerator. I left the fridge door open and motioned to the two Agents to help themselves, which they did, taking cans of soda, nuts and chips and a couple of candy bars.

Less than an hour later the Cleaners packed up, nodded to the two FBI Agents, and left. Their job done, no one would ever know that a man had had his head blown apart in the suite's bedroom just hours before. There wasn't a microscopic spot of blood, not one thin strand of hair, not one small shard of glass, nothing. Patrick Chesterson, as far as anyone was concerned, had never walked into my suite and jolted me as I woke.

When the Cleaners had closed the hallway door behind them, I asked the two Agents, "Is that it? What happens to Patrick now?"

"Patrick who?" Morrissey asked. "I have no idea what you're talking about."

"That's it?" I asked. "I've heard your people speak about being 'disappeared'. Is that what's happened to Patrick?"

They looked at each other, and then Morrissey asked, "What else do you want?"

"OK," I said. "I'll leave it like that. I want to speak with Ryan Russell. I'll go to the safe house where he's being protected. Just tell me where it is."

"You can't do that," Chandler said.

"Why not? You were told to cooperate and tell me whatever I want to know," I demanded.

"You can't," Morrissey said. "Because Ryan Russell is dead. Someone attacked the safe house two nights ago. They killed the three Marshalls who were supposed to be guards, and they killed Russell, and they left. It was like a slaughter house. All four people were literally torn apart. Bones were crushed; Ryan's skull was cracked like an egg. It was like some animal got them. No one in the neighborhood heard or saw anything."

"Oh my God!" was all I could say. The madhouse killings weren't coming to an end. The killer – who I was sure was the man who had been held at The Levels – was wiping out everyone who had even a minor knowledge of the CIA traitor. And, at least on the surface, it seemed nothing was being done to stop this murderer.

And so I asked, anticipating the answer, "Is anything being done to stop this guy?"

"What guy?" Chandler asked. "If you know who killed Ryan Russell and the Marshalls you need to tell us."

"Come on," I said. "Stop trying to kid me. We all know what's going on."

"Tell us," Morrissey demanded.

I was being used and laughed at. I knew it. And I wasn't going to fall into their trap. So I said, "Bring me Willis' personnel file . . . Today . . . This afternoon. And if there's anything else on him in another file, I want that, too. Now, you'd better leave and get on that."

They left, laughing together at their little joke. When they reached the hallway door, I stopped them and said, "Oh, by the way. When you come back, I want a gun. Something big; something that can stop a bear. A 10MM semi-auto will do. And small enough to conceal. And you'd better bring two extra full ammo clips."

Morrissey opened the door and stepped into the hall.

"You aren't licensed to carry concealed," Chandler said, as he started through the doorway.

"Yeah. I know," I said simply as I closed the door.

I took the opportunity to shower and shave and phone for housekeeping to make up the room and bring fresh towels. I also needed to have the suite's bar and refrigerator restocked. I found the last bottle of beer in the honor bar and opened it. While I waited for all that, I turned on the TV. I was right in the middle of the news hour when Sandy walked in.

THIRTY-TWO – A Little Like Mike Hammer

As it turned out, we were in bed when housekeeping showed up. Sandy jumped to the floor and threw on my shirt. I pulled my underwear on, went to the door and said, "Come back later."

A woman's voice on the other side of the door said, "I do room, yes?"

Sandy said, "Let me try. I think she's a Spanish speaker. Let me try."

She spoke loudly at the door, "Por favor, vuelva más tarde."

The housekeeper answered, "OK, I come back."

I made sure the suite's door was securely locked before Sandy and I shared a leisurely shower that took the better part of twenty-five minutes. An hour later we decided we had better get out of bed, throw some clothes on, get some food and be prepared when . . . And if . . . Morrissey and Chandler returned.

Sandy ordered green salads, turkey sandwiches and coleslaw instead of the fries that were supposed to be with the sandwiches. I guessed correctly that my vacation from healthy food was over. Housekeeping returned to do up the bedroom as we ate in the sitting room, and I brought Sandy up to date on what had happened.

"So you really think the FBI is going to bring a CIA

personnel file and a gun to you?" she said maybe just a little sarcastically.

"I'd bet my last million on it," I said, and as I did, there was a knock on the hallway door. "See, I told you so," I said pompously.

It was, in fact, Agents Morrissey and Chandler. And they weren't happy. They had a large and very fat manila envelope and a small brown metal box with them.

"Sandy, I don't believe you have met," I said. "These are the FBI's best, Agents Chandler and Morrissey," but neither Morrissey nor Chandler apparently were in the mood to be polite. They said nothing to her.

Morrissey handed a manila envelope to me and said, "That's a photocopy of Willis' complete file. You can thank Ian McCauley for that. Your request was turned down flatly by the DCI. Ian made copies himself and managed to sneak them out to us. He said he wants to know what you find . . . To repay him for taking the risk," he said.

Chandler hesitated but finally handed a metal box to me. I opened the double latches and inside was a very lethal looking pistol and two spare clips as I had asked for.

"You know," he said. "If a traffic cop stops you for speeding and you're carrying that, you're gonna be in big trouble."

I decided to be a little nasty, a little like Mike Hammer, and I said, "Hey Agent Chandler. Trouble's my middle name."

Sandy snickered, and Morrissey burst out laughing so suddenly he started choking and coughing. When he was able, Morrissey said, "I'm going to put a couple of agents on you . . . For your protection . . . 24/7."

"I don't think so," I said. "I need a free hand."

"You need protection," Chandler said. "Personally, I wouldn't shed a tear if somebody blew your friggin' head off. But you've got influential people who, for some reason unfathomable to me, seem to want you to stay alive."

I was about to say something childishly smug again, maybe get the two Agents really mad at me, when Sandy stepped in between us, as she has become accustomed to doing when I start pissing people off.

"Agent Chandler," she said sweetly, smiling beautifully, and locking eyes with him. "We do appreciate all you're doing for us. I'm sure your people would protect us wonderfully. But I think having two or more of your very qualified Agents with us would just draw unnecessary attention. If you don't mind, I think we'll just go on alone. And if you want, we'll sign a release that will take the pressure off of you and Agent Morrissey if we do get ourselves killed."

Morrissey said, "That's very nice. Not too smart, but very nice. If that's what you want, that's what you'll get. But that doesn't relieve you of your duty to report evidence to us. Whatever you find needs to be given to us. If you don't, you will be committing a crime, and I will see you charged. Understand?"

"With all due respect, Agent Morrissey," I said as seriously as I could manage, "I've been warned of that before . . . Many times as a matter of fact. I've been in jail, I've been charged and brought to court, I have . . . Unfortunately so . . . Been forced to kill people. Whether you like to admit it or not, I will be successful once again. I've said this before to several different kinds of police . . . You will know what I know when I know it. Now, if you will please excuse us, my wife and I need to read the file on Henry Willis."

They left us alone.

I opened the manila envelope and dumped the contents onto the small dining table in the suite's sitting room. I guessed there were close to a hundred 8 ½ by 11 photocopied pages. Sandy and I sat side by side at the table and started to read.

The first thing that struck us was the detail of Henry's

personal life in the file. There were school records going back to the fifth grade running through his college years at Stanford. Henry was an outstanding student apparently. He excelled at mathematics and was taking advanced college level math in his freshman year of High School. He left his classmates in the dust studying all sciences. In the early days of computers he was called a genius by more than one teacher and Professor. His one failing was that Henry was uncoordinated and totally incompetent at all sports. Sandy said, “Henry must have been one of the original nerds.”

Henry’s adult life wasn’t as easy as his school years. He apparently had no friends in school; girls shied away from him; no one felt comfortable being with him because he would talk above them, around them, and through them. He carried this into his adult years, which according to the file, must have been very lonely indeed.

He was recruited by the CIA directly out of Graduate School where he had obtained a PHD at the tender age of twenty-two. He spent five years working in a small corner of CIA headquarters as an analyst of scientific data. He spent six days a week reading everything given him, in Russian, German, Korean and Mandarin Chinese – scientific journals, newspapers, magazines, and any papers and files field agents could get their hands on. The seventh day he spent writing overly detailed reports of what he read, linking details together that other analysts would miss.

And then came the Second Gulf War. Henry saw something in a few pages of grease stained paper, innocently folded inside a copy of a little known German pharmaceutical magazine that had been the property of a Syrian Intelligence Agent who had been kidnapped by the CIA. The papers were vehicle rental agreements for six 2 ½ ton Mercedes Benz trucks. The rental agency was located in Baghdad.

Henry did something he had never done before. He left his crowded little cubicle and ran from floor to floor, trying to find someone in Operations Section. Ian McCauley was the first to take the time to hear Henry out.

Henry and Ian sat together for three days trying to get someone to believe what Henry saw as so obvious. The Syrians were moving six truckloads of something – Henry was sure it was chemicals – out of Iraq. By the time satellites were redirected and Special Forces were flown in to Northern Iraq by helicopter, the six trucks had vanished across the border into Iran. To this day, no one knows exactly what was on those trucks.

But Henry was quickly moved from his dusty little cubicle up to an Operational Planning Unit, where his ability to apply analytical minutia to Field Operations was put to good use. In short order, he was at the center of Top Secret Field Operations.

It was during his first year on that job that he first suspected there was a traitor inside The Company. He put bits and pieces of seemingly disjointed data together in what he knew was mathematical precision leading to – in his vision – irrefutable evidence. But once again, no one would listen. Even Ian McCauley wouldn't believe this one. It turned into an obsession and it brought Henry to a CIA run mental facility, where he died.

The file was nearly a biography of Henry Willis. Sandy sighed several times and mentioned that she felt sorry for him. He had no life outside the agency and no friends. He had one obsession and that was fine Belgium chocolates, which he was never without.

The rest of the file consisted of performance appraisals and supervisor notations. There were regular background checks and financial record reports. There were the standard annual polygraph tests every Company employee who had access to confidential material took. He had received two commendations for work he performed and regular raises. He took vacation only when ordered to do so and when he did, he spent most of his vacation time in the office reading everything he could. There was nothing remarkable in the file, at least nothing that was obvious.

We read the last piece of meaningless paper, and when we were done, I felt the need to go immediately to the suite's bar. Sandy joined me and put together a large vodka martini for herself as I poured a stiff bourbon over ice for myself. We retreated to the couch in the sitting room.

"There's not much there to go on," Sandy said.

I put my finger to my lips and wrote on a telephone pad that was on the end table, 'The room is bugged.'

Then I said, "Hey, it's been a long day so far. How about joining me in the shower, babe?"

"Are you propositioning me, big boy?" Sandy said after reading the note and nodding. "Only if you scrub my back, OK?"

In the shower, with the water turned on full, I whispered, "I have a hunch where Henry's file is. Here's what we're going to do."

****

There is a small house in Forest Heights, Maryland, across the Potomac River from Arlington, Virginia. It's a nice house on the outskirts of a nice neighborhood, located at the very end of a cul-d-sac, at the edge of a few acres of trees. An equally nice family of four have lived in the house for the past seven years. They are good neighbors who take good care of their property, who talk to all their neighbors, who host a party for the neighbors every now and then. Their children have friends in the neighborhood; the boy plays little league; the girl just started kindergarten.

Dwayne and Terry Ballinger and their children, Dwayne, Jr. and Mary, live in the nice little house. Dwayne, Jr. and Mary were born in Forest Heights. Dwayne, Sr. and

Terry were born in Smolensk, Russia. They were children when they came to America with their parents, who were Russian sleeper agents, as are Dwayne and Terry, who inherited the job as well as each other. But with the fall of Russian Communism and the KGB, Dwayne and Terry now work for a gray, ghost-like reincarnation of the KGB that is closely associated with the Russian Mafia.

Their nice little house is now a safe house, available for those who need it. That day a strange man was using their house. He was a big man, and the few words he spoke were spoken in a heavy Russian accent. There was an aura surrounding the man that frightened Dwayne, his wife and children.

The phone rang. Terry answered it. The same metallic, electronically altered voice that had told them the man would stay there asked to speak with the man. Terry brought the phone to him and walked away quickly.

The man listened, said nothing, hung up the phone and left the house. His car was parked in the driveway. He drove away.

Five year old Mary hugged her mother around the knees and asked, “Mommy, is the bad man coming back?”

****

We stepped out of the shower, and as we dried ourselves Sandy asked, “Are you hungry?”

We knew someone, somewhere, was listening to what we said. I was positive that the FBI and CIA would not have passed by the chance for the cleaners to leave ‘bugs’ everywhere. The Intelligence Agencies wanted to know what we knew, and the traitor inside the CIA needed to know, too. So we spoke the script we had agreed on.

“Tell you what,” I said. “I need to go see Senator

Hubbard. How about we go to one of those extravagant restaurants Washington is famous for?"

"You wanna do that first?" she asked. "It's kind of early for dinner."

"No, after I see the Senator. I want to catch her before she goes home."

"Well, if I'm going to be seen at some high class place, I need to find a dress. I packed light to get here quickly," she said.

"OK, you do that, babe. I'll be about an hour. Is that going to be enough time to spend a fortune on a dress?"

"I'll try," Sandy said. "Should I get something very formal or a cocktail dress?"

"Not too formal, Sandy. I'm not wearing a tuxedo and that's final," I said.

We dressed and talked casually about Caroline and Betsy, without mentioning where they might be. Before we left the suite, I made up a couple of drinks for us, vodka martini for Sandy and bourbon and club soda for me. I made them strong, figuring we would need them to do what we needed to do.

I tucked the pistol I had been given tightly at my waist, under my belt, and we left the suite. Outside on the street, the doorman waived down a taxi. Sandy kissed me lightly and quickly, I hoped not too nervously as I was sure someone was watching us. She jumped into the cab as the doorman waived down a taxi for me. I watched a grey, nondescript Chevy pull away from the curb across the street from the hotel. It stayed three cars behind Sandy's taxi and followed her as she rode away.

As my taxi took me away, I turned to look behind me and saw a blue, equally nondescript Chevy pull away from the curb, again across the street from the hotel, and follow me. Morrissey and Chandler were intent on keeping an eye on us. At least I hoped it was the FBI and not someone even more dangerous.

I had to pass through security at the Senate office building. Before walking through the metal scanner I told the guard to phone Senator Hubbard's office to tell her I was there. They did, and I was able to bypass the scanner and keep my pistol.

While I waited to see Senator Hubbard, I flipped through a two month old copy of Newsweek. After waiting a half hour to see her, I was finally ushered into her office where we talked about her visiting Sandy and Caroline and me in California soon – light and meaningless conversation that I dragged out for as close to half an hour as I could make it. I hoped it would be enough time for Sandy to make it to the very upscale Georgetown Mall.

The taxi dropped Sandy at the main entrance to the mall. Inside she first stopped at a Starbucks and sat near a window as she drank a large coffee and pretended to read the Wall Street Journal. She glanced outside occasionally and found the two men who were assigned to follow her. They were dressed casually, no dark suits and white shirts, but even so they stood out like a couple of sore thumbs. Two fairly young guys hanging out together in a mall may not be unusual to most folks, but to Sandy they were just too obvious.

After leisurely finishing her coffee, while the two men following her started to impatiently shift from one foot to another, Sandy went from store to store in the mall. She peered through racks of clothes, tried on many, one at a time, bought nothing, and kept looking. After almost an hour of this, her two shadows were starting to wonder just what the hell they were doing. Maybe, they agreed, it was time to just pick her up and drag her in to the J. Edger Hoover Building in handcuffs.

Sandy strolled through the mall and finally found what she was looking for. At the entrance to the mall's restrooms, on the wall, was the small red box. A fire alarm. She sat on a bench outside the restrooms, checking her makeup with her pocket mirror, until there was a crowd of shoppers around her. She stood and walked past the alarm, reached up and pulled it without stopping. The entire mall was filled with a loud, screeching alarm of bells and sirens. Panic set in, and hundreds of shoppers all started running for the exits.

Sandy inserted herself in the middle of the frightened mass of people, hunched over because Sandy was taller than most of the crowd, and found an exit. The parking lot outside was a bedlam of people running in every direction. There was a bus stop at the far end of the lot and a bus arriving at it. Sandy ran and pushed her way onto it. She looked out the windows for the grey Chevy but it wasn't there.

Two more buses and she was back in downtown DC, where she got off and ran for the DC subway. She changed trains three times, as we had agreed she would do, and then emerged onto the street. She looked carefully for anyone who might be following her but saw no one. She waived down a taxi and rode to Arlington, Virginia.

The personnel file we had read on Henry Willis listed his home address, phone number, Social Security Number, blood type, bank account numbers, hair and eye color, and even his damn shoe size. Sandy's taxi stopped at the curb in front of Henry's home.

He had owned and lived in the right-hand side of a very nice Georgian duplex in a very good neighborhood. There was a tall, green, leafy tree in the front yard. There were roses and hedges and a green, well maintained lawn. We had agreed that there was no need to get inside Henry's house; the FBI and CIA would have been over every microscopic inch of the place and would have found nothing. There was no need to redo what they had already failed at.

It was a warm, clear day, and Sandy took great pleasure in walking the neighborhood. Block by block she strolled casually and seemingly aimlessly, taking in the beautiful yards. Birds were singing overhead, and a few butterflies fluttered around some sweet smelling flowers. Then she found what she was looking for.

Henry's file had some interesting information in it about him, but Sandy and I agreed that there was one very, very interesting fact. Henry, reports in the file indicated, was obsessive about secrecy. He never took the same route to anywhere twice in a row. He even went to different dry cleaners every time he wanted clothes cleaned. Nothing was ever the same in his life. Except for his one overpowering compulsion – Belgium chocolates. He ordered his chocolates online *almost* all the time. Each time from one of seven online retailers that carried what he loved. But when he was out and he couldn't wait for a delivery to arrive at his door, he went to a small, exclusive chocolate shop in a small, out-of-the way little group of shops four blocks from his home.

Sandy almost walked past the alleyway of small galleries, gift 'shoppes', tea rooms, and one chocolate shop. Along the sidewalk at the entrance to the picturesque alley were three white, wrought iron, filigreed tables, each with two matching chairs. Small glass vases on each table held a single red rose. And bordering the entrance at each side of the alley were thick climbing roses of bright pink. She smiled, very satisfied, and walked to the gourmet chocolate shop she had been looking for.

Inside she was greeted by the owner, Sissy Torrey.

"Hi," Sandy said with a big, broad, beautiful smile. "This place smells like heaven."

"Heaven is chocolate," Sissy said happily. "I'm sure of that. Would you like to sample something?"

"Thank you," Sandy said. "Maybe another time. I'm Virginia Willis. I'm Henry Willis' sister."

"Mr. Willis?" Sissy said. "He's one of my best customers. But I haven't seen him in awhile."

"I'm afraid Henry died . . . An auto accident . . . It was terrible," Sandy said managing to create a tear in her eye.

Sometimes I think she would have made it big in the movies.

"Oh my God! That's awful!" Sissy said.

"He was in the hospital for several days before . . . Well, they did all they could for him but he was just too badly . . . I'm sorry. It's hard to talk about."

"I understand," Sissy said. She came around from behind the counter and took Sandy in her arms. Sandy did a good job of sobbing on Sissy's shoulder. She pulled away and dabbed at her eyes.

"Before Henry died he said he had left a package with you. He asked me to pick it up."

"Oh, sure," Sissy said. "Mr. Willis asked me to keep it for him. You know, he bought the most expensive Belgium chocolates there are. I kept a small supply of them for him. Let me get the package."

"Thank you," Sandy said. "And let me have a box or two of those chocolates. You know, sort of a remembrance of my brother."

Sissy returned from her backroom with a battered and well worn package, wrapped in newspaper and tied with a rough hemp cord. And on top of the package she carried three boxes of the Belgium chocolates that Henry Willis was addicted to. Sandy handed Sissy two $100 bills but the look on Sissy's face told her that wasn't enough. A third $100 seemed to make her happy. Sandy thanked her and walked out with the box of 'evidence' Henry Willis had put together and the three boxes of very expensive chocolates.

It took some walking, but Sandy managed to find a cab driving by. She waived it down and slid into the back seat. She told the driver she needed to stop at a store that sold cell phones. He found one quickly enough, and Sandy bought three pre-paid 'throw away' phones. In a second cab, she started away, out of Arlington, and she phoned me on one of the cell phones.

"I got it!" she said. "You were right."

I had wasted all of Senator Hubbard's time that I

could and decided to walk awhile, forcing my two followers to leave their blue Chevy and take to foot.

"OK," I said. "I'm going to lose my friends and meet you. If I'm late, just do what we planned, and I'll catch up."

"Got it," Sandy said. "You be careful, Morgan. I don't want to lose you."

"Hey babe, the most that will happen is that I wind up in Gitmo sharing a cell with some son of Allah."

"Be nice, Morgan," Sandy said. "I keep telling you, they're not all bad people."

"Yeah," I said. "That's yet to be proven to me."

THIRTY-THREE - Henry's File

Our house, in the hills overlooking the San Marcos Harbor, was dark that evening. The car pulled to a slow stop at the curb, scraping tires along the curb. The driver, a big man in a grey suit, sat inside and left the engine running for a couple of minutes. The sun had set dramatically, lighting the sky over the pacific on fire. The neighborhood is one of large, wooded lots and the few neighbors we had were inside preparing dinners and talking about their days at work and school.

The driver got out of the car, took one final look around, and then approached our house. He knocked on the door and listened and looked. No sounds came from within, and no lights were turned on. He knocked again, a little harder, and rang the doorbell. Still nothing.

He tried the doorknob and found the door locked. One twist of the knob and he ripped the big brass handle from the solid oak door. He stepped inside the dark house. His eyes adjusted to the dark quickly as he walked through our house. He searched each room without making a sound.

The woman with the child would not be out late, he thought. The child was young and needed to be put to bed early. The man sat in our dark living room and waited. At ten to midnight he had to admit and accept the fact that the child had been taken away and he would not be able to take it from the young girl as he had been told to do. He got up and left our house.

****

The Greyhound bus ride from DC to Virginia Beach was long, slow, uncomfortable, and as clean as Sandy could hope for. We figured correctly that the FBI would have some access to airplane and train passengers and be watching for us. But bus travelers were something that would be hard to keep track of. And so it was The Greyhound system that took us out of DC and to some relative and perhaps short-term safety.

On the bus Sandy, travelling without me, was bothered by a fat, smelly man who needed a shave and a change of clothes. For some reason unfathomable to her, this guy thought he had gotten lucky, sitting next to a beautiful woman. After a half hour of his droning on about what a great salesman he was, Sandy opened her purse and took out a long and not friendly looking metal nail file.

She held it pointed at his groin and said, "How'd you like your nuts filed off?"

The man decided to change seats, and the rest of her trip was just long and slow. She arrived at the bus station in Virginia Beach a little after one in the morning. She carried Henry's file and left the three boxes of chocolates on the seat of the smelly bus as she stepped into the cold night air. She rented a nondescript Toyota using Peter Jascro's Amex card and drove to the coast. Our plan was to find a remarkably plain, cheap, and unnoticeable motel on some side street where we would spend a day or two figuring out what to do next.

She found a place called The Wave Crest Motel that fit the bill and checked in, using cash and ignoring the leers of the surfer type manning the desk as night clerk. She used the second of the pre-paid cell phones to phone me, and when I answered she said only, "Wave Crest" and hung up. She tossed the phone into a street corner trash can and drove back to the motel to wait for me.

I had not made it to the bus station in time to ride with her, but after making sure I dumped my FBI friends, I caught the next bus out of DC. I had to change buses in Richmond and arrived in Virginia Beach at a few minutes before three in the morning. I managed to find The Wave Crest Motel just as the sun was showing its face out on the Atlantic.

The surfer-type desk clerk was sleepily looking forward to his day shift relief to arrive. It took only a twenty dollar bill to convince him I was the beautiful lady's husband. I had no idea what name Sandy had used when she checked in, and with the twenty in hand, the clerk didn't care. He gave me a key to Sandy's room.

I unlocked the door to room #7 and stepped quietly inside. Sandy was curled under a sheet and light blanket, asleep. I undressed and slipped under the sheets next to her. It was a long and exhilarating day. Our adrenalin had had a field day pumping up our heart rates and blood pressure. The bed, as lumpy as it was, was like falling into a cloud. We slept until 2:30 in the afternoon.

I awoke to find Sandy lying at my side, eyes open, starring at me. "You're awake," she said, smiling at me.

"Ummm," I mumbled through a dry mouth. "How long you been awake?"

"Not long," she said. "A few minutes. You wanna' get up or . . .?"

"You know I can never get enough of you," I said. "But we've got a lot to do today. Let's get at it."

We showered in a moldy tub/shower. I had no razor, so shaving had to be put off. We dressed in yesterday's clothes and went out to find a place to get a meal. Sandy drove, and as she was about to pull onto the street, she suddenly threw the car into reverse and spun tires to get back to our room.

"We forgot the damn file," she said. I jumped from the car and retrieved Willis' file. She was right, of course. We shouldn't let the damn thing out of our sight.

We found a little breakfast and lunch grill on a side street a couple of blocks from the beach and, because we hadn't eaten since lunch the day before, we ate a lot of stuff we wouldn't normally have eaten. I thought the meal of fried stuff and coffee was great, but I wasn't about to admit that to Sandy who has spent the last several years working on my weight.

As we left, I debated mentally if I should suggest we stop somewhere and get a box of donuts to bring back to the hotel, but I knew what Sandy would say about that, so I just kept my mouth shut.

Back in our room at The Wave Crest Motel, we sat on the bed that had been made up by housekeeping, the newspaper wrapped package between us. Sandy managed to untie the cord and carefully pull the newspaper away, revealing a stack of papers and file folders and newspaper clippings and articles that had been ripped from magazines.

Page by page, we started to read everything in the five inch thick stack of stuff. Most of what was there was hand written – really hand scribbled – notes made presumably by Henry Willis. Most, we agreed, were decipherable only by Henry himself. They were cryptic and meaningless to us.

There were photocopies of parts of internal reports, some copied well and clear, and others poorly done and hard to read. There were clippings from newspapers from all over the world, some in English and others in foreign languages that we couldn't read. Interspersed throughout were articles torn from magazines, most about American politics and a few about military actions around the world.

The most interesting and confounding thing was a paper-clipped together stack of obituaries. They were the final memories of a few elderly people, a couple of soldiers who died in foreign places, and people who died in mid-life. There seemed to be no connection between these people however.

When we had read everything, being careful to keep everything in its original order because that, we agreed, might be important, we were mentally exhausted. Sandy lay back on the bed, her arm covering her eyes. I was pacing around the room. We were both wondering if maybe Henry Willis really was crazy, like the CIA thought.

Sandy said in a voice that revealed her near despair, "Maybe there really isn't a traitor inside. Maybe we're just being used. Maybe we should just bring the damn papers to the FBI or CIA or whatever and go home."

"You could be right," I said. "You're right more often than you're not. But explain the murders. Explain who raided The Levels. Explain T. J. Kohl who's not exactly stupid. She believes there's a traitor. Explain that man . . . Everyone seems to be referring to the guy as The Spy Who Would Not Speak."

Sandy remained on the bed, her arm still covering her eyes, and said, "I can't explain any of it. This world of spies and spooks and mercenaries and killers and lies and subterfuge . . . It's not real to me. It's maybe a maze that once you're in you can't get out."

Still pacing, my mind whirling around inside my head, I suggested, "Look, Willis began his career as an analyst. He apparently was a genius at what he did. He was also a mathematician. Unless he really was over the deep end, he saw some connections in all this mess. Maybe we should try to look at it like he would."

"How?" Sandy asked. "Hell, you have a hard time balancing your damn checkbook."

It would do no good for me to defend myself. She was right of course. All my life I had an unlimited supply of money I could dig into. And all my life I left it to other people to handle the record keeping, the accounting, the management of the businesses the family owns, the taxes, all of that. But I had an idea.

"Let's take some time and try changing the order of all this," I said waiving at the stack of papers. "Let's see if there is anything . . . Names, dates, places . . . Anything that connects one paper to another. Let's put stuff in chronological order if we can and then see if there are connections anywhere."

Sandy pulled herself off the bed, sighed and shrugged her shoulders. "OK, let's get started. What can it hurt?"

As we started, a knock on the door made us jump. I reached for the gun Agent Chandler had given me, and Sandy carefully stood to the side of the door as she opened it. The surfer type night clerk was standing there. I hid the gun quickly.

"You folks gonna' stay?" he asked. "You gotta pay since we ain't got no credit card for ya'."

The room, in spite of the very cheap and basic furnishing and the mildew and mold, was $99.00 a night, which in my opinion was $90 a night too much. I gave the guy two $100 bills and closed the door quickly. The door had a chain lock on it and a bolt lock, both of which I fastened.

Sandy said, "You know, some really bad guys may find us here. Are you really intent on using that gun?"

"My dear," I said trying not to sound too morbid. "The opposite of my not using it is something I don't want to think about."

And so time slid by as we laid out the papers across the bed, and then across the floor, because the bed wasn't big enough. First we put everything in as good a chronological order as we could. Some things, particularly the notes Henry made, some of which were barely readable, could not be placed in any order. These we laid out separately. Then we tried to find linkage . . . Any linkage, overt and obscure . . . Dates, places, names, anything . . . And moved papers with a link next to each other.

The photocopies of papers and files internal to The Company carried the most sense with them. These we moved around with the linked papers as we saw some linkage to other papers – perhaps meaningless to us but maybe obvious to Willis.

The day moved on into night, and hunger began to sound loudly. Without asking, I phoned a pizza delivery place and ordered two large pizzas and two liters of diet Pepsi (Diet, as a compromise to Sandy's complaint about the pizza that I was expecting, but it surprised me when the complaint never came).

We continued to work until the knock on the door stopped us. We were on our knees shuffling through the papers. We stood quickly, and I handed the pistol to Sandy. "Can you shoot someone if necessary?"

"If necessary," she said but there was reluctance and fear in her voice.

Sandy stood against the wall, on the hinged side of the door. I stood on the opposite side and called out, "Who is it!"

"Pizza delivery."

I opened the door a crack and saw a young black man in a wrinkled red and white shirt with a red and white baseball cap on. He was holding a red and white 'hot bag' case with two bottles of Pepsi on top.

"You want it or not man?" the delivery guy asked.

I opened the door enough to take the pizzas from him. I took the two bottles of Pepsi and handed him a hundred dollar bill.

"Hey man, I can't change that. I take credit cards," he said.

"Keep the change," I said and closed and locked the door.

Sandy breathed a sigh of relief, laid the gun on the

nightstand next to the bed, and said, "This is crazy. My God! We were ready to kill somebody! This isn't right."

"So what do you suggest?" I asked as I opened the pizza boxes. I wasn't as unsure about having to kill as Sandy was. Maybe it was the old caveman – macho thing. But I felt sure I could protect my wife and daughter. I had killed before when it was necessary; I knew I could do it again. Without telling Sandy, I told myself that from that point on, I would keep the pistol. I kept to myself that I'd be ready to use it.

"We're not safe," Sandy said. She took a slice of pizza and took a couple of big bites. "We need to move and find someplace safe," she said through a mouthful of cheese and pepperoni.

"Where?" I asked. "We can't go home. If we use credit cards they'll find us. We can't phone anybody we know because somebody, good guys or bad guys, probably are listening in and waiting for us to call someone. We can't get on an airplane. If we try to use passports they'll be waiting for us."

"Who is 'they'?" Sandy asked.

"The FBI, the CIA, any of the other ten or twenty intelligence agencies the Feds have, and more likely and more dangerously, that guy who's going around killing everybody."

"Do you think we have to protect ourselves from the FBI? From the CIA?" she asked.

"From the Agencies themselves? No, of course not," I answered. "But maybe there's one person in one of those Agencies we do need to protect ourselves from. Maybe Henry Willis wasn't crazy. I mean, somebody wanted Henry and the others dead for some reason. Maybe he was on to something. And now we have his file. Maybe that person is trying to find us and kill us."

"Oh my God!" Sandy almost screamed. "Caroline!"

She ran for her purse and pulled out the third pre-paid

cell phone. I took her hand in mine and said patiently, "Sandy. Don't waste the only throw away phone we have. There's a pay phone out by the office. I'll go use that. You stay here."

It was dark when I stepped into the parking lot. There was a dim light hanging outside, next to the door to our room. I reached up and loosened it enough to turn it off, burning my fingers, but I ignored it. There was light traffic on the road running in front of the motel. The parking lot had a handful of cars in it, all old and dirty except for the rental Sandy had driven. That wasn't good, but there was nothing I could do about that at the time. A young couple was walking by, hand in hand, enjoying the warm evening and moonlight. The cab of a big truck was parked at the curb across the street. It looked safe enough, but what the hell did I know? One of these spooks could be hiding in a shadow for all I knew.

I kept looking everywhere as I walked to the motel office and the pay phone. In my mind every shadow and every corner held a killer waiting to pounce on me. I dropped a quarter in the slot and dialed in Betsy's cell phone number. More coins in the slots and I could hear the ringing start. She answered on the second ring.

"Don't say my name," I said quickly.

"Oh, Hi Bubba," Betsy said. "How you doing, man?"

"I'm fine. How about C?"

"C's an A+," Betsy said. "You on the road . . . Headed for home?"

"No," I said. "Stay safe. Be careful."

"No problem," she said. I could almost hear her grin mischievously. "I've got this nasty biker gang looking after me."

I hung up and restrained myself from running back to the room. I walked slowly and watched for anything that moved. Inside Sandy was waiting anxiously.

"Caroline's OK," I said. "I'm still not sure Betsy's a

good influence on her, though."

"Why? What's she done now?"

"I think she's hiding out with some Hell's Angels types."

"As long as Caroline's safe, and she doesn't get any tattoos, I guess I can handle that," Sandy said, smiling happily for the first time in a couple of days.

We ate some now cold pizza and drank some warm Pepsi as the night wore on. We kept at the papers that were spread all over the room, shifting some from here to there, talking about ideas and possibilities, and walking around and over them hoping that a different angle might open a door. Sandy fell asleep on the bed, fully dressed, as I continued with it. I tried, in my tired mind, to place everything that Willis had put together inside the walls of the CIA, inside what I knew of The Company's operations, of the hierarchy and people who did the work. Exhaustion was setting in, but I fought off the urge to sleep.

Willis was a mathematician. Numbers started to race across my blurry eyes. I started to add numbers unconsciously to no avail. Maybe sleep after all, I thought. And then I started looking at everything in reverse and there it was. I saw what Henry saw. I saw the progression, step by step, fact leading to fact. Each piece was fitting together like a jigsaw puzzle, but a puzzle I had found the correct answer to. Henry was right, I could see it. I knew who the traitor was. And the best part of discovering what Henry Willis knew was that my guess was right. I had guessed some days before who the traitor had to be, and I was right.

THIRTY-FOUR - Here's What I Want You To Do

I woke Sandy and showed her what I had learned. I went step-by-step, explaining each connection and what I had gotten from each that led to the next. Her reply after I was done was, "Oh my God! If you're right . . . How do we get out of this?"

"We need to go to somebody we can trust who's powerful enough to handle this," I said.

"OK, genius. Who do we trust?"

Now that was a good question. Was the traitor working alone? Was the traitor in it for political reasons or money? If it was money, was there enough of it to buy the assistance of others inside the Intelligence Community?

"I think there's one person we have to trust," I said. "I think we should go see Senator Hubbard."

"I agree," Sandy said. "Let's leave as soon as possible. I hate this damn rat trap motel."

So we gathered all the papers together, trying to keep them in the last order we had separated them into. Sandy tied them into a neat bundle once again using the newspaper and cord Henry had used. One look around to make sure we hadn't missed anything and we started for the rental car waiting outside for us. I left the room key on the beat up old dresser and turned the lights off.

Outside there was a cool ocean breeze moving through the night. Sandy handed me the keys to the car, and I was unlocking the doors when the head lights of three cars flooded on us and we were momentarily blinded.

"Mr. & Mrs. Crew," a strangely accented man's voice said softly. "Please do not move. A man will come to you. He will want your pistol, please."

From out of the lights, from the right, a man wearing a leather jacket against the night air walked toward us. I was holding Henry's file; Sandy was holding onto my arm. I could feel her nervous shivering. The man reached inside my jacket and pulled the pistol from my waistband. He walked away with it and disappeared behind the headlights.

"Thank you," the man said. I seemed to recognize the accent. I remember hearing something like it before. Unless I was wrong, I thought that it might be South African. "I don't want to hurt your wife, Mr. Crew. So please do as I say. Please step two paces away from each other . . . I am sorry, I mean you should both take two paces to the side away from each other. My English is often halting, I am sorry. Please be patient with me."

Sandy looked up at me and whispered, "Do as he says, Morgan. Nothing stupid, OK?"

We took the two steps, Sandy to the right and I to the left.

"Very good," the man said. "That's the file, correct Mr. Crew? No need to answer. I know you found it. I want the file, Mr. Crew. That is something you cannot stop. I also am told to bring you and Mrs. Crew with me. If you resist I must hurt both of you . . . But in the end you will come with me anyway."

"No need for violence," Sandy said. "We'll come with you. But where are we going?"

"I cannot tell you that, Mrs. Crew. But now a man will come to you. He will take the file."

A man came from the left this time. He was bigger than the other man and wrapped in a trench coat. He took the bundle of papers from under my arm roughly and grinned maliciously at me. I didn't argue; I let the file go easily. The man walked away into the lights.

"Now if you will both stay perfectly still, a man will come to you. I am sorry that I must have you blindfolded. But I will not handcuff you if you promise you will not run away. Do I have your promise?"

Sandy spoke up before I could. I think she was trying to keep me from one of my all too usual snide remarks. "We promise. No handcuffs, please," she said.

A third man came towards us. This one was shorter than the first two and shorter than me. He wore a wrinkled, khaki army field jacket. His black hair covered his ears and he wore a beard that was cut short and close. From behind me, he reached up and tied a black silk scarf over my eyes. Sandy was next, and neither of us complained.

He took us by our arms, he in the middle, and walked us toward a car. Sandy was helped in first and then me. The driver, who was the man who had spoken from behind the headlights, said, "You've been very good to do as I say. Now sit back and stay quiet. It won't be a long drive."

Of course, we could have reached up and pulled the blindfold down. In the past, Sandy and I have taken on a few people, and between the two of us, I felt sure we could beat the crap out of any one, maybe two people. But I had no idea if the driver was alone, if the other two cars were still with us, or if there were a whole lot of guys in the three cars with us. So we sat still and silent and waited to see where we were going.

The route we took must have been on city streets, as there was a lot of stopping and starting. I could hear traffic passing in both directions, which told me our South African driver was taking it slow. Then it occurred to me that he probably was not used to driving on U.S. roads and maybe had a halting knowledge of where he was taking us. It was stupid to think he'd get lost . . . But what the hell, I hoped it anyway.

There was no talking in the car. The radio was turned off. It was an eerie feeling sitting in the back seat, blindfolded, with our hands folded meekly in our laps. But one thing did ease my mind. Wherever they were taking us, whoever wanted us, we were still alive and I figured we were going to stay that way. If they wanted us dead, we would be lying in the parking lot of The Wave Crest Motel rather than sitting in the back of the car.

And then the car slowed to a stop. I heard a metal garage door being opened. I was tempted to pull up the blindfold and take a sneaking look but I had Sandy to worry about. I couldn't risk doing that.

The creaking of the metal door stopped, and the car moved again, I assumed into a building. The car stopped, and I heard the car's door open and the driver get out. Sandy leaned against me and whispered, "I don't know where we are, but we just pulled into a creepy old warehouse."

"How do you know that?" I asked her.

"I pulled up the edge of the blindfold a couple of times," she said. "Didn't you?"

"Yeah, of course," I lied so I wouldn't sound like a pansy. I had to keep my manhood intact after all.

The rear door opened and the man with the South African accent told us to get out.

"Leave the blindfolds on," he ordered. "There are two chairs."

He took us by our arms and led us a few feet away from the car. He sat us in what felt like metal folding chairs. The warehouse was cold and damp. There was a definite odor of age and mold. Somewhere overhead a fan was spinning. It hummed quietly and made things even colder for us.

Our driver then said, "You can take the blindfolds off now. But just stay where you are. Don't turn around. Don't move at all; just listen."

We did as we were told and were met by a dark, black building. It was so dark inside that it was impossible to see walls in front or to either side. In front of us, maybe ten feet away, was another metal folding chair. On it was a small speaker with a wire running from it off into the blackness.

The still quiet was broken by a very weird, metallic like voice. It was like something out of a cheap horror movie.

"Mr. and Mrs. Crew," the voice said slowly. "You two are becoming a real pain in my ass."

"Can you hear me?" I asked.

"Of course," the disguised voice answered. "Do you have a question?"

"I have a couple of questions," I said.

"Then we will trade. I will endeavor to answer your questions if you will answer mine."

"Deal," I said. "First, are you going to kill us?"

"That is always an option . . . But it is a last option and only if all else fails. Now it's my turn. You've read Henry Willis' file. What did you learn from it?"

I looked at Sandy and she looked at me. We've been together long enough that we are used to thinking the same thoughts at the same time, especially when we're in trouble. She nodded and I turned to the speaker on the chair and said, "I guess the only thing we could figure is that Henry Willis really was a nut case. Your guy has the pile of papers everyone thinks is a file. It's just a crazy assortment of papers and stuff that have no meaning or relationship. I think Willis might have been paranoid or maybe a schizoid, but I'm not a doctor. If you're really crazy, and you got a pile of crap . . . You look at it and see what you imagine is there. I suggest, since you now have that pile of crap, that you look at it and see what you think."

"Yes, I'm going to do that," the voice said, as the speaker squeaked with static.

"Now it's my turn," I said. "Do you work for the CIA?"

The voice laughed over the crackling of the static. "You're not going to walk out of here knowing who I am. Do you really want to know? Because if I tell you, then you will die."

Then a voice I recognized spoke up from behind us, "Don't say anything else, Morgan!" Colonel Masterson said. He walked very quickly to the speaker, pulled the wire from it, and threw it away from him.

He looked up and turned in a full circle as he said, "I told you I'd bring them here. I'll have no part with murdering them. I like them, and I won't kill them."

He walked the few feet to us and stood in front of us. Masterson is a big man but not young, as reflected by the grey in his buzz cut hair. But he is powerfully built, square jawed, and with deep set piercing eyes. His face bore scars as testament to the wars he had fought. But as he looked at us, there was a look almost of shame clouding his face.

"I'm sorry," he said simply and softly.

"For what?" Sandy asked.

"For bringing you here. I thought all he wanted was the file and to throw a scare into you. Had I known there was a chance you'd be killed . . . Well, the money's not all that important."

"You were paid?" Sandy asked.

"Of course," Masterson said. "They call me a mercenary you know. I work for pay."

"Just out of curiosity," I asked. "How much did you get paid?"

"Twenty-five thousand," he said.

"More importantly," Sandy said. "Who paid you? Who was the guy who had to disguise his voice?"

"I really don't know," Masterson said. "I received an envelope with cash inside and one page of instructions. I did what I got paid to do. But I'm not a murderer of people who I like."

I'd heard that before. When Sandy and I were in

London we recruited the assistance of an American expatriate, Joseph Cross. He is a criminal, but I realize now he is a criminal with standards. Cross had fought as a mercenary in Africa, and in fact he helped us to get out of trouble and profited by it. I hold no animosity to professional soldiers – they do what has to be done for most people who can't do for themselves. But murderers who call themselves professional soldiers or mercenaries are lying. They are murderers and nothing more.

Masterson looked over our shoulders and said, "Gustave, please take Mr. and Mrs. Crew back to their motel. See that nothing happens to them."

We stood and looked behind us. A man, not as old as Masterson but equally as military looking, stood there grinning broadly at us. In the dark of the warehouse, we could see Gustave and Masterson but no one else.

The Colonel said, "Gustave Hendriks is one of my Lieutenants. He'll see you back. My advice is to go back to California. This is no place for you."

"That's your advice is it?" I asked. "Give me a minute to speculate here, will you? You want me to go home, right? But maybe you thought I would say 'no'. You want Willis' file. But if you asked me for it, maybe you thought I would say 'no'. So maybe you thought up this little stage play. You brought us here and rigged up that Halloween speaker gadget to make us think you're helping us. So now you have Willis' file, and you're going to let us go with advice to go home. We have nothing, since you've taken the file. Why not go home? No matter if T. J. Kohl is waiting there for us and kills me and my whole family."

Masterson looked bewildered. He glanced at Gustave and then asked Sandy, "Do you believe that, too?"

Sandy looked him directly in the eye. "Sounds about right to me," she said.

"Gustave," he called out. "Do you have the file?"

"Yes, sir. Of course."

"Give it to . . . Give it to Mrs. Crew." He said. "And then drive them anywhere they want to go. Don't let any harm come to them."

"You got it, Colonel," Gustave said. He opened the rear door to the car and held the string wrapped shabby pile of papers for Sandy. Colonel Masterson walked away, into the darkness and out of our sight.

Without words being spoken, Gustave drove us back to the motel. He drove a little faster this time, and we weren't blindfolded. In the parking lot, as we got out of the car, Gustave rolled down his window and said, "You're making a mistake not trusting him. He's a good man."

He pulled away and left us alone in the lot, next to Sandy's rental car.

"So what now?" she asked. She looked at the ugly blue painted door with the light above it still out and said, "I don't want to go back in there. That room stinks."

I thought about what we could do and found the choices to be very limited. DC wasn't our territory. I felt like the proverbial fish out of water.

"Let's go home," I said simply. Sandy nodded agreement, and we drove to the airport in Richmond. We were exhausted both mentally and physically. We hadn't changed clothes or had a good meal in days. And perhaps worst of all, most depressing of all, we were completely out of options.

We each had two drinks in the First Class cabin of the non-stop to San Francisco and then fell asleep. We slept all the way to San Fran; we slept right through whatever meal service there was – I had lost track of time and I didn't really care anyway.

At the airport I phoned a limousine company and twenty minutes later a car and driver picked us up and took us back to San Marcos. Sandy slumped in the back seat, holding the tattered bundle of papers on her lap. There were two crystal decanters of some kind of booze, but I was too fatigued to care. We drank whatever it was without caring what it was.

It was still morning West Coast time when we walked up to the front door of our house and saw that someone had broken in. I made a quick search of the house and found no one.

When I joined Sandy in the living room, she was already on the phone. Betsy answered on the third ring. "Come home," Sandy said her voice barely audible.

"I'm on my way," Betsy said. "Be there in a couple of hours."

I reached for the phone and dialed in Peter Jascro's private number. Peter, being my father's lifelong friend, almost an uncle to me, managing partner of Harper, Harper, Jascro and Nettles, and my personal attorney, has never refused me anything. When he answered, and after the usual admonitions to get out of whatever trouble I was in, I said, "Here's what I want you to do."

****

Betsy and Caroline arrived home as evening began to set in. Caroline was as happy to see Sandy and me as we were to see her once again. Betsy stood off to the side, smiling and feeling satisfied that she was needed . . . For the first time in her life. And as Sandy hugged Caroline, I hugged Betsy and whispered in her ear, "Thank you".

Later, Betsy and Sandy took the baby into her room and got her ready for bed as I paced around the living room. T. J. Kohl was still out there . . . Perhaps even outside our house waiting to kill us all. Add to that the fact that we were deep in a swamp with alligators and snakes all around us. I had to find a way out and keep us all alive at the same time.

We made some sandwiches and Betsy joined us to

eat out on our back deck, overlooking the San Marcos harbor and the Pacific. The darkening sky was overfilled with stars. The air started to cool off around a breeze coming in off the ocean. After finishing the sandwiches, we agreed that it would be more comfortable if we settled inside, and I told Sandy, "I'm going to phone Senator Hubbard."

"I agree," she said. She started mixing a couple of drinks for us. "But should we go back to DC? I really don't want to."

Betsy said, "Look guys. It's not just you. You got C to think about, too. I mean, you're sitting here where everybody knows you live, with no protection at all. Wouldn't it be easy for someone to find us here? How about I get some of my friends to hang around? I mean, some of these guys are huge and really mean."

I said, "Betsy, I appreciate you wanting to help but some very professional soldiers were killed just outside in the yard. I'm afraid your biker friends wouldn't stand a chance against whoever is out there. Besides, I want you to be able to go back to them with Caroline if necessary, and if you get some of them killed, they probably wouldn't want you around anymore."

"Yeah, I guess you're right," she said. "Look, it's late and I'm tired. If you guys don't want nothin', I'm gonna' hit the sack."

Sandy and I stood in the living room and stared into our glasses. After a minute or two, I said, "I think I'm probably right about who the traitor is, Sandy. And we're about as far away from the traitor as we can get. I think we're safer here, on our own territory, than in somebody else's backyard."

"But Betsy's right," Sandy said. "We're sitting ducks here. We need some protection."

We lingered over three drinks, then I phoned Senator Hubbard's office, and as usual I had to leave a message for her. But I emphasized the importance of the call. And we waited.

"Right now," I said, "I don't know where to get protection from. Who do we trust?"

It was three in the morning – six AM in DC – when Senator Hubbard phoned.

"Morgan!" she said brightly. "You're not in Washington anymore."

"Senator, thank you for returning my call. I've got a pile of papers Henry Willis called his file."

"You found it!" she said. "Where? What's in it?"

"I don't want to talk over the phone, Senator. Too easy for people to listen in. But I know who the CIA traitor is."

"You mean Willis was right?" she exclaimed. "He wasn't crazy? There really is a traitor?"

"I'm 99% sure," I said.

"Will you come to Washington and testify before my Committee?" the Senator asked hopefully.

"Sorry," I said. "There are too many people back there who want me dead."

Senator Hubbard paused for a moment or two and then said, "I'm coming to you."

THIRTY-FIVE – We Played, We Laughed

Betsy was stretched out on my Italian leather couch once again. This time she had pulled off her studded boots however. Sandy and I sat crossed legged on the floor. Betsy was laughing, I was laughing, Sandy was laughing, and little Caroline was having such a good time showing everyone how she could run from Sandy to me and then back to Sandy without anyone holding her hands, that she was laughing, too.

I had had a new front door installed that morning; the new one solid oak and much heavier than the old, and with two four inch deadbolts on it. But I also knew that anyone who could have broken down the old door would probably be able to do the same to the new one. I also had more outdoor lighting installed, just in case.

Betsy had brought Caroline safely back home in mid-afternoon the day before. I didn't ask where she had taken Caroline, but I knew there was a gang of bikers taking care of her. I considered the possibility that she might have to take the baby away again before all this was over. But she had done a good job at keeping her safe. I figured if she could go underground – even if that meant staying with a biker gang – then Caroline would be safe.

I was about to suggest that we have something to eat when the doorbell rang. I had my little .38 tucked into my waistband at my back. Sandy got up off the floor and picked

Caroline up. Betsy jumped from the couch and pulled Sandy back into a corner next to the big stone fireplace. And then she did something that both surprised and impressed me. Betsy stood in front of them. My opinion of her keeps getting better.

I went to the door and looked through the peep-hole. It was evening but almost as bright as daylight with all the new lighting outside. But all I could see was a shadow of a heavy set man, his back turned to the door.

"Who is it?" I yelled, but the door was too heavy. I made up my mind to have an intercom installed the next day. So I pulled the gun out and unlocked the door. I edged it open and looked out.

"For Christ sake, open the damn door," Bob Sommers said.

Bob is the sole Police Detective on the San Marcos Police Department, and today he runs the whole place. He and I spent four years in college together, having a lot of fun, chasing a lot of girls, and drinking a lot of beer. He is my best and closest friend.

I opened the door, and he pushed his way in. Bob is a big guy. Sandy has been trying to get him to lose some of the 240 pounds he carries around. She has been successful at getting him to quit cigarettes, but point at food when Bob is around, and he will eat it, no matter what it is or what time of day it is. So when he pushed his way into the house he very nearly floored me.

I closed and locked the door using my left hand as I held the .38 in my right hand. Bob looked down at it and asked, "What the hell is that all about?"

"That's a long story, Bob," I said and tucked the gun back into my belt.

Sandy rushed up to Bob and would have thrown her arms around him except for holding Caroline. "Hey! How's my best girl!" Bob said grinning like a kid as he took Caroline into his arms. He held her high up above his head and spun around. She giggled with delight. "You being a good kid? You keeping your crazy folks outta' trouble?" he said and laughed with her.

Betsy was standing with us. She took Caroline from Bob and said, "You're going to talk with Sandy and Morgan. Me and C will go into the kitchen and make some tea, OK?"

"A cold beer would be better," Bob said.

"Tea is what you get," Betsy said as she walked from the room. "You want a beer, go someplace else. You should be showing C a good example," she said and grinned to herself.

We watched Betsy and the baby until she closed the kitchen door behind her. Then Bob said, "OK, now tell me what the hell's going on in my town."

"Bob, this has nothing to do with you," I said.

We followed him as he went to the living room and sat in the chair he always sits in at our house, which just happens to be my favorite chair. He crossed his legs and looked around the room before saying, "There's this really odd looking black van parked out on the street. The windows are all blacked out. There's a counterfeit plate on the damn thing . . . I ran it. I pounded on the doors, front and rear. I think there's people inside, but they ignored me."

Sandy and I looked at each other and again our minds were in sync. It could be anybody. Maybe T. J. had picked up a van. Maybe the guy who was out there killing everybody was waiting in the van. But why be so obvious? A killer would be in the shadows, not in broad daylight, and very, very obvious. It had to be some kind of good guys out there. We nodded, and without words we were able to agree, and Sandy said to Bob, "We don't know anything about it."

"Then I'm going to call a tow truck and three or four patrol cars," he said waiting for our reply, but we said nothing. He waited, but all we did was stand there and look at him, both of us grinning casually, trying to look like we didn't care.

Sandy turned and headed for the decanter of Wild Turkey I keep nearby and poured two healthy glasses of it over ice. She handed one to Bob . . . With the thought that it would at least delay him in what he wanted to do . . . And one to me. I nodded just enough to let her know I knew what she was doing.

We sat next to each other on the couch and stared at our friend as he drank the bourbon. The silence was almost painful. I wanted to shout out that a bunch of spook murderers were after us, but I didn't.

Bob finally broke the silence, "OK, if you two don't know anything, then I'll use your phone, if you don't mind, and get a crew out here. That van's gotta' go."

"Wait," Sandy said. "Why don't you and Morgan go out there first? See if you can get anybody inside to say hello."

"That sounds like a good idea," I said. "It's probably just some kids smokin' pot and getting' nookie."

Bob followed me to the front door but stopped me before I could open it. "You got a permit to carry that peashooter you got tucked at your waist?"

I pulled the little .38 from my belt and laid it on the entryway table. Walking slowly ahead of Bob we reached the sidewalk. Then the thought occurred to me that Bob had a gun and I didn't. Just in case, I stepped aside and waived Bob to go ahead of me.

The van was still there, parked a hundred feet down the street from my house, at the curb in front of an area of trees that stretched down a hillside too steep for a house. It was jet black and very clean. The sides and back were without windows; the front windows were heavily blacked out so that it was impossible to see inside.

"See those tires?" Bob asked. "They're military. It would take a .50 caliber to blow them out."

We circled the van, and as we did Bob pounded on

the walls and back door. He yelled, "Anybody inside! Get your friggin' clothes on and come on out! I'm a cop!"

I let Bob walk around the van again, pounding harder and yelling louder. A car pulled up to the curb and stopped a few feet behind the van. The driver's door opened and Colonel Masterson got out. He was smiling and shaking his head as he walked to Bob and me.

"You guys are something else," he said shaking his head and trying to hold back laughter.

Bob pulled his gold shield out of his coat pocket and held it in front of him. "I'm a cop," he said. "Who the hell are you, and what the hell are you doing here?"

"Bob," I said. "This is Colonel Masterson. Colonel, this is Detective Lieutenant Bob Sommers, San Marcos Police Department. He's also a very good friend of mine."

"Colonel?" Bob asked. "What branch of service?"

"Sort of my own," Masterson said. "Look, I don't know how much Morgan has told you, but I'm here to protect him."

"Protect me?" I asked. "Why? Who's paying the bill?"

"This is pro bono," he said. "I owe you for being suckered into taking you to the warehouse."

"What warehouse?" Bob asked. He was getting angry. I knew him very well, and I knew there was a point where our friendship meant nothing. He put me in jail once . . . But I have really great attorneys.

"Bob," I said. "Come inside. I'll tell you what I can."

"What about him?" Bob demanded. "I know what that damn van is. Look up on top. See what looks like a satellite radio antenna? That's a CCTV camera. And it keeps moving. Whoever's inside is watching your house."

I asked Masterson, "Can you tell Bob who's inside?"

"You know him, Morgan. It's Gustav Hendriks. He's got two other of my men with him."

"Are they going to stay?" I asked.

"As long as I tell them to. Of course they're working in shifts."

"And what if I tell you to get the hell outta' town?" Bob demanded.

"Then I'd let you arrest me and see what happens when you can't charge me with anything. Assuming of course that Morgan wants us to stay," Masterson said. He was smirking as he said it. Masterson was taller than Bob. Bob may have outweighed Masterson by 60 or 70 pounds, but the Colonel was 100 pounds meaner, and both of them knew it.

Bob turned to me and asked, "Are these people your guests?"

I had to think about that one. T. J. Kohl was still out there somewhere and apparently the best the CIA and FBI had weren't good enough to catch her. Colonel Masterson had kidnapped us, albeit politely and gently, and brought us to that warehouse where the disguised voice threatened us. What real part did he have in that? But if he and his soldiers were outside, locked in their van, what harm could it do?

So I said, "They are my guests, as long as they stay outside my house."

"What about that counterfeit license plate?" Bob demanded.

Masterson looked at me for an answer or maybe an excuse that Bob would accept. I said, "Bob, as a favor to me, ignore all this for a couple of days. I'll explain inside. Let the Colonel stay here until this is all over."

Bob agreed but added, "Colonel whoever you are, you can stay here, but break any law, especially using any violence, and I will bust you and throw your ass in my jail. My friendship with Morgan goes only so far."

We left Masterson on the street and walked back to the house. Masterson pulled a small radio from his jacket pocket and spoke to Gustav inside the van. I heard him tell Gustav that the orders have not changed. Then Masterson walked to his car and drove away.

Inside the house Betsy had a platter of ham

sandwiches and a bowl of potato chips waiting. Bob, as usual, without waiting to be asked, dove in and finished a big sandwich before saying a word. He looked at the pitcher of iced tea, then glanced around the room for some beer or anything but tea but found nothing. He ignored the tea as Betsy filled four tall glasses.

With his mouth full of the last of the sandwich, he managed to say while spitting only a few crumbs down his shirt front, “You got something to drink? Maybe a coke or something? Beer would be better, but I guess your little biker chick pick-pocket ain’t gonna let me have any.”

As Betsy went to the kitchen for a can of soda, Bob asked, “OK, tell me, what’s going on?”

Sandy, holding Caroline, said, “Morgan, I’m not sure Bob should be involved in all this.”

“Involved?” Bob said. “I’m the friggin’ cops around here! I get involved in everything in this friggin’ town. Now tell me what’s going on.”

“I agree with Sandy. It would be best if you weren’t involved,” I said.

“Morgan . . . Sandy . . . You’ve got some guy who thinks he’s got his own little military force out there. I’d say he’s some kind of mercenary, and that bothers me. Don’t think I didn’t see the bulge under his left arm. The guy’s carrying, and I’d bet he doesn’t have a permit or license.”

“Please. Bob,” Sandy said. By way of trying to bend him around her little finger she put Caroline in his arms. The baby gurgled happily and reached for his nose. “Let this one go for the time being. There’s stuff going on that you can’t be involved in.”

“You know, Morgan,” Bob began. “I’ve busted you before. All your money and power and influence don’t exempt you from the law. You and Sandy are my best friends. Hell, for some unknown reason you made me godfather to Caroline . . . I’ve not figured that one out yet . . . But if you pull one of your stunts like you’ve done before, I’ll see both of you in my jail and maybe even the baby, too."

Betsy returned with an open can of Pepsi and almost laughed when she said, "Does C get her own cell? How do I get copies of her mug shot?"

Bob left with me following him. He stopped at the door and looked down at the .38 I had left on the entryway table. He shook his head as I picked it up and tucked it securely under my belt.

****

The next two days could have lasted forever; at least I wished they would. We played, we laughed, and Sandy and I took Betsy and Caroline to The Country Club for lunch on a clear and warm day. Sandy, Betsy and I all saw the black van following us to the Club and back home, but no one said anything about it, maybe not wanting to jinx the spell of good times.

Caroline was showing off how she could walk all by herself, all over the place, and finding things on table tops that interested her enough to pull them off onto the floor. We took turns following her around and tried to keep her and all the interesting things safe. I managed to extricate myself from the room whenever it was diaper changing time.

On the morning of the third day, as Sandy and I enjoyed a bright clear morning out on the deck, finishing a pot of really good and very strong coffee, Senator Kelly Hubbard showed up. The short time away from the world of spies and spooks and killers had almost cleared my mind of the fact that our lives were in danger.

Betsy walked onto the deck and told us, "There's a woman here. Says she's Kelly Hubbard. She looks rich, so I figured you guys know her. I let her in. She's in the living room."

THIRTY-SIX - Rock Solid Evidence

Senator Hubbard greeted me with a big hug. She had never married and had no real family. I was as close to a nephew as she would ever have, and she made the most of it. She had not met Sandy before and as everyone else when first meeting Sandy, she was taken with her beauty.

"My God!" she said to Sandy. "What do you see in that big lug you married? You're much too pretty for him, you know."

Sandy laughed and thanked her as Betsy came into the room with Caroline. The Senator took the baby into her arms, and after a few minutes of the usual flattery, with little Caroline enjoying every minute of it, Betsy took Caroline and left the room. "I'll make some fresh coffee," she said as she walked away.

We found seats in the living room, and for what was the longest minute in my life, we said nothing. The three of us just looked back and forth at each other, very uncomfortably.

Senator Hubbard broke the silence. "The van . . . Out front . . . That's Masterson, right?"

I wasn't sure if I should tell her everything, so I said nothing. Senator Hubbard nodded knowingly. Being on the Senate Intelligence Oversight Committee, she knew how secrets were handled.

"You've got Henry's file." It was a statement, not a

question. She was sitting on the edge of the chair, nervously twisting her hands in front of her.

"It's not so much a file as a pile of papers," I said. I asked Sandy to get it and bring it into the living room.

"You said you know who the traitor is," the Senator said. Again it was a statement, not a question.

"I do," I said as Sandy carried the tied up bundle and handed it to me.

"That's it?" the Senator said, surprised at the tattered stack of what appeared to be garbage.

"That's it," I said. "Let me explain . . ."

"OK," she said. "Give it to me and I'll take it back to Washington. It'll be safe with me. I have a private plane waiting."

"Senator," Sandy said. "Whoever you give this to would think it's just a pile of papers put together by a man who had gone over the deep end. It wouldn't make any sense to anyone."

"And what happens if it gets into the wrong hands?" I asked. "There is a traitor out there somewhere, and if Henry's file is spread around enough it could just disappear."

She thought about that and then said, "But it made sense to you? Why? . . . How?" Hubbard asked.

Sandy and I looked at each other again, once again sharing that mental connection we have. I said, "We'd have to explain it, Senator. We'd have to go through it page by page or it wouldn't make any sense to you or anyone else. But the connection is there once you put everything together."

"OK," she said and smiled at having gotten at least a suggestion that the answer lay in the pile of paper. "Then come back to D.C. with me. We'll take it to my Committee. You can explain it there."

"We aren't going back to Washington right now," Sandy said. "There are just too many people out there who would love to see us dead. We're safer here."

"You're safer here?" the Senator said. "You're kidding, right? I can have the FBI, the Secret Service, Federal Marshalls . . ."

I interrupted her and asked, "Can you guarantee that one of the people protecting us isn't the traitor?"

Hubbard sat back in her chair. She was frowning, in deep thought. "OK," she said. "So what do we do? If there is a traitor . . . I've got to stop him."

I said, "Let us go over the papers with you here. If you see what we see then the problem's solved. But we're not leaving here, Senator. If necessary . . . Bring your Committee here."

Betsy brought a very formal silver tray and coffee service into the room. It was a little bit too much for morning coffee, but what the heck, she was trying. "Can I watch? This stuff is fascinating." she asked as she carefully started to fill Sandy's best china cups with the coffee.

We said she could, of course. In the back of my mind, I hoped that she could use what I was beginning to believe was really good 'smarts', as she had in the last few weeks. She had shown me she had a brain capable of solving puzzles and coming up with good questions, if not answers. I was even beginning to appreciate having Betsy Concanon around. I was beginning to trust her.

And so Sandy untied the string holding the bundle of paper together, and we started to lay out what we had across the living room floor. It was Sandy's well thought out suggestion to go step by step through what she and I did at the Virginia Beach Motel. We started chronologically and explained each piece of paper as we laid it out. It took over an hour to do that, and when we were done I said, "As you see, it doesn't make much sense."

"You're right," the Senator said. "It seems Henry Willis really was insane."

I looked down at the mess of papers lying across the carpet. There were photocopies of CIA papers, photocopies of FBI papers, photocopies of Military Intelligence papers. There were shards of paper scotch-taped together that appeared to be handwritten notes from anonymous people who could be in any one of the several score of Intelligence Agencies the U.S. has out there. There were articles torn from a number of newspapers from around the world, most in English, some from foreign countries. There were a number of multiple page articles from news magazines that had been stapled together. And there were dozens of scraps of paper on which Henry Willis had scribbled notes in pencil or pen. On the surface, they made little sense.

The photocopies were bits and pieces of what must have been intelligence operations. They were in English but in an intelligence-bureaucratic form of English strange to us. Neither Sandy nor I knew enough of intelligence language to know a lot of what they referred to. We knew they had to be important, because most of them had been stamped in large red letters: 'EYES ONLY' or 'CLASSIFIED' or 'TOP SECRET'. And when we put them with other papers in the pile, we knew what they meant.

The newspaper articles seemed like disjointed reports of house fires, auto accidents, and armed robberies; from all over the world. Of the twenty-one news magazine articles Henry had ripped out, only three had any immediate and obvious relevance. These were articles about operations some Special Forces Units had been involved in. And each described operations in which a lot of men had been lost in failed operations in Afghanistan.

That was what Sandy and I had seen in the Wave Crest Motel. Meaningless jumbles. Then Sandy and I working together started to re-sort the papers on our living room floor as we had at the motel. We explained in detail all we had done and moved papers around as we explained. The Senator was standing and walking around the papers, following us, looking down, and trying to follow as we spoke. She asked pertinent questions that we tried to answer based on what we knew to be true.

What was obvious to Sandy and me was rapidly becoming obvious to Senator Hubbard, that Henry Willis had collected all he could on failed intelligence operations; spies captured or killed, military Special Operation raids gone bad when the bad guys were waiting for them. It was all just bits and pieces of what would appear to be mere unassociated data, but when put together in the right order, those bits and pieces made it clear that someone was giving information to our Nation's enemies, and as a result, people were being killed and secrets were lost.

Sandy and I agreed that American Intelligence Operations had to be planned as perfectly as that type of thing could be planned. I mean, the Boy Scouts weren't doing the planning. Yet all of a sudden, three years ago, operations began to fail; agents were killed; secrets weren't secret anymore.

The Senator was getting excited as we started to mix and shuffle the papers into their final order. In fact she made suggestions of where a few sheets should be placed, based on what she knew of intelligence operations.

After more than two hours of unscrambling paper, I stepped back and said to Senator Hubbard, "Ok, that's it. Do you see it?"

She said nothing. She walked in a circle around the papers. And Betsy was doing the same thing: looking and studying, and by the look on her face, she was beginning to understand. Betsy took a step backward, put her hand to her mouth and gasped, "Oh my God!"

"You see it, don't you," Sandy asked her.

Betsy took a couple of more steps backward, staring down at the flood of papers. Her face turned scarlet, and then the color washed away, leaving her looking sick.

She looked up at us and then back to the papers. "You mean I'm right?" she whispered.

"I think so," I said, excited at the fact that someone

else saw what Sandy and I had seen. I was actually starting to feel a little bit of pride in our little biker-chick nanny. "Tell us," I said.

"Well . . ." she started, hesitating, but wanting to go on. "Each of these things that were screwed up . . . I guess you call them operations, right? Each of these things is about different people. I mean, a few are from the CIA. But some are operations by the FBI, some by the DEA, some by the Army, some by the Navy. Look at that one over there," she said pointing to four pages layered together. "That's about some CIA guy who was blackmailing some North Korean scientist guy. The CIA guy disappeared while getting some secret stuff there in Korea. That last page there is from a South Korean English language newspaper saying the North Korean scientist guy turned up dead on a beach in South Korea."

She took a step or two to the right and pointed down. "This here is about some Navy spy guy who was supposed to sneak into Iraq, steal some stuff, and get out. He never came out. Some Israeli guy undercover inside Iraq said the Navy guy got caught and killed. And over there it's about some secret stuff something called the NSA couldn't keep secret. It's all different," she said.

"And what does that mean?" Sandy asked her.

"You guys said your traitor dude was in the CIA," she started. "That don't make sense."

We waited as Betsy walked around the piles of paper again. "Why doesn't it make sense, Betsy?" I asked her anxiously.

"I can remember 9/11, when those Arab guys flew planes into buildings. I was young, but it really shook me up, you know? I watched the news for days. I can remember all the stuff about how our Intelligence Agencies weren't talking to each other. There was a lot of stuff in D.C. about that. You know, the guys in Congress doin' all those hearings on TV. They said if all the Agencies would have shared what they had, maybe they could have stopped the attacks."

Betsy paused again and circled the papers on the floor once again. I asked, "So what? What does that mean, Betsy?"

"It means your traitor dude isn't in the CIA," she said proudly. "Anybody inside the CIA wouldn't know what the other agencies are doing. These spy guys don't talk to each other, do they? And nobody inside the other agencies would know what the CIA is doing. It has to be somebody who knows what they all do."

"You're right, Betsy," Sandy said. "And who would that be?"

Betsy stepped carefully into the middle of the laid out papers, bent, and picked up a scrap of paper with greasy finger prints over quickly written pencil scribbling on it. She held it up as she turned to us and asked, "Who wrote this?"

I answered, "We believe it was written by Henry Willis. There are dozens of handwritten notes like that. What does that one say?"

She read, "'Nathan Strasburg liaison for 'Intel SenComm'. Intel SenComm. That's your committee, Senator, isn't it? You and the other dudes on that committee know all the secret stuff that goes on, no matter who is doing it, right? That means this Nathan dude had access to all the different agencies and what they were doing, doesn't it?"

"That's exactly what that means, Betsy," I said. "It means that Nathan Strasburg worked for the United States Senate Intelligence Oversight Committee. He was the go-between man. He could get his hands on anything he wanted."

Senator Hubbard was in shock. She was looking for a place to sit down before she fell down. She felt faint; she felt sick. "You're saying Nathan was the traitor?" she asked, stunned and unbelieving.

"I don't think so," I said. "I mean, yes he was selling secrets but he wasn't working alone. If he were the traitor everybody is looking for, he wouldn't have just disappeared. If he were the traitor, he would be too important to be killed or pulled out and sent out of the Country. That guy who was at The Levels was sent to kill everyone who suspected Henry Willis might have been right. If Strasburg were the traitor, and if he simply left the Country to save himself, all those people who were killed wouldn't be dead right now. No, I think Nathan Strasburg is among the dead. And all the others were killed to protect the traitor.

"I asked my lawyers to do some work for me. They did some background on your Intelligence Committee . . . You know, how it operates and all that. I'm ashamed to say that I've never taken an interest in how our Government operates. I think that maybe if more people took an interest in the things Washington does, we might see a different kind of Government running things. Anyway, it seems that Nathan Strasburg was classified as an Investigator for your Committee. He earned $58,000 a year, and he had a CIA retirement payment of $32,000 a year. Washington, DC and the suburbs are very expensive places to live. That money wouldn't go very far.

"But my lawyers were able to find a little bank account Nathan had in a Private Bank down in Grand Cayman. It's a numbered account, but we were able to break into it with some tricky computer hacking. Nathan shows up as owner. The balance in that account is exactly 338,540 American Dollars as of the day before yesterday."

"So Nathan is the traitor," the Senator said. She was confused, and I think she didn't want to admit that someone was selling secrets right under her nose. I knew, and I'm sure she knew, that when that got out, her career would be over. The media would roast her and all her colleagues on the Committee over really hot coals.

Sandy said, "No, he was the person who stole the secrets. What he stole was worth a hell of a lot more than what he had hidden in the Caymans. He handed off what he stole to the traitor who is a mole somewhere inside the Intelligence Community. And the mole was controlled by someone else. I have absolutely no evidence of this but I'd bet Morgan's last million that person is or was in the U.S. and controlled not only the traitor but ordered all the killings, too."

"Then who?" she asked and her blazing stare was like knives thrown at me.

"Right now," I said. "It's more important that my family is protected and safe. If I tell you who we suspect, and you go back to Washington, you have to report it. Who do you report it to? And once you do, it becomes public that Sandy and I know who the traitor is. Then our lives are in jeopardy. No, until I figure out what to do with this, how to expose the traitor and protect my family at the same time, I'm not going to tell you or anyone else."

Senator Hubbard said, "And if I send the FBI out and toss you and Sandy into jail . . . What will you do then?"

Betsy spoke up grinning broadly, "Hey! Don't forget me and C. I think I may know who the traitor guy is, too. I been in jail before but it would be a new experience for C."

"How about it, Senator?" Sandy asked. "Are you going to put all four of us in Jail? Are you going to take our baby away, maybe? Or are you going to trust Morgan for a few more days?"

The Senator, Kelly Hubbard, my mother's childhood friend, said nothing. She turned suddenly and stormed from our house, slamming the front door behind her.

THIRTY-SEVEN - I Had A Hunch

"We did it, Morgan!" Sandy said dancing into my arms and spinning me around. "We did what all the spies couldn't do! We actually figured it out!" Sandy wasn't worried or frightened; in fact she was as happy as I was. Then cold reality began to edge its inevitable way through the cracks in my good mood. And our little biker-chick Betsy was the chauffer who drove reality to us. She watched unbelieving as we smiled and laughed and danced around the room.

"Hey guys," she said. "Get real, will you?"

"What?" I said. "We were right, weren't we?"

"Sure," Betsy said. "You were right. Almost, anyway."

"What do you mean 'almost'?" Sandy said, almost whispering. She stopped dancing but held onto me.

"OK, sure," Betsy said. "Remember that this Strasburg character was walking secret stuff to some spy guy. He was getting paid. Yeah, he's probably dead now. But the guy he was giving that stuff to ain't . . . I mean isn't dead. That killer guy is still out there. And that killer guy knows your name, doesn't he? Are you guys really happy? Are you really safe? Who you gonna' go to? Who's gonna' bail you guys out?"

As she said it, it became so obvious to me that I was ashamed not to have seen it myself. My guess was right, of course. There had to be a person receiving what Strasburg stole. That person was still in the dark, even though I had a hunch who that person was.

"Plus," Betsy said. "You just let the Senator lady walk away. You think she's just gonna' do nothin'? Hell, she'll put the Country over you guys in a New York minute. And if she exposes all this shit . . . I mean stuff . . . She'll turn out to be the hero. She's gonna' be the one who caught the traitor guy. The TV news people will eat that up. She'll be famous. A real spy catcher. She might even run for President when all this is over. She's probably on the phone to the FBI right now."

Betsy's reality-slap-in-the-face made both of us aware of the many, many dangerous things that could be waiting for us just around the corner. I wasn't feeling so safe in my own house and my own little town anymore. Sure, Kelly Hubbard could run to the press but she didn't know who the inside man was. If I was right about the traitor, he would be in a position to call down on our heads the person or people who had been killing everyone involved with The Levels and Henry Willis' file. He would have plenty of time to kill us before he could be exposed, if he could be exposed at all.

There was a knock on the door. It was a hesitant knock, almost too soft to hear and too slow to mean anything but danger for us.

Sandy said, "Betsy, go to Caroline's room. Run with her if necessary."

"Go with her," I pleaded with Sandy.

"Not a chance, big boy," she said. "We're in this together." She raced around the room gathering up the papers and for lack of any other place to hide them she quickly shoved them under the couch.

I grabbed the .38 and hoped that it would be big enough to do the job if that became necessary.

The slow pounding on the door continued. I went to the door and opened it a crack. Senator Kelly Hubbard was there, her face pale; her eyes were wet and filled with fear.

"Let me in," she whispered.

"Why?" I asked.

From behind her a heavily accented, deep voice said, "Open door please, Mister Crew."

"Why?" I asked again. "Who's there? Who are you?"

"He's going to kill me, Morgan," Hubbard said. "Please. Let us in."

I started to close the door, but the big man behind Kelly pushed with one hand and the force of it threw me backwards. The Senator was pushed forward and fell into my arms. The man was big, muscular, handsome, and he smiled broadly, but his smile was like a snake that was ready to strike. He was dressed well in a light gray, very European suit, cut with double vents. It had to have been custom made to fit as well as it did across his massive chest and around his thick arms and neck. His blond hair was cut short in military style. His eyes were dark like the sea during a storm. He carried a big, black, semi-auto pistol that was much bigger than my little .38.

He spoke slowly, menacingly, "I take gun." It was a command not a request. I hesitated, wondering if I could get a shot off before he could. It would be a risk, one I would have taken gladly except for Sandy and Caroline. So I handed the .38 to the man.

"Who are you?" I asked him.

"I come for you, Morgan Crew," he said. "I say name right?"

"Who are you?" I repeated. I started to edge backward, toward the living room and Sandy. He pushed Kelly Hubbard in front of him as if he were carrying a shield and followed me as I walked backward.

I have just enough education in psychology to get me in trouble. But I tried some psychology on him anyway. Keep him talking, I thought. Maybe find some point that we could agree on. Maybe he would have a hard time killing people who were friendly and people whom he had gotten to know.

"Excuse me," I said. "Your accent? I mean your English is very good, but you sound maybe Russian. Where are you from?"

"Where is file?" the man asked, ignoring me. He spoke each word separately and struggled to get the words right. I guessed psychology wasn't going to work on this guy.

"What file?" I said and smiled as best as I could. I was determined not to push too far. Something told me he wasn't going to be pushed. This man, I felt certain, was the stone cold killer who had been going around killing everyone who had been near Henry Willis' file. In the past I have been pretty lucky by tossing bullshit at danger. I would try that, but when I figured he wasn't going to take any more of my bullshit, I'd give him whatever he wanted.

"You joke," he said. He tried to smile, but it looked like he didn't have a lot of experience in smiling. It was forced and mean looking. "You don't joke with me. Give me file . . . Now."

"Let's make a deal," I said. "You give me your gun, and you can walk away with the file. Without the file, I have nothing, and your people are safe. My family and I are safe in return. How's that? Do we have a deal?"

He said nothing.

"Tell you what," I tried. "I'll even throw in a bunch of money. How's a million dollars sound? You can run away with that and live pretty good. How about it?"

"Give me file," he growled. "Give file or everybody die . . . Slow and with hurt."

So I tried. This guy wasn't about to listen to common sense, and he apparently couldn't be bribed. So I turned and nodded to Sandy. She bent and pulled the pile of papers from under the couch. She reached out with it toward the man. But rather than take it he said, "You put papers in . . . What you call it? Place for fire? What is it you call such place?"

"You mean the fireplace?" Sandy asked, more than a little astonished. "You want to burn it?"

"Do as I tell you," he demanded in an animal like growl. "Put papers there. Burn."

"Wait a minute," I said. "Look, if we burn the file, do we walk away? Will you let us go?"

"Don't talk," he said in a low whisper. "Burn papers now."

Rather than do as he commanded, I said, "If we don't burn the file . . . You're going to kill us. If we do burn it . . . You're going to kill us anyway. Why the hell should we do what you tell us to do? We have nothing to gain."

"You die quick," The man said. "Or you die slow. You make choice. All three of you will die anyway. Make it easy for me and you."

Senator Hubbard cried out, "Wait just a damn minute! You can't get away with killing a United States Senator. The power of the entire Nation will come down on you. You can't kill me!"

"Shut up, woman," the man said cruelly. He pushed her hard and she fell onto the couch. "Burn papers and I kill all quick, easy. Don't burn and much pain, yes?"

From behind the big man a voice I thought I recognized said, "Drop the gun Demchak."

It was Noah Goldberg, the man who got Sandy and me involved in this whole damn mess. Noah Goldberg, who was a Mossad Agent, who T. J. Kohl had said was recalled to Israel. And from the kitchen, from around the corner, T. J. herself stepped into the room and stood next to Noah. They both held pistols pointed at the big man's back.

The big man, Demchak, turned quickly, almost too fast for me to see. Noah shot him four times in the chest. It slowed Demchak, he took a step backward, but the four shots didn't stop him. His arm holding the pistol lowered slightly and then he raised it again, not so fast this time. T. J. pumped four more bullets into him. He was stopped, still standing, but the gun slipped from his hand. He slumped slowly to his knees and looked up unbelievingly at Noah and T. J..

Noah took a few slow steps toward Demchak. He looked down at the monster of a man, kneeling on the floor, staring up, unbelieving still. Noah slowly raised his pistol and shot Demchak once in the middle of his forehead. The big man crashed backwards and lay in an unnaturally twisted pile on the floor.

T. J. looked at Senator Hubbard and deliberately raised her pistol, pointing it at her.

"Wait!" I shouted. I quickly moved in front of Hubbard and raised my arms. "You can't kill her."

"She allowed my parents to be killed," T. J. said menacingly. Her eyes were like those of a wolf fixed on a kill. "Get out of my way, Morgan. I don't want to hurt you, but I will if I have to."

"She didn't know!" I pleaded. "The real traitor is a mole inside CIA, and he's still out there."

"What the hell do you mean?" T. J. asked. She lowered her pistol slightly, but not enough.

"This guy," I said pointing down at Demchak's body. "He was sent here to kill everyone associated with Henry Willis' file. Henry's file has evidence of a three-year-long sale of secrets to people who don't much like our Country. It was Nathan Strasburg who was stealing secrets. But he wasn't selling it directly. There's someone else . . . A middleman so to speak," I said. I hoped I was right, but even if I wasn't, it might stop T. J. from killing Kelly.

"She hired Strasburg," T. J. said. "She let him run loose, and she's ultimately responsible. She should have stopped him."

"Senator Hubbard had nothing to do with what happened at The Levels. Demchak was killing people to protect whoever Strasburg was giving the secrets to. It was Nathan Strasburg who was turning over classified information, not Senator Hubbard," I said. "Damn it, T. J.! Don't you see it?"

"Explain," T. J. demanded.

I said as I took a few careful and slow steps toward T. J., "Strasburg had a great reputation in the CIA. You know that. But he was old, and he wanted a few years of the good life. He was approached by an old friend inside the CIA. This person . . . this mole . . . this traitor . . . couldn't get his hands on the valuable information his buyers wanted from more than the CIA. But Strasburg could. Strasburg had access to all venues of intelligence. That was worth a fortune to the mole."

I took another step forward, still standing between Kelly Hubbard and T. J., and said, "Lower that gun just a little bit."

She did, and Noah Goldberg sat in a chair, crossing his legs, but still holding his gun.

"T. J., you have to understand. Money corrupts. Few people in the world would turn down a retirement fund of hundreds of thousands of dollars. He has the money stashed away in a bank down in the Caymans. I'd bet Strasburg was feeling angry that he had spent his whole working career risking his life for a Country that put him out to pasture on a miserly pension. He took the money.

"Senator Hubbard couldn't have known," I continued, trying to keep everybody alive. "Strasburg was good as an Agent, and he was as good at stealing secrets for the traitor as he was as a CIA Field Agent. The Senator's only mistake was trusting Strasburg and giving him free reign. But how was she to know? Strasburg was a lifetime spy, and he was good at it. Everybody trusted him."

T. J. was weighing everything I had said. It made complete sense to me, and I hoped it made sense to her. Her gun, hanging down at her side now, was still cocked, and her finger was still on the trigger. I hoped I sounded convincing. Saying Nathan Strasburg gave the secrets to a mole inside the CIA was little more than a guess on my part. I felt sure I was right, but could I convince T. J.? I looked at Senator Hubbard. Her face was pale and beaded with sweat.

T. J. was thinking about it, wondering if I was lying to keep Senator Hubbard alive. "Strasburg!" T. J. said. "That's not possible. He's old school CIA. There's no way . . ."

"I agree," I said. "But he was liaison between the Senate Committee and all the Intel Agencies. No one else except Kelly's Committee and the White House knew all the secrets from all the agencies. And why has he disappeared? If he were the traitor he would still be around; he would be protected by Demchak. Demchak was killing everybody to protect the traitor, even after Strasburg disappeared. If he's safe somewhere why would the killings continue? Hell, Demchak was about to kill us for Willis' file. If Strasburg were somewhere safe, outside the Country, why continue looking for the file? Was Strasburg in hiding somewhere . . . Moscow or Iran or someplace . . . and was he just going to show up one day? He would have to explain where he was. Strasburg was a liability, not an asset when the crap started to hit the fan. The real traitor . . . Inside the CIA . . . Had to be protected. Strasburg wasn't as important as the mole. Why do you think he's not around anymore?"

"So now you're telling me there really is a traitor inside the CIA?" T. J. asked.

Sandy had walked up behind me, leaned in and whispered, "Are you out of your freakin' mind?"

I had to go on with it. Maybe I was completely off base, but I had to at least stall T. J. killing Kelly Hubbard.

"Yes," I said answering T. J. and ignoring Sandy. "There is someone inside the CIA who is selling all of this and probably a lot more. And if you think about it, there has to be someone inside the U. S., a foreigner, and agent paying the traitor. Nathan Strasburg was the spigot of secrets, but he couldn't be the center of all this. I think if you consider everything in Willis' file and everything that has happened since The Levels, you'll see that there is someone inside who was controlling Strasburg. Otherwise Strasburg would be in front of your gun right now."

The sounds of sirens began to fill the air. Bob Sommers and most of the San Marcos Police Department were racing to our home. Too many gunshots had killed Demchak. Even in my neighborhood, where neighbors weren't very close, someone had to have heard.

Sandy stepped beside me as we listened and said to T. J., "You'll have to kill both of us before you kill the Senator. And that would be murder . . . Nothing more. Listen. The police are almost here. There are a couple dozen cops on the way here. They'll be here in a minute or two. I don't think you want to risk that."

"You killed that guy to protect us," I said, pointing down at the dead and twisted body of Demchak. "I'm certain he's responsible for all the deaths in the past weeks. I know who your traitor is. Let the law handle the rest of this."

"So who's the mole?" Noah asked.

I wasn't ready to tell anybody that, and thankfully Bob Sommers and his cops burst in before I could say anything.

****

Bob Sommers didn't bother knocking or ringing the doorbell. He stormed in, wrapped in a bullet proof vest and with his biggest gun raised. Behind him was almost every cop he had. They had rifles with scopes; they had automatic rifles; they had shotguns; and they even had a few pistols.

They filled the room, and we found ourselves surrounded. They were all crouched in combat positions.

Bob shouted, "Drop those guns! Everybody! Now!"

Noah, still comfortable in his chair, laid his gun on the side table at his right. T. J. bent and carefully laid her pistol on the carpet.

"Morgan!" Bob shouted again. "Your little pop gun, too!"

"He has it," I said, pointing down at Demchak.

"OK!" he continued shouting, too loud for the little living room. "Everybody! . . . Hands on your heads!"

Noah, still not moving, started to say in a very calm voice, "I am Noah Goldberg . . ."

"Shut up!" Bob screamed. "Hands on your head or I'll drop you where you stand!"

"I'm not standing, officer," Noah said softly, relaxed in the overstuffed chair.

"Get up!" Bob screamed. "Get on your feet! Hands on your head!"

Noah stood slowly, smiled, and calmly put his hands, fingers intertwined, on top of his head. T. J. did the same.

Sandy and I were standing next to each other, still in front of Senator Hubbard. Sandy, as she does all the time when the situation is getting out of hand, said calmly and softly, "Bob, it's all over. Let us explain."

Bob hesitated a moment and then relaxed. He stood up straight and holstered his pistol. The officers with him didn't move, however. Their rifles and shotguns and pistols remained pointed at us. "Sandy," Bob said in a lower voice than he had used since breaking down our front door. "There better be a really good explanation for all this."

Before Sandy could say anything, three more of Bob's officers walked into the house. Their side arms were holstered, they were not threatening, and they had looks of disbelief on their faces. They told Bob that the three people inside the black van parked at the curb near our house were dead. The rear door of the van, thick with bullet proof steal, had been ripped off its hinges; the metal had been torn as if it was paper. They also said that a man in a black Cadillac, parked a block and a half away, was dead. His skull appeared to be crushed.

"Oh my God!" Sandy gasped. "That must be Colonel Masterson."

I turned to Sandy and said, "Demchak must have done that."

"Who the hell is . . . What you said?" Bob demanded.

"Bob," I said, "This is going to take some explaining. Look, let's put the guns away and calm down. I suggest we all sit, and then we can explain everything to you."

Senator Hubbard stepped from behind Sandy and me and said, "I am Senator Kelly Hubbard. That woman there is T. J. Kohl, and she is wanted by Federal Authorities. She tried to kill me. I insist you take all these people into custody and hold them for the FBI. I need to leave now. I need to get back to Washington."

"Bob," I said. "Do yourself a favor . . . You'll be saving our lives if you keep her here. Call in the FBI. Ask for Agents Morrissey and Chandler. They've been involved in this and they know what's going on."

Bob looked around the room. He knew Sandy, and he knew me. The others were strangers to him. Trust is a rare thing today. People see lies as a common, normal part of politics and business. Lies, as a way to acquire power and money, are accepted, are understood, and are unfortunately no longer a bad thing in our society. Politicians lie and are re-elected, honored, and become heroes in history. Truth is rare, and with that rarity comes the rarity of trust. Bob had no option but to trust Sandy and me once again.

Bob said, "OK, everybody sit. Nobody leaves." Noah casually took his seat again; Kelly Hubbard sat hard on the couch; T. J. looked around and finally sat on the couch next to her. Hubbard tried to get up and move away from them, but T. J. grabbed her arm and pulled her down.

Bob turned to the cops behind him and said, "Stand down. Secure the area. Secure the crime scenes outside. Rope off the street in both directions. Nobody in and nobody out. Phone the FBI, and get Morrissey and Chandler here quick. And get the Crime Scene people in here. Get something to cover that body once they're done but don't move it yet. Bag and tag all the guns."

I took one of the chairs next to the fireplace; Sandy took the chair on the other side. We watched as the police did their job. Bob stood off to the side, near the front door. He watched them, and he watched all of us also and said nothing. After an hour of work and several hundred photos of Demchak's body, it was zipped tight inside a black body bag, put on top of a gurney and wheeled out. As the front door closed behind Demchak, Bob told the last cop standing with him, "Get something to cover that." He pointed at the blood stained carpet.

A black plastic tarp was placed over the wide stain, and Bob stood where it was between him and the rest of us.

"OK," he said. "Let's start with who you all are. How about you?" he said looking at Noah.

"I'm Noah Goldberg. I am a Mossad Agent . . . A citizen of Israel."

"Sure . . . Right . . . Mossad . . . Right," Bob said not sure if Noah was being a smart ass or not. "How about you?" he asked T. J..

"I'm T. J. Kohl," she said. "And I am . . . Or I was . . . Special Assistant to The President of The United States for Intelligence Affairs."

"Special Assistant," Bob said. "Oh sure . . . Alright. To the President, right? Damn! I wish I had something to write all this down on."

"And you," he said looking at Senator Hubbard. "You said you were what? A Senator or something?"

"Yes," Kelly answered. "And you're making a big mistake keeping me here."

"Well, I'll tell you lady," Bob said. "I make a whole lot of mistakes. I don't care about making mistakes anymore. So you stay until I tell you to leave."

He started to pull a cigarette from a pack he had stored in his bullet proof vest pocket. Sandy said, "Don't even think about it, Bob." He shoved the crumpled pack back in the vest's pocket.

I decided this was going on long enough and wasn't going anywhere anyway. So I said, "Hey Bob. They're all telling the truth. He is Mossad . . . She works in the White House . . . She really is a Senator. That guy you bagged is some kind of killing machine probably from Russia. How about you sit down and let me tell you what's going on."

As Bob shook his head and found a chair to sit in, Betsy walked into the room with a big pot of coffee, seven mugs, and a stack of freshly made sandwiches. She put the tray on the coffee table and said, "Let's eat. Bob you ain't gonna' believe this."

"I got a better idea," he said. "How about I slap cuffs on all of you and take you downtown. I'm gonna' keep everyone there until I get at the truth."

"The truth about what?" Sandy asked. "Everyone here has been truthful with you."

"How about the truth about who killed that guy we just bagged?" Bob said.

"I killed Demchak," Noah said quickly. "He was Demchak Kolesnik. He was sent here to kill people. He was about to kill Morgan and Sandy. I put four bullets in his chest and T. J. put another four into him. I put a bullet in his head. That's what killed him."

"You killed that guy? You saying that guy took eight chest shots and you had to put one in his brain to kill him? Did I wake up in some kind of comic book or something?" Bob said, astonished at the admission. "You tryin' to make this too easy for me? You want me to arrest you and let the rest of these people go? Do I look that stupid?"

"I suggest you phone your own State Department," Noah said. "I am an Agent of the Israeli Government. You'll find that I was sanctioned to kill Demchak by both your Government and mine."

"You've got to be kidding," Bob said, and he tried to laugh, but he couldn't. "You're telling me you're some kind of James Bond with a license to kill? Not in my town, buddy."

It was time to end all this. It was apparent that Bob wasn't going to believe any of what he was being told. I had to try to bring him around, and the only way I was going to do that was to tell him the whole story . . . Or at least parts of the whole story.

"Bob," I said. "I'm going to tell you everything. It's a long story." So I started at the beginning and told Bob about a man being caught and interrogated by various intelligence agencies, without mentioning The Levels. Both Kelly Hubbard and T. J. Kohl interrupted me and told me I was illegally revealing a classified State secret. I ignored them and went on. I told Bob that this man, rather than be killed, spoke my name.

"I believe," I explained, "that this man was waiting to be rescued. I believe he knew that if he were captured, his people would come for him somehow, so he could finish the job he was sent here to do. The plan was that rather than be killed, he say my name. Use my name as a red herring, to throw people off the trail and give him time to be set free. Unfortunately, my name has become very public in the last few years. By implying that this man knew me, he opened a whole new set of threats and a whole new set of suspects. His execution would be delayed while a couple dozen spy types started wasting time investigating me."

I told him about a rescue mission by unknown military types that freed who I believed was Demchak Kolesnik; I told him about T. J.'s threats to kill me and Sandy if she didn't find out who freed Demchak and killed her parents. I told him about our visit to the secret prison in Colombia, but I didn't mention names of the people who helped me with that. I told Bob about the killings of everyone associated with Henry Willis and his file that contained information about a CIA traitor.

Sandy picked up the file and she explained how we found it and what it meant. T. J., the Senator and Noah all were in disbelief that we had been able to find the file when the entire intelligence apparatus of the United States couldn't. Between the two of us it took several hours to explain everything and answer all of Bob's questions.

It was well past midnight, rapidly approaching the very early morning hours, when we had finished. But was Bob convinced? After all, it was like something out of a movie plot, but it was all true. Yet it was obvious he remained unconvinced.

"That's the whole thing?" he asked. "There's nothing more? Like how did Alice get out of Wonderland? I think I'm gonna' take everyone downtown. Everybody is gonna' stay in my jail until I get all this crap straightened out."

"Wait a minute, Bob," I said. "Let me ask a couple of questions first. Another couple of minutes aren't going to hurt anything."

"OK," Bob said. "You ask your questions while I get transportation for all of you folks. I'm sure there's enough room in my jail to hold all of you."

Bob stood and went to a phone. While he made his call, I asked Noah, "What the hell are you doing here? I thought you went back to Israel?"

"T. J. and I thought it better for everyone to think I was back home," he said.

"So you stayed in the States?" I asked. "What for? Why?"

T. J. sat forward and answered, "Noah and I knew that we probably would never find Demchak on our own. And no one was going to help us find him. I was on the run, and that fact didn't give me the time to find Demchak. Mossad agreed to place cover out there for Noah. He would stay here, and while I let everyone chase me, he would be free to find Demchak."

"You didn't do a very good job," Sandy said. "Demchak killed a lot of people. Could you have stopped him earlier?"

"You have to understand who Demchak was," Noah said.

"So tell us," I said. "Who the hell was this guy?"

Noah explained, "For decades before the fall of Soviet Russia, the KGB was experimenting with creating a super soldier. A human killing machine without a conscience who would be stronger than normal soldiers; who was smarter than normal soldiers; who could be severely wounded and keep on fighting; who was incapable of feeling pain. Mossad has known about the program for years. Your CIA has known also. But none of us knew that the remnants of the KGB were successful at creating that geschöpf . . ."

Betsy interrupted and said, "That means creature . . . German . . . In case you didn't know."

I should have guessed our little biker-chick would know that.

Noah continued, "Until Demchak showed up, we thought they were still experimenting. We have people in Ukraine. There's a well hidden facility in a valley deep inside the Carpathian Mountains. It's being financed by al Qaida and a bunch of money from the Russian Mafia. Our people there found out that the former KGB people working at the facility have developed a chemical cocktail that produced Demchak's strength and what Doctor's call Idiopathic Neuropathy. Of course, we think we now know what chemical compounds caused the Neuropathy, so if we're right, what was induced in him shouldn't be called Idiopathic."

"What the hell's Idiopathic?" I asked.

"It means a condition whose cause can't be determined," T. J. answered. "But that's not important right now. The fact is that Demchak Kolesnik couldn't feel pain. He was tortured in The Levels and felt nothing."

Noah added, "And his strength was unbelievable. He was capable of crushing bone and cracking skulls like they were eggs. You saw it . . . It took eight shots to bring him down, but they didn't kill him. I had to finish him off."

"Did you enjoy that?" Sandy asked.

Noah ignored that and said, "We've stolen a sample of the chemical cocktail from the compound, and so far it looks like although the chemicals work only after two years of injections, it will surely kill whoever the recipient is in six to eight months after the injections are stopped. Short term but very affective."

"Anyway," I said, hoping to get everyone back on the subject. "Why were you here, Noah? Did you follow Demchak here?"

"No," he said. "T. J. and I agreed that hunting Demchak was futile. He was just too good. But we knew that sooner or later he would be coming after you, Morgan. So I've been with you for weeks."

"You've been following me?" I said, astonished and even a little bit pissed off.

"It was to protect you, Morgan," T. J. said.

"It was to use me as bait!" I said. "You put me on a friggin' hook and trolled, waiting for that freak to bite!"

"If you have to see it that way . . ." T. J. began.

I wouldn't let her finish with her excuses. I asked, "And what about those guys in the van? And what about Masterson? You were here but you let them get killed?"

Noah answered blandly, as if I should have known the answer already, "They knew what this was all about. They knew the risks. They knew they might be killed. They were professionals. They just weren't good enough."

"You people disgust me," Sandy said.

T. J. smiled understandingly. She said, "We keep you safe. If you knew what we do to keep you safe . . . You'd thank us."

"So tell me," I said. "Why not kill Demchak out on the street while he was killing the people out there? Why here and not there?"

"Because on the street he wasn't trapped," Noah said. "He's an extremely tough kill. You saw that. On the street he could run . . . He could fight . . . It would be nearly impossible to get close to him . . . He was a machine that needed to be in a trap to be killed."

Before I could say anything else, the front door opened and one of Bob's cops walked in. Bob had finished his phone call and was standing at the edge of the living room, listening. I hadn't noticed him, and I wondered how much he had heard. The cop whispered in Bob's ear, and Bob said, "OK, bring them in."

The officer went outside and returned with Ian McCauley and Colonel Masterson.

Everyone in the room – except for me – was astonished to see Masterson walk into our house. Everyone was talking at once, "But you're dead! . . . What the hell! . . . How! . . . Why! . . . Oh my God!"

Bob was staring at me as everyone was talking. He saw I wasn't surprised or shocked. He saw that I knew something no one else in the room knew. He took control finally. "Everybody! Shut up!" And the room fell into quiet once again.

He turned back to me and asked, "Morgan. How come? You're not surprised."

"You're right," I said. "I had a hunch the Colonel wasn't killed out there."

THIRTY-EIGHT - Later I'll Kill Him

I told Bob, "I don't want anyone leaving here, Bob. Get a couple more of your cops in here. Cops with very big guns. And have you been able to contact the FBI?"

Bob spoke into his radio and listened to the reply in his earpiece. He said, "The local FBI office in San Fran has contacted Washington. They said two Agents are on a jet right now."

"Would that be Morrissey and Chandler?" I asked.

"As a matter of fact, yes," Bob said.

"Good," I said. "Betsy, please get two chairs from the dining room and bring them in here for our new arrivals."

Masterson said, "I'll help the little lady."

"Colonel," I said stopping him from leaving the room. "I'd like it better if you stayed right here, please."

As I spoke, two more of Bob's officers walked into the house, carrying mean looking and very big M-16 rifles and stood between Colonel Masterson and the dining room. The Colonel had taken two steps and stopped. I smiled as the two cops moved to the side to stand behind Bob and to his left. There were now four San Marcos Police inside, armed and controlled by me.

No one spoke as Betsy carried the chairs, one at a time, into the room. When they were there I said, "Colonel, Ian, please sit. Betsy, have you ever fired a gun?"

"Once or twice," she said, wondering just what I was getting at.

"Bob, I'd like my .38 back, please," I said. "You're Caroline's godfather. I need it for her." Reluctantly, Bob handed the little revolver to me. I held it out for Betsy. She took it and I told her, "Go to Caroline's room. If anybody but Sandy or me walk in that room . . . Or try to get in through a window . . . Or do anything else . . . Kill them."

"You got it, boss," she said and hurried to the baby's room.

When she was gone I said, "Bob, I'm going to expose some stuff no one is supposed to know. Once I'm done there might well be some violence here. A couple of the people in this room may try to run . . . Or even try to kill me because I know what's going on. These people don't need guns to kill. They're very dangerous. I need you to stop whatever happens and keep everyone here until the FBI gets here. If anybody makes a sudden move of any kind you may need to kill them. Will you do that?"

Without answering Bob turned to his three officers and, taking his meaning without having to be told, they raised their guns at the ready. I was satisfied; I trusted my friend Bob Sommers.

"I want to deal with what everybody has been calling the traitor," I began. "As I said, Nathan Strasburg may have been a traitor to his Country, but he isn't the traitor everyone's been looking for."

Ian, surprised, said, "Strasburg! You've got to be kidding!"

"Be patient," I said. "Just take my word for it. We've been all though that part already."

I looked from person to person, looking for expressions that would reveal what they were thinking, what they were feeling. Sandy broke the silence, "OK, Morgan. Who is it then?"

"Let me diverge a little bit," I said. "I want to go back

to The Levels and the attack that set that guy Demchak free."

Bob interrupted, "The Levels! What the hell is that?"

"Later, Bob," I said. "My understanding is that an extremely professional group freed him. The group was paramilitary and very well equipped. Hell, they even had a couple of black helicopters! They were the best I guess. Noah . . . T. J., correct me if I'm wrong there."

T. J. said, "They were the best. They killed everyone there except for Noah and me. They killed my parents. And I haven't given up wanting to kill all of them and the person responsible."

I said, "I'm pretty sure that you won't be able to kill the people who did the killing at The Levels. I have a hunch all but one of them is all dead already."

"Dead!" T. J. said. "I don't get it. There must have been more than two dozen men in that force. How can they all be dead now?"

"I'm speculating here," I said. "But I've never been able to bring myself to believe in coincidences. Blame that on a couple of college psych courses and Sigmund Freud. The group who attacked The Levels weren't amateurs. They must have worked together before because the job was carried out so professionally. Add to that the fact that they seemingly knew everything there was to know about the physical setup of the levels. They must have had codes to unlock doors and elevators. They knew where everything was.

"So where did they come from?" I asked, knowing the answer. "We have Special Forces in our military. We have a Delta Force. But The Levels was a U. S. Intelligence Operation. Why destroy our own operation to free what everyone thought was a dangerous spy or something like that? I'm speaking about the guy who had been referred to as The Spy Who Would Not Speak. Thanks to Noah there, he never will speak. No, there's no reason for our own

Government to destroy The Levels.

"So anyway, it had to be some outside force but a well connected and informed outside force to have known all the codes that unlocked doors. A foreign Country? I doubt it, because if the attack failed, it would be an unexplainable act of war. Not even Hugo Chavez is crazy enough to risk war with the U. S..

"Maybe it was a Mexican or South American drug cartel? I mean, they apparently have the guns and money to finance such a raid. But I doubt it. If anybody would hire them, they'd open themselves up to blackmail by the cartel. I don't think anyone who is smart enough to be the traitor would be dumb enough to do that.

"So it had to be a paramilitary group," I continued, still watching faces. And I saw what I was looking for on the face of one of the people sitting in my living room. Fear is something almost no one can hide. Oh, a brave man, a well trained man, can outwardly laugh at danger when it approaches, but that man will still fear what is approaching him, and only an insane or mentally incompetent person will not show outward signs of understanding that fear.

"It had to be a group of people no one would know, yet was trustworthy enough to handle the raid without danger to the traitor who arranged the raid. But what group was it? As I said, I don't believe in coincidences. Colonel Masterson, you recently have had more than a dozen of your best men killed in action. T. J. here killed a couple of them. That Demchak guy killed a few more tonight, out in the street.

"When you were working in Uganda recently . . . With Ian, you said . . . you lost more of your best men, seemingly unnecessarily, at least to me and experts in the field. My attorneys did the research on that. Uganda Government records and newspapers and witness statements gave them details about the work you did there. That whole operation was a stupid waste of human life. I mean, what the hell was the purpose? I understand you were going after the leader of a rebel group, right? But I'm told that group consisted of fourteen poorly armed boys, the oldest was seventeen years old. You sent your men in at two in the afternoon on a bright, sunny day. They were slaughtered by these children. You got away.

"I believe you're too much of a professional . . . You're too experienced, and you plan too well to suddenly lose so many of your best men. I believe those men were the people who attacked The Levels, and you know, as I do, that keeping a conspiracy secret is never absolutely possible. One person can keep a secret. With two or more it's difficult. I keep remembering that old Sicilian Mafia saying, 'Three people can keep a secret if two of them are dead.' The more people involved, the more unlikely it is to keep the secret. So you had to get rid of everyone who took part in the raid to protect yourself and the person who hired you."

"That's a load of bullshit," Masterson said. He started to get up out of his chair until Bob took two steps to him and pushed him down.

"Sit down," Bob said. "Shut up. Listen."

"You came to me," I said to Masterson, "with orders from Ian there to cooperate with me fully, to tell me anything I wanted to know. Yet you lied several times. Why? If you were paid to tell the truth, why did you lie? I think I know why you lied. I think someone paid you to lie, to throw me off the trail, to cloud the truth." As I said this, I watched the faces in the room. I saw what I wanted to see, and what I saw told me that my hunch was correct.

"I'm gonna' make a deal with you, Colonel," I said. I stood up and began pacing back and forth in the middle of the room, carefully avoiding the plastic tarp covering the remains of Demchak Kolesnik. I knew, inside of me, that I was right. But I couldn't stop my stomach from feeling like a storm at sea. I was having a really hard time controlling my nerves. "You tell me I'm right, and I'll give you one million dollars and a free ride out of the Country. I have enough influence to get that done. How about it?"

"You can do that?" he asked.

"I told you I can," I said. I stopped pacing and stood a few feet in front of the Colonel, looking down at him. I forced a smile; it was difficult, but I smiled. "I have access to more money than you can ever imagine. I have politicians in my pocket. I'm sick of seeing your face, but I'm more interested in the man who hired you than in seeing you in some jail somewhere. Tell me where you want to go, where you want the cash deposited, and it'll be done today."

Masterson thought for what seemed like an eternity, but was actually only a moment or two. He said, "OK. I have friends in Peru. I'll go there and I'll take cash."

"You got it," I said. "Tell me who hired you to make the raid on The Levels and you'll be out of here with a lot of money."

Masterson grinned like the cat that caught the canary. "OK," he said and flicked his thumb to the left. "McCauley hired me."

Ian jumped to his feet and lunged at Masterson. "You son of a bitch! You lying son of a bitch!"

Bob pulled Ian off of Masterson and threw him off his feet and onto the floor. But he wasn't able to stop T. J. from leaping across the room at the Colonel. She had a short, slim bladed knife in her hand. Before I could focus or react, Noah Goldberg was up and had grabbed T. J. from behind and twisted her around, away from Masterson. He had hold of her wrist and twisted it hard, forcing the knife from her hand. He then turned quickly and threw her to the floor.

Masterson was on his feet. He pulled a small pistol that had been tucked inside his right boot but before he could point it and kill T. J., Bob rushed at him and fell on top of him, pushing him down onto the floor. Masterson's gun flew from his hand. Ian, lying on the floor, reached out for Masterson's pistol but Noah kicked it away, towards me, before Ian could get his hand on it. I picked it up, but I knew I wouldn't need it.

T. J. was on her face on the floor, her arm twisted behind her and held by Noah. Bob had his 250 pounds on top of Masterson holding him down on the floor as Masterson tried to tell him he couldn't breadth. Ian McCauley was on the floor, looking up at me as I held Masterson's pistol pointed at him. Bob's cops, small town San Marcos cops to the end, hadn't moved. They stood frozen, their jaws hanging open, I guess waiting for their brains to catch up to the action.

I needed to get control back, and I saw that the three dangerous people in the room were no longer dangerous, so I said, "Bob, get off of him before you suffocate him, and put some cuffs on him."

Bob struggled to push himself to his feet. He pulled Masterson up and quickly handcuffed him at his back. He pushed the Colonel back onto the couch, and I said, "Do the same for Mr. McCauley."

Bob waived at one of his officers who bent and handcuffed Ian as he lay sprawled out on the plastic sheet covering the blood stain from Demchak Kolesnik.

I turned to Noah and said, "Please, let her get up. I don't think she's going to do anything stupid now."

Noah slowly let T. J.'s arm go, and he helped her to her feet. Her knife lay on the floor at their feet. He said, "I'm sorry T. J.. Now isn't the time or place."

T. J. stood and looked down at Colonel Masterson like a lioness fixed on her prey. "You're right, Noah," she said. "Not now. Later I'll kill him."

When things had calmed down a little, I said, "Ian, I know you weren't in Uganda. You were in D.C. at the time. You led everyone to believe you had been out of the Country to keep the trail away from your behind."

"That's crazy," Ian said. "I was with Masterson. Ask him."

I looked at the Colonel but said nothing. He shifted from looking at me to looking at Ian. I helped him along a little by saying, "Remember. A million bucks and a free first class ticket to Peru."

Masterson finally admitted, "OK, he wasn't with me. He paid me to lie."

I was angry; I was feeling the heat rise in me. I said, angrily, "You killed that young guy who was driving your car away from CIA Headquarters. A young guy with a young family and a good future ahead of him. But he had to die to protect you, you son of a bitch. You killed Patrick Chesterton when he wouldn't do what you wanted him to do. As weird as the old guy was, he couldn't bring himself to turn Benedict Arnold on his own Country."

"Bullshit!" Ian said. "Demchak killed those people!"

"I don't think so," I said. "That freak killed with his bare hands. You used a long range rifle to kill them both. Demchak wouldn't do that. Patrick told me he was taken to someplace . . . A dark warehouse, he said . . . and someone spoke to him by way of a loud speaker and a disguised voice. You killed Patrick before he could tell me he thought that voice was you. The same thing happened to Sandy and me when we were taken from the motel in Virginia Beach. Except the voice wanted Masterson here to kill us. He refused. Tell me who the voice was, Colonel. Who hired you to pick us up back there in Virginia Beach? And keep in mind there's a million dollars riding on your answer."

Without hesitation, Masterson said, "OK. It was Ian. He set the whole thing up but he didn't pay me to kill you . . . So I didn't.

Sandy asked, "And if he had paid you, would you have killed us?"

Masterson answered like it was a foregone conclusion and a stupid question, "Of course."

I reached out and handed Masterson's gun to Bob, and then I picked up T. J.'s knife and handed it to Bob, too. I said, "Bob, you can take Ian and Masterson to jail until the FBI shows up. I'll contact Washington and make sure they know what's going on."

Masterson's dead gaze lit up suddenly as his head shot up, and he glared at me. "You said you'd let me go," he said to me.

"Yeah," I said. "I lied."

THIRTY-NINE - When A Plan Comes Together

Bob and his officers searched Ian McCauley first and found a small Browning .380 semi-auto strapped to his right ankle and a 9 inch long switchblade knife in his jacket pocket. Colonel Masterson was next, and they found he had a Marine's K-Bar knife tucked in his left boot, a Colt .45 1911 under his jacket in a shoulder holster, a stiletto dagger strapped on his left wrist under his sleeve, and a small 9 MM pistol in his back pocket.

"My God!" Sandy said, astounded at all the weapons. "Do you always walk around ready for a war?"

Senator Hubbard stood like a statue, staring off into nothingness. I think she knew her career as a United States Senator was over. The Senate Intelligence Oversight Committee would take the hit. Nathan Strasburg was using his position with the Committee to sell secrets. The Committee, supposedly the best and brightest in the Senate, let him do that under their noses. Heads would roll, including Kelly Hubbard's. Without a word, she walked out the front door, and no one tried to stop her.

Masterson and McCauley were taken away, hands cuffed behind them. Bob offered to stay, looking suspiciously at T. J. and Noah, suggesting that maybe Sandy and I shouldn't be left alone with them. I laughed and said, "Oh, Bob. These are the good guys. You don't have to worry about them."

He argued, but in the end I walked Bob to the door and thanked him for being there when I needed him.

When the door was shut, T. J. and Noah both stood and said they would leave, too.

"Nonsense," I said jovially. "Stay and have a drink or two . . . To celebrate! Hey, we got the bad guys, you know."

Noah said, "I really have to be going. My Government will be waiting for a report. I don't want to get in trouble back home."

"Oh, don't worry about that," I said. "I've already got my people working on getting you a pass. Now, Sandy why don't you mix up a big batch of your famous martinis? I'll have a Wild Turkey, but I'm sure Noah and T. J. will appreciate your martinis."

"Wait a minute," Noah said. "You're getting me a pass?"

"Sure," I said. "No problem."

"How the hell can you do that?" he asked, not just a little astonished at what I had said so casually.

"Hmmm? What? Oh, of course. You see a couple of my companies do a lot of business with Israel. Military stuff . . . You know. We're on very friendly terms," I said. "Ahh, I see Sandy has the drinks ready. Time to celebrate a job well done."

Sandy carried a silver tray holding martini glasses and a large silver shaker filled with her martinis and my glass of Wild Turkey with just a splash of club soda. When she held the tray out for me to take the drink she whispered, "I hope you know what you're doing."

I cracked a smile and winked.

"OK," I said maybe a little too loudly . . . I was feeling a little excited and a little happy at bringing this all to an end. "How about a toast to figuring out who the hell the traitor was? Wait a minute . . . How about a better toast? Here's to getting the last guy involved in all this crap?"

T. J. asked, "What the hell does that mean?"

"Drink your martini, T. J.," I said. "You too, Noah. I'm about to burst a bubble."

Noah looked sideways at T. J., and she looked at him. She put her glass down on a side table; Noah drank his down.

"Stop all this shit, Morgan," T. J. demanded. "Say what you're going to say and stop all the dramatics."

"That's a great idea, Morgan," Sandy said. "You're beginning to scare me."

"Oh, alright," I said as dramatically as I could manage. "If you insist."

I walked across the room slowly, enjoying every second of it, and put my glass down on a table near the couch. "It's just that this is going to be fun, and I wanted to keep it going as long as possible. But anyway, let's go back to the beginning. I've read the reports on the attack at The Levels . . ."

"How the hell did you get your hands on that?" T. J. demanded.

Sandy grinned widely and said proudly, "I've learned that his damn family's money can do anything."

"Getting back to it," I continued. "The raid was to free that freak Demchak. We know why and we know who . . . Well, we know *almost* everyone involved."

I waited and watched for truths to be shown on faces. But T. J. and Noah were the best, and I'm sure they had been able to hide their emotions from better people than me.

"So when Masterson's people broke in they started killing everybody. I can only imagine what the slaughter looked like . . . But the two of you survived. Everybody else was killed, but you lived to walk away."

"Are you saying we were involved somehow?" Noah asked.

"Be patient, Noah," I said. "I'll get there. But first, the reports I've read didn't have anything about how the two of you managed to survive. How about letting me in on the secret?"

T. J. looked at Noah who had his eyes locked on me. His blank, emotionless expression was that of a very experienced poker player. But there was something there; I could feel it, even if I couldn't see it.

T. J. turned slowly and looked at me. She said softly, "We were in a sort of an apartment . . . Set aside for VIPs who might visit The Levels. I was going to stay there that night, although I had plans for dinner . . . Outside of The Levels, I mean. Noah visited me there. We go back . . . We go back many years and many operations. The power went out in the apartment and we were left in the dark. We heard the gunshots. I wanted to go out, into the hallway, to see what was going on. Noah was smarter than me, and he stopped me. I'd be dead if he hadn't."

She waited for me to say something I guess. But I knew that wasn't the end of the story. The two of them didn't just sit around some apartment drinking beer and eating potato chips, waiting for the shooting to stop.

"So?" I said.

"So what?" she asked.

"So go on. I mean everybody was getting killed. How did you two survive?"

T. J. looked at Noah once again. His stoic poker face had not changed. She said, looking down at her feet, "We hid under the bed in the back room." I could almost believe she was embarrassed.

Sandy stifled laughter, and I came close to chuckling myself. I asked, "Wait a minute. A bunch of very professional killers were all over the place, killing everyone they could find. They were tossing hand grenades and they used high explosives to blow open steel doors. They didn't toss a couple of grenades into your room? And you were hiding under a bed? You've got to be kidding me."

Neither said anything, so I kept going. "OK, whose idea was it to hide under the bed?"

T. J.'s brow frowned as she thought, then she said, "It was my idea to go back to the bedroom. I wanted to go outside, but Noah was right. Neither of us was armed. We couldn't do anything. So we locked the heavy steel door to the suite, and it seemed like retreat was a good idea."

"So it was your idea to hide under the bed?" I asked her.

She thought again and then said, "No, Noah pulled me under."

"What happened then?" I asked her.

"The door was blown open. I saw the feet of several men enter the room. They came into the bedroom . . . and then they turned around and left."

"They just left?" I asked. "They didn't search the room or maybe spray some bullets around? Were there closets in the room? Did they look inside?"

T. J. said, "No, as a matter of fact . . . They just turned around and left. I thought it was weird at the time. I mean, if it were me, I would have torn the place apart. I wouldn't want anyone left alive."

I smiled because I then knew I was right. I love it when a plan comes together. I said, "Noah. I know something you don't know."

"You sound like a child playing games, Morgan," he said. "Just say what you're going to say."

"OK," I said. "When T. J. asked that Mossad assign you to The Levels and the Demchak guy, they initially refused without telling T. J.. They didn't want anything to do with The Levels. Israel seems to think that the methods being used there were something like a throwback to the Gestapo. But you insisted. You wanted to go, to help your friend T. J., you said. And they let you go. But what you don't know," I continued, "is that your insistence stirred a lot of suspicion back at Mossad. They're waiting for you to come home, Noah. I think you're in trouble."

"That's bullshit!" he said. "You said you were fixing

things up for me. You're lying."

"No, I'm not lying now; I was lying when I said I was getting you out of trouble." I said. "The truth is, you're in deep shit back home. You see, a lot of people back in Israel are starting to believe what I believe. You didn't come here to help T. J.. You were there to supervise the raid, to supervise the extraction of that Frankenstein guy they had there. You didn't expect T. J. to show up at The Levels that day. She surprised you and everyone else with her visit. Your long friendship with her made you keep her alive that day. You've stayed with her since to keep her from killing Demchak, Ian, and the Colonel if she were to discover who killed her parents. You're involved with them, and I think that bank account you have hidden away in those banks on Malta, in Monaco and on Grand Cayman will be the rope around your neck once the Mossad gets those bank records. My attorneys will have them in a day or two. They'll send them on to Israel."

"You're a fool, Morgan," Noah said. "I killed Demchak Kolesnik. If I was protecting him from T. J., why would I kill him?"

"Yeah, well, it only took me a minute or two to figure that one out," I said, bragging a little because I knew I was right. "Demchak had completed his assignment. He had killed the people he was supposed to kill. Everyone who knew about the file was dead. Except for me and Sandy, of course.

"T. J. was with you. If you had not killed Demchak, or if you had stopped T. J. from killing him and let Sandy and me be murdered by Demchak, what would T. J. think? You were protecting yourself. You were sure you could take care of me and Sandy yourself, later. You could kill us and get Willis' file. But your secret bank accounts reveal the lies, Noah. You were a part of it."

Noah sat frozen for a moment; maybe for the first time in his life he was frightened. But he was still a highly trained

Mossad agent who could react and move quicker than a jungle cat. When T. J. launched herself at him, he jumped to his feet before she could reach him. From under his light tan jacket he pulled a gun.

"Stay where you are, T. J." he said. "I don't want to kill you, but I will if I have to."

I was still on my feet, as was Sandy. I moved a step or two to my left to stand in front of her.

"Noah," I said carefully and slowly. "There are San Marcos police outside . . . Armed and ready. When I walked Bob Sommers to the door I told him to leave some people outside. There's no place for you to go."

"Morgan," he said. "I've gotten out of tighter spots than this. I'm going to leave here, and your lovely wife is going to come with me."

"No one's goin' anywhere," Betsy said from behind Noah. "Don't turn around. I've got Morgan's gun. Drop your damn gun."

Noah didn't turn around. He didn't move. He said calmly, "Young lady. I'll kill Morgan and Sandy before you can pull the trigger. You carefully lay that little gun on the floor and kick it towards me."

Betsy took a step closer to Noah's back and said, "They die . . . You die. They live . . . You live. It's up to you."

"Betsy, you're just a child," he said softly without turning. "Don't be silly. You can't stop me."

"Try me," Betsy said.

Noah turned without warning. Before Betsy could react, he was facing her, but in the one or two seconds before he could get his gun pointed at her she shot him three times in the chest. He fell backwards, hard, onto the plastic sheet covering the blood stain left by Demchak Kolesnik.

FORTY - All The Friggin' Evidence, Too!

Sandy ran to Betsy and took her in her arms. The .38 slipped from her fingers and fell onto the floor. The four cops Bob had left burst into the house. Betsy was in shock, and she began to cry. Sandy walked her out of the living room, away from the man she had just killed.

The four police officers seemed unable to come up with a quick idea of what to do. They were confused. They knew me and the influence my family's money carried in San Marcos. They looked back and forth at each other and didn't move until I told them to call Bob Sommers and get some more people there.

T. J. had collapsed onto the couch and sat, for the first time in her adult life, astonished and overwhelmed.

I pulled a corner of the plastic tarp over Noah's head and shoulders. I remember thinking that this was the man who first got me involved in all this. This was the man who showed up at our door and brought all this black danger into my house. This was the man who said he wanted to protect me from T. J. Kohl's murderous wrath. But this was also the man who had sold his soul for money. Oh, he hadn't worked against his own Country; he took money for selling out the only friend his Country had in the whole world. There it was once again. Money! God damn money!

Bob Sommers arrived with more of his cops and an

ambulance to take the body away. As the medics zipped Noah inside a black body bag, Bob stood by and watched, shaking his head in disbelief.

As Noah was placed on a gurney and wheeled out, Bob turned to me and said, "OK, explain this one, Morgan. Did you kill him?"

"Bob, my friend," I said. "You're gonna need a stiff drink."

As I said it, T. J. started to get to her feet. Bob turned and pointed a finger at her. "Sit!" he commanded like a Marine T.I., and she did, still in shock at the death of her friend. He told two of his officers to take her into custody, to search her, to handcuff her, and to take her to Police Headquarters. He said, as they were leaving, "And keep her away from those others we got down there."

I poured bourbon into two heavy, very expensive, hand-cut crystal glasses – not the kind of glass I would normally offer Bob and his slippery fingers – and said, "When the FBI gets here, you're going to want to turn T. J. over to them. The CIA will want to talk to her. I'm going to spend a few days explaining all this to the FBI and probably to some spooks from D.C., too. I think you should be there. It's a really long and totally unbelievable story, Bob."

Bob took his glass and drank half of the good sipping bourbon down in one mouthful. "You bet I'm gonna' be there," he said. "This is still my damn town. I gotta' write some damn reports about all this, ya' know."

"Bob," I said and smiled. "I'll bet my last million you're not going to write any reports at all. I'll bet you're going to get orders from up high in D.C. to turn over all evidence to them and destroy any and all paper on all of this. I'll bet you'll be threatened with life in Gitmo or something even worse if the newspapers ever hear a word of this."

"Screw all that," Bob said with feigned and strained braggadocio. "It's still my town. But I asked you a question, Morgan. Did you kill that guy?"

Before I could answer, Sandy walked into the living room and said, "No, I did."

Bob turned around to face Sandy and said incredulously, "You killed that guy?"

"I shot him three times with Morgan's gun," Sandy said with a straight face, pointing to the .38 lying on the floor. "He was about to kill Morgan and me."

"So you used your famous quick draw technique on him, Sandy?" he said mockingly. "You got the drop on him, right? Come on! Who the hell are you kidding? I may not be the best cop in the world but I got two eyes that work just fine."

"Bob, darling," Sandy said smiling sweetly. "I'm confessing, and you won't believe me. My heart is broken. I thought we had this special thing going between us."

"So that's the gun?" Bob asked, looking down at my little revolver lying on the floor.

Sandy hesitated, smiled and turned to me. I said, "That's what I killed him with."

"Wait a damn minute!" Bob said. "I thought Sandy killed him?"

"She was lying," I said. "She was trying to protect me."

"That Noah guy was lying on his back. He was shot in the chest and fell backwards. That would put you two between him and your front door. Did you think you had him trapped?"

We grinned, maybe a little nervously, but said nothing. Bob is a good cop, and he can catch lies easily. So we thought the best thing we could do to protect Betsy . . . If she needed protection . . . Was to not say anything.

"He had a gun," Bob said. "I know that. He was threatening your lives. I can believe that. But I can't believe you're telling me everything. Remember, I've got a witness. The T. J. woman will talk to get herself out of trouble. Eventually she's going to tell me the truth. It'll go easier on the both of you, if you come clean with me now. Who the hell really killed that guy?"

Sandy looked at me, and I looked at her. We weren't smiling anymore. Bob was right, of course. He had T. J. Kohl who wasn't about to protect anybody. She would spill her guts freely trying to get a little leniency for herself.

From behind Bob we heard Betsy's voice. "I killed him," she said almost proudly as she walked into the room. "He was gonna' kill Morgan and Sandy. I killed him before he could."

"That's ridiculous," I said. "They're both trying to protect me. I killed Noah."

"Morgan!" Sandy said. "Don't try to protect me. You know I killed him."

Betsy took a few steps towards us, and she was trying not to smile broadly, knowing what we were doing. She said, "That's a load of crap, Bob. They're trying to protect me. I killed the guy."

I continued the line by saying, "Hey, Bob. You know me. I've killed people before. I killed the guy, and the girls are just trying to protect me."

"Girls!" Sandy said, laughing. "Hey! I ain't no girl! I'm a woman in case you didn't notice! And I killed the guy, Bob!"

"Ok," Bob said. "That's enough of this bull. I've got a witness, remember? You can play this game only so long."

As he said that, the phone rang. Betsy answered it and handed the phone to Bob. "It's for you," she said.

Bob listened for a second or two, and then shouted into the phone, "NO! . . . NO! . . . Don't let them do that! . . . I don't care! . . . What! . . . Stop them! . . . What'ya' mean you can't! I said stop them!"

He slammed the phone down and turned to face me. His face was scarlet red; he was breathing hard. He looked like he was going to have a stroke.

"What happened?" I asked. "Are you OK? You need

to sit down, Bob."

"The damn FBI took everybody into custody," he said. "They even took the damn bodies and all the evidence, too. They're on the way to the airport. National friggin' security, they said."

Sandy ginned like the cat that just caught the canary. "So you have nothing then," she said.

"No," Bob said as he pulled a pair of handcuffs from his belt. "I got you three."

"On what charge, Bob?" I asked. "Who you gonna' charge with killing Goldberg? You saw that he had a gun. I killed him in self defense. You can't prove I didn't. You know if you don't have hard evidence, my lawyers will eat you alive in court."

"You've got a huge friggin' blood stain on your damn carpet," Bob said.

"And you've no evidence where that blood stain came from. You have no DNA to match it to," I said. "So you tell me where it came from."

"You're still going in, old friend," he said. "This is my town, and I say what happens here."

"OK," Sandy said, still grinning. "But I think we should phone our attorneys first. You know. Those guys who will sue you and the city for a couple of million bucks when they find out you arrested us without evidence of a crime."

Bob's shoulders sort of slumped, and a look of defeat crossed his red face, draining the color from it. He knew Sandy was right. The FBI would not be returning any of the evidence nor the witnesses. The news media wouldn't know anything, and they wouldn't report anything. The fact that The Levels ever existed would never become public. The secrets would be filed away in some top secret vault, and maybe in a hundred years or so, maybe even longer, the files would be opened, but who would care then?

Oh, Bob could file a report but who would believe it? Now, looking back on all this, even I have a hard time believing any of it really happened . . . But it did.

Bob slid the handcuffs back in their leather case on his belt. He seemed lost as to what to do next.

"Come on, Bob," I said. "Let's go out on the deck. I'll buy you a beer."

FORTY-ONE - Life Goes On

Four months later Bob Sommers had given up trying to make a case against anyone. No one would cooperate with him. The FBI wouldn't return his phone calls. He wrote letters on official SMPD stationary and mailed them off to everyone in Washington, DC he could think of . . . None of them were answered.

Sandy and I took Bob to the Country Club for dinner one night. As usual he overate and drank too much, but we didn't mind. He is our closest friend and Caroline's godfather. We each took an arm as we walked him out, down the stairs, and to the parking lot. Waiting at our car were FBI Agents Morrissey and Chandler. Morrissey was leaning against the driver's side door. Chandler was pacing back and forth in front of the car. They didn't look happy.

"Hey guys!" I said. "What's up? Long time no see!" I had a gut feeling I was in trouble, but I wasn't about to let them know that.

"It's not you, Mr. Crew," Morrissey said. "Lt. Sommers, I've got a FISA warrant in my pocket. It's got your name on it."

Bob was drunk. He shook loose of my grip on his arm and spat out, "Bullshit! . . . D'hell's goin' on here! . . . Screw you guys!"

I moved in front of Bob and took him by his shoulders. "Sandy," I said. "Back him off. Knock him out if you have to, but shut him up and walk away while I talk to these guys."

Sandy took Bob's .38 from its holster and handed it to me. She struggled to push him away. He kept shouting and swearing, but Sandy managed to move him ten or fifteen feet back.

Morrissey and Chandler didn't make any effort to stop Sandy. Chandler said to me, "You know he's going with us. You can't stop that."

"Why?" I asked.

"He's causing too much trouble," Morrissey said. "Too many people are beginning to ask questions."

I knew they were right, of course. I had warned Bob not to keep pushing it. But he couldn't bring himself to believe me when I said that everything that happened was in the realm of National Security. I didn't want him to wind up in Gitmo. But Bob wouldn't stop. He made too many phone calls and wrote too many letters.

OK," I said. I wanted to reason with them; I needed to keep my friend out of trouble. "What can we do to make this right?"

Morrissey pushed himself off my car and took a step closer to me. He said, "Just let us take him away. You don't want to go with him."

"You know me," I said. "You know I've got influence . . ."

Chandler interrupted me. "This comes from the top," he said.

Morrissey added, "From the White House."

There was nothing I could do. Not right then, at least. I walked away and grabbed Bob by his shoulders again. He had been pushing Sandy, but she had held onto him. Even with his more than 250 pounds, he was in no condition to be dangerous.

"Bob," I said quietly and calmly. "Listen to me. You're drunk. These guys are serious. You've been shooting off your mouth too much. Now go with them and go quietly. Don't say anything and don't sign anything. I'll get you out of this in a few days."

"No! Bullshit!" he slobbered and tried to push me away. I knew the two Agents would hurt him if they had to, and I didn't want that to happen, so I hit Bob hard at the side of his head and let him slip from my grip to the ground, unconscious.

The Agents walked slowly to us. Chandler rolled Bob onto his stomach and handcuffed him behind his back. It took both of them to pull Bob's dead weight bulk up and drag him across the lot to a waiting black SUV. They roughly tossed him onto the floor of the back seat. I stopped them as they started to get into the car.

"Wait a minute! I want to see that warrant," I demanded.

Morrissey pulled the two page document from his inside coat pocket and handed it to me. I, of course, had no idea what I was looking at, but I made believe I was reading it and understanding it.

"I want to keep this," I said to them. "I'm going have some lawyers with him in a few hours."

"You can't keep it," Chandler said as he ripped it from my fingers.

"Where are you taking him?" Sandy asked.

"You're not cleared to know that," Chandler said and grinned.

The thought ran through my mind that my closest friend was about to disappear off the face of the earth, and there was nothing I could do about it.

So I decided to try humility and pleading before trying to take Bob forcibly, which I knew was stupid but I'd try anyway. "Look, you guys know I helped you out in the past. You know I was dragged into this thing unwillingly. This guy here is my oldest friend. He's like a brother to me. He's my daughter's godfather, for Christ's sake. He's a small town cop with nothing but me and his job in his whole damn life. He didn't know what he was doing . . . At least he didn't know everything that went on. He was just trying to do what he thought was his job. Please. Let me help him. Let me get a lawyer for him. Where are you taking him?"

Chandler laughed and got into the SUV. Morrissey whispered, "He'll be held in DC . . . At the Hoover building . . . For a few days anyway . . . For questioning. After that, I don't know."

He pulled himself into the black SUV, and Sandy and I watched as they drove out of the parking lot and into the dark of night.

****

Harper, Harper, Jascro and Nettles, my family's law firm, had a staff of attorneys fanning out all over Washington, DC, in every Federal Court there was, and in every political office the Crew family had any influence in, as well as flooding FBI headquarters at the J. Edger Hoover Building with reams of paper, before Morrissey and Chandler could get Bob halfway across the Country by jet.

They had writs of habeas corpus, they had orders signed by Federal Judges, they had letters written by Senators and Representatives, and they had Federal Court filings claiming illegal detention and even a Civil Court filing asking for 10 million dollars in damages. And the next morning they had me and Sandy and Betsy and Caroline there, too.

It took three days, but we managed to get Bob released into our custody. The deal I made was to use the three newspapers the Crew family owns to publish whatever the FBI and the CIA and the NSA and any of the other acronyms that our Federal Government sports, to publish whatever they wanted for up to six months. They would make up stories to cover up the rumors going around, and we would publish them.

The second part of the deal was that Bob would keep his mouth shut. I put up 1 million dollars in bond that I knew would never be returned to me, but I really didn't care. And any record any Federal Agency had on Bob would be sealed under National Security so his job back in San Marcos would not be put in jeopardy.

Bob had sobered up, and he knew he was in trouble. He silently sat in on the negotiations and agreed quickly to forget about all that had happened in San Marcos.

When he was led into the room we were in, he was sporting three days' growth of beard and the same clothes he had been in when arrested, which were stained with vomit he had spit up in the back seat of the black SUV. He smelled bad and looked worse, but we bought him a First Class ticket on the first jet out of DC and back to San Francisco. I arranged to have a limo waiting there that took him home to San Marcos.

****

Rather than go home, Sandy suggested we all needed a little vacation. I agreed, Betsy said, "Hell, yes!" and Caroline giggled and gurgled happily because everyone else was happy. So I rented a car and we drove north . . . To New York's Hudson River Valley where all this started.

We, of course, knew where Brown's Farm and The Levels were. We'd been there, and someday both Sandy and I hope to be able to forget we were ever there. We took our time and stopped at a couple of really nice Country Inns and Bed and Breakfast places. The weather treated us well, and we had fun, even stopping for a picnic alongside a tree shaded brook one afternoon. We searched through a couple dozen antique stores and gift shops and bought some useless stuff.

One morning, I woke early. We had stopped at a nice motel with a little stream running behind it. I decided to dress and walk to the stream in the early morning light. Outside the office, a newspaper in a coin box caught my eye. I slid a couple of coins in the slot, and I pulled the paper out. Senator Kelly Hubbard had committed suicide. She had been found in her Capitol Hill office, at her desk, a small pistol in her hand and a large hole at her right temple. The article said she had been suffering from incurable cancer.

But I knew the truth was the news media, and her political enemies could not let her go. She had to die because she had no future, no family, no real friends, and no career left. She was alone with nowhere to go.

Ian McCauley and Colonel Masterson could easily disappear, which they did because my enquiries at the CIA were answered that they had no record of an Ian McCauley ever working there. The Colonel, on the other hand, lived in a dark, hidden world not accessible by very many people. If he were to disappear, who would know? Who would care? I didn't even know his real name or where he lived. Military specialists like Colonel Masterson can be easily and quickly replaced. As long as there is enough money, military specialists can be bought.

Everyone who had any part in what Henry Willis had discovered was dead. Everyone that is, except Sandy and me. But they could not make us disappear because of the Crew family name. And any accidental death would be investigated by my attorneys until the truth was revealed. So I felt comfortable . . . Sort of anyway . . . That we were not in danger.

I dropped the newspaper in a trash bin near the Motel's office and went back to our room. Next door I could hear Caroline giggling and Betsy talking baby-talk to her. Sandy was just waking up. There was no need for her to know about Kelly Hubbard. She would learn about it soon enough. Why ruin a good vacation?

After a so-so breakfast at a nearby truck-stop diner, we drove off to find Brown's Farm. When we arrived at where we knew it was . . . We easily recognized the surrounding area . . . All we found was an empty field, overgrown with weeds. There was no rusty mailbox, no pitted gravel driveway, and no old, age-battered house. Sandy and I got out of the car without saying a word. Betsy sensed that there was something wrong, so she stayed in the back seat and hugged Caroline tightly.

We walked through the weeds to where the house used to be. There wasn't even a rusted nail or shard of termite infested wood left. Where the old barn was, now stood a tall oak tree that wasn't there when we had visited before. It could have been a hundred years old by the looks of it. We searched for some remnants of an entrance down into the levels but found nothing.

"I wonder what we'd find if we dug down a few hundred feet?" Sandy asked.

"I'd bet my last million we'd find nothing," I said stoically. "They can't have any evidence of a place like The Levels having ever existed. Henry Willis' file has probably been burned and the ashes spread. I'd bet only the most secure computers in the most secure basement at Langley has any record of what happened."

"So what do they do?" she wondered.

"They go on like it never happened," I said. "The spooks keep playing their dangerous games. Money is spent on stuff nobody will ever know about. We'll send spies to other places, and they'll send spies here. People will die. Nothing will change.

We turned and walked back to the car. There wasn't any more talk of The Levels or of all the people who had to die. We spent another ten days driving around New England, trying to have a good time.

It's been a year since we returned to San Marcos from our second trip to Brown's Farm. Gradually the tension and the nightmares have dissipated, and our life goes on . . . Until the next time, that is.

THE END

www.ingramcontent.com/pod-product-compliance
Lightning Source LLC
LaVergne TN
LVHW050923080826
845145LV00001B/193

* 9 7 8 0 6 1 5 8 3 2 4 7 0 *